DOMESTIC

ALSO BY JEFF WISHARD
Available from Port Fannin Publishing

Redemption Avenue

DOMESTIC

JEFF WISHARD

PORT FANNIN PUBLISHING
FORT WORTH, TEXAS

This book is a work of fiction. Names, characters, places, and incidents are the product of the author's imagination or are used fictitiously. Any resemblance to actual events, locales, or persons, living or dead, is coincidental.

Port Fannin Publishing
6245 Rufe Snow Drive
Suite 280
Fort Worth, TX 76148

First Edition: October 2017

ISBN 978-0-9834653-6-2 (Paperback)

*To domestic violence victims,
survivors and advocates everywhere*

August 1992 - Indiantown, Florida
Julia

THE last day of Patricia's life started with a hangover. It held her head firmly in a vice, briefly taking her mind off the squalor about her. The sheets she was wrapped in and the mattress were no longer on speaking terms, begging to be put out of their suffering. The bedroom floor was likely just as miserable, but an assortment of clutter kept the ugly truth from view. A fly buzzed by the window, as if realizing it had chosen the worst trailer in the park, looking to go back out the way it came.

The hot pink name tag atop the dresser read Trish, a name she tolerated. Her given name was Patricia, which she despised. Her boss freaked out when she covered Patricia over with masking tape and wrote Trish on it. She nearly quit on the spot, but he finally compromised to let her go by Julie, using the name tag of the girl she replaced until a replacement arrived from headquarters in Atlanta. Like a dozen other jobs she had held since turning 16, the effect on an asshole once given a title as spare as assistant night manager was amazing.

The rent for the trailer was too much, even after splitting it with her boyfriend, a strapping, engaging loser named Neal. He was the alpha of his band of overserved, underemployed buddies he met at the local bowling alley. He was the operator that could win at small stakes like conning someone into buying a lemon car, or talking someone like Patricia into bed, but always came up snake eyes in the bigger games, when the results could tangibly change his life. When the losses exposed him to criminal risk, his father, a county judge, invariably cleaned up after him.

The reason a character like Neal could make his way into her life was expectations lowered by bad experiences, and a worse self-esteem. She expected to be killed by every boyfriend she ever had, surviving several close calls in her 23 years. Choking, stabbing, and gunfire were among the attempts that, fortunately, had failed.

Neal was not above getting physical, most recently slapping her after she mouthed off to him at the bar in front of his disciples. He had it coming, grabbing the ass of their waitress after coming on to her all night. Once he sobered up the next morning, he profusely apologized and promised it would never happen again. Since then, two months had passed without incident. Neal still had the wandering eye that led to his earlier transgression. However, he hadn't come close to anything like it since and Patricia had accepted it as a blip on the screen.

It also helped that those same two months were the start of her career at the Flamingo Grill, a makeshift diner retrofit from an abandoned Denny's in Stuart. Previous jobs had been sabotaged by significant others with repeated phone calls, intrusions at the workplace, and drama that caused excessive absences. The jealous boyfriend camping in a booth by the front door throughout consecutive shifts were usually the last straw. The lack of interference from Neal at work was what passed for stability to her.

The trailer park where they lived hid neatly on the side of a county road behind a row of palm trees, with a discreet entrance and a non-descript sign that was painfully honest about its age. Halfway between I-95 and Lake Okeechobee, few travelers on the road ever noticed the park. Their trailer was in the back corner, with weeds obscuring most of the rust and disrepair of the structure.

Patricia knew Neal wasn't forever, but he was better than other available options. In her few quiet moments, she realized he was merely a placeholder. She also realized that was part of the problem. The absence of that other person was too lonely, too frightening to endure for very long.

Off the early shift at noon, then back at midnight was enough to drop her into bed and have her sleep soundly for hours. In her slumber-deprived state, the phone ringing was disguised as an element in one of her dreams. When she made no effort to answer, the answering machine kicked on.

"Trish, I feel like shit and I'm not going in tonight. Thanks, bye."

The mumbled words of her friend Beth swam away harmlessly, not connecting with her consciousness. She awakened an hour after she was supposed to rise and saw the alarm clock. She jumped out of bed, put her hair in a ponytail, found her uniform and dashed for the door. She stopped at the sight of the blinking answering machine and punched the play button. After hearing one of Neal's many creditors on the first of ten messages, she figured whatever Beth had to tell her could be repeated when she arrived and rushed out of the house. Maybe Beth would drive and let her apply her makeup on the way.

Her beaten subcompact tore out of the trailer park and onto Highway 76 in an awkward cloud of dust. The little coupe she had driven since getting her license had just passed 150,000 and didn't figure to see 160,000. She refilled the oil and coolant levels every few days because repair wasn't an option and a new vehicle was a fantasy.

She and Beth met at a dead-end job just out of high school. Their schools were cross-county rivals and they knew many of the same people. In the previous four years they moved together, switched jobs together, and they partied together. Their tastes in men were similarly disastrous, although Patricia felt Beth was more to blame for her relationships' unfortunate endings. She was routinely unfaithful to her boyfriends, and always had a convenient excuse for finding her way into another man's bed. She had bailed Beth out from the explosive fallout of these choices more than once. With each rescue, Patricia feared she would not be able to save her friend the next time.

The distance of five miles to Indiantown seemed across the country for how far it felt in her sleepy state. The fatigue of work wore on her, far more than she should feel at only 23. Each awakening felt more labored than the one before.

Even three or four days off in a row didn't have the expected recuperative effects. She only smoked when she drank, and she only drank when she had the money, which was payday Friday. By Sunday, the money was gone and she had to wait another five days to experience a release that was taking more than it gave in deceptively growing increments.

The house Beth rented wasn't much more luxurious than the mobile home. The landlord had left parts of several cars in the back yard. Calling the ground in the back a yard was also generous, as there was more dirt than grass, and what grass was there was dead or wished it was. Beth's only recourse when the money ran short was to find a new man with a better job, a nicer car, and a seemingly more mature outlook on the future. Despite the personal risks, this strategy had managed to keep her solvent.

Beth's car was in the single-file driveway. The flat tire was the first clue to her need for a ride, but Patricia also knew the transmission was miles away, in the process of getting rebuilt. She stepped around the various objects scattered in the yard and knocked on the front door. No answer came.

"Beth, it's me."

To the left of the front door, the dingy curtains inside the master bedroom window moved. She knocked on the door.

"Beth, wake up. It's me. We're going to be late."

Patricia opened the front door. It certainly wasn't something she would have normally done, but she sensed something wasn't quite right. She took a step or two forward.

"Beth?"

"No!"

Beth's protest was halfway between a scream and a wail, right as Patricia opened the bedroom door.

"No, Trish! Don't—"

She saw Neal and Beth, naked in bed, and they saw her. He attempted to cover his face, hiding behind the sheets, but it was a moment too late.

Patricia stood dumbfounded in that moment where time freezes and you feel the full brunt of embarrassment. You're the fool, the whole world's laughing, and there is no recovering from the shame that will never go away. Once that moment had fully taken hold, she turned and bolted out of the room.

Before she could reach the front door, she felt Neal's firm grip, grabbing her left arm. When he turned her, Patricia tried to swing at him. He caught her by the wrist and she struggled with him. The struggle didn't last long, as he was a foot taller and 100 pounds heavier. She wasn't sure whether it was the anger at being caught or being attacked, but he promptly decked her. The fist connected squarely with her left eye and she fell in a heap.

Everything went dark and dizzy. As she recollected her senses, the sounds were growing louder and sharper. As her vision slowly cleared, she saw why. Beth had responded to Neal punching Patricia by jumping on top of him and putting him in the best chokehold she could manage. At barely 100 pounds, Beth's clench had Neal's face red, his eyes bulging, his lungs struggling for air. Finally, the two naked bodies tumbled backwards, their combined weight toppling them against the bar in the kitchen. In the fog of her pain, Patricia saw them fall and heard a sickening crack.

Neal struggled to his feet. Beth didn't move. Her head was leaning at an odd angle and her body was still.

He quickly turned and saw Patricia. She saw him.

They both knew Beth was dead.

They also knew each of their lives hung in the balance. Patricia would not help Neal cover up a crime, let alone the killing of her best friend who he had cheated with. She also knew Neal would never let her live to tell the truth.

Patricia scrambled toward the door, but Neal was on top of her before she could make it halfway to the door.

"Like hell!"

He shoved her to the floor, putting his hand on her neck.

"You killed her!"

"Dammit! You know I didn't mean to."

She looked at him and saw conflict. Maybe he was having remorse, something that caught her off guard. He loosened his grip slightly from her throat, and turned toward Beth, as if he noticed something.

"Oh, shit. She moved."

He released Patricia, and rose to his feet, moving toward Beth.

"Maybe she's not dead."

Patricia regained her breath and saw him looking over Beth's naked body, as if searching for a pulse or breathing. She slowly crawled over to them.

"I'm going to call the ambulance," he said, moving away from her to the phone. Patricia went in closer to her friend, but only needed a moment to realize she was dead.

That moment of indecision was all Neal needed. Before Patricia could turn, Neal had struck her from behind, knocking her cold.

When Patricia came to, she felt like her head had been chopped in half. It ached horribly. Once she had registered that pain, she sensed her hands bound together.

She was in a moving vehicle. After listening to the motor, the feel of the seats, and the rough ride, she knew it was her car. Despite the blows she had taken, the memories of how she arrived at this point quickly returned.

Patricia remained as still as possible, letting the undulations of the road rock and bounce her body as if she were still unconscious. Her head was lying on her left side, slightly downward. She opened her eyes just enough to see the floorboard of her car. The shoes on the driver's side were Neal's. He had clearly chosen to cover up Beth's death, rather than take his chances with explaining what happened to the authorities. Patricia was next.

She barely had time to think through any scenarios for escape before the car slowed, turned right, and descended at a sharp angle. She remained limp, trying to simply let her body move naturally. When the car finally stopped, she cracked her eyelids open a bit more and saw water ahead of her, at the end of a boat ramp.

Patricia was tempted to test the limits of her restraints, but that had to wait. As fearful as death by drowning was, death while tied up was a certainty if Neal realized she was conscious.

She saw him pulling the emergency brake, then putting the car in neutral. Then, he produced a rag in his hand, heading toward her face. The bastard wasn't going to chance her escaping in the water, aiming to suffocate her first. She had only one chance, and it was now.

Patricia jerked her tied, fisted hands upward and hit Neal perfectly under the jaw. It stunned him just enough to give her the time and room to lift herself over him, now using the ties to strangle him from behind. He began thrashing about, and he was stronger than she had ever imagined. In his struggle, he kicked the emergency brake and the car rolled forward.

Neal's effort increased to the point where she was not sure he wouldn't knock her out again. She kept pulling back on his neck with everything she had. He reached back and dug his fingers into the left side of her face, desperately clawing at her to try and loosen her grip. She shook off his hold, his uncut fingernails drawing blood. The water rushed in through the open driver door.

Something told her she could make it up for air, even bound. She couldn't leave him alive, because he would never leave her alive. She waited until she didn't think she could hold her breath any longer and finally let him go. Neal dropped limply into the windshield above the dash.

She no longer had time to make sure he was dead, having to escape herself. When she emerged from the car, she realized the water was shallow. She could see the surface and even see the shore. She semi-dog paddled toward the shore and climbed up the edge to where she came up for air once, then twice.

Alive.

Patricia collapsed on the shore, gasping for air. Once her breathing returned to normal, she turned to her restraints, using a nearby jagged rock to cut the twine enough to work her way free. She dropped back to the shoreline, letting the water harmlessly splash against her. Eventually, the discomfort of the rocks exceeded her exhaustion and she sat up and examined her surroundings.

It was Lake Okeechobee, in an area barely deep enough to submerge a vehicle, even at its deepest depths. She spotted the small boat ramp that Neal had used. No one appeared to have witnessed his attempt to kill her. His last living act was so typical of him. He was devious enough to think ahead about a contingency, but too sloppy to carry out the plan to completion.

It now occurred to Patricia that she wasn't anxious to explain the night's events to the police. Unlike Neal or Beth, she had no close family that would mourn her loss, or demand justice for her demise. She had no money to provide for a reasonable criminal defense. She had also watched far too many TV shows where innocent poor people take the rap for deaths when details are sketchy. With Neal's father enforcing his version of the law, it was a virtual guarantee she would lose.

Patricia picked herself up and walked away from the lake. The lights of vehicles travelling on the nearby road drew her. It was US 441. She waited until there were no cars in sight, then crossed to the shoulder on the northbound side. North was out of Florida, for good. She had only left Florida twice in her life, once to bury her father across the border in rural Georgia, the other to bury her mother beside him less than a year later.

A semi slowed, easing up next to her.

"Hey, sweetie. Where are you headed?"

"Out of this shithole," she said as she hopped in, hoping for the best from the stranger. The trucker looked over the uniformed waitress. She had a swollen eye and blood streaming from the side of her face.

"You okay?"

"I'm alright."

"I'm Jim," he said with a nod, handing her a handkerchief. She sensed a humble respect, something she could usually count on her instincts assessing correctly. Her regrettable personal choices had always been against her better judgment. She nodded back, dabbing the wound.

"Julia," she finally blurted out, extending her hand.

Jim shook her hand gently. "Buckle up, Julia. Out of the shithole we go."

"Thanks."

"Not a moment too soon. You think it's bad now, just wait till Andrew comes through. That bastard is looking like it will take no mercy."

She took a deep breath, the first in her new life. She had always hated the name Patricia. Every Julia she saw or heard about had fun and loved life. She had no choice but to start fresh with that new name, far away from every type of bastard the old life presented.

With each mile down the road, the fog of what had just happened faded, and the gravity of reality set in. She fought back the tears, realizing she was recreating herself with no plan. Nothing worthwhile had been left behind, but it didn't ease the fear of being all alone, in a place she had never been.

ONE

THE blow from the back of his open left hand stunned her, dropping her to the kitchen floor. It shouldn't have been a surprise, as his moods could lie dormant for days before exploding without warning. The sheer force of his hand connecting with her face was so jarring, it was impossible to brace for, even when it could be expected.

She stayed collapsed on the floor, trying to collect herself as she heard a stream of angry shouting through the fog. Over time, she had learned to use the moments after his attacks to anticipate what he would do next and how she could help end the episode as quickly as possible. Her best strategy was to drop to the ground where she could cry, but not scream. A shriek would only infuriate him more, prompting a longer session. If she remained on the ground too long, it would agitate him further and the next hit would be worse. If she rose too quickly, he wouldn't consider the punishment sufficient and would continue until her pain reflected enough remorse for whatever had set him off.

The offense was twofold. First, the refrigerator was empty of beer. Second, the explanation why she had not bought more beer on her trip to the store was rejected before she could even finish.

Through her tearing eyes, she saw her own blood on the tile. She struggled to rise to her feet, but was surprised that simply moving sent waves of pain coursing through her, from too many places to account for. She kept her face shielded from him, leaning against the fridge. The empty bottle in his other hand quickly became a missile, thrown down on the floor close to her feet. Angry shouting laced with profanity trailed after him as he marched out of the house.

The slam of the door and the subsequent roar of the pickup's engine as it tore away removed her internal restraints. She began openly sobbing, sliding down the front of the fridge and dropping to the floor, knocking off magnets, photos, coupons and appointment cards, unconcerned about the glass underneath her. Her life felt just as shattered as the bottle, ready to be disposed of with the rest of the garbage.

The assaults had accumulated, blurring into a frightening montage that she couldn't escape. They would occur one after another in a flurry, then stop for a tantalizing stretch, fooling her into believing something had changed. The activating events ranged from running low on beer to her daring to request that he put his dirty laundry in the hamper. The most common was imagined infidelity, often triggered by something as trivial as a pleasant exchange with a clerk at the grocery store.

And just when it seemed they might end, he would come home drunk once again, igniting his demons. At first, he had been the type to unleash his fury and moments later collapse in tears next to her, begging forgiveness. The episodes gradually became longer and more brutal, the apologies fewer and less genuine.

Once her raw emotions were exhausted, she slowly picked herself off the floor, returning her thoughts to survival. Still dazed, she staggered to balance herself, leaning against the kitchen table. For most of her two years with him, she wondered when the breaking point would arrive, when an attempt at escape was worth the possibility of death or worse.

The clock on the wall read 8:24 PM. He would vent his frustrations with his crew at the bar until it closed at 1 AM. What he would do upon returning could range anywhere from continuing his terror throughout the night to half-hearted contrition and an overture for make-up sex that she didn't dare refuse. If she was lucky, his night would end with a simple grunt before passing out in the nearest chair.

For most of her time with him, she had dreamed of running. She had rehearsed in her mind every step and every precaution. She had conducted more escape dry runs than she could count, methodically covering her tracks and removing any evidence of her tests. Two changes of clothes were folded neatly in the drawer, ready to be placed in a small duffle bag once the moment finally arrived.

Tonight, she had no choice. There would be no more practice. She dared to promise herself that this attack was the last.

She took her purse and opened it. In between a fold in the leather where the seams had weakened was a small fissure, just wide enough to discretely slip three items inside. The hiding place was crucial. If he saw the information on the items, any hope of escape would be doomed.

The first item was a card that read "The Shelter - 24/7/365" in large, bold letters. She held it gingerly, her wrist sprained or worse. Below it, in a smaller font, a five-digit number was listed with the instructions to text "HELP" for an immediate response. The card was obtained months earlier, and caused her to find the hiding spot in her purse.

The second item, a pay-as-you-go flip phone was purchased the same day she received the card. To avoid arousing suspicion, she paid a friend in cash to keep the minutes for the burner topped off online and kept it turned off except to test it periodically. She had typed out the four letters many times before, unable to muster the nerve to complete the text.

The third item was placed there today, a single sheet of paper from her doctor, folded several times over. The results of the tests were shown clearly.

She was pregnant. The baby was his, but she would die before bringing a child into the same house as her abuser. It was this item that convinced her to finally press "send."

After sending the text, a minute passed, and then her phone buzzed with a call.

"Hello," she mumbled, using a tissue to slow the blood dripping from her nose.

"Hello. I'm with The Shelter. Are you in immediate danger?" The caller on the other end of the line was a female. Her voice had both urgency and calm.

"No," she replied. She was still breathing heavily, something her caller noted.

"Are you alone?"

"Yes."

"Good. Take a deep breath or two. What is your name?"

"Sophia."

"Hello, Sophia. If you left without word or warning right now, when is the earliest you would be missed?"

"Probably 1 AM."

"Do you have a vehicle?"

"Yes."

"Is downtown too far to drive?"

"No," Sophia quickly replied, anxious to get as far away as possible from the area.

"There is a Starbucks at the corner of Congress and 6th. What are the chances you will see anyone you know this late?"

"Not much."

"How soon can you be there?"

Sophia had prepared to leave, but she hadn't considered all the implications of actually leaving, or what would transpire after she was gone. They had little contact with their neighbors at her boyfriend's insistence. Anyone near their home had been conditioned to ignore them. But what if someone noticed?

"Thirty minutes. What about the car?"

"That's fine. We'll deal with your car. Go into the Starbucks, order something and have a seat. An attractive black woman will order a caramel latte. Do not approach her. She will approach you."

"Okay. Do I pack—"

"No. Just bring your purse or whatever you would take if you were going right back home. We'll worry about the rest later."

"Alright."

"Be careful."

The line went dead. Sophia found her purse, and then stopped to look around the house. It had been her home for nearly a year. The nightmares outpaced the joys several times over, but the abuse had a perverse security to it. The unknown carried its own set of fears.

Inside the garage was a small, beaten pickup which used as much oil and coolant as gas. The only part of the pickup that had worked properly since it was purchased was the odometer, a fact not lost on either Sophia or her boyfriend. He watched the miles carefully, making sure his girlfriend had been exactly where she claimed. Sophia watched the same mileage, so that any deviation from her reporting could be reasonably justified.

Out of habit, she memorized the six digits shown on the dash. Sophia shook it off, vowing to herself it was now an unnecessary exercise. She said a prayer, backed out of the garage, and drove off without looking back.

Once out of their neighborhood, the chances were slight that he would spot her driving by in the evening traffic from one of his favored watering holes along the way. Still, she bristled with chills as she passed each one until she turned to go south on Mopac toward downtown. She couldn't believe the day had finally come for her escape, and suspected it was a trick of her mind or someone in league with her boyfriend.

Sophia found a parking garage a couple of blocks from the arranged meeting spot, another precaution in case she was tracked. She took the ticket from the automated gate without a thought of whether she would ever pay to retrieve it. The countless permutations of logic she tried to employ began to overwhelm her brain. She was ready to hand the reins to someone else who had more energy and power to fight for her.

She emerged from the parking garage and began pacing up Congress to the coffee shop. She alternated looking downward, afraid to meet the eyes of those passing by, then occasionally raising up to spot any threats. She failed to notice a young black woman, sitting on a bench, just beyond the glow of the security lights from inside a clothing store. By appearances, she was simply looking at her phone, perhaps waiting for someone to join her for dinner or a drink.

That impression was exactly what the woman intended, furtively scanning the area in front of the Starbucks, watching each person pass back and forth intently. As Sophia shuffled across the street and into the coffee shop, the woman observed every person coming and going within the area for several minutes.

Sophia placed her order and waited until it was ready before sitting down. Taking her first sip, she saw the woman at the counter, and their eyes connected. The woman gave her a subtle nod before turning back to the barista.

"Grande Caramel Latte, please."

"Your name?"

"Cassie."

With the order placed, the woman surveyed the people inside, then scanned the streets outside before walking toward Sophia. Her contact was only a little taller than she was, but her long legs made her look even taller. She was indeed beautiful, with a soft smile and a confident demeanor.

She sat at a table across the aisle from her, but did not resume eye contact. The place had several customers, but the area around them was relatively quiet. The baristas behind the counter were making the only perceptible noise.

"Sophia?" she asked softly.

Sophia's head moved slightly, enough to see the woman was looking straight ahead. Her hand made a subtle motion, as if to wave.

"Hi," Sophia mumbled, halfheartedly. Scared and alone, her body language confirmed her plight as much as her bruises.

"Any chance you were followed?"

"I—I don't think so."

The woman nodded. "Wait five minutes, then walk out and go right on 6th. I'll pull up beside you and pick you up. Black Cadillac."

As if on cue, her contact's order was called. The woman retrieved her order and walked out. Sophia waited as instructed, and then walked outside. She looked in both directions, waiting for the car. Only a few seconds passed when a black XTS rolled up, but on the far side of the street.

The number of people in the area should have given Sophia comfort, but it somehow made her feel more vulnerable. Once the crowd had dissipated and there was a clear gap between her and the Cadillac, she rushed across the street.

Sophia raised her foot to step on the curb, but it never landed. She was yanked back from the sidewalk, her coffee cup flipping harmlessly to the pavement. She let out a desperate shriek that never reached outside of the rough hand clenched around her mouth.

"What the hell are you doing here?"

The angry voice that rang in her nightmares was unmistakable. Her boyfriend began dragging her toward the alley where there was more darkness and less potential interference from some nosy good Samaritan. She struggled and kicked, desperately seeing the black XTS sitting there, its driver unaware of her plight. Her fighting finally forced him to shove her to the ground, punctuating his fury with a full fist. He raised her up by the neck with both hands, holding her against the brick wall.

His grip was suddenly torn away, cutting her to bleed in the process. He had no choice but to let go, as one arm was somehow bent backwards, taking the rest of his body with him. When he looked to see how this had happened, he saw a black woman glaring at him, taking a position between him and Sophia.

"Mind your business, bitch. This doesn't involve you."

"It does now."

He saw her confidence, but didn't possess the common sense to factor this into his next move. He rushed forward, only taking a step before meeting her fist and falling back to the alley floor. The punch was so quick that he wasn't exactly sure which side it had come from. He staggered back to his feet, only to be flattened by another shot he never saw coming. The blow was a kick, delivered by an expert who clearly had no fear of him.

He struggled up, looking at the woman burning a hole through him with her eyes. Sophia leaned up against a wall a few feet behind her, breathlessly watching her life hanging in the balance.

The sound of a blade ripped from its sheath brought a gasp from Sophia, but it was no surprise to the woman. After a couple of awkward swipes, she twisted his arm, wrenching the knife from his grasp. She threw him against the wall and began to pummel him with shots, one after another, until he dropped, exhausted and half-conscious. Certain he was defeated, the woman backed away, retrieving his knife and leading her away.

"Let's go."

Sophia complied, following the woman to the car. Once inside, the Cadillac whipped 180 degrees on 6th, turned right on Congress and roared away. After several blocks, she darted into an underground parking garage and backed into a parking spot where the entire lot could be seen through the windshield.

"You okay?" the woman asked, producing some tissues and handing them to Sophia, pointing at her neck which was bleeding, but not profusely.

"I think so."

"I'm Cassie," she said, extending her hand.

"Sophia," she replied, taking her hand in response, exhaling deeply.

"I take it that was him." Cassie gently touched her face, examining each of her wounds.

"My boyfriend."

"His name?"

She swallowed hard. "Brad. Brad Benton."

"Did you tell anyone about this?"

"No. I was careful. I can't believe he followed me."

"It's 2016. He has some way to track you. Probably in your phone."

She groaned in disgust, angry at herself for letting it happen.

"Any children?"

Sophia shook her head. "Not yet."

Cassie paused for a moment at her response. "What about your family?"

"My mother and sister live in Houston. I haven't seen them in six months. Brad won't let me go, and he refuses to let them visit me."

"Friends?"

"Mostly in Houston. I've tried to make some here, but—"

Sophia's resolve weakened and tears welling in her eyes began to spill, tracking down her cheeks.

"Do you have a job?"

"I worked at the Angel Boutique until last month. He got me fired." Sophia's eyes stayed fixed on the floorboard.

"Sophia, look at me."

The directive was firm, but not harsh. Sophia slowly lifted her eyes to meet Cassie's. Her eyes were the kindest she had seen in a long time.

"I can help a little or a lot. It's up to you."

"How?"

"If you're prepared to leave now, we can make that happen. If you're not ready, we can help a little. Sooner or later, you'll likely end up right back here."

"Can I go back to Houston?"

"Eventually, yes. For now, you'll have to lay low and let us do our job. You understand?"

Sophia shook her head in agreement.

"I'm about to take you to an undisclosed location. I'll have to blindfold you so that you are unable to later tell someone where you were. Everything you see from here on is confidential, now and forevermore. Are you agreeable to this?"

"Yes."

"Are you ready? If so, it starts right now."

Sophia took a deep breath. "I'm ready."

Cassie motioned to get out. They left the vehicle and moved toward the rear. The trunk opened.

"Give me any cell phones, tablets, or electronics that you have."

Sophia hesitated, and then fished out both her regular phone and the burner. Cassie produced a handful of Ziploc bags from the trunk. She took the phones and stripped out the batteries, GSM cards, and the micro SD cards in seconds, then slipped the pieces of each phone into its own bag. She then dropped the bags into a heavily padded duffle and zipped it closed. As Cassie moved, Sophia noticed a very large pistol in its holster at her side, discretely covered by her jacket vest.

"This duffle bag blocks RFIDs, or electromagnetic signals."

She then retrieved a wand like the security people at the airport wielded.

"Spread your arms and legs."

"You take this seriously," Sophia noted, as she followed her instructions.

"If I were you, I wouldn't have it any other way."

Cassie turned on the wand and passed it along her body. After a few moments, she nodded in satisfaction.

"Very good," she said, dumping the duffle and wand into the trunk and closing it. "Let's go."

They dropped back into the car. Cassie handed Sophia an eye cover and tapped on the screen on her dashboard. Sophia slipped the blinds over her eyes.

"Ready?"

"Yes."

"Hang on."

The XTS took off, tearing out of the garage and back down Congress to its destination.

TWO

S HE liked being there after dark, when the subtle lamps and candles scattered around the church provided just enough light to see what was important, leaving the trivial in the shadows where it belonged. In the fallen world outside, the shadows chased you, invading your soul and holding you prisoner. Even those who found the strength to face them would only enjoy a brief respite until new shadows emerged.

Julia had learned to live with these realities. She was a believer, but had a healthy reserve of skepticism about the man-made institutions that built their earthly empires on servicing expressions of faith. There was no doubt about the meaning of the sacrament she put to her lips, the rosaries clutched inside her fist, or her motions making the sign of the cross. There was no need to describe it to others or herself. It was for her, and her alone.

Once she left and stepped into the night, her refreshed spirit turned steely. The perspective gained inside the church walls would now be tested, travelling alone in an unforgiving world. The road home was a constant reminder of her solitary existence, street lamps only providing the illusion of order and safety to the rats racing through the maze.

She saw her house, welcoming despite her uneven maintenance regimen. The 3-2-2 in North Austin had been nursed like a newborn by the previous owner, an elderly woman who had developed a nasty reputation by chasing neighborhood kids off her front sidewalk. When her children talked her into selling it, the new owner reaped the benefits. All 42 trees and plants in the yard had been named, their planting dates recorded, and their care instructions carefully written in a spiral notebook that the woman had left for her. Julia often joked that, despite collecting many enemies over the years, her life would ultimately end at the hands of the previous owner after seeing what she had done to her old home.

The rest of her life consumed her far too often to improve her home's upkeep. For all the negatives that had resulted from discarding her previous life, one of the positives was that she quickly developed a work ethic. But all that work was centered around building her career, and the house's appearance fell down the list of priorities. Besides, few of the people she counted as friends even knew where she lived, let alone had visited.

A grey tabby met Julia at the door. She knew Ozzy's greeting was more of a plea for dinner than a welcome home. Once fed, he dutifully followed her around like a security guard. After she changed clothes and sat behind her desk, Ozzy took his place on top of it as if protecting her with his life, periodically marching outside of the office on patrol. It was one of her favorite things about him, not that he would strike fear into an intruder like a tiger or lion, his wilder, larger ancestors. His spirit gave her comfort, a karma that a human being couldn't replicate. People were flawed and given to corruption. Animals were truer companions.

She had also learned how to live by herself, though it still wasn't comfortable to her. Her fear of being alone had created many of her problems, especially keeping company with less than desirable companions. At 47, she had never married. Her life had seen many relationships, but she had never shared a residence since leaving Florida.

Like Ozzy, she had developed a vigilance that had helped her through her chosen vocations, including her current one. Because of it, her cell phone sat nearby, fully charged, volume at maximum. The calls and texts came like the weather, several days passing without it sounding, followed by stretches of days where it wouldn't stop. When the phone did sound, it reminded her of that day 24 years before. It's why she did what she did for a living.

She produced a whiskey bottle from her desk drawer and poured into her empty coffee mug, taking a swig. Next to the mug, her cell phone chirped and vibrated on the desktop. She pressed a button on the phone.

"Yep."

"Cargo retrieved," Cassie said. "En route to the Manor house."

"Any issues?"

"Nothing I couldn't handle."

Julia paused. "Alright. Be safe."

"Will do. Good night."

The line clicked off. With no more extractions to confirm that evening, she drained the mug. High ball glasses were in order, but the mug secured the illusion that the drinks were impromptu. Now the mug taunted her, flaunting her feeble attempt to fool herself.

Julia rose from the chair, pacing back to her bedroom to make a payment on her sleep debt. She stopped at the door, looking back to the desk where the unseen bottle in the drawer beckoned her.

You'll sleep better.

The bottle had made empty promises throughout Julia's adult life, but she wanted to believe them, wanted to surrender. She walked back, steadying her hand on the desk, two steps from the bottle. She saw the newsprint underneath the glass of the desktop.

The clipping was from the front page of the Statesman, two years before. The above-the-fold feature told of the mysterious drop in domestic violence cases over a five-year period, when the rates in the rest of the United States continued to rise. Rumors of a rogue vigilante group who defended survivors, protected the underground and attacked abusers were the source of wide speculation by advocates and authorities alike. Those who were quoted for the piece either pled ignorance or responded cryptically, lending credence to the growing legend.

Like all wars, the war with domestic violence came at a heavy toll. Whatever her sobriety cost, it was a price she couldn't ever imagine affording.

Julia pulled the bottle from the drawer and poured once more into the coffee mug. She took the mug back to her bedroom, turning off lights as she went. Ozzy watched her knowingly, trotting after her. Some demons even he could not protect her from.

THREE

TWO hundred miles north, on a suburban street where no house was valued less than seven figures, it was quiet enough to hear the rustling of a few leaves that had escaped the meticulous care of landscapers. The entrance to every residence in the neighborhood was gated. Some of the homes had secrets more precious than their valuables to protect.

The most famous homeowner was rarely spotted by his neighbors. When seen, he was often surrounded by an entourage of four or more men, hurriedly rushing him off by SUV or limousine to some important commitment on the calendar. There were two known attempts to obtain his autograph when caught by himself at his home. Both the 10-year-old and the 12-year-old were met with profanity-laced refusals.

These experiences were in stark contrast to the carefully crafted image Trent Tanger displayed on the TV screen. High definition coverage on professional baseball's best player in a generation never seemed to catch him in such poor behavior. Not only did he have all five tools on the field, his demeanor on camera always displayed the "good face." He smiled and laughed with teammates in the dugout, opposing base runners who he held on at first base, and fans he willingly signed autographs for before games. He could also show edge, barreling into a catcher covering home, or charging the mound when thrown at once too often by a hot-headed pitcher who refused to pay homage to the golden child after he admired a home run shot one moment too long.

The view of Tanger from baseball and the vast number of media outlets that covered the sport was nearly unanimous. He was the best thing to happen to America's pastime since the steroid era had turned its brightest stars into punch lines.

These trappings had cleverly hidden the fact that Trent Tanger was an abuser. The shrill crying of his beaten wife would go unheard outside the mansion. Inside, a security staff of four loitered, imagining away the desperate screams while occupying themselves with diversions. Each had been told that the superstar's wife was crazy, strung out on prescription drugs and a danger to herself and others. That story had long since worn thin, leaving each man's conscience to wrestle the numbers in their bank accounts. They would remain silent and their checks would keep coming.

The volume cranked up from the stereo tried but failed to drown out the auditory evidence of violence. Sandy and Bonner, two former collegiate offensive linemen, were shooting pool. Gordon, who dwarfed over them, spread his 6-8 frame on the couch, watching the wall-sized television in the media room. He never played ball past high school, primarily due to having never graduated.

Junior, the leader of the security team, watched the bedroom activity from his tablet. Two hidden cameras relayed a feed that could be accessed from each man's smartphone, and that one member of the team monitored at all times. Once things got too "rowdy" in the suite, he was to alert the group, and two of the men would go in and remove Tanger. The definition of "rowdy" was a grey area, but generally meant saving the slugger from himself, preventing him from causing his wife serious injuries or worse. Entering too quickly would unduly anger Tanger, but a murder would force them to choose between risking their ongoing paychecks and risking prosecution as an accomplice. Concern for his wife's welfare was not expressed in the instructions.

The shrieks of the woman were so tortured and piercing, the video was no longer necessary. The noise stopped their attention from their distractions just as Junior gave them the signal. The two men playing pool dropped their cues and jogged down the hall, meeting Tanger at the door as he emerged from inside. They could still hear her crying, confirming that she was still alive.

"Don't let her leave!"

Tanger always said this despite his wife not being allowed to leave on her own for years. When she did leave, one or more of the men were assigned to "protect" her.

Once Tanger had left, Junior went in to see the woman. What he saw confirmed his suspicions. Instead of rendering aid, or even communicating with her, he left the room, and called the number at the top of his speed dials.

"This is Junior at the Tangers."

Inside the bedroom, a young woman was crumpled on the floor, her face dripping with sweat and tears, and blood trickling from the corner of her mouth. Whatever pleasant memories that existed for April Tanger, they were clouded by the pain her husband caused her and by the drugs coursing through her veins that masked those pains. When the effects of the drugs faded, the memories that never left were the nightmares of a man who dominated her, unwilling to control himself and his violent impulses.

Trent Tanger was not the same man she met at a college party at such a tender age, and perhaps he never was what she thought. She knew nothing about sports, her only attraction to him being his looks and magnetic personality. Only later did she learn most of his presence was manufactured, carefully honed by his legion of handlers. Already a coveted baseball prospect by then, Tanger was more image than reality. Now she was trapped with who he really was, someone she would have never fallen for if given a preview of his darker side.

The drugs inside her were mostly legal, dispensed by a doctor handpicked by her husband's team. Unlike normal people who made decisions for themselves, she did not have the option of seeking a second opinion. Her doctor's diagnosis was the only one she would get, due to the controlling desires of the man who paid the bills.

She had also learned the most prudent mode of behavior after being assaulted. Loud screaming would prompt action from one of her husband's assistants, most likely a call to the doctor, or worse, her husband's master. She had fallen into a rhythm of life, in accordance with their design. Having her sedate, pliable and able to function when needed for public events served their purposes.

April had escaped once, a little over a year after their wedding. He had come off a long, horrendous road trip and her mere presence made her a target of his frustration. A broken nose and busted lip would not have avoided the press if she had made it to the Nashville hospital. Instead, he dragged her from her car and added bruising to her arms and legs to the injuries.

The doctor making house calls had become routine. She had long since distrusted the purpose of the prescriptions. There had been a succession of many physicians, ironically protected by the very privacy laws that were supposed to protect her rights. All of them had ignored the most important oath. Their willful compliance with Tanger's handler had done harm above all else, his schemes going far beyond the exploits of modern medicine.

In a tenth-floor suite overlooking the Dallas Tollway, Damon Cash watched the late-night traffic rush back and forth beneath him while he did what he was best at, and what earned him his generous income.

Cash talked. And talked. And talked. He talked to his clients, their parents, friends, spouses, children, attorneys, accountants, doctors, pastors. He talked to team owners and executives, movie producers, directors, record executives, politicians, judges, police officers. He schmoozed them, cajoled them, pushed them, placated them. He made things happen, and he made his clients money.

He worked tirelessly and played recklessly, with an appetite few of his clients could match. The agent could hang with the most seasoned partiers, and yet hit the ground running the next morning. A lifelong bachelor, he routinely vacationed with swimsuit models and B-list actresses. The mother of his five-year-old daughter was a former Miss March centerfold.

When someone referred to him as a sports agent, he smoothly but arrogantly chided the individual for selling him short. In addition to a small army of athletes from all the major professional sports and most of the high profile Olympic sports, he also represented celebrity entertainers, including actors and musicians. Damon Cash was a household name for anyone who consumed even a nominal amount of celebrity-driven media.

With his feet propped on his desk, he conducted business on behalf of Cash Legacies, LLC, without an ounce of restraint or shame. The autographed jerseys, footballs, basketballs, bats, hockey sticks and platinum albums lining his office walls quelled any intruding thoughts that he should consider a nobler solution to any problem. Life was a zero-sum game, and he was rarely on the losing end of the equation.

It was commonplace to receive calls to troubleshoot the personal lives of his clients. Most issues could be delegated to an armada of assistants who would discretely handle them without incident. He occasionally had to put his own boots on the ground and extinguish the larger fires. The number from the Tanger residence appearing on the caller ID display usually indicated an inferno in progress.

"Cash."

The mouth that never seemed to quit was silent as the caller explained the situation.

"Where did he go?"

The answer produced a long sigh.

"Alright. Call the doctor. No one sees her until I get there."

He hung up the phone and opened one of his larger desk drawers. Inside was a safe with the combination lock facing upward. He quickly unlocked it and looked over its contents. He ignored some files and two pistols, instead reaching into several rows of cash. He pulled a few stacks, still bound from the bank and reached for his sport coat, tucking the stacks into the pockets before darting out of the office.

Inside the elevator, Cash shook his head, accepting the frustration. Once the elevator door opened in the basement, he marched to the ivory Escalade, parked with several of his other luxury vehicles along his reserved wall in the garage. His duties at the Tanger residence were a nuisance, but they generated more than enough income to justify the inconveniences.

FOUR

THE room was dimly lit, with six wall sconces providing just enough light for the woman working behind the desk to see. The desk was an L-shaped, two-tiered workstation, also serving as a bunker facing the door to the room. On the two tiers sat four monitors, two notebook computers, and one separate keyboard. Three computer mice of different colors sat next to their respective keyboards. All the equipment was wired to a closet down the hall where the guts that ran all the ones and zeros were housed.

The woman tapped away on a keyboard, intensely focused on her chosen screen. Her blonde hair was pulled back in a ponytail under a Texas Rangers cap, and black rimmed glasses over her brown eyes. There was plenty of work, more than enough to justify her odd hours. There were projects on the board for half a dozen clients, ranging from designing a website for a mom and pop burger joint to conducting white hat security tests on the network of a Fortune 500 company. When the money ran low enough, she donned a grey hat to keep the bills paid.

A cell phone sounded with a ring that would set off a sensitive car alarm within shouting distance. She grimaced, not wanting to stop the flow of her work. She yanked the earbuds out of her ears and snatched the phone from the desk.

"Yeah."

"It's me, Noelle," said Cassie. "Pickup made and delivery is seven miles out."

"Is she alright?"

"I've seen worse. Should be fine."

"Full name?"

"Sophia Jane Ricks."

"DOB?"

"6/12/94."

"His name?"

"Brad Benton."

"Got it."

"I also have two of her cell phones. The one she used to contact us is a burner she said he doesn't know about."

"Good. Bring them to the office and I'll take care of them."

"Anything else?"

Noelle looked at her three monitors and they exploded with data on their newest client.

"That's plenty. I'll get her file worked up and we can talk about it with the others when we meet."

"Great," sighed Cassie.

"Alright."

"Bye."

Noelle put down her phone. Before she could put the earbuds back in, the door to the room opened and a teenage girl stumbled in, rubbing her eyes.

"Momma, your phone is so loud."

"Sorry, sweetie. I can't hear it with my headphones."

Noelle watched her daughter, Megan, fall into her lap. The resemblance was so striking, it was like looking in the mirror 20 years before, when she was 17.

"Why are you working so late?"

"I'm a night owl, and we've got clients waiting. Someone's got to pay for those designer fashions you wear to school. I have to settle for sweats and sandals."

"That's what you want to wear, Mom."

Noelle laughed. "You think so?"

"I know so."

"Okay," she said, pushing her off her lap. "Back to bed. I'll turn the phone down a bit."

"When are you going to bed?"

"When the work is done, sweetie. Good night."

The girl trudged off, closing the door behind her. It seemed like yesterday Megan was all elbows, knees and acne. Before her mother's eyes, she was evolving into a woman.

From the phone bill, it was clear the boys had taken notice as well.

The protective instinct was more than that of a responsible mother. Noelle knew the dangers far better than most mothers did. That knowledge was a big reason she pushed her schedule and her scruples to the edge, for money and for principle.

She returned to her work, motivated by those principles. The data she saw in front of her, and the thought that a sweet, innocent girl like Megan could easily fall prey to an animal like the one now displayed on her screens pressed her forward. Within moments, what she saw brought disgusted looks to her face.

"Bastard."

As Noelle continued reading about Brad Benton, she shook her head. She began the methodical process of digging into every nook and cranny of his life. As his vulnerabilities multiplied, the smile on her face grew. Whatever sad circumstances had led Benton to the twisted nature of his current life was of no concern to her.

The duties of Noelle and her partners were twofold. First, rescue and protect the victim. Then, punish the abuser accordingly. The court system was sometimes utilized. More often, the law was found insufficient and other means were used to exact justice. As Benton's history unfolded, Noelle began to customize his punishment from a lengthy menu of choices.

I hope this one is dumb enough to put up a fight, she thought. It's always fun watching them get a taste of their own medicine.

Sophia heard the Caddy's rumble and felt its forward motion waning. After a sharp turn, she felt the car slow and finally come to a stop.

"I'll get you out. Keep the blinds on."

Sophia did as she was told. She felt the door open and Cassie gently taking her hand.

"Right this way."

Sophia carefully stepped out, allowing Cassie to guide her. They walked several paces and up one step. She heard a door open.

"Hey," a cheerful voice said.

"Sorry it's so late."

"Never mind that. Come on in."

Cassie turned to her passenger. "You can remove the blinds."

Sophia removed the cover and found herself in the entry of a home. A woman with silver-gray hair and a wide, sweet smile extended her arms.

"Hello, Sophia. I'm Molly."

"Hi."

Molly gently hugged her guest. "It's so good to meet you. I'll be your host for a while."

"Rest well," Cassie said, patting Sophia on the shoulder, then leaving quickly. Molly led Sophia to a living room and they sat in chairs next to each other.

"Are you hungry?" Molly asked.

"Not really," she said. "I'm almost sick to my stomach."

"I understand, sweetie. Let me get some information from you, then we'll get you to your room and you can get some sleep."

"Thanks."

"What are your sizes?"

She replied and Molly wrote them down on a notepad.

"Do you have any prescriptions you need?"

Sophia said yes, but could not remember them all. She did know her doctor's name and pharmacy, and that was enough for Molly to get them refilled.

"Good. We will cover all the rest tomorrow. Come with me."

She followed Molly down a hall and opened the first door on the right and motioned her in. The room inside was like a motel room, but with an interior much more like a guest bedroom. An old tube TV sat on a stand with a small refrigerator underneath it.

"There are towels in the bathroom, along with soap, shampoo, and all the other toiletries you might need. There's some water and juice in the fridge. I'll have some clothes sitting outside your door by morning."

Sophia nodded, still trying to take in the blur of the last four hours.

"You have a neighbor across the hall, a real sweet young lady named Renee. You'll be sharing the bathroom with her."

"Okay."

"Once you're ready in the morning, come to the kitchen for breakfast. If you have an emergency, just come knock on my door at the end of the hall."

"Thanks."

"Sure, sweetie."

Sophia closed the door to her room and crawled into bed. The transposition from a life in hell to being treated like an honored guest in only a few hours was welcomed, but jarring. It took a while for her to relax, but once the fatigue overcame her nerves, she curled under the covers and slept soundly.

FIVE

THE Escalade stopped abruptly inside the front gate of the mansion. Several vehicles were parked ahead at odd angles, taking up all the space in a wide court that could have accommodated twice as many cars parked in an orderly fashion. Cash left the SUV and walked to the front door purposefully, entering without a knock. The mental checklist for things to do in situations clients like Trent Tanger presented quickly went through his brain.

Inside the door, a lean, yet muscular man named Vance waited in the entryway. He stood 6-3, and wore a jacket, open collar button down shirt and slacks. Unlike the others, he looked like he belonged in business attire. The others were dressed similarly, but somehow didn't belong in what they wore. Whether it be shirts with one too many buttons undone, deviant facial grooming, or tattoo sleeves peeking from underneath the cuffs of their shirts, their appearance gave away the true nature of their work.

Vance served many purposes, the primary one being a layer of distance from Cash. Technically, Vance was the owner of a security firm that Cash hired through a blind corporation. Most of the profits ended up in Cash's pockets, but Vance earned a healthy salary and bonuses, the bulk of which went untaxed. It was relatively easy work for Vance, who had spent most of his career making less money with far more hazards across the pond. His pay was earned by taking on the liability risks, financially and legally, for the questionable tasks Cash assigned his charges.

While the evening's events were not uncommon, they required a specific response. Junior, the leader of the security team was entrusted with knowing when to report events, and when to let matters settle on their own. When he reported, he called Vance. Vance then determined whether or not to call Cash.

The men inside knew what to expect once Cash arrived. He would only approach Vance, taking him out of earshot of the other men, usually in an ornate sitting room off the entry. Vance would then give the men their marching orders.

After only a few moments of conferring, they emerged from the room as the men watched them.

"Is the doctor here?" Cash asked Vance.

"She's in with her now."

They walked down the long hall, their boots clicking on the marble until finally arriving at the door of a bedroom. Just before Cash could knock on the door, a woman appeared and looked expectantly at Cash. Inside, loud cries of protest couldn't be ignored. As the door closed, the cries elevated to wails.

"Dr. Pelson. Good to see you."

She gave him an ugly look. Cash realized it's inappropriateness and waved his statement away, leading her from the room a short distance.

"What happened?" he asked.

"She has multiple bruises and lacerations to her face. She also has a sprained wrist."

"Did she hit him?"

"No, Mr. Cash. She did not." Her words were firm and angry.

"Calm down, Janice. Can you care for her here?"

"I can, this time. I don't know about the next time."

He glared at the doctor, preparing to brace her properly. Before he could speak, the volume from inside the bedroom increased, as if to beg anyone within her voice to somehow help her.

Cash shoved the doctor to the side and bolted into the bedroom. He found his client's wife prostrate on the floor, next to a king size bed. Her face and eyes were red and wet, both of her arms were visibly bruised and blood trickled from the right side of her mouth.

When April saw him, she froze, her eyes exploding in fear. She instinctively scrambled away from him, even though there was no exit. Cash leapt across the bed and tackled her, pinning her against the vanity cabinets in the adjoining bathroom.

"No!"

"Shut up!"

They kept wrestling until he pressed her firmly enough to where she had no choice but to take whatever he would give her.

"You listen, and listen good."

April was breathing heavily, her teeth bared like an animal fighting for survival. With one of Cash's hands clenching most of her hair and the other around her neck, she had little choice but to comply.

"I bought your ass for a hundred grand because you caught the eye of the best baseball player of a generation at a frat party. I could have bought you for ten if your pimp hadn't recognized me. All these years later, he wouldn't give me twenty bucks for what's left of you."

The taunt achieved its intent, covering her in even more shame, sedating her spirit to fight. Cash paused with purpose, waiting for her to quiet before continuing. He drew closer, whispering in her ear.

"In fact, I bet they'd charge me to take you back, and I'm about this close to paying the freight just to be done with you. That's exactly what I'll do if you don't start being a good girl."

She tried to shrink away from him, but his grip was too firm. He strengthened his hold and drew closer.

"You think it's rough with Tanger? I'll get you shipped off as a slave whore in some third world country. And you know all about that, don't you?"

April knew it was no bluff. She had seen enough from Cash to know he wouldn't hesitate.

"Count your blessings," he hissed in her ear before shoving her by her face back to the floor and marching out of the room, closing the door behind him. He walked back to the doctor and reached into his jacket pocket, producing two stacks of crisp bills. He snatched her right arm and shoved the stacks into the palm of her hand. Janice tried to turn away from the sight of the bills, but was unable to do so.

"That should cover it. If it doesn't, I'll need an explanation."

"Mr. Cash, how long are we going to do this?"

"For as long as it takes."

This reddened her face. Cash read that she was getting close to the edge of her moral limits. He had already stretched those limits gradually for over a year, but he didn't want to push her too far.

"Janice. We are—"

"It's Dr. Pelson, Mr. Cash."

"Be careful, Janice."

Pressed by the snap in his reply, she lowered her gaze. Vance loomed over his shoulder, his stare reinforcing Cash's attitude.

"We are working with Mr. Tanger to get him some help. It takes time. The best-case scenario will be to get these two away from each other for good. We're a few months away from accomplishing that."

She shook her head in regret. Cash read her thoughts.

"We're in this together, Janice. That practice you want to open in Colorado is within sight. You have made some great sacrifices on this family's behalf. That won't be forgotten. There will be a day when everyone involved will thank you. Just think what would have happened if a lesser physician had been working with us."

This seemed to calm her. Now that he had pulled her back from the edge, Cash resumed control.

"Get her ready to go. She and Trent have an event next week."

"Next week?" she asked incredulously.

Cash nodded. "Can you up her dosage?"

April Tanger was on numerous medications, but Janice knew which prescription the agent was referring to.

"That's not wise. We're already well past the recommended level for ongoing intake."

"Either make her understand or up the dosage. If we can get her to December, he'll hit free agency, get her a generous divorce and we're all done with this."

Janice said nothing, brushing past him on the way back to the bedroom. When she entered, the woman inside resumed wailing. The talking inside slowly settled to a level not heard in the rest of the house.

"Where is he?" Cash asked Vance as they returned to the entryway.

"He didn't say where he was going."

Cash motioned for Vance to follow him outside. Once there, Cash lit a cigar and took a long drag, strolling into the perfectly manicured lawn.

"You need to start drawing up a plan."

Vance watched him blow smoke into the night air. He knew exactly what the agent meant. They had debated the merits of the plan for months. The first mention of it was years before, when the stakes weren't as large or as certain.

"Are you sure you want to do this?"

"Don't tell me you have a problem with it."

Vance chuckled. "Don't be silly. It's just a task with a dollar figure attached to it. However, there is significant risk. Are you sure offing his wife carries less liability than paying her and sending her away?"

"She's not rational, not even to comply with a generous divorce agreement. If she were to violate it, all she would lose is money. We could lose everything. Burying her quietly carries far less risk."

Vance noted the meaning in Cash's wording. When there were problems or risks, it was "we." When there was profit to be gained, it was "I" or "me." Since Vance's compensation had proven worthy of his efforts until now, there had been no need to challenge the agent's perspective.

"I'm assuming you want to get the divorce and get him some distance from her first."

Cash nodded. "We'll do the divorce, then after a couple of months leak the drug problems. Then, when she disappears, no one will wonder about her fate."

"Very well."

The pair nodded to each other. Cash went to his vehicle and Vance went back inside to his team. They would continue to ignore the cries at the end of the hall. The doctor would take the money, heed Cash's instructions, and leave quietly, undeterred by the desperate pleas of a drugged, semi-conscious woman.

As Cash settled in the Escalade, he shook his head in bemused disbelief. What a mess these people make of their lives, he thought. What a fabulous life I've made of it.

SIX

JULIA'S landing in Austin was more a function of happenstance than forethought. She was not used to good fortune, but the three-day trip from Florida, and everything that happened along the way, turned out to be the best stroke of luck in her life.

The capital city of Texas was merely the outbound destination of the trucker who met her in Birmingham. Jim, who picked her up in Indiantown, paid for a hotel room for her and arranged for a friend named Fred to hitch her further west the following day. Fred would have typically travelled directly to Austin, but the pair diverted to Texarkana on purpose.

Like Julia, Fred had disposed of his birth name out of a necessity he did not detail. A local bail bondsman a mile off the Texas-Arkansas state line had been arranging new identities for years. As luck would have it, he had a Julia Ann Caldwell in the queue, complete with a Social Security number, passport, and a stellar credit rating, waiting for a human being to give the data flesh and blood. The original Julia was dead, killed with her parents in a car crash in 1972. The bail bondsman had harvested thousands of identities over the years, and was protected by authorities in five states who unofficially used his services when urgently needed. There were similar off-the-grid services available in Chattanooga, TN and Bullhead City, AZ, but only if you knew where to find them.

She instantly took to Austin, an eclectic melting pot of friendly free spirits. A steady influx of transplants like herself, and overwhelming highways that were still hopelessly behind the increase in population had completely transformed the city since her arrival. Locals lamented the changes, longing for the Austin of the past that would never be again. Still, the vibe that had attracted her and many others was there once you snuck through the cracks of urban sprawl.

With safe houses dotting a seven-county area, she lived out of her pickup. Eating, grooming, makeup, and work got wedged in between her appointments that seemed to cluster, leaving stretches of days without travel. It was a rhythm she had adjusted to, but she longed for a smooth routine. Every so often when the schedule was too calm for too long, she realized it wasn't really who she was or would ever be.

Molly's safe house was used more often than the others. The widow lived to take in battered women and help them get a fresh start. Her place was east of town on 290, just outside Manor. Her first rescue was her niece, who had since successfully relocated to Oregon. Protecting her required brandishing a shotgun outside her front porch, trained at the head of her estranged boyfriend. The same weapon remained at the ready, but had not been required since.

Every time Julia neared a safe house, her senses sharpened to watch everything around her. She had not yet been tailed by an abuser that she knew of, and their track record for keeping victims safe when under their protection was perfect. She was intent on keeping it that way.

Sophia barely remembered her father, who left when she was four. Stepfather number one routinely whipped her and her sister until they bled as children. This paled in comparison to her mother, whose eye was permanently damaged after the last night in their marriage. Stepfather number two treated her similarly, but she again did not have the worst of it. Her mother and her sister protected her from harm, in ways she wished she could forget.

It didn't occur to her until after moving in with Brad that he was frighteningly similar to each of her stepfathers. It took little time for the dark side to show itself. Angry and uncontrolled at one moment, calculating and manipulative the next. The pain strangely seemed normal, up until yesterday. The stakes had changed.

On a trip to the hospital months earlier, the RN made a point of handing her the business card. She took her bandaged right hand, gently but firmly, sliding the card underneath the bandages and out of view of her boyfriend coming to get her. The RN looked deeply into Sophia's eyes.

"When you are ready for it to be over, as in over for good, call."

She punctuated her words and looked with a nod before walking away. As the months passed, that look from the nurse never faded. It grew with memory as she considered the possibility of calling the number and taking her chances with a new life.

Looking around the room, she considered what it had brought her. The bedroom had a small, narrow window at the top of the wall, giving away the age of the house. The furnishings were spartan, but not uncomfortable. The double bed was a tad firm, but the sheets and comforter were soft and it slept okay. The old 19-inch tube TV didn't appear to have cable, but a small DVD player sat next to it on the desk. The bathroom was clean and stocked with all the necessities, as promised.

When she rose from the bed, she noticed two things. The first was a distinct smell of cigarette smoke. The second was a note, clipped to the top of a file folder, slid underneath the door. She opened the note.

Good morning, Sophia.
There are several breakfast choices in the kitchen. Make yourself at home.
Please look over the forms inside the folder and begin filling out what you can. A friend named Julia will stop by and help you with any questions you have until I return.
Enjoy,
Molly

Sophia looked inside the folder. There were several forms with too many questions to consider without the benefit of nourishment. She walked into the kitchen and dropped the folder on a small, round breakfast table. While the house itself was modest, the appliances were updated, and a large Keurig sat with a full reservoir of water. She selected her preferred blend and a large pink mug, and closed the pod into place. Once the coffee was in the cup, she followed the sunshine to something she couldn't see last night. A sliding door revealed the backyard, now visible by daylight. Outside, a woman was stretched out on a lawn chair on the porch, taking a drag from her cigarette.

Sophia stepped outside, and the other woman measured her curiously.

"Are you the new neighbor?"

"For now."

"Renee," she replied, extending her hand.

"Sophia."

Renee looked at her cigarette. "I hope you don't mind if I finish this off. I can't try to quit in the middle of this shit."

"Go ahead. How long have you been here?"

"About a week," she said, as she displayed her left forearm in a cast, almost as if to brandish it as a badge of honor. Sophia didn't know much about life after the decision to leave, but she knew that was a cover. It was just different from hers.

"Where do you think we are?"

"Probably east of town. We had a strong storm a couple of days ago, and the news said it was heavier on that side."

"It still feels weird, not knowing where I am."

"It bothered me at first, but then it started to feel safer and more comfortable. Since I don't know where I am, I can't be tempted to tell him."

Sophia nodded knowingly. Fortunately, contacting her abuser was the last thing she was tempted to do at the moment. She stopped to wonder if that would change.

They spent nearly an hour on the porch, talking about light topics with natural stretches of silence. Like two strangers on a flight, they took comfort in their compatibility and a lack of future commitment.

Four coasters sat atop the small table between their chairs, piled together at odd angles. Renee watched Sophia unstack the coasters, then place them at the four corners of the table, spaced exactly the same distance from each other.

"Did you eat anything?" Renee asked, stifling a chuckle at her new neighbor's behavior.

"No, I didn't."

"Why don't you go get some of that breakfast casserole while I burn another one of these?"

Sophia nodded and rose from her chair. "Is it good?"

"Very."

Sophia went inside and opened the fridge, finding a casserole pan with only a few squares missing. She cut herself a piece and put it in the microwave. Five minutes later, she was sitting at the table, absorbing the first stress-free meal she could remember.

Three firm knocks sounded on the front door. This gave Sophia a start, taking her breath away. She shook off a chill, then slowly walked to the door, but didn't reach for the door handle.

"Who is it?"

"I'm Julia Caldwell. I'm a friend of Molly's."

Sophia looked through the peephole. She saw a pretty brunette of about 5-8, dressed in a business suit. She looked legitimate.

The door cracked open, and Sophia peeked around it.

"Sophia?"

"Yes."

"I'm Julia."

"Hi."

"Hello. Do you mind if I come in?"

Sophia slowly opened the door. Julia eased her way in.

"Molly said you might be coming."

"Good."

"I was about to eat something. Is that okay?"

"Go ahead."

Julia recognized the timidity, the habit of asking permission to do simple things like speaking or leaving the room. They sat at the table and Sophia dug her fork into the slice, letting steam escape.

"Is that Molly's casserole?"

"Yes."

Julia smiled. "I can't resist that." She rose and went to the fridge, retrieving a slice of her own. Sophia saw her helping herself, putting her plate into the microwave, clearly comfortable in the home.

"Did you get a look at those forms?"

"They look long."

Julia laughed, making her own cup of coffee from the Keurig. She could feel the flask in her purse on the couch drawing her, even though she wouldn't dare produce it in front of a client.

"We don't like them either, but they're important. Just relax here and try to finish them. In the meantime, Molly will take good care of you. The casserole is one of many recipes at her disposal, and they're all to die for."

"And then?"

Sophia watched Julia turn toward her as she finished a bite, wiping her mouth with a napkin.

"It's mostly up to you. What do you want?"

The question made her pause. Maybe she never really knew. For as long as she could remember, it was simply to be somewhere else, with someone else.

"I don't really have any idea."

"Why don't we start with where you've been?"

Sophia nodded. "Okay."

Julia produced a folio and opened it to a legal pad. Ordinarily, this would have frightened Sophia, the mere idea of another human being knowing what had happened to her and putting it on record. Julia had quickly put her at ease, however, without pretense or manipulation.

"I met him shortly after I moved here."

"From Houston?"

She nodded, realizing Cassie had given her some of the details. "Pasadena. Me and two of my high school friends moved together. A year later, they moved back and I moved in with him."

With that, Sophia poured out her heart, recounting every bruise and cut she had taken, and every tear that it produced. It later surprised her how much had been pent up, and how freely it now flowed. She was ready, but it took Julia to make her comfortable enough to release it. She mostly listened, making less than a page of notes to document a painful journey. Throughout the narrative, she massaged eyes fixed on the floor, swollen with tears. Julia produced tissues while listening, serenely steadfast.

Once Sophia finally fell silent, she looked up at Julia.

"What now?"

"Are you ready to move on from him?"

"I should be, shouldn't I?"

"That's a decision only you can make."

Sophia saw in her new friend's eyes that she had been in her place once before. It was like a frequency that only those who had absorbed such wounds shared. Julia watched her knowingly, wrestling with her own soul.

"I don't want to love him anymore. I wish I didn't, but I still do. If he could only just—"

"Change?"

"Yes. Silly, isn't it?"

"No. But it's not likely."

Julia watched the young woman, her face twisting with the internal turmoil.

"Do you know what it means to compartmentalize?"

"I've heard of it."

"It means you put your life in separate boxes. You are going to have a lot of conflicting thoughts and emotions resulting from your trauma and what you have to do to stay safe. Mixed together, all this stuff will drive you crazy. If you sort them, and put aside the items that hurt but that you can't solve, it makes it simpler. The scars won't ever go away. There's a part of you that will always be vigilant, like a soldier. Hopefully, the only battles you have left will be with yourself."

"I can't go back there. I just can't."

"Okay. We'll start working on it." Julia rose from the chair and put her folio in her bag.

"What happens now?"

"Once that paperwork is completed, we'll file for a temporary restraining order. That will last for twenty days. Hopefully, by then we'll have him out of your life, and keep him out for good. We'll map out a plan with a tentative schedule. We'll make sure we get your history cleared through the system and get you lined up with a job. When you're ready, we'll get you to a safe place to relocate. Then, you can start again."

"How exactly will you do all that?"

"We have our ways. The specifics I can't tell you. To protect you, as well others before and after you, it's confidential."

Sophia nodded. "Okay."

They hugged each other. It wasn't something that always happened. Julia could usually tell when an embrace was appropriate. Some clients were just too traumatized for any unwarranted contact. She and Sophia had connected and it furthered the bond they had quickly built.

"I'll be in touch," Julia said. "Relax and take care of yourself right now. We'll do the rest."

"Alright."

Julia walked to the door. Sophia stepped toward her.

"Tell me it will get easier. Tell me the pain will go away."

Julia turned back to her. The way Sophia asked and the intent in her eyes let Julia know it was a personal question about her own experiences.

"That I can't do. There will be more pain, and more tough things. However, I can help you get stronger. I can help you get your life back. And, I can make sure that bastard never dares touch you again."

Sophia saw Julia's firm, but gentle gaze. She meant what she said.

"Thanks."

"Sure."

SEVEN

THE throng of reporters crowded in front of the gate was so large, it spilled onto the two-lane road. The vans representing all the major networks parked on the shoulder of either side of the road served as the only warning to oncoming traffic of the human obstacles ahead.

The Jupiter Island estate belonged to John Skilby, the All-Pro passer who had held out the entire season, refusing to accept the $23 million salary due a quarterback with the franchise tag. Minnesota had attempted to negotiate a multi-year deal with his agent ever since the tag was applied in March, but little progress had been made. Skilby had fired numerous missives at the club via Twitter and Instagram, draining any sympathy Minnesota's fan base had for him in the standoff.

Through the estate's gates, reporters could barely make out the compound through the leaves of the palm trees. The drive from the compound's front door to the street seemed so long and winding, even the quarterback might have difficulty arming a pass to the mailbox. Most of them had arrived prior to the scheduled 2:00 PM press conference, despite knowing it was unlikely the diva passer would show on time. True to form, at 2:43, a limousine began navigating the drive slowly, finally stopping just short of the gates. Skilby took great pleasure striding out of the limo and having the gate doors part just far enough to let him step through as the cameras and reporters eyed his every move. He wore sweats, sandals and sunglasses, despite the overcast skies. He was so above what he was doing, but it was necessary.

Minnesota's refusal to give him a long-term extension at market value after his first five years in the league was an insult, he explained. Three playoff appearances and one conference title deserved the franchise's respect. The worst performance in league history by a quarterback in a title game had nothing to do with his involvement in the Bourbon

Street brawl days before, he argued. Sure, he had underperformed in his contract year, but with scrubs for an offensive line and an offensive coordinator who spent the whole season with his head up his ass, who could blame him? $40 million guaranteed might seem like a lot, but was reasonable for a legitimate passer in a league where several teams had gone decades without sniffing a championship.

Mercifully, Skilby's tirade and a short Q&A had only taken 37 minutes of their lives. As the limo carried him through the gate, parting the unwashed media, Gil Hawthorne turned off his digital recorder and considered the nonsense he had witnessed. The young reporter could have written his story before Skilby had spoken a word and arrived closely to what he would end up submitting to his editor.

The more prestigious members of the fourth estate brushed by him without a word, sharpening their knives to carve up the quarterback in 500 words or less. They knew the truth, as did Minnesota. Their multi-year offer was generous for a player who was just as good at making an ass of himself as making plays on the field.

Hawthorne was still taken aback how ignorant celebrities were of their public perception. The media was too powerful to take for granted, especially when not given their just pleasantries. This much was clear to Hawthorne, even at a startup like Neon Megaphone, or neonmega.com. For three years, the owner of the digital tabloid promised it would be the next big online tabloid, but that hadn't happened yet. His journalism professors promised him several years of paying dues before reaching the top. Once Hawthorne had the chance to jump to a respected source for sports news, he was gone. Until then, he bided his time, waiting for the story that would send him to a legitimate gig.

He quickly composed his story on his notebook computer, sitting precariously on the armrest of the subcompact rental sitting on the shoulder of the road across from the estate. As he typed, it occurred to him how much of an outlier John Skilby was for his agent, the most powerful representative in sports. Damon Cash's clients rarely broke from his firm guidance, wise given his impressive track record.

Hawthorne made a mental note to watch the situation closely in the days ahead. Cash was crafty enough to spin the most preposterous situation into a palatable narrative. He was also not above distancing from clients who had become more trouble than they're worth. Right now, Skilby had to be testing his agent's patience to its limits.

Cash watched the TV screen on the far end of his office and could feel the dollar signs disappearing with every word Skilby uttered. His mindless grandstanding in the driveway of his mansion was a brutal display of tone deafness that did the agent no favors.

With each passing week, the quarterback's worth dwindled. Every victory made him more expendable, while every defeat made his return less relevant. Minnesota had already given Cash the parameters of what would keep the quarterback on the team. $42 million over three years with $16 million of it guaranteed was their best offer so far. While the $23 million franchise tag was possible, it was no certainty. After Skilby's sound bites, Cash hoped the $42 million was still on the table.

The agent rose from his seat and sent a text to two of his employees. Plan A was a trip to Minnesota to convince Skilby to take the reduced deal. However, Cash fully expected to be forced into Plan B, a contingency he had put in place months before. That option would be far worse than unemployment for the spoiled quarterback.

After telling his staff he would be gone through tomorrow, he took the elevator to the parking garage and paced to the Escalade. The agent also had an S63 and a Continental GT patiently waiting for their turn. Cash especially preferred the Bentley when expecting clients, but preferred the Cadillac or the Mercedes for everyday driving.

The drive would not be long. The country club was just down the road from the offices of Cash Legacies, LLC, in the cradle of North Dallas money the wealthy bathed in. The club was accustomed to serving the whims of the privileged, but certain members were particularly difficult to satisfy.

Cash entered the clubhouse and approached the desk.

"Is he here?"

"He is, sir. Should be right around number 6."

Cash motioned to the attendant and he handed the agent a key. Outside, Cash selected a cart and rolled down the path. He passed by several groups without a word or a wave.

Unlike Skilby, Trent Tanger radiated a magnetic personality in front of the camera that sold millions of dollars of products and brought millions more to a long list of charities. He was a media favorite who always sounded smooth and genuine. A few moments without any recording devices would paint a much uglier picture of the most popular baseball player of his generation. But the negatives about Tanger had always been cleverly hidden, and were difficult to uncover.

Tanger was groomed as a child by doting parents who were intent on living out the career his father was denied due to one too many surgeries. From the boutique "select" leagues until high school, he was always the best player on the field. The phenom from Austin was the first pick of the major league draft at eighteen years old, selected by the Nashville expansion baseball team. The new owners spent nearly a billion dollars on the franchise fee, and then were held up by a ridiculous list of demands by the most powerful agent in the business. Faced with an unprecedented PR disaster if they refused, the front office had no choice but to comply, paying the largest rookie bonus in history.

The instant multi-millionaire spent his first year of pro ball in double-A and quickly set records for home runs and batting average at that level. Promoted the following year to the majors, he made the all-star team as a rookie and every year afterwards. After seven years, he owned every significant offensive team record. With only a few weeks left in his final season until unrestricted free agency, the world was his for the taking.

The team constantly made the necessary adjustments to keep the superstar in the good graces of the public and the media. They would gladly continue doing so, if only they could win a bidding war with the big market teams, a longshot at best. One of the coasts beckoned, but could the kid handle the pressure? Would an untamed media be able to expose his warts?

While Tanger's inner circle and entourage saw him wrestle daily with his demons, he could escape the constant scrutiny on the golf course. Curiously, he found peace from the rage in a place that stole the self-control from most of its patrons. He insisted on golfing alone in his own cart, with a club caddy driving a cart of his own to attend to all of his needs. The clubhouse kept an extra space before and after him to keep friction from other members and nosy fans to a minimum.

The golf cart discreetly approaching registered with him, entering his consciousness just enough to ruin his focus. The shot sliced to the right of the green and disappeared under a row of bushes. Tanger looked back to see the biggest pain in his ass, and the biggest reason he was about to break the bank.

"Dammit, Cash!"

"Don't open up your clubface, T."

"What the hell do you want?"

Cash pulled a roll of bills out of his pocket and peeled off a fifty, handing it to the caddy. "Go grab some lunch, and then catch up with us."

The caddy scurried to his cart and rolled away.

"Cash, give me some space."

"What happened last night?"

"She just pissed me off."

"This is happening too often, T. You can't keep doing this."

"I just don't want this anymore. I'm sick and tired every day. I need a break."

"Trent."

Cash punctuated his sharp words, grabbing Tanger by both arms firmly. The agent was five inches and 75 solid pounds short of his client, but it was clear who the alpha of the relationship was.

"Do you know how many illegitimate children my clients have, altogether?"

"No. How many?"

"I have no idea. Never bothered to count them, and I don't much care. Do you know how many employed clients I have guilty of beating a woman?"

Cash formed his five fingers into a circle.

"That would be zero. None."

Tanger turned away from the agent, shaking his head in frustration.

"Trent. Look at me."

He turned back to Cash reluctantly, like a child about to be grounded.

"You have only a few weeks until free agency. There are 500 million reasons for you to keep it together. Trust me."

"You really think you can get that much?"

"If you don't fuck it up, absolutely."

Tanger's eyes fell to the ground. He had yet to feel like an adult, had never been required to mature like the rest of normal society. His parents had treated him like a commodity to be mined. Handing him over to Cash wasn't that drastic of a change, and the agent had no reason to have him start thinking for himself.

"Spend the night at the hotel," Cash said while removing a ball from Tanger's bag on the cart and casually tossing it in front of him on the fairway. The agent selected an 8-iron and began casually swinging the club.

"You already made a reservation?"

The agent nodded. "Room 514. The key is in the glove box of your car."

"Alright."

Cash lined up with the ball. "Your personal life is in a slump. It happens, just like in baseball."

The swing was perfect, the delicate knock of the ball skying into the air and dropping three feet from the hole.

"The key is to relax," Cash said, handing him back his club. "When you wake up in the morning, call me. I'll tell you where we go from here. Understand?"

Tanger nodded meekly, as his agent jumped into the cart and rolled back to the clubhouse.

EIGHT

THE sound of water falling from the rock fountain into the pool outside was soothing to the woman standing on a stepstool, cleaning the windows inside the house. Through the glass, she looked out to a clear afternoon sky, dotted with a few clouds. She displayed an easy smile, relishing the simple, physical work that transported her one more day further from a horrific past.

The pain Lily felt with lifting her right arm was a stiff reminder that returning to her estranged husband was not an option. Tearing her rotator cuff in her final struggle with him was an equitable trade for her life. It still smarted when she stretched to reach the corners of the windows on that side, an ailment the doctor said would ease with time. She knew the terrible memories of what caused the wound would take longer to fade.

"Here we are," a female voice said, as the door opened. A couple entered, escorted by a real estate agent in a classy, conservative pant suit that tried in vain to mute the lady's curves. As she spoke of the home's attributes with the hint of a Hispanic accent, the husband made a conscious effort to not look too long at her. He was not alone as she had a hypnotic effect on many of the men she encountered.

"Plenty of natural light," she exclaimed, leading the couple from the entry into a formal living room, with the sun shining through windows stretching to the ceiling. They nodded in approval as she listed the home's features effortlessly. As the wife pointed out something to her husband, the realtor looked to the lady cleaning the windows and nodded subtly.

Yardley Ramirez was one of the top realtors in Austin, but few knew how difficult it had been to get there. Eighteen years earlier, the young mother of two arrived in town without a penny to her name. She ignored the logical, reasonable voices encouraging her to find a modest, stable paying job to keep the rent and utilities paid. Instead, she shared a two-bedroom apartment with another woman for eight months to help finance a real estate career. A year later, she sold her first property. Another year later, she purchased her first home. Three years later, she led her broker in sales. Now, two years after starting her own agency, she was on the short list in Austin for luxury properties at seven digits or more.

She also had interest in a property management service. Her stake was small enough to limit her exposure, but large enough to ensure she could hire whoever she wanted. Numerous victims assisted through the Shelter, like Lily, had worked for her in this way, earning money to live until making the transition away from their abuser into a new life.

"The sellers are the original owners," Yardley continued as she led them up one of the two spiral staircases from the entry, their feet thumping firmly on the hardwood covering each step. "It was custom built with several unique touches you'll love." When they reached the top of the stairs, she pulled back, letting them lead the way into the spare bedrooms, game room, and balcony overlooking the pool.

Yardley knew this house, their fifth showing of the day, had hit the mark once the tour was complete. The facial expressions on both spouses were telltale signs that this home, nestled in the hills of Lakeway, was a winner.

"How much was it again?" the wife asked. Yardley showed her the worksheet, pointing at the asking price.

"We're interested. How much would you offer to start?"

"Let me work up some comps this afternoon. In the meantime, let me know how much you want to put down. You're already pre-approved for enough."

With that, they shook hands and the couple walked out to their car. Yardley watched them walk away, then went to the dining room table that could easily feed two dozen guests and pulled out a chair. She tossed several files on the table and produced her cell phone. She was the top seller for 7 of the last 8 quarters, but it was not without producing its share of grey hair, expertly hidden by brown hair color with just a hint of auburn.

"You alright, Miss Yardley?"

"Just drowning in opportunity, Lily. Like always."

"You work so hard. When are you going to take a break?"

"My little ones have to eat, sweetie. You just keep on top of me and I'll do it one of these days."

Lily continued cleaning the house as the afternoon fell into dusk, finishing her work as darkness had nearly finished taking the skies outside. When she descended the stairs, Yardley remained, grinding away at her work, her cell phone sitting atop a pile of paperwork, her computer in front of her. The only evidence the realtor had moved was that the lights above the dining room had been turned on.

"Isn't that enough for today, mija?" Lily asked.

"Just a little more, then we'll go."

Yardley often utilized Lily for security purposes as well. She rarely felt vulnerable, but had heard the stories of realtors working alone being assaulted or worse. Safety was the rule, which meant having a companion tag along whenever possible.

She and Lily shared a strong bond, stronger than many of the others Yardley had employed in her business to maintain market properties. The realtor had an aunt who had suffered much like Lily had. Yardley's aunt had never escaped and was still in her living hell. She was still plotting an out for her, but the plan had not come to fruition, in large part due to the aunt's hesitation.

For now, Yardley shoved those thoughts out of her mind to focus on the tasks at hand. There was the buyer who focused on the Bee Caves area for four weeks and over thirty houses, but now wanted to look at Georgetown instead. There was the seller who couldn't understand why her house remained unsold despite insisting on a price many thousands above the comps in the area. There was the seller who rearranged Yardley's painstaking staging, a skill for which she was paid handsomely before her sales made enough to live on alone. And then, the paperwork. She entrusted some of the paperwork to her transaction coordinators, but she was too much of a control freak to let it go entirely.

The phone rang several times, some of which she let go to voice mail. She would always call back clients she had under contract. One exception was the Georgetown maniac, who probably saw an internet listing even farther from where he was the last time he called. Finally, one call came from another realtor, one Yardley had started with. They cried on each other's shoulders during those lean early years when they learned the hard lessons, and celebrated together when they climbed the ladder to the next levels.

"Hey, sweetie. What are you up to?"

Her friend wasted no time in getting to the point. As Yardley listened, she pushed away the paperwork in front of her and moved her legal pad within writing range.

"Absolutely."

She scribbled something on the pad, then pulled her computer closer. It came to life and she found what her friend was describing.

"Yeah, I'm looking at it. That's exactly what I'm talking about."

Her friend told her a few more details, and Yardley nodded as her brown eyes widened as she looked at the photos.

"Definitely, sweetie. Let me look it over and I'll call you tomorrow. Thanks."

Yardley kept scrolling through the photos, astonished that somehow the oddball property she had been searching for was right in front her. She warned the buyer that such an opportunity was rare, and to consider alternatives. But she kept her eyes peeled, despite the long odds.

She snatched the phone and dialed. The voice mail prompt came on.

"Julia, it's me. Sweetie, it's a miracle, but I may just have what you're looking for. If you're interested, we can see it tomorrow."

January 1999 – San Antonio, Texas
Yardley

THE bus rolled into the station, slowly easing until its brakes hissed as it stopped. Travelers began filing off, collecting their luggage as they passed. The last passengers to exit the bus were a young woman and two small children. She held them close, as if she feared they would fly away, or be snatched by some unseen threat. She took her duffle and slung it over both shoulders with difficulty, taking each of her children by the hand. One of the mother's hands was encased in a hard cast.

"Don't let go," she said firmly, turning out of the station and down the street. It was dark and cold, but she had been given little time and no choice prior to this journey. Her life and the lives of her son and daughter were at stake.

The activity of downtown San Antonio buzzed on the other side of the street. She had made several trips to the city, but only had experienced the Riverwalk once, with her parents when she was very young. The Monday after New Year's was relatively tame, but the streets to the south she had remaining to travel on foot were cold, dark and foreboding.

Her five-year-old son was to her right, nearest to the street. She could sense him steeling himself for the fears of the unknown that lay ahead, looking directly in front of him. Her daughter was three, looking all around her, still naïve to the dangers of the world.

Three blocks down from the station was a tavern, more lively than the rest of the Riverwalk. The sounds of joy and laughter were of no comfort. Everyone inside was a stranger to them, seemingly oblivious to the young mother's plight, shuffling by in the cold.

* * * * *

The New Year's Eve festivities had stretched several days for Julia, and for that she was thankful. The party down by the Riverwalk on the last night of her vacation was not nearly as appealing as the days before it, comfortably ensconced in the guest house of a wealthy friend's parents. It wasn't the sheer opulence of the estate that recharged her. It was instead the departure from her usual surroundings that gave her needed perspective.

Her new life was just over six years old, but the events that led her to erasing who she was and rebooting never left her. The numerous "domestics" she answered on patrol kept the epidemic in front of her. She was being drawn to a mission that was bigger than her, and that she was passionate about, but that hadn't yet fully formed.

Like any police officer, her observation skills had increased exponentially with the passage of time. She could spot potential dangers on sight, but couldn't always act before events unfolded in front of her. Trailing one individual who was likely to commit a crime was not feasible, for the candidates were too numerous. She was also not omnipotent, and reminded of it frequently.

These skills did hold value in her passion for the battered woman. Julia could seemingly spot them in the crowd. The same people had been there all along, but her senses were now attuned to the classic signs, in ways that she couldn't fully comprehend. Their non-verbals, their posture, their gait and numerous other clues were like sirens to her. She occasionally had the time and means to direct them to a place where a life-changing choice could occur, to save themselves and others they loved.

It could have easily gone unnoticed, three figures walking down the street outside. Some would call it pure luck, but Julia was both spiritual and superstitious, a combination that demanded that everything happens for a reason. She grudgingly admitted this was debatable, but her heart pulled her in this direction, sometimes to the detriment of her profession.

She couldn't explain exactly what struck her about the mother and her children. Maybe it was the size of the children, or the time of the day, or the extreme cold that had descended on the Alamo city over the weekend. But she always remembered seeing the cast on the woman's forearm, with a little boy hanging on to it with hands that couldn't fully enclose around the claw left from the plaster.

Her eight friends barely noticed her leave the table, thinking she was going to the powder room. She walked straight outside and crossed the street, approaching them. When the mother saw her coming, she instinctively retreated, looking over the woman carefully.

"Hello," Julia said.

The mother's grip on her children got tighter, releasing their hands and pulling the children's bodies closer, next to her legs. She had a large shiner on one eye, confirming Julia's instincts regarding the cast were correct.

"My name is Julia. Everything okay?"

The mother nodded slowly.

"It's really cold tonight," Julia continued. "Where are you headed?"

"A friend's house. That way."

She looked over the mother, who was barely more than a child herself. She was no more than 25 and very pretty. She noticed the duffle across her back, worn and bursting at the zippers.

"How far do you have to go?"

The young mother considered the woman, concluding she was not an enemy. She handed Julia a piece of paper with an address and directions scribbled on it.

"That's at least two miles. Let me give you a lift."

The mother shook her head violently. "No, no. That's okay."

"Don't be afraid. I'm a cop, see?"

Julia produced her badge. The mother leaned forward to look at it, both arms holding her children back. She looked back at the officer, measuring her once more before nodding.

Her children were just as guarded, perhaps shaking from more than the chill in the air.

"C'mon."

Julia led them across St. Mary's to the lot where her pickup was parked. She helped load the woman and her children into the cab.

"Stay in here. I'll be right back."

Julia ran back into the restaurant and a few minutes later ran back out to the pickup. She cranked it up and turned back onto St. Mary's.

"Show me that address again."

The mother handed her the paper. Julia nodded and pressed the accelerator.

"Have y'all had supper yet?"

"No."

"Is your host feeding you?"

"I don't know."

"Who are you staying with?" Julia watched the road as she asked the questions.

"A friend."

The short, clipped answers gave her pause as she turned into the neighborhood. She found the address and pulled into the driveway of the small frame house. No lights appeared to be on.

"Are they home?"

"I don't know."

Julia turned back to the mother. "They know you're coming, right?"

The mother shook her head.

Julia killed the ignition. "Okay, let's start over. I'm Julia Caldwell. I'm an Austin police officer."

The young woman looked at her, then hung her head in shame and began to weep.

"No, no. It's okay. I'm just trying to help."

Her two children watched wide-eyed, too alarmed at the events of the day to cry.

"What's your name?" the officer persisted.

"Yardley."

"Yardley, good. Where are you from?"

"Brownsville."

Julia nodded. "So, you came here by bus, then planned to walk all the way here?"

"I—I had no choice. I—"

Yardley collapsed into Julia's side, sobbing. She held her tight for a few moments, letting the cries subside.

"In Austin, I have some friends you can stay with. You don't have to tell anyone where you are. We can protect you from whoever it is you're running from. Do you want to go?"

Yardley pulled back from the embrace and looked into the driver's eyes. She slowly nodded.

Julia cranked the truck up and pulled back out of the driveway. She produced a cell phone and pressed it to her ear.

"Molly, it's Julia. I'm good. Hey, I need a favor. Mother and two small children. Can you swing it?"

Julia looked back at the children in the back seat, huddled next to each other. She winked at them confidently.

"Maybe an hour and a half. Okay, thanks."

She hung up the phone.

"I am going to take you to a friend of mine. She'll feed you, take you in for a few days. Then, we'll figure something out."

"Thank you."

"My pleasure."

They rode on quietly. She had made such offers many times before, with varying results. Some of her passengers she would never see again. Some would receive the needed help and restart their lives anew. Some regrettably returned to the pain, unwilling to face the fears of the unknown. This one felt different for some reason. Only years later would she realize how significant this one was to her future and dreams that were evolving, years away from maturity.

Yardley kept looking Julia over, envious of her quiet, serene poise.

"How did you know?" the mother softly asked.

Julia looked in the rearview mirror, then turned to her passenger.

"Because I've been there."

NINE

CASH, Vance and Gordon left the limousine purposefully outside the IDS Center. It was a cloudy day, windy and cold for early October, even in Minneapolis. Each of the men turned the collar of their overcoats up for the short walk to the lobby of the skyscraper. Inside one of the building's thirteen elevators, Vance punched the button for the 20th floor.

The elevator door opened to reveal a grand glassed entrance. THE SKILBY FOUNDATION was stenciled on the glass. Through the windows, a striking young blonde woman smiled as they approached and entered.

"Hello. Can I help you?"

"Yes, we're here to see John Skilby."

"Damon Cash?"

Cash smiled. "You must be new."

"I am, two months in. Heather Moore." She stood and shook his hand, smiling at him. Cash nodded approvingly while looking her over.

"Right this way. Mr. Skilby should be with you shortly."

They followed her down the hall. The walls were filled with framed posters of Skilby in action poses on the football field, as well as vanity photos with other celebrities. There were also shots of him and his wife with sick children the foundation supported.

"Nice, isn't it?" Cash asked.

The two men nodded in agreement with their employer. Vance had been there a few times before, but Gordon never had. Of course, none of them were looking at the items on the walls. Their gaze was fastened on Heather's ass.

She showed them into Skilby's office, where he was in an animated conversation with someone. It was an angry exchange, characterized by profane adjectives. After about a minute, Cash stepped forward to the edge of Skilby's desk.

None of the three men had bothered to sit. He made the cutthroat sign, telling him to finish.

"I've got to go," he muttered, abruptly ending the call.

"Good morning, John."

"Have a seat, Damon. I wish you'd have—"

"John, come over here," Cash said, waving him out from the desk to the sitting area on the far side of the office.

Skilby hesitated, but saw the stern gaze of Cash's two companions. Vance was similar in build to the quarterback, but he looked dangerous. Gordon was bigger than any of his teammates, and could probably kill him with one hand tied behind his back. The quarterback complied, pacing out toward them. Cash grasped him by the neck and pulled him close, like a father would. But the non-verbal psychology of their physical contact was more manipulative than affectionate.

"Remember when I told you to skip the combine altogether, and wait for your pro day?"

"Yeah."

"The media burned you for a month. Then, what happened?"

"I went second."

"Second. Second in the whole damn draft. You'd have gone first if Detroit hadn't have drafted a quarterback the year before. Remember?"

The man nodded meekly. "I remember."

"Trust me."

His client breathed deeply, then shook his head violently.

"I'm worth more than they're offering."

"John, this guarantees you more than you'll get if they cut you. If you get waived, you won't get half that on the market. It's no guarantee you'll even get a starting job."

Skilby looked at Cash, then at the large, expressionless goons on either side of him. His pride finally overcame his common sense.

"Who the hell do you think you're talking to?" Skilby retorted, face to face with Cash, trying to regain a measure of control. "Two passing titles, an MVP, and a conference championship."

Cash's posture and expression had not budged. "Two concussions last season. Two knees that wouldn't pass another team's physical."

"I don't give a shit."

"And a losing battle with the bottle."

Skilby paused, snorting defiantly. "I'll take my chances."

Cash could tell when he hit the wall with a client. No amount of logic, reason, or intimidation would move them. That time had come.

He grasped his client's shoulder and squeezed it. "Even if it's your last chance?"

Skilby shook Cash's hand off of him. "You let me worry about that."

Cash watched Skilby march behind his desk. The agent then motioned for Vance and Gordon to follow him out of the room. Walking down the hall, he turned to the men behind him to get their attention.

"Take a good look at all this. In a few months, this suite will be empty. What a shame."

When they had left the building and were in the car, he called out an address to the driver. The limo abruptly changed lanes. Cash produced a thick, padded mailing envelope and handed it to Gordon.

"When we get to the place, hand this to the woman. Wait until she understands before you return to the car."

They both nodded affirmatively as the limo moved further into the suburbs.

The condo was nice, far more than she would consider renting, let alone buying. The 3-3 also had a kitchen that would satisfy a master chef and two spacious living areas that mostly collected dust. Most of the activity happened in the master bedroom. Fortunately, it was selected for its discreet location as well as its proximity to the local football team's facility.

She had only met the man who paid the bills once. The agent was a cocky asshole who had all the answers and thought he could read every person on sight. The problem was that he was usually right. His guesses at her life story were frighteningly accurate.

What she didn't know was that Cash only appeared to be a sorcerer. He simply knew more about her territory than she did, spotting her as the most likely of the groupies milling in the night spot to take the money and put up with the inconvenience and indignity of occupying a famous athlete's off hours.

John Skilby wasn't an altogether unpleasant experience. The petulant superstar was relatively easy compared to most of the powerful men she had been paid to keep company over the years. What was new was escorting a client who had no idea she was being compensated for her time.

Outside the condo window, light rain began to fall. Two men left a limousine and stepped up to the door. The knock was rough, shaking the frames on the wall. She rushed to the door, wrapped in only a robe.

"Yes, what is it?"

Two large men stared back at her.

"Mr. Cash would like to speak to you," Vance said abruptly.

The woman glared back at them. "Right now?"

In answer to her question, Vance took the envelope from Gordon and handed it to her, along with a flip cell phone. As if on cue, the phone rang. She answered it, watching Gordon standing behind Vance, looking down at her.

"Hello."

"Robin, this is Damon Cash."

"What's going on?"

"Starting tomorrow, we will no longer need your services. Thanks so much for your help."

She stepped back into the condo and dropped into a couch nearby. The men followed her inside, stopping a few feet in front of her.

"Well, okay. Where do I go now?"

"As long as it's out of town, I do not care."

"This is where I live, Mr. Cash."

"Not for the next 6 months, you don't."

"But—"

"Robin, look inside the envelope."

She glanced inside and saw several stacks of money, and a bottle of pills.

"That's a final payment, along with a bonus. Just put four of those pills into my boy's drink tonight. Once he falls asleep, you pack up and take a nice, long vacation. We'll tell you when you can come back and get the rest of your shit."

Robin considered the turning upside down of her life. The money had been nice, but she was unprepared for the end. She had been warned it might last months, or even years, but the end would arrive suddenly. Now it was here.

"And the car?"

"Leave it at the airport. We'll take care of it."

"Okay."

The two men took the phone from her and immediately left. She glanced at the money and the pills and almost couldn't believe what had just happened.

Once she realized it wasn't a dream, she began debating her next destination.

TEN

QUIETLY nestled in the wooded area west of downtown Austin, a small business complex escaped the notice of most of the nearby traffic from Mopac. Four buildings with four units each surrounded the parking spaces for the buildings. The buildings were older than many of the newer developments in the area, but were managed well and meticulously maintained.

CIG Incorporated, a private investigation firm run by Julia Caldwell, occupied a unit in the far corner of the complex. To get to her office, you would have to be looking for it, which was how she wanted it. Almost all her business was from referrals, and profit was not always the first consideration when taking on clients.

Julia arrived early as usual, rolling up in a pickup that hid over 100,000 miles well. She stepped out carrying her attaché, a folded copy of the Statesman and a Grande Mocha Latte. This was a constant source of amusement for her younger neighbors, calling both she and her newspaper quaint relics from a simpler time.

Once inside, Julia cranked up her computer and scanned the email. The inbox number was well into the thousands, something that never seemed to bother her. Her life outside the sanctum of her home was messy and her business was cleaning up messes. Unread emails she wasn't waiting on were not automatically reviewed. Only correspondence from a small list of senders would be inspected upon arrival.

Her desk lacked even more organization, but the clutter was not work related. It was the peripheral items that arrived in the mail and throughout her travels during the week. Ads, receipts, pamphlets and anything else that never merited attention couldn't find its way to the circular file underneath the desk.

Julia's mind was a far different matter. She had a clear vision of who she was, where she had been and where she was going. She was not always able to convey that vision to others, or even use verbal or written words to capture what she saw. In her heart, despite the personal burdens she carried, she knew she would arrive at that place someday in the future.

Two permanent items on her desk were the markers on the road she was travelling. The first was a replica of her Austin Police badge encased in a clear frame that served as a paper weight. She had great memories of her time on the force, and had maintained friendships with those who were still there, as well as some who had moved on like herself.

The second was a small vanity mirror. The item was unremarkable on its own, and she was unsure where exactly she got it. She did know it predated the line of demarcation in her life. It also clearly showed her face's reflection and its defining features. Wavy, shoulder length tresses framed a pretty, rounded face with pert lips and fiery hazel eyes. The one feature she looked for was the one most out of place. Others only saw it up close, and were rarely bold enough to ask about its origin.

The scar started deep above her left cheek and continued up at an angle, just past the edge of her left eye socket, until it faded altogether. A normal application of makeup made the scar unnoticeable except from a conversational distance. However, she never wanted to completely hide the mark. It was a part of who she was, and what she was about.

In the clutter of her inbox, Julia spotted a message with several attachments and links from a neighboring tenant, Noelle Gardier. The email advised a review of the contents by all recipients ASAP, which was a relative term since Noelle was a notoriously late riser. She reached into her lower desk drawer and inside an empty box of envelopes sitting on its end. She pulled a small flask from the box and poured some brown liquid into the coffee. She told herself there was plenty of time before the meeting, but there were plenty of other ways to justify it if need be.

She took a sip and noticed the XTS roll by to its destination parked outside the office next door. Cassie Snow, attorney at law, was also an early riser. From the email, Julia knew that Cassie was already privy to its nature. The details would be part of the meeting later in the morning. Reviewing the files was not necessary as Noelle would debrief the group on the details. She quickly scanned them to get an idea of what to expect.

After Julia killed off over 100 emails, a cherry red E63 with "YARDLY" spelled on bright pink Texas plates pulled up to the opposite building. Yardley Ramirez specifically selected a suite facing the road, wanting more visibility than her neighbors. Julia was happy to have her friend occupy center stage, enabling her to work in the shadows.

The landline had buzzed several times after Julia arrived and she ignored them all. A call finally came in that she was willing to accept.

"Yeah?"

"It's me. You busy?"

"No. Come on over."

Moments later, Cassie walked in, a cup of coffee in her hand, sitting across from Julia's desk.

"Did you look at Noelle's stuff yet?"

Julia nodded, casually perusing other emails. "What do you think?"

"Another redneck asshole."

"Probably."

They looked through the windows at one of the adjacent buildings where Yardley Ramirez was animatedly talking with some clients, her hands adding to her narrative. The joke was if they tied her hands behind her back, she would explode in seconds.

"Did she sell the Greene property?"

Julia shook her head no. "Financing fell through. Noelle told her it would."

"Shaking that ass doesn't sell them all, does it?"

They both noted the custom Mini whip into the lot at a speed that would have most other vehicles on two wheels. Noelle was awake earlier than normal.

One hour later, the four ladies assembled in the conference room in Julia's office. They gathered around the table, caffeine in hand. Cassie handed Noelle the Ziploc bags with the stripped cell phones and their guts as they sat down in their traditional spots and began their meeting routines. Julia, Cassie and Yardley produced folios with note pads, while Noelle opened her laptop.

"Any surprises?" Julia asked Noelle. As the de facto leader of the four, Julia usually called the meetings and chaired the proceedings. Noelle took a remote from the table and changed the channel on the flat screen TV against the wall to pair with the laptop in front of her.

"Not really."

After a few taps on the keyboard and clicks of her mouse, a Texas driver's license appeared.

"Bradley Wayne Benton, 23. His stepfather, who married his mother when he was five is serving 15 years in Big Spring for manslaughter. His mother is on disability and lives in Lufkin near her family. He has several step-siblings, only some of which I have located, but he appears to have little to no contact with any of them."

She clicked keys again, and a credit report appeared.

"He's currently employed at a local body shop, but his job history is sporadic. That explains the princely sum of $23.12 in his checking account. He has several credit cards, all charged off except one. There is also one repo on record."

Another click. An arrest record appeared.

"Graduated from Blanco High a year late, due to two suspensions. He also has some priors. Two MIPs, possession with intent, aggravated assault."

"Is he still in the system?" Cassie asked.

"Yes," Noelle replied. "He's still got a few more months with Travis County on the assault. The PO is Clarence Adams."

"I know him," Julia said.

"So do I," added Cassie.

Both ladies shared a knowing smile.

"What else?"

More clicks, then a cell phone bill appeared.

"The usual items. His cell calls were primarily to Sophia's cell, and the cell of a Marcus Miller. I still have some background to do on him. He called Miller almost as much as Sophia, but the calls abruptly stopped about a month ago."

Noelle took the remote and killed the screen.

"That's all so far."

"Adams could help us," Cassie said.

"Yes, he could," Julia clicked her pen excitedly. "Noelle, work on Marcus Miller and see what you can find. Once we get that, maybe we'll have something to take to Adams."

Each of the ladies took turns providing updates on various survivors currently under their protection. Once the Shelter took in a victim, she and any children were taken to one of a list of "railroad" stops, safe houses where she could stay indefinitely until they chose the next steps in their future. Once the updates were done, the meeting closed.

Cassie left first, darting out for an appointment. Yardley motioned towards Julia as they stood.

"You get my message?"

"I did. When can I see it?"

Yardley smiled. "How about now?"

As those two women left the conference room, only Noelle remained, clicking keys on the laptop. Before she started work on Marcus Miller, she remembered a detail of another case that needed to be taken care of.

She had been doing this for years, but certain tasks never got old. After the last keystroke, she closed the laptop with a wide smile, picking it up and taking it back to her office.

* * * * *

The last few months had been a rough stretch for Seth Rimmon, a sales executive for a networking firm in Round Rock. He had always been able to hold his own in his field, consistently logging healthy numbers selling to clients on several continents. His personal life had always been up and down, but recently his fortunes had been sliding south along with his relationships.

His wife had finally left him, disappearing like a thief in the night. Rimmon had always threatened the "til death do us part" vows were literal, and that there was no living escape from him. Whether it was the truth or not, he wasn't sure. Until three months ago, she had not tested him. His verbal threats and physical displays of domination had kept her home. Whatever changed, it happened quickly. One day, she was home. The next, she was gone.

He barely slept, trying to keep his busy work schedule while trying to hunt her down by night. It was exhausting work, driving to every one of her friend's houses, parking down the road and waiting for sight of her. After a month with no clues, he invested in a private investigator, who quit after two weeks, calling it a dead end.

The details infuriated Rimmon, but were humorous to the detective. Clues branched out to multiple cities. His wife's credit cards were being used in Cleveland and Phoenix at the same time. Her cell phone was making calls in Atlanta while the IP address of her tablet was active in Vancouver. New accounts had been opened in each of the four cities, but were all ruses. Utility bills led to addresses that did not exist. Calls to the cell phone were forwarded to the Austin Police Department. The investigator quickly deducted that finding the wife was not worth the time and expense required.

Meanwhile, Rimmon's financials began leaking holes. Despite never missing a payment of any type in his life, four of his six credit cards were cancelled. The other two accounts, each with healthy credit limits, were almost maxed out. Delinquent medical bills from years earlier appeared out of nowhere. The doctor had already filed a judgment. The cable bill was promptly charged off. Predictably, Rimmon's three attempts to open new credit card accounts were declined.

He tried to shake off the last few weeks of hits as he sped to the airport for a big pitch in San Francisco. It would be his biggest score ever, if he could close it. The client had dozens of satellite offices across the country and would use his firm's services until he retired. This sale wouldn't let him retire, but the residuals might ensure that retirement would remain comfortable if he lived to be 100.

The state trooper who pulled Rimmon over on his way to the airport could have made his life miserable, and was inclined to do so given the salesman's surly attitude, but he simply gave him the ticket for 72 in a 55 and sent him on his way. After sprinting and growling his way through airport security and the gate, Rimmon found his first-class seat headed for the Bay area.

Once he walked through the doors to his presentation, he had calmed down. Everything changes here, he told himself. He made his classic introduction, cracking light jokes that were received well. He then opened his laptop and connected to the screen. He found his presentation and clicked twice.

Rimmon's carefully crafted words to accompany the visuals that normally focused his future clients on the benefits were wasted as his audience displayed a mixture of open mouths, chuckles and gasps. He turned to see a browser window stretched across the screen, filled with pornography, in HD color.

"Shit!" he snapped under his breath, running to the laptop, trying to click the window closed. Instead another screen of adult video popped up, this stream in black and white, with both the video quality and content a bit dirtier.

"No!"

With each attempt to close the windows another screen would pop up, each screen seemingly naughtier than the previous one. Finally, Rimmon wisely disconnected his computer from the video screen.

"I'm so sorry. I don't—"

"I think that will be all, Mr. Rimmon."

With that, the dozen or so assembled clients filed out. As if shot, he fell into a chair and dropped his head to the table with a thump.

What the hell is going on, he thought. Only now did he begin to wonder if it was the karma of his conduct as a husband. Somewhere on the flight home, the possibility that someone was deliberately out to destroy him crossed his mind. Shortly after he deplaned, his boss called to explain the severance package and managed to wish him well in his future endeavors.

After several drinks in a house that would hit the market the following day, he decided it was time to let his wife go and begin rebuilding his life.

ELEVEN

"IT'S a basic 3-2-2," Yardley explained, while she navigated her Mercedes effortlessly through the midday traffic on Bee Caves road well above the speed limit. "Built in 1972. The roof was replaced in 2002. Foundation is not bad. The inside could use some updating."

Julia listened as the realtor explained the mundane details of how her friend discovered the property. She had the gift of gab, and it was difficult to keep from tuning her out. She rambled, something that Julia figured didn't happen with clients she was less comfortable with.

Yardley turned off the highway and wound up and down hills, passing several older, rural homes on lots with acreage. Most of the residents had been there for decades and weren't going anywhere. It was non-descript, something Yardley knew would appeal to Julia's preferences.

They slowed and turned into an uphill gravel road that disappeared into dense tree cover. The trail meandered through the trees for a quarter of a mile before entering a clearing with a simple house. The concrete on the circle drive was cracked in several places and needed repair years earlier. The car stopped and Yardley jumped out.

"What do you think?"

"It's odd," Julia replied, looking it over. "I would have expected that this property would have been developed long ago."

"This is a critical water shed zone. The corresponding easement only allows for a small amount of impervious cover."

"Impervious cover?"

"Pavement, roof. Whatever God didn't make."

"You told me the inside is what matters."

"It is."

Yardley walked to the front door and unlocked it. As she approached, Julia noticed a large deck on the side of the house that badly needed treatment. The deck was empty with no table or chairs. She wondered why the realtor hadn't said anything about it.

Julia walked inside to find it was much like the outside. Outdated furniture and fixtures, all dusty and musty.

"What else?" she asked, clearly not yet impressed.

Yardley smiled and led her to the kitchen. Nothing appeared out of the ordinary, except for two large doors on the back wall. It looked like a large pantry, but the doors had a lock on the knob, as well as a deadbolt. Yardley unlocked both and swung the doors open to reveal an elevator.

Julia laughed. "I don't suppose it goes up."

"No, it doesn't. There's a shed out back with a stairwell in case the elevator is out."

They walked into the elevator and went down. The door opened into a parking garage with two dozen parking spaces clearly marked.

"Who was this guy?"

"Some wealthy widower. The guy made a lot of money in the stock market, then his wife died fifteen years ago and he lost it. No children, no heirs. He had a gorgeous mansion in the Tarrytown section that he never set foot in after she passed. He lived out here and rarely left the house."

The walls of the garage were barren with the exception of two doors, one to each side and what appeared to be a ramp that extended into nowhere. Julia paced to the ramp and looked up to see nothing but darkness.

"Let me guess. The deck?"

"Very good. The doors open just enough to let a two-axle vehicle through."

Julia walked back toward Yardley who opened the door in the wall nearest to the ramp and let her into what looked like the hall of a hotel.

"How many bedrooms?"

"Four. There's also two bathrooms and a small kitchen."

Julia peeked into the rooms. Each had a double bed with modest furnishings and dated wallpaper.

"Surprisingly, he stayed up on technology," Yardley added. "Everything is wired, with three backup generators. They look in decent shape. He also used materials that made everything below ground a 21st century Faraday cage. He was plenty paranoid."

Yardley could talk you into an ice cream sundae on the North Pole, but no sales push was needed here. Julia had told the group of hoping to find such a place to harbor clients. She also knew Yardley was truthful when she said it was a longshot.

They returned to the ground floor and walked outside. She walked to the deck.

"Can this be operated by remote?"

"Already is. There are controls above and below ground."

Julia got quiet, slowly taking in what she was seeing.

"Okay, now let's have the bad news."

Yardley smiled and handed the folder in her hands to Julia, who looked it over carefully.

"Not bad, but still a bit out of our price range."

"What is our price range?"

Julia continued looking at the folder, but not for more data. A singular fortress to protect the most at-risk victims was a dream so incredible, so ethereal to imagine. Now that a nearly perfect scenario had finally presented itself, she wasn't sure how to feel. The reality now required action, and doubt about her own motives crept in. Whatever benefits an ideal location offered, it wouldn't protect her from the demons of her own internal battles. Those forces required a different type of security.

"I don't know."

She handed the folder back to Yardley, still looking over the house. She walked around it once more, as if she was absorbing the grounds spiritually. Yardley knew why, for she had suffered the same trials and understood the significance. Julia's response to her experiences had turned into a mission, a quest so noble that words were too ordinary to dignify it. This was a decision that had to resonate inside her, regardless of its practical merits.

Yardley knew that the source of their group's funding was a grey area. Julia had expertly delegated according to skill sets, and plausible deniability. Noelle had the keys to the technology and finances. Cassie was the legal expert. Yardley's real estate prowess and connections had proven useful, but she was out of the loop with the other three in some regards. She knew that Julia had done this in part to protect her.

"What are you looking for?" the realtor asked. "Something missing?"

"Nothing but the money," Julia quipped.

"Don't be too sure. I want in on this."

"We'll see. Let me think about it."

"Alright."

Yardley closed her folder and walked toward the car. Julia watched the house for a few moments more before joining the realtor in her car.

"We'll never know until we try," Yardley said as she cranked the car, reading her friend's mind. Julia smiled in response, knowing she was right.

TWELVE

WHILE it was difficult not to blame John Skilby for his bad behavior, he had clearly come by it honestly. Like many millennials, his father and mother's world revolved around their only child's athletic dreams. Their marriage was built mostly on the foundation of young John's destiny, facts obvious to even casual observers. They evolved from an annoying pair of helicopter parents in little league to the ringleaders of a bombastic entourage at the high school level. The Skilby machine was only tolerated due to young John's consistent success for his teams in the athletic arena.

College programs are wired to placate talent, and Utah gave in to every demand, even forcing a new offensive coordinator on the current head coach. A pro-style offense was promptly installed that would best serve Skilby's prospects after he completed the three requisite years to be draft eligible. Their purpose was achieved, as Skilby posted record collegiate numbers and delivered three dazzling bowl performances to whet the appetites of professional football.

The spring before the draft provided no surprises, live or on film. His arm was a cannon, able to make all the throws. He had a sturdy 6-5, 250 frame, and his mechanics were excellent. His teammates appeared to respond to him on the field, but red flags of character were whispered throughout the league. Some of his teammates thought him a bit of a diva.

In the end, the negatives cost him only one spot in the draft, down to the 2nd pick. Minnesota, desperate for a quarterback, agreed to exceed the 1st pick's guarantees in a complicated deal that used seemingly every loophole in the CBA. And for five years, Minnesota was a contender. Skilby piled up stats, but the team made only one title run, ultimately sabotaged by the quarterback's arrest for assault days before the championship game. The contest was a misnomer, ending up as the worst playoff defeat in the team's history.

The disaster behind the scenes was carefully designed for the public eye to seem like a career destined for the Hall of Fame. The artist was Damon Cash, and he considered Skilby such a masterpiece precisely because of how far he had distanced the perception from reality. But Cash viewed his vocation less as a craftsman, and more like a hedge fund manager. His instincts spotting trends on and off the stages of athletics and entertainment were incredible. The clients he parted ways with had a habit of dropping down the totem pole. Did Cash's absence cause the downfall, or was the agent a puppet master, orchestrating his client's eminent demise? The chicken-or-the-egg question was now a popular debate in the media.

Skilby's ignorance of the trend showed how myopic his perspective was. Most of Cash's clients could feel him pulling away, and would either change agents or make efforts to regain his interest. The quarterback's refusal to accept Minnesota's renegotiated deal despite Cash's forceful presentation was the final straw.

The discovery of Skilby, passed out in his Lamborghini on the side of the highway, was headline news. The DUI itself was bad enough, but the drugs in his system were likely the death knell to his career. After bonding out, the star quarterback hid for days.

Predictably, the media found him first, puffing on a cigar while entering one of several country clubs of which he was a member. With the storm warnings ignored, the hurricane force of the press blindsided him. The arrest and Minnesota's swift waiving of the star quarterback made ambushing him even more tantalizing.

"Were you surprised Minnesota waived you?"

"Do you think the commissioner will suspend you?"

"Do you have an addiction problem?"

"Is your career over?"

Skilby muttered something unintelligible, perhaps even to himself before disappearing into the clubhouse. As inane as the questions were, he began asking them of himself. Cash had repeatedly listed his concerns, which seemed paranoid at the time. But with the arrest, and as a repeat offender in the drug program of the league's CBA, the trouble now seemed real.

He went over in his mind the beverages from the previous night. A few drinks were not usually an issue for him, as Robin, his current female companion, was good about limiting him when he pushed the limit. She had not the previous night, however. In fact, she encouraged him to relax and enjoy himself.

He remembered that Cash had warned him against the woman, telling him she was trouble. Skilby now realized he should have listened to Cash. What he didn't know was that it was the advice he had been given last week he should have heeded. The advice he was given last year was simply setting the stage for the trap door that had been poised to open all along.

From the cramped LA office of neonmega.com, Hawthorne watched with interest while sipping on convenience store coffee. He could have and perhaps should have predicted this. Damon Cash wasn't averse to letting clients make asses of themselves. Once they started throwing money away, his clients quickly self-destructed.

While the dim-witted Skilby might never do the math on what just happened, the confluence of events made Hawthorne wonder. Cash had neatly avoided being on the scene of several disasters his clients had become. What if it wasn't just instincts, or premonition? Was the agent brazen enough to arrange the end of clients he no longer had the trouble for?

As he struggled to put intelligent syntax into another fluff story about a million-dollar athlete's reality show girlfriend getting into a pissing contest with fans on Twitter, his mind kept drifting back to all of Cash's dealings with clients, both in sports and the entertainment industry. He had surprisingly few setbacks, and his percentages of separating with clients before a sharp career downturn were striking. Try as he might, his instincts wouldn't stop shouting.

The reporter shook his head, dismissing his own thought. He was game for just about any conspiracy theory, but a sports agent taking the trouble to ruin his own clients at the risk of his own career was too much of a stretch to fathom. Hawthorne wouldn't be dismissed as a hack for reporting such a story, simply because he wasn't a big enough blip on the screen for public opinion to matter.

But if he was right, the story could change his career overnight.

He had only a small portion of Cash's clientele committed to memory, simply because the number of individuals was so vast. He pushed aside the fluff piece and googled Cash. What came up was a veritable phone book of athletes, actors, musicians, and celebrities.

Of all of Cash's clients, Trent Tanger was the most prominent. Cash's brave talk of a half-billion-dollar contract in next year's free agency period would be a fascinating story to cover on many levels. Drafted out of high-school with the first pick in the draft, Tanger had helped Nashville steadily build from an expansion team to a contending club with youth and investment in their farm system. They were incapable of bidding on big money free agents, just like other teams in smaller markets. Now, the five-tool player that was their foundation would be lost, or the club would have to blow up their whole budget for a decade to keep him.

Hawthorne knew, like even the most casual of baseball fans, that none of this would concern Cash. The agent was an amoral predator who cared nothing about the sports his clients competed in. He would extract every penny possible from the club winning the bid, and lose not one wink of sleep.

The next item he could find on Tanger's schedule was a party in Nashville where he would be presented with the league MVP award. The event was expected to be a celebration of sorts of the first playoff appearance in the team's short existence. Executives, coaches, staff and many players were expected to attend even though the season had ended weeks before. It would be no surprise to see Cash there as well, playing for the camera with the world watching.

Hawthorne turned back to finish the fluff piece, hoping his editor would approve the red-eye flight to Nashville after receiving it well in advance of the deadline. Since Neon Mega had only a fraction of the resources of other online tabloids, it would take some smooth talking to get that reservation made.

THIRTEEN

BRAD Benton walked twelve minutes late into the county offices for his appointment with his probation officer, Clarence Adams. To and from all other places, he strutted. He was the classic attitudinal twenty-something, arrogant with no reason to be. His required meetings were one of the few events that checked his reality at the door.

Inside the PO's office, he saw an attractive black woman smiling as she watched him enter. The smile was not a friendly one, and he returned it with a "go to hell" look of his own that he had at the ready to intimidate anyone who opposed him. He did a double-take, recognizing her from their encounter days before. She was clearly pleased to see him.

"You're late, Mr. Benton," snapped Adams.

"You. What—"

"Shut up and sit down." Adams walked over to the window of his office and closed the blinds. Benton continued glaring at Cassie. Once he realized she seemed to be enjoying it, Benton turned his attention back to Adams.

"I had more than enough to violate you before Ms. Snow walked in. I'm going to let her do the talking."

Cassie rose from her seat and stood in front of the corner of Adams' desk, leaning on its edge.

"I'm Cassie Snow."

Benton nodded casually. *Whatever. Get on with it.*

"Sophia Martin."

"Where is she?"

"Someplace safe."

Cassie considered him for a moment, then turned to Adams and pointed at the file on his desk.

"May I?"

"Be my guest." Adams handed Benton's file to her.

"Hey! You can't—"

"Two MIPs," she continued with a grin, "possession with intent, aggravated assault. All that is impressive, but there is something missing."

Cassie handed Adams back the file and produced another, opening it.

"Does the name Marcus Miller mean anything to you?"

"Uh, no." Benton's reply was less than convincing.

"Marcus Miller, Mr. Benton. You attended school grades 1-12 with him in Blanco, Texas."

Benton nodded. "Oh, yeah. I remember him now."

"Perhaps you also remember that he did not graduate with you and your other classmates in the spring of 2012."

Benton's cocky demeanor began to fade. He tried to show no reaction, but his mouth opened in confusion of whether to speak or stay silent.

"He was incarcerated. Arson. Evidence strongly suggests he had an accomplice. He denied this and evidently took the rap for whoever was with him."

Benton's eyes narrowed defensively.

"Turns out Mr. Miller's eight months were not enough to completely rehabilitate him. He was recently picked up on an assault with a deadly weapon. The going rate on that conviction is anywhere from 2 to 10 years. I showed Mr. Miller photos of Sophia Martin from several days ago. I told him about Ms. Martin and her plans for the future."

Now, Benton's eyes shifted away from Cassie's laser gaze, and down to his feet. He adjusted his sitting position slightly.

"I also brought along the arresting officer from his arson case. Mr. Miller must have a quirky memory, because he's starting to remember the events of the night he set fire to that teacher's house a lot more clearly than four years ago."

Cassie stopped talking and smiled at him.

"What do you want?" Benton mumbled.

Cassie lifted another sheet of paper from the file. "This is a warrant for your arrest, pursuant to the complaint Sophia Martin has filed against you, along with her medical records from the night in question. You're going to plead guilty, and you'll do no more than six months. The judge will also impose a permanent restraining order against you for Ms. Martin, and you will not petition the court to discontinue it."

"And if I don't?"

"In exchange for a much lighter sentence, Mr. Miller gives you up. Those months in prison turn into years."

Benton snorts in disgust. "You're bluffing."

Cassie pulled a nearby chair and sat, easing up next to him.

"Am I?" she whispered. "That's the same mistake you made the other night in the alley. Do you really want to bet against me one more time?"

Benton turns away, with no more chips to bet and no more cards to play.

"How do you know all that shit?"

"That's not all, Mr. Benton," Cassie said. "I also know plenty of people in the Texas penal system. If you think the ride you've taken Ms. Martin for is rough, just wait until you go back inside. Your dance card will be full before you walk in. I'll make sure of it."

Benton bared his teeth in frustration, stamping his boots on the linoleum floor. This stranger had boxed him in with no hope of escape. Without looking up, he nodded.

"Wait here," Adams said to Benton as he and Cassie left the room to make the arrangements.

"Can I talk to her for a minute?" Benton asked. Adams looked at Cassie expectantly. She smiled and nodded, closing the door behind Adams as he left. Cassie sat back down next to Benton.

"Six months is not that long," he said, "and my memory is a lot better than Marcus Miller's."

"Then remember this, Benton. If I hear of you inside the same area code as Ms. Martin, I won't call the police. I'll hunt you down, take my pistol and shoot your testicles off. And if I ever see your face again, I won't bother with your balls. I'll just gun your ass down cold."

She gently slapped his face twice with her hand and smiled.

"Enjoy your time."

Cassie left the room. Adams met her a few feet away from the door.

"What did he say to you?" Adams asked.

"He very graciously thanked me for giving him the chance to take stock of his life and change his ways."

Adams chuckled. "I'll bet."

"Thanks, Clarence."

"Anytime," he said. "Hey, how did you find out about that arson thing?"

"A little birdie told me."

"Did you really talk to the arresting officer?" he asked quietly.

"I never even talked to Miller," Cassie whispered, slapping him on the shoulder before walking out of the county building. Once she was in back in the STS and cruising down Mopac at 75 MPH, she touched her nav screen and a dial tone began to sound.

"Hello."

"Noelle, it's done. Benton's gone for six months."

"How much do you want to hit him for?"

"Whatever you can safely take. He's not the sharpest knife in the drawer. He won't know any different."

"Nobody would buy his story, anyway."

"No one with any sense, at least. Later."

"Bye."

When Noelle heard Cassie hang up, she turned back to her bank of monitors. Within minutes, the remaining $273.24 of credit in Brad Benton's name was shaved down to $48.24. Benton had unwittingly contributed $125 in gift cards and $100 in gas cards to the Shelter.

Noelle had long since dispensed with the guilty conscience associated with her Robin Hood tasks contributed to the cause. The acts were done with a clear mind and heart, far different from how she learned the tradecraft she employed.

September 2001 – New York City
Noelle

THE baby stood up in her bed, waving to her mother with an open-mouthed smile, the kind of smile a well-rested, well-fed toddler displays without a care in the world. The mother smiled back wistfully, keeping up appearances to not transfer the fears and shame she carried inside her heart. A day was coming when the bruises on her arms and the swollen, busted lower lip would bring tough questions, questions she would not have the answers to.

The baby's father was a common grifter, good enough to keep just enough food on the table and just enough scratch to keep the multiple bookies he owed at bay. The stakes kept mounting, however, with no end in sight. Pickpockets in the city were the small, steady streams that paid the bills. Fencing office equipment and electronics evolved into boosting cars. Though many felonies had been committed, he had only served 30 days for a shoplifting arrest he had managed to plea down.

The mother's name was Kendra, and she had a dozen different plans to get away from the father, an asshole named Jack. Her biggest mistake was in telling him she was pregnant. He was not the loyal, monogamous type, and she knew that going in. But he viewed the child as a claim to be staked, so he moved in with her, despite maintaining an assortment of relationships, rotating as needed.

She quickly learned that sex was not the only utility the other women served. When the wrong team scored the late touchdown preventing the right team from covering, the wrong people began knocking at the door. The inquiries were becoming more confrontational, despite Kendra's honest testimony that she did not know Jack's whereabouts. Eventually, things would come to a head and someone would pay the price. Kendra thought more than once about asking his creditors to just take whatever they wanted from him, as long they could guarantee her a 24-hour head start.

The previous night had been a rough one. Jack took New York and the under, and now owed $2000 more than he or Kendra had. The default move in such situations was to go to Manhattan and work the business crowd. He was not above picking pockets on the street in broad daylight, but moving from floor to floor in either of the World Trade Center towers presented the best possibilities for the least risk. Clad in a generic package delivery uniform and a messenger bag, enough could be secured to pay off the bookie and arrange to try his luck again next weekend.

It wasn't until Kendra was clearly pregnant that she realized his attraction to her was more than physical. Her two semesters at the community college had exposed her to computers, something she had never worked with much before. Once she started, she discovered a surreal knack for technology. The coding would engross her mind for hours. She would start with a tutorial one Saturday morning, then blow off her weekend plans to build a new application.

Faced with the real possibility of no food for her baby along with physical abuse if she declined to assist him, she prepared coffee with her internet connection live, ready to take credit card numbers of stolen wallets over the phone. The gaping security holes in the world wide web were easy to exploit for grade schoolers, let alone a burgeoning IT student. The numbers were used in the first one or two hours after theft, ordering anything from formula to light bulbs to garden tools. The items were used or fenced. Rinse and repeat.

The phone rang and she picked it up. Jack or one of his partners read off account numbers, CVV numbers, and expiration dates for three credit cards from his cell phone. She wrote them down and hung up, preparing to hit the websites with the most favorable security profiles until the cards were declined.

A big screen TV that nearly covered the wall of their little apartment showed the news of the day. The noise of the morning shows annoyed her, so she put the studios on mute, only turning on the sound when something on the screen distracted her from the ones and zeros she bended to her will.

The smoke had been emanating from the World Trade Center for a few moments before it caught her attention, and she turned on the sound. Commentators speculated that a small plane may have hit one of towers. From the video, Kendra thought that was ridiculous. Having been to the towers many times, she knew the gaping hole was likely from a jet. While she recognized that the accident had tragic consequences, the pain she had suffered at Jack's hands had her hoping against hope that he would be one of the casualties and would not return.

When the second plane hit the other tower, the same wave of emotions that hit everyone in the country crashed into her. She left her computer and dropped into the couch absently, stunned by what she was seeing. She remained transfixed by the horrors, shaken away only by the cries of her toddler. When she went to her daughter, she picked her up and took her back to the couch, holding her tight. The world she had brought her child into had just turned darker and more dangerous.

Her phone began to ring. First her mother called, then her sister, but she did not answer. Outside her apartment, the sounding sirens began to multiply into a cacophony. That noise, and the rush of people on TV running from what remained of the towers strangely brought a serene focus to her mind. The darkness falling over her heart did not trump her survival instincts.

Kendra had never rehearsed running. She had thought about the practice many times, but no preparations had been made. There was a mental list of what she would take and she began working off that list, grabbing a duffle bag and throwing things in without much order. She gathered roughly seven days for her daughter, and only three days for herself. As she started, she picked up the phone and called her mother.

"Come pick me up at the apartment, right now."

She listened to her mother point out the obvious traffic problems at the moment.

"I know, Mom. Just do it."

Her protest continued for a few seconds before Kendra cut her off.

"I'm serious, Mom. Do it now. Bring all the cash you have with you."

She hung up the phone and continued her packing. Once she had everything together, she raided Jack's stash, one that she wasn't supposed to know about. She took the five $20 bills and the .22, leaving the dope. She carefully placed the baby in the stroller.

"Alright, sweetie. We're going to go see Nana!"

Her daughter fidgeted, nonplussed at the prospect. Perhaps she sensed that the trip was not for the same reasons she was used to.

Ten minutes after Kendra left the front door of the apartment building, a maroon Buick LeSabre pulled up. Kendra quickly threw her bag in the back. Her mother rolled down the passenger window.

"What the hell is going on?"

"Sit over here and hold your granddaughter. I'm driving."

Her mother hesitated, but followed the instructions. Kendra folded up the stroller and threw it in the back as well. Once all three were loaded in, the Buick bolted away.

"What are you doing?"

"Bugging out. I need your wheels."

Her mother looked at her daughter's face and arms, and understood. She knew there had been some incidents, but did not realize the extent of them.

"Where are you going?"

Kendra shook her head in uncertainty. "Somewhere far from here. West and warm."

"Is he in one of the towers?"

"I pray to God he is. If not, hopefully it takes him all day to get back to the apartment."

"What do I tell your father?"

"Whatever you have to. I will let you know where I leave the car."

The traffic began to pile up. It would be another hour before they got back to her mother's house. The two older generations fell silent for the remainder of the trip, but the youngest cooed gently, as if it was just another day.

The car finally pulled to a stop in front of the house she spent most of her formative years in.

"Can you go get her car seat?"

"Sure."

Her mother dashed out, coming out with the car seat a few moments later. She strapped her granddaughter in and hugged her daughter, unsure of when she would see either of them again.

"Remember, you haven't spoken to me and don't know where I am. It doesn't matter who asks."

"Right."

"I love you, Mom."

"I love you. Be careful."

The LeSabre sped off. The toddler began to fuss in the car seat.

"It's okay, sweetie. We're going on a vacation, just you and me."

The road west stopped for the first night in Staunton, a small town in Virginia. She risked the use of a stolen credit card at one motel, and was refused when ID did not match. Her explanation of the abuse, corroborated by the bruises she displayed, did buy her some mercy, preventing the front desk attendant from reporting her to the police. Choosing to save the cash she had left for gas and a minimum of food, she elected to find a quiet place to park the car for a night's sleep.

She found the parking lot of what looked like an abandoned grocery store, and parked facing the main road. Across the road was an old bar and grill, with an exterior that the owner had neglected to update. It reminded her of the places Jack dragged her to meet the shady people he did business with, and it gave her an idea.

She walked inside, carrying her daughter with her. A few patrons were scattered throughout the place, with a lonely bartender wiping down the bar. He turned his attention away from the news on the TV overhead, and gave the woman and her cargo a curious look.

"Hi. Can I bring her in here?"

He looked at the toddler, quietly fidgeting, then nodded.

"Fine by me. What'll you have?"

She looked at her roll of cash, then thought, what the hell.

"Corona Light."

He turned to retrieve it and she grabbed the nearby basket of nuts. She pulled a handful out and tossed them in her mouth. He noted her consuming them ravenously as he delivered the bottle.

"Hungry?"

She realized he had noticed her not-so-subtle approach. "A little."

"The nachos are great, and so are the sliders. Don't do the fish."

She smiled. "I'll think about it."

He walked off and she looked him over. He had a tattoo sleeve that snuck past his short-sleeve shirt down past his elbow. His cropped haircut and his long goatee suggested that he might match what she was looking for.

"Crazy, huh?" the bartender prompted, pointing to the TV.

"It's horrible," Kendra agreed.

"Yeah. One thing's for sure. We're gonna get those bastards, wherever they are."

She took another long swig of the beer. "I can't believe I brought her into a world like this."

"If it makes you feel any better, our parents thought the same thing. Want another?"

"One will do. That's all I can afford."

He looked her over. She was too young for whatever she was doing, wherever she was going.

"Where are you from?"

"Not too far from there," Kendra replied, motioning toward the tape of the burning towers on the screen overhead.

"It may take you a while to get back."

"I don't think I'm ever going back."

The finality of her statement caught his attention. She motioned for him to lean closer.

"Can I trust you?"

"Of course."

"You look like a man of action."

He smiled. "I'm a man who can get things done."

Kendra nodded. "Let's say a friend of mine comes to you and tells you her man is beating her. She wants to run away to somewhere she'll never be found."

"Never?"

"Never, ever."

"Does this woman have children, hypothetically?"

"Yes."

The bartender looks back down at the toddler.

"The child is six to eight months? Just a guess?"

"Hypothetically, let's say seven."

"How dangerous is the man?"

"Deadly."

The man leaned on the counter, twisting the cup towel as he considered the scenario. Kendra knew this was a lie. If Jack was still alive, he wouldn't have the courage to kill her, unless it was required to save himself. But her new friend needed as much motivation as possible.

"There's a person I've heard of that helps with problems like that. He calls himself a 'life harvester.' Births, deaths, credits, debits, Social Security numbers, driver's licenses. He's a one stop shop."

"Can you call him? I would—my friend would really appreciate it."

"I can't do that. I can make some inquiries, see if anyone knows how to reach him."

"Thank you."

He turned away from the bar and lifted the phone, dialing the number. He pulled the receiver out of view, the cord stretching around the door to the back. A few minutes later, he emerged, scratched something out on a notepad, tore off the paper and folded it in half.

"Here you go."

She reached for it, but he pulled it back with a wry smile.

"Wait a minute. That was quite an ask. How are you going to repay me for this?"

"I can't say what my friend would do," she said, laughing. "All I can do is give you a nice, big tip."

She laid as many bills as she dared on the bar, saving only enough cash for two days' worth of gas and a few snacks. The man looked at the bills, then back at her. He handed over the sheet of notepaper. She read the note carefully.

"Chattanooga? As in, Tennessee?"

"The only one I know of," the man replied. "Follow the instructions to the letter. Otherwise, everything on there is as hypothetical as the conversation we just had."

FOURTEEN

JULIA had learned to accept the slow traffic in Austin, expecting delay with every venture into the city. It was impossible to travel even a mile or two without construction or an accident bringing motion to a standstill. Tonight, she was pleasantly surprised to find the roads tolerable. She took a few serpentine moves to arrive at a parking space labeled "private property," owned by one of many friends she had collected over the years.

Her destination was a 6th Street club that started out as a honkytonk in the early seventies, when the outlaw country of Willie and Waylon found they didn't need Nashville to thrive. Four decades later, the place had been redone countless times by several owners. The current incarnation might host a Hip-Hop act one night, and Death Metal the next.

The opening act was an outfit called Arrogant Punk, a cover band replicating the glam metal hits of the 80s as best as they could. Watching them parade onto the stage with teased hair, cut-off muscle shirts and ripped jeans made the crowd cheer, welcoming a much-needed escape from the reality of the 21st century. Julia reminisced often about the era as well. She knew all the songs on their set list, having seen every band they covered from the nosebleed section as a teenager.

While the twenty-something band members visually replicated the era, the sound didn't do the original bands justice. The drummer and bass player were adequate, but hardly impressive. Neither guitarist had the chops to do anything but shame the legends they patterned themselves after. The frontman's mullet was spot on, but his voice had very little range and zero emotion.

Julia had never heard of the band before a client, a big insurance carrier of worker's compensation claims, presented her with the case of Norman Parrs, AKA Zeddy

Paris. Zeddy fancied himself a lead guitarist, and duplicated the classic stage movements from all the videos he had seen, but butchered most of the chords. Her client was mostly interested in Zeddy's range of motion. His claim listed him as an invalid, even though his factory work rarely included lifting over 50 pounds in his three years with the insured factory.

She elected not to go glam with her attire, choosing a normal outfit for a night on the town. When she arrived, she discovered she fit right in. There were plenty of glam band T-shirts and leather, some which fit well, more that didn't. There were a few college kids, but it was mostly the MTV generation, having a blast reliving their glory days.

In all the YouTube videos of the band, Zeddy spent most of his time to the right of the stage and to the crowd's left, only strolling to the other side once or twice a show. She ordered a vodka tonic and took a seat at a table on the elevated portion across from the bar and left of the stage. Fortunately, she could leave after the opening act, avoiding the common hazards of flying solo on the club scene.

"Good evening."

She was barely into the first sip of her drink when bachelor number one presented himself, sitting on the stool next to her before the words left his mouth. He was not unattractive, she thought. His hair was starting to thin and he had a bit of a belly. But he was at least 6-3, and his large physique was clearly more muscle than flab. His was an earnest confidence, not the phony bravado of the desperate guy who would come out firing until a woman finally gave him a bit of encouragement.

"Hello."

"I'm Tom," he ventured, extending his hand.

"Hello, Tom." She didn't return her hand in reply. "I don't mean to be rude, but you are in my boyfriend's seat."

"I saw you sit down alone, so that means either he went to little boy's room, or—"

"Or, it's because he had to work late and didn't get home before I left."

"Or," he continued, "for whatever crazy reason, you decided to give me brush-off scenario number 9. Why you would give a charming rogue like me that treatment, I have no idea."

He turned her firm grin into a chuckle. "Okay, guilty as charged. I'm flattered, Tom, but tonight's just not the night. Thank you for paying me the compliment of introducing yourself, though."

"Fair enough," Tom said, rising from his seat and picking up his longneck from the table. "It was worth a try."

"Enjoy your evening, Tom."

"You do the same."

He smiled and paced back to the bar. She chuckled, flattered by the attempt. On another night, she would have let him continue to see where it went. But the band was scheduled to begin any minute, and she had missed their last two local dates due to conflicts on her calendar. Their schedule wouldn't bring them within a hundred miles of Austin for at least another month.

"Another one bites the dust."

She turned and saw a burly black man who was even bigger than Tom. They quickly embraced and the man's bear hug nearly made Julia disappear.

"Hey, Cheese. What are you doing here?"

Robert Chisum was her first partner after leaving the police academy. They became fast friends, but rarely saw each other since she left the force.

"Working."

"How's that?"

"Club security."

"When did you start moonlighting?"

"When my kids started browsing for colleges."

"The last time I saw them, they were barely this tall."

"Now they're taller than you."

They fell into several minutes of catching up on shared colleagues and the news between them that had been missed. Julia's face suddenly lit up, remembering her old partner's off-duty activities.

"You still have your GC license?"

"I do, not that I use it much."

"You want to dust it off? I might could use your help."

"Anytime. What's up?"

Julia smiled. "I found it."

"Found what?"

"The fortress."

"Really?"

"Yes."

"Tell me about it."

Julia described the property, describing every detail she could recall. Cheese nodded earnestly, making a mental note of what he was hearing. He was modest about his status as a contractor, as he regularly took jobs to make ends meet. He only worked off referrals and was selective about what jobs he agreed to. Her band of freedom fighters could not afford his regular rates, but he had a soft spot for his old partner, and the cause was worthy. They would work something out.

She was nearly finished with her description when the lights began to dim, he motioned upwards.

"I've got to head to the stage. When do you close on it?"

"Don't know yet."

"Once it's done, count me in."

"Thank you."

They hugged and he waved as he walked toward the backstage door. Julia thought back to their nearly two years they spent together. As the grizzled veteran, Cheese taught her so much of the wisdom she used in her days on the force. He was so steady and sure of himself, balancing a serene home life with his wife and children separately from stints on patrol, vice and the SWAT team. Those lessons were still applied in her current pursuits. The day they were assigned new partners still broke her heart. The thought of him working alongside them, restoring the house, made Julia smile.

The band emerged on the stage and began their set. True to the reports, Zeddy was quite an athlete on stage. Their play had also not improved from the YouTube clips. They closed with two predictable favorites, "Livin' On A Prayer" and "Pour Some Sugar On Me." They successfully worked the crowd into a stir, not so much by the music, but by the era it represented, when the bulk of them were young and crazy. Once she had finished her drink, she had already collected plenty of video on her cell phone, acting as if she was texting. She took her purse and started to walk toward the door.

Julia saw Tom at the bar, chatting with the bartender and a couple sitting next to him. He still looked at ease, as if he regularly stopped here to unwind after a pressured day at work. She turned back, took a drink napkin off the table and pulled a pen from her purse. She quickly scribbled on it, folded it in half, and then eased up to him. He turned and she extended her hand.

"I'm Julia."

"Good to meet you, Julia."

"Sorry that tonight wasn't your night. Try again some time."

He accepted the napkin and nodded. "I will."

Julia strode out the door and he watched her go. Tom correctly guessed that this was a woman who did everything on purpose. He was looking forward to learning why.

FIFTEEN

AT first glance, Trent Tanger and his wife made an elegant couple. Like most superstar celebrities, the best hitter of his generation fit the red carpet nicely, giving all the requisite nods and poses. Tanger was all confident smiles, nods and laughs. Unlike the shallow bravado John Skilby displayed a few weeks earlier, this client of Damon Cash didn't have to sell anyone on his worth.

To the trained eyes of Gil Hawthorne, the demure persona of April Tanger was another matter. Like most media members, the reporter fancied himself an amateur psychologist, reading the athletes and coaches he covered like a scientist observing a lizard trapped in a holding tank. Her demeanor was uncomfortable, squinting at lights with half-hearted grins and telling body language. Visually, the young woman was a knockout, but she had zero presence to accentuate it. Her empty gaze had an odd vacancy about it.

Even though Hawthorne got paid for the tabloid dirt that wasted bandwidth and megabytes clogging the arteries of American brains, he was determined to be a columnist with a legitimate media outlet. Long before he had mastered reading and writing, sports was Hawthorne's first language. It didn't take him long to realize it was his brain that was fast-twitch, and not his body. He quickly applied his enthusiasm to the written word and memorized games and statistics moments after the contests ended.

Since Hawthorne wasn't even a pawn on the board of sports media, he wouldn't dare air his suspicions about the couple. The reporter would love to ask her even a couple of questions to gauge the nature of her reticence, but would never get the chance. The closest he would get was the brush of Tanger's custom tailored suit against his shoulder as he led his wife past the media into the restricted area and the elevators leading to the luxury suites above.

Besides, it wasn't even the story he was after. He would file away his observations for future reference, and return to the party for quotes from the remaining patrons. His focus was Damon Cash and his infectious salesmanship for the slugger. The agent was the story, and he would provide his digital recorder with more than enough material to work with.

What the reporters, including Hawthorne, didn't notice was the grip of Tanger's large, viselike hands on April's thin forearm. As they disappeared into the elevator, the grip got tighter and more painful. Only the drugs kept her from crying out before the door closed and the car moved upward.

As they darted into the presidential suite, April dropped into the loveseat inside the door, instinctively wincing as if expecting the forearm clench to be punctuated by something worse. She knew her reactions were dulled and was trying to protect herself from attacks she would not have the reflexes to avoid. She sloppily moved to her clutch to look for something, so that she would not have to face him.

Tanger watched her and the resentment began to rise. Everything around him compelled rage inside. Though the world was seemingly made for him, it took all he could muster to not explode out of control. His fury had him wound far too tight, but it was a mania he felt powerless to control, an edge he had not been forced to bank. It was a necessary evil, because his payday was within sight. Somewhere in the distance, relief would arrive.

The frail, fragile woman in front of him had caused him nothing but trouble. In their seven years together, she had produced no children. Lacking the strength to stand against him and the leverage to leave him, she was unnecessary baggage. And with only enablers around him, she was a convenient punching bag to release tension when there was no athletic obstacle to rid him of his demons.

"What's wrong with you?" he snapped.

"What's that?" April answered distantly. It was common for no words to be spoken between them for days, even when they were forced to travel together.

"You couldn't even smile for the cameras."

"I did—I did the best I could."

"Your best. Like hell. It was bad enough only five players showed up."

Not to mention no coaches and members of the front office, she thought. She raised her eyes to look at him, but dared not say what crossed her mind. He was just as much an asshole to them as everyone else. When he got his payday and left Music City for good, no doubt many high-fives and barroom toasts would be shared by ex-teammates.

April's brief unintentional look lit the fuse. He rose back to his feet, pacing toward her.

"Say it."

"What?"

"Say what you're thinking. They didn't show because they hate me. And you don't blame them."

April was an honest person by nature. With her system compromised by chemicals, any attempt to deny his assertion would be clumsy, at best. Her silence was the only answer she could muster.

"Why can't you—"

"Can't I what?" she mumbled. "All that dope your goons shove down my throat—"

At this, he yelled and leapt toward her, grasping her chin.

"Shut up! Shut the fuck up!"

He threw her against the wall, the collision thundering throughout the suite. To outside ears, it would have sounded like furniture was being moved and accidently dropped.

"You will never, ever say that again! Never!"

April wailed in terror, coiled in defense in a corner behind a chair. The nightmare continued, even through the fog of chemicals. With all the nearby suites kept vacant at Cash's insistence, no one would hear the painful sounds that followed.

The zipping of Tanger's belt leaving the pants' loops caused her to scream, for she knew what was next. He snatched her from the corner and threw her back into the center of the floor. The belt slapped against the woman, her screams occasionally shrill, but mostly muffled by his hand clamped over her mouth. When the struggle became too uncomfortable, the slugger dragged her from the couch to the other room and the master bed. She fought to stay away from it, for what waited there was even worse. After a brief wrestling match, he pinned her face down into a pillow propped up between the headboard and the mattress. He ripped off her dress and panties and grabbed her hair to control her resistance. Able to easily snap her neck with his raw strength, she had no choice but to surrender to his will.

In a suite several doors down, Sandy watched from his cell phone, realizing activity had escalated past the line he had been conditioned to monitor. He waved to Junior, who sat at the edge of the bar in the kitchen, his mouth full of a bite of his burger from room service. Junior took his associate's phone and watched for a few moments. The small camera was positioned behind the bedroom TV, looking out to the king-size bed.

"Let it go, as long she's breathing. Just keep an eye on it."

When the long night was over, Tanger left to whatever commitment Cash had scheduled for him next. The two bodyguards would escort April to the airport and then back to Texas. With all the horrors she had endured, what April truly feared was being locked away again, back in her multi-million-dollar prison. There she was merely marking time, forced to wait for another assault from her husband, or a visit from his handpicked doctor who would pump more drugs into her. That wait, and the fear and dread of it, was even worse than the actual abuse.

SIXTEEN

ONLY a few days in the safety of Molly's house had done Sophia wonders. Once freed from Benton's terror, Sophia saw how imperative it was that she made the move not a moment later than she did. There was another life out there, something that seemed mere fantasy days before.

Both Molly and Renee were gone, something she was happy to see. Her host and fellow guest were pleasant enough, but she relished some alone time in a safe place where she didn't have to dread the opening of the door to someone who would hurt her.

She fixed some coffee from the Keurig and opened the newspaper sitting on the kitchen table. She hadn't read a newspaper in some time, relying on the internet for that task. Even that had been a walk of tension before leaving, making sure she avoided a website that would incite her abuser to take some offense, and in turn take it out on her. The Statesman had nothing out of the ordinary. A battle in city council loomed over a rezoning measure. A Federal judge was nabbed with cocaine in a traffic stop in Kerrville. The Longhorns won again, continuing their winning streak.

The lock of the front door began to click and Sophia's heart jumped into her throat. She held her breath for a moment, then began looking for something solid to throw or swing at the coming intruder. As the lock finally turned, the best she could do was a nearby floor lamp, training the end of it toward the door.

Molly tumbled through the door and both women jolted with a start. Sophia caught up with herself and her fears, and Molly held her hands open in surrender the best she could with both arms full.

"It's just me, sweetie."

"I'm sorry. You never come through the front door."

"That's because I haven't had to haul in framing studs until today. They're too long to come through the garage. You want to get the door?"

"Sure," Sophia said, exhaling deeply as she followed in her pajamas and sandals. She did not know how long she would be with Molly, but she hoped to leave with some of her skills. In four days, she watched her fix multiple meals that were chef-worthy, tear out a wall to open up a room, and replace the starter on her car.

"Thanks," Molly said, as Sophia laid the materials where her host had pointed.

"Where is Renee?"

"She's pulling the wheelbarrow around to pick up the rest. She agreed to help extend the patio out back."

As if on cue, she heard commotion out back. Through the back window, she could see Renee unloading bags on the ground.

"Where did you learn all this?"

"I went to a few Home Depot classes, picked up a few pointers. Then, I just started."

Molly looked at Sophia as if to make a point of emphasis, then returned to measuring one of the holes she had created in the bathroom.

"I didn't try anything that would do permanent damage to the house. That way, I could always clean up any mistakes."

"Did you make a lot?"

"Plenty of them. That's how I learned."

Sophia continued to watch her work, effortlessly executing a plan her brain had down cold while casually conversing.

"The most important thing I learned is to not second guess myself. I started with an idea, then followed through on it. I had to learn to let my mistakes be setbacks, and not defeats. The setbacks then became stepping stones. Once I learned that, I trusted myself not to make fatal errors."

Sophia nodded, taking in her host's command of her project.

"So, you want to help?" Molly asked.

"Sure."

"Take this."

Molly shoved a large bag with assorted contents into Sophia's arms, while she dragged in several studs of lumber. She carried them back into the hall and set them on the floor, dusting herself off vigorously. Sophia was a neat freak and a clean freak, resisting the urge to rush to the bathroom to wash her hands.

"What are you doing in here?"

"You see this bathroom?"

"Yes."

"I want to make it private to the bedroom you are now in. But first, I want to build a bathroom in my other bedroom. That way, when more young ladies follow after you two, they each have a private bathroom to use."

"Alright. What do I do?"

Molly led Sophia to the bedroom she mentioned. Between that bedroom and the one where she slept was a large set of built-ins. She handed her a sledge hammer.

"You take this, and destroy these shelves, the wall between it, and the closet on the other side. When you're done, come see me for the next job."

"Molly?"

"Yes?"

"You know that I'm pregnant. Will I—"

"What are you, about eight weeks?"

Sophia nodded. Molly smiled in return.

"You're fine. I had four myself. Just don't push it. I'll get you moved to light duty long before it'll hurt your little one."

Molly winked at her, leaving to retrieve more items from the truck. Sophia lifted the sledge hammer, using both arms. She eyed the built-ins carefully. They were functional, but worn. One door hung askew from its upper hinge, begging to be repaired to its proper right angle. However, its owner had determined otherwise, choosing to discard it and replace it with something newer, with better purpose and utility.

It was a dramatic change for Sophia, tearing something down completely instead of trying to fix it. Some structures simply outlive their usefulness. Some relationships, built on flawed foundations, were never meant to survive.

Sophia took a deep breath and hurled her first blow at the crooked door. It collapsed in, unwilling to fight the coming progress.

SEVENTEEN

THE four vehicles turned off FM 1826 onto a road that was alternately gravel and asphalt. Attempting to drive above the speed limit of 25 was unwise, as was passing another vehicle. The dusty trail eventually stopped in front of the aged house, tucked inside the trees. The two newcomers looked curiously at the structure as they emerged from the vehicles, wondering what the fuss was about.

Yardley began her tour with Cassie and Noelle without the usual fanfare reserved for prospects she had just met. Julia soaked it all in again, trying to note the things she missed before. She found herself watching her colleagues more than the property.

The strengths were clear. The eccentric widower's original specifications perfectly suited the Shelter's needs. A subtle location so close to the city would attract a minimum of unwanted attention. The location was built on a rise facing the road, making the place defensible if need be.

However, the secluded lot was also a weakness. If any of their transports were tailed, there was nowhere to hide. The narrow road used to access the property would bottle any escape from their hideaway and trap them there. Also, construction to suit their intentions for the property would cost more than a cable channel rehab.

Cassie ran her fingers across wallpaper at least three decades out of style, then smacked the dust off with her hands. The kitchen was just as dated with a built-in microwave that had a dial for a timer. Noelle quickly found the corner of the den where phone and cable connections had once been. She popped off the wall covers and investigated the lines as if she was about to go to work.

When they looked at the bathrooms, Julia spotted some details she had overlooked. The fixtures were all original and well past their prime. Both toilets were small and needed to be replaced. The cheap linoleum tile was peeling away from the walls in several spots.

After they loaded into the elevator, Noelle produced a device with a digital display. Slightly bigger than a TV remote, the display showed digits fluctuating as they descended. When the door opened into the parking garage, Cassie burst out laughing.

"What the hell?" Noelle said. The four women walked out on the pavement, stunned at the enclosed garage that seemed to serve little purpose. Yardley pointed out the doors, disguised as a deck above the ground, in the far corner, sloping up to the side of the house.

"You wonder what kind of cars he kept down here," said Julia.

"I don't see much in the way of grease or oil between the white lines," Yardley said. "It may not have been used much."

The four considered the garage in wonder for a few moments before Yardley's heels clicked toward another door next to the elevator.

"This way, ladies."

The door opened to a hall with doors on either side. While the décor and upkeep of the rooms was similar to upstairs, the bones looked just as solid.

"This is a real doomsday prepper setup," Noelle said. "I might have bought this myself."

As Yardley described the downstairs, Noelle moved along each of the walls, watching the results from her device. Before entering the elevator to go back up, they noted Noelle nod in satisfaction, putting the device back in her purse.

The four stepped outside into bright afternoon sunshine, comfortable now that fall had set in. As Yardley finished her tour, Cassie asked to see the file. Noelle edged behind Cassie, looking over her shoulder. Once they appeared to have finished reviewing the paperwork, Julia raised her eyebrows, as if prompting discussion.

"I like it," Noelle declared, breaking the silence. "Very ordinary on the outside, blends in. The electronic shielding below ground is good."

"Yardley?" Julia asked.

"I do too. It's rough around the edges, but we're not trying to make the parade of homes. We'll have plenty of time to do the work to suit us. Below ground, we can start moving victims in soon."

All eyes turned to Cassie. The attorney sighed, handing the file back to the realtor.

"I only have one question. Why?"

"Let's flip it over," Julia replied. "Why not?"

"I know shelter and safe house space is lacking, but is this the answer? We have four rooms down there. That's throwing a rock against a tidal wave. Surely there's a better way to use our resources, if we had enough."

"We can do this, Cassie," Julia said.

"No, we can't."

"Yes, we can," said Yardley.

"I'm not counting the money we've stolen from abusers and hidden away," snapped Cassie. "We start laying out that money in large chunks, that's not going to escape notice."

"Not necessarily," said Noelle. "There's plenty of ways. We can do this."

"Noelle, just because someone hasn't knocked on your door doesn't mean it's escaped notice. They could pull the trigger at any time and this whole thing is over."

Yardley slapped the folder shut and stepped forward. "So, our badass attorney is the one among us not willing to run a red light or two to make this happen?"

"I don't see you dodging any bullets with those fancy realtor signs of yours."

"Enough!" snapped Julia. She exchanged looks with each of them, then looked at the ground. In their time together, each of the other three women had invested in the cause in their own way. A unified decision hadn't yet been required.

The friction between Cassie and Yardley was not new. They were usually cordial, but they sparred regularly, often over the most trivial details. Julia was determined not to interfere with them, other than to keep things civil. If they ever established a bond, it would have to be negotiated between them alone.

"Cassie's right," Julia admitted with a shrug. "We don't have to do this. And, it is a risk, far larger than the ones we have been routinely making. But this could change everything, for our community and for future efforts far away from here. We have no idea what all the little things we do add up to.

"Every shelter and safe house in a hundred-mile radius sends us their toughest and most dangerous cases. What we do needs what this property provides."

After a few moments, Cassie felt the other three women measuring her. The pressure of being the lone holdout made her dig in firmer, determined not to be pushed against her will.

"I'll think about it."

"It won't last forever," Yardley replied sharply.

"I said I'll think about it," Cassie replied, turning and walking away. The XTS quickly roared away.

"I'll get my attorney started on getting an LLC set up," Yardley said, closing her folder, sending both herself and Noelle toward their cars. Julia remained standing in place.

"No, we won't."

"What?"

"We're not doing this without all four of us on board."

"What are you going to do, Julia?" Yardley snapped. "Hold off decisions like this until she feels good about it? You can't handle it that way, and you know it."

"Stop it, Yardley."

"No, I won't, Julia. You have been babying her from day one. It's time she invested herself in this. It's not enough for her to ride in, save the day, and collect her fee."

Julia appeared resolute in her position, watching Yardley carefully. Noelle stepped towards them.

"Yardley speaks for me as well."

"Does she?"

Noelle was not comfortable challenging Julia, content to go with the flow of things. On this, Yardley and she agreed. While she did not have the personal issues Yardley did, she shared her view of Cassie's level of commitment.

After a brief pause, she nodded, meeting Julia's gaze firmly.

"Yes, she does."

"Ladies, this is not up for discussion. It's either unanimous, or we don't do it at all."

"Maybe I'll just buy it myself," Yardley shot back.

"You're at liberty to do so," said Julia, "but you better be planning a doomsday shelter for you and your family. Or flipping it. Not one of our victims will be staying there under that arrangement."

"Julia—"

"That's it!"

Julia's interruption of Yardley's protest was the last word spoken. Yardley abruptly slapped her portfolio shut and marched to her car.

"What is it with those two?" Noelle asked.

"Clashing personalities, shared stubbornness. I'd like to think they'll work it out eventually."

Noelle rolled her eyes. "See you later."

The Mini took off leaving Julia behind. She leaned against her truck, looking over the house and acreage, considering what it would be like.

She wanted that place badly. Instead of shuffling the most at-risk victims back and forth across town, juggling the schedules of a dozen kind-hearted sponsors, they could all stay here. It would be a castle, a fortress where women could heal, gain the strength to begin new lives, never to let an abuser dominate them again.

Julia shook herself away from her vision and cranked the truck. Her dream now had a location attached to it, but it couldn't be hers alone to make it a reality.

August 2005 – New Orleans, Louisiana
Cassie

HANNAH had always called her stepfather by his first name, Antonio, knowing from the start he wasn't really her father and did not merit being called by that title. His mother married Antonio when she was only four. By the time she realized they were poor, she also realized that her mother did not have the same capabilities as normal people her age. She walked with a decided limp, the result of one leg being shorter than the other. Her mental capacities were also compromised.

As Hannah grew older, she realized that Antonio capitalized on her mother's weaknesses, feeding them to make her even more dependent on him. Hannah recalled him striking her mother in her early years, but the attacks lessened as Hannah grew older. Though it had been years since Hannah had seen him get physical, his overall treatment of her mother remained brutal and unforgiving.

Stress seemed to bring out Antonio's worst. Once Katrina had passed over Florida and was scarcely impeded, Gulf residents were forced to choose between mobilizing to safety, or rushing to the stores for provisions. Antonio chose the latter in the final days, shouting marching orders to each of them as he went back and forth from the hardware store. Her mother argued some, but Antonio's harsh rebuttals ended any potential debates.

Hannah had never directly defied her stepfather, but she had provided just enough resistance to earn a measure of restraint from him. He sensed her strength of will, perhaps saving her and her mother from more extreme levels of abuse.

At 21, she was nearly living her own life, and would have been completely if not for her devotion to her mother. She longed to leave New Orleans and see what the rest of the world offered. Her mother, under the thumb of her stepfather, kept her tethered to the Crescent City. She never left town for longer than a weekend, and never farther than she could return in a few hours' drive.

Instead of openly refusing to remain with Antonio, Hannah planned to whisk her mother away while her stepfather was gone, eventually coming back with her to manage whatever storm Antonio created upon their return. Once he left Saturday morning, she would send her mother to travel north with her relatives.

Her compact car wobbled up to the curb and she jumped out, running to the little house she had called home most of her life. She opened the door, and found the house in shambles. The sparse furnishings were strewn about like a storm had already hit. A few moments after she took this in, she found her mother sobbing, on her knees in the bedroom.

"Momma, what's wrong?"

Hannah lifted her from the ground. Her mother's face turned to show multiple deep bruises. Her daughter gasped from the sight.

"I—I can't do it anymore, baby! I'd rather die than keep doing this."

Hannah looked beyond the wounds and into her mother's eyes, seeing a desperation she had never seen before. She hugged her tightly, knowing she could not allow it to go any further.

"You need to go with the rest of the family up to Jackson."

"What about you?"

"I'll follow shortly after. You need to get away from him. This is your chance. Get what you need and let's go."

They quickly packed and drove the two miles to her relatives' house. Hannah stopped just long enough to gingerly hand her mother over to her sister.

"What happened?" she gasped. The look on Hannah's face told her everything.

"I'm going back to get a few more things, then we'll go."

"What if he's there?"

Instead of answering, Hannah turned quickly, running back to her car and driving off.

Her aunt's question was all she thought about on the drive over. The possibility of confronting Antonio scared Hannah, but the anger from seeing her mother in that condition made her determined to leave that house on her terms, not his.

When she returned to the house, she opened the door cautiously, even though Antonio wasn't home. It was as if she was preparing for when he would enter. If he gave her any trouble, she would respond accordingly.

Hannah first went to the photo albums, sitting inside a worn TV stand. There were so many more than she remembered, documenting every step of her life. When she pulled them out, they tumbled to the floor, sending her line of sight narrowed at her feet.

"Where the hell is Lana, girl?"

His voice always boomed, but this time, it shook Hannah to the core. She turned abruptly and lost her breath at the sight of him, then collected herself.

"You scared me."

"Where?" he demanded.

She sighed, as if exasperated by the question. "In case you haven't heard, there's a storm coming, Antonio. I already sent her with the family." Hannah continued gathering the albums, acting as if nothing had happened to her mother. Her stepfather grabbed her forcibly by her arms.

"Call her and get her back! Now!"

"They're in Mississippi by now," she said, lying to keep him from chasing after her. Hannah would have said more, but he pinned her against the wall. In that motion, he could feel something unnatural at her side, a hard, solid object inside her jacket.

"What is this?"

They began wrestling, Antonio correctly guessing what the object was. Hannah had wisely chosen to take her stepfather's pistol before she left with her mother. Any element of surprise she might have had was gone.

"I knew you'd try this shit! I knew to never turn my back on you!"

As Antonio pressed against her, gradually winning the struggle, she screamed. This enraged him even further and he finally won the battle for the firearm, ripping her jacket in half in the process. He then whipped her with the butt of the pistol and she dropped limply to the floor.

He caught his breath, watching her. His stepdaughter appeared to be unconscious or dead. He reached down and slapped her face. She did not respond.

Antonio picked up the pistol and left her. He would pack his things and go after her mother.

But how would he explain what had just happened?

He turned back to see her, motionless. He thought of the house, its deteriorating condition and the looming storm. If he made sure she never moved again, the story would be his to tell. His stepdaughter would die tragically due to Katrina. If Katrina somehow spared the house, he would burn it before she returned, the fire likely to be attributed to storm damage.

He packed a bag in moments and dropped it by the door. He went back to see that his stepdaughter still hadn't moved. He considered her there, bruised by the blow of his pistol, but still pretty in sleep. There had been plenty of moments he had thought about her, in ways too contemptible to mention. He knelt by her, removing his handkerchief from his pocket. He would suffocate her first, then explore her in ways his imagination had only allowed before.

Antonio's plan might have worked if he had done it in that order. Since she hadn't moved, he decided to begin looking her over prior to finishing her. He undid one button on her blouse, then another. Then, he moved his hands to the belt around her pants.

Hannah began to move and he panicked. He quickly brought the handkerchief up to her nose and mouth, pressing firmly. She started to twist, then thrash about in desperation. Her arm banged against a small end table. She somehow wrapped her hand around its leg, grabbed it, and lifted it with one last surge.

The corner of the table was sharp enough to cause damage, especially in Antonio's left eye socket, just above the eyeball. He dropped on top of her like he was shot. He yelled angrily, which somehow prompted her to swing it again. This time it hit him square on the temple, and he fell against a nearby wall.

When Hannah came to full consciousness, moments later, she discovered that her clothes were barely on her. Only one button held her blouse in place, her bra in full view. Her belt was unbuckled and her jeans were unzipped. At this, she no longer needed the nerve to act.

Antonio groaned against the wall, his pistol nearby. Hannah wisely chose to ignore the gun and scanned the room for a blunt instrument. She remembered the large wrench kept underneath the sink for the frequent plumbing issues the house suffered. She grabbed it and moved toward her stepfather, still crouched, semiconscious, his back to her.

The first blow to the crown of his head caused a sickening crack, so sickening that she immediately threw up. Once she was done retching, she swung again. She continued the process until there was nothing left in her stomach and there was no life left in Antonio.

Exhausted, she dropped to the floor. Once she regained her breath and nerves, she had to decide how to proceed.

She felt zero guilt, but would a jury of twelve agree?

In a moment, she knew the answer. For the time being, Hannah would take her chances with the road.

Julia did not begin her career in law enforcement to pursue justice for domestic violence victims. She could not count how many domestic calls she responded to, or even one incident that stuck out in her mind. The horrors blurred together, adding to a mosaic that chilled her spine and made her doubt how effective her profession was in combating a growing epidemic.

She had already retired from the force when the Castle Rock versus Gonzales decision came down from the Supreme Court. SCOTUS voted 7-2 against a suit that would have considered financial damages after three children were taken in violation of a restraining order and killed by their father, apparently as revenge against their mother, a domestic abuse victim.

That decision confirmed what she already knew. The law was often either unwilling or incapable of protecting women in peril from domestic violence. Justice for many victims would have to come from outside the legal system.

It took well over a year after starting as a private investigator before she began making enough money to support herself, another before she was confident it would continue as a career. Once certain of the viability of her business, she began working with her old friends in law enforcement. The connection quickly evolved into a unique quid pro quo relationship that spread mutual benefits throughout the Austin area.

It began with a simple request from her friend Robert Chisum. Cheese had a robbery case that he had been unable to crack. It was a team of young men who scouted and hit businesses in Travis and Williamson counties with no discernable pattern. They knew the ringleader, but did not have enough to bring charges that would equal sufficient prison terms. They also did not have the resources to follow his every move.

Coincidentally, his girlfriend had taken three trips to the local urgent care clinic, all claimed as "household accidents." Enter Julia Caldwell. She birddogged the ringleader for two months and discovered their next target. When the burglary attempt was greeted by four Georgetown police officers, the crew was arrested and all of the participants pled out to terms of 3-4 years each. The leader's parole after 18 months was on the condition of a lifetime restraining order for his battered ex.

The stories began to collect as the months and years passed. As Julia built a cohesive system out of a disconnected group of police, judges and good Samaritans, the tangible effects began appearing on domestic violence rates in the area. It had a dozen nicknames. Underground. Shelter. Whatever it was, the word soon made its way throughout Austin and the surrounding community. Commit violence on your significant other or a child and the penalties were severe. Apart from maximum sentences and curious misfortunes once they were released, a leper-like stigma also followed the guilty around. It would take years for the rest of the country to begin following suit.

The growing tide gave Julia latitude in a number of situations. She often sought circumstances where the poor and disenfranchised congregated, trying to spot victims to save in the crowd. Over time, she became almost a savant at reading the non-verbals of such individuals, plucking them out one by one.

Serving as an emergency volunteer, Julia picked her most noteworthy victim out of the thousands of Katrina evacuees milling about the Astrodome. She somehow looked out of place at first glance, but it was the eyes that gave her away. In the midst of all the pain and suffering on display, there was a different desperation in the eyes of an abuse victim on the run.

She was maybe twenty years old, alone, and without a group, glancing back and forth like someone was chasing her. When her eyes met Julia's, both women froze.

"Can I help you?"

"I—I don't know."

"Care to talk about it?"

In-depth conversations with white people had not been common in her life. She had been conditioned to not trust other colors under any circumstances.

They sat on a crate on the edge of the Astrodome concourse, the chaos flowing in all directions past them.

"What's your name?"

"Hannah."

"I'm Julia. Where are you from?"

"The lower Ninth Ward."

"I know you're scared from the hurricane."

The young woman shook her head. Julia's instincts were correct.

"What is it?"

What happened hours earlier was eating away at her. She couldn't hold it in forever. Though she knew better than to trust her instincts, she chose to follow them now.

"Something bad happened before I left."

The woman measured her carefully, then casually looked around. No one was paying any attention to them. The storm was still blowing people around, just in different ways. Julia made a point of sitting next to her, close enough to hear her whisper, and she began telling her story. A few minutes later, the victim's new friend sighed, taking it all in.

"Okay. Come with me."

The woman led her out of the Astrodome and made the long walk to her truck. Once inside, she produced her cell phone and dialed.

"Carol, this is Julia. I got an emergency call from my sister's boyfriend. She was in a car wreck back in Austin and is in the hospital. I'm in the car driving now."

Hannah watched Julia talk and listen to the well wishes of whoever she checked in with back at the Astrodome. Her new friend was a smooth liar. Hopefully, the words she had told Hannah were the truth.

"Thanks so much, Carol. I'm sorry about this. I will let you know as soon as I know something. Thank you."

Julia killed the cell phone. "Alright. Let's go. I'm guessing Austin will do for now."

"Does your sister even have a boyfriend?"

"I don't even have a sister."

Hannah took it all in. The previous ten days weren't enough to get used to the fact that she might never see New Orleans again, after never leaving the state of Louisiana all her life.

"So, what now?"

"We get you to a safe place for a few days. We get you fed, get you some sleep, then we figure out the future later."

"We? How many of you are there?"

Julia smiled. "Enough. Until we figure out where you stand back in Louisiana, we'll get you a new name. Off the top of my head, the names they have available include Amanda, Madeline, Britney, Deborah, Nadine, Cassandra—"

"Cassandra. As in Cassie?"

"Sure. It could be."

And with that, the SUV sped up 290, chasing the sunset. Hannah considered life as a Cassie, and hoped her mother would understand someday when she explained it to her.

EIGHTEEN

THE XTS was cruising east down I-10 at 90 MPH, as effortlessly as if it were rolling through a school zone in single digits. It held what little curves the South Texas interstate had to offer as if the car was magnetically fastened to the asphalt.

With only Cassie's purse in the passenger seat and a small duffle in the trunk, it couldn't be a pleasure trip. She was as concerned about her appearance as any female, but she would see few people who would care how she looked, and none who knew her in her new identity or the old one.

She always had an eerie sense of history on these trips. Not so long ago, it was unthinkable for a black woman to travel South Texas and Louisiana alone in a late model Cadillac. When she left her car for gas, food or a restroom break, she was acutely aware of glances she received. Times had changed, but some hearts were still hard, some spirits poisoned beyond reason.

Seven hours after leaving Austin, the XTS rolled through the Ninth Ward, turning right off Claude Avenue, toward the Mississippi, and into the neighborhood she called home. Twelve years before, houses that had stood for decades disappeared, leaving empty lots. Now, the houses were splotched here and there, like a new development that had yet to complete sales of the subdivision's inventory. Instead, it was the winds and waves of Katrina that had destroyed the structures. Those who chose to rebuild remained, as did the memories of what was before.

Cassie carried those memories with her. She often wished she could leave that part of her behind, but it was impossible. Too much trauma had taken place on that street. Too many horrors in a house that was no longer standing. It was still just as real to her, as she could return to that day in an instant. She had disappeared with the storm, resurfacing at a place of her choosing with a new name and a new life.

She stopped across the street from an empty lot that was the focal point, her cue to let her emotions roam. In Austin, such thoughts blurred her focus. Here at home, she could safely feel them, letting them center her. Her new life came with unknown freedoms, but untold pain remained that time and distance couldn't erase.

Cassie drove west on Claiborne, turning on Louisa. She crossed Robertson and parked on the left, next to the cemetery. She got out, walking deliberately. The sun was setting and it would be unwise to let night fall in the area, even with the pistol at her side. The pain inside her dismissed any fears.

Three rows back and eleven plots to the left. The moss had grown around the engraving, but it was still legible.

LANA ANNE WILLARD
1958–2006

She could see her mother being dominated, so helpless to escape, and Cassie so powerless to help her. Today she could have easily come to her rescue and taken her someplace safe. Today, with the wisdom of twelve years and a law degree, she knew her flight off the grid was unnecessary. But today was twelve years too late.

Rarely did more than two or three months pass before she would make this trip and return as swiftly as she left. It was an anchor, a familiar place she returned to when considering a decision. It reminded her of where she had been, and where she wanted to go.

The permanence of her mother's grave gave her some perspective, despite the pain. Signing a contract was nothing as dramatic as disappearing in the bedlam of Katrina and assuming a new identity, but something told her it had just as much potential in defining her life. Maybe a few more moments wouldn't have changed anything twelve years ago, but she wasn't about to rush such decisions ever again.

When she had enough and walked to her car, her phone rang.

"Hello."

"What are you doing?"

Julia's voice broke Cassie out of the memories.

"I took a drive to clear my head."

"Long drive, huh?"

Cassie laughed, dropping back into the Caddy. "Yeah, I guess."

"What's in your head?"

"Just thinking about yesterday."

"Second thoughts?"

"Once we do this, there's no turning back."

"It's only money, Cassie."

"It's not the money.

"Then, what?"

"I watched the body count in my city rise every day for weeks from the safety of a safe house 500 miles away. The cops and firemen were just cleaning up the mess. A lost cause. You know how empty that leaves you?"

Cassie paused. Julia sensed the coming tension.

"You're trying to do the same thing, Julia. You're building a castle among a field of ruins. We're not builders, we're recyclers."

"What does that have to do with the house? It's a business transaction."

"What I don't know is why. Why is that house so damn important?"

Julia stopped to consider the question. The answer was from somewhere else, a deep reservoir she usually only navigated at home alone, moments before sleep. It was an idea that resonates so clearly, you couldn't ignore it if you tried. Words never did it justice, but spirit filled her heart, prompting her voice to make the attempt.

"Are you still at the graveyard?"

"Yes," Cassie replied.

"Look at those gravestones. Do you ever wonder how many of those people took dreams they never finished chasing with them?"

"What are you getting at, Julia?"

"I turned 47 a few weeks ago. Once you get to this age, you start losing people. Not to car wrecks or freak accidents. The expected stuff. Cancer, heart attack, stroke. It's happening to classmates, colleagues, friends. People that all thought they had more time. You start to realize that you don't have much time. You probably have far less than you think.

"That dream that you've always had, you get determined not to let it die with you. When your body finally gets put down, you just want to make sure you gave that dream of yours everything you had. You don't want to get up to heaven and find out that you almost made it. You just needed one more push, one more step before the dream came true."

The call fell silent. Cassie absorbed what she had heard, then nodded in understanding.

"This thing we do," Julia continued, "that house is a symbol of that to me. It's the unicorn, the fortress that cannot fall. I want it. I'm not quitting until I get it."

The line went silent for a few moments. Cassie wasn't a dreamer, but Julia was her mentor. She still didn't fully understand her, but she respected her. And she knew Julia wouldn't stop.

"Come on back to Texas," Julia said. "You marinate too long in those memories, they'll take you over."

Cassie chuckled. "Okay, Mom."

"Be careful. Good night."

"Night."

NINETEEN

TRENT Tanger's entourage was modest in comparison to many of Damon Cash's clients. The two bodyguards walking at his side into the Cash building had eased into other roles in his life. Once inside the safe confines of his mansion or hotel room, assistants quickly became friends, drinking buddies and then confidants. This was planned well in advance by Cash, as he selected bodyguards not only for security, but compatibility as well. The few friends Tanger had from his younger days had all been run off by the agent.

No one ever looked at the floors changing on the elevator ride. Once you rose above ground level, you could see the trappings of the Cash machine on full display. To the left was a massive workout facility with every conceivable piece of equipment proudly on display. A handful of million-dollar athletes roamed the gym, with no fear of an autograph or selfie hound to ambush them. To the right, basketball and tennis courts. Tenants in offices circling the five-story building were able to watch the athletes working below.

The bodyguards walked Tanger into a conference room. At one end of the room was an HD screen that covered most of the wall. The other walls were covered with photos, posters and framed jerseys of various Cash clients. Tanger belting a home run in the playoffs last year was intentionally placed right across from where he would be sitting.

"Have a seat, Trent. Let me make some introductions to some of my staff you may not have had a chance to meet."

Cash went around the room, naming each of his experts. There were two men who had once been baseball executives, now employed by Cash. One had been a general manager for a major-league team, the other had been the director of pro scouting for another team.

There was a man and a woman, both with advanced degrees from Ivy league schools. Their sole purpose was to crunch every baseball statistic, including advanced analytics, and produce data in support of Cash's clients.

There were two men and a woman representing marketing and branding analysis. Two had experience with shoe companies, one had experience with both a soda brand and a luxury vehicle division.

There was also an accountant and an attorney, both in-house representatives of Cash's firm. Next to them were Tanger's accountant and attorney, who were acknowledged as well. Next to Cash's seat was his personal assistant, who would operate the video screen and handle any other tasks that were necessary.

The only other person in the room was Vance, who sat in a back corner, several feet away from the table. He was not introduced.

The primary source of discussion was a two-inch thick leather binder that sat at each of the fourteen places at the table. Each section was coordinated with the video aids that had been prepared. On the cover of the binder, Trent Tanger's cheery laughing face standing near a batting cage in bright sunshine was punctuated by his autograph embossed in gold.

"Now that we all know each other, let's show Trent what we have."

The lights dimmed and the monitor came to life. The former general manager began by listing eight potential destinations, but only going into detail on four teams. New York, Los Angeles, Chicago and Houston were widely regarded as the most serious contenders. The GM listed the pros and cons of each, as well as the likelihood of their making a play. The former scouting director reviewed the rosters of the teams as well as projecting the future of their farm systems.

One of the analytics experts spoke, outlining the keys that Cash would stress in negotiations, as well as the differences in how Cash would approach each of the teams based on their particular preferences and their manager's style of play.

Both of the marketing experts spoke, outlining the brands who were already preparing their separate presentations in various categories of commerce. They detailed what they knew about their plans and the projected revenues to be gained from each.

The accountant and attorney both spoke briefly regarding the potential business opportunities that might be available in each of the four cities. The accountant was quick to point out that there were no state income taxes collected in Texas, giving Houston a small edge that might only be of benefit in playing the teams against each other in a bidding war.

After an hour and a half, the meeting closed. Tanger offered the group polite thanks, and they respectfully acknowledged this in passing out the door. Tanger rose from his seat to follow.

"Hang back for a second, T."

Tanger nodded dutifully and sat back down in his chair. Cash walked over next to him and sat astride the conference table, with one leg hanging off comfortably.

"We have to talk about the elephant in the room. The one only you, myself and the attorneys know about."

"What's that?"

"The wife."

Tanger sighed in resignation. "What about her?"

"She has to go."

"Dammit, Cash! I—"

"Trent, you can't keep her. She was a liability long before you hit her. You know that."

"I love her."

"No, you don't. You love the idea of her. You love that she looks good on your arm, and that she puts up with your shit, once we pump her full of chemicals."

Tanger fell silent. He felt rage rise inside him, as it constantly did without warning. Only the fear of Cash kept those emotions in check. The agent watched the fires inside him quell, then continued.

"We're going to keep you away from her in the coming weeks. Once your contract is signed, we'll do a quiet divorce, pay her off, and we're done."

"I want to see her. One more time."

Cash paused tellingly. "Maybe. We'll see."

Tanger's eyes fell. He felt like a child so often, but especially in the presence of his agent. He had never felt in control of his own life, but Cash made it feel even more restrictive. He glumly walked out of the office.

Vance rose from his seat at the far end of the room, walking up to Cash.

"Well?"

"I think it's time. Do you have a plan ready?"

"I have several, depending on your timeline."

"Let's make it a few days after the signing," Cash said. "We'll have the story of the first season in his new home dedicated to her memory."

Cash nodded, mostly in agreement with himself. Vance watched him processing the decision.

"How do you suggest we do this?" Cash asked.

"Maybe a car accident," Vance ventured with a shrug, "with clues to the drugs handy."

"Perfect. We can add the drug advocacy angle to his media profile."

"What about the next woman?" asked Vance. "And the one after that?"

Cash waved his hands in protest. "No relationships for him, not for a long time. One night stands only, with your men in the next room for every minute of them."

TWENTY

CASSIE eased the XTS to a stop outside her office well before dawn. She thought she would be the first in the complex to arrive, but the lights were already on inside Ramirez Realty. She had to give Yardley credit, as she wasn't just a pretty woman charming her way through life. She burned the candle at both ends for business, and her customers swore by her. Vacations were hard-earned luxuries she grudgingly took when she reached total exhaustion. She and Cassie fought like siblings, but it wasn't for lack of respect.

She stepped outside the car, looked back toward the Ramirez Realty offices, then threw the leather case back inside the car. She walked inside and found Yardley in her office alone, stacks of paper surrounding her on the desk, and stacks of paper lined on the table across from her desk. She stepped inside, gently knocking on the door frame. Yardley saw her and gave her a sleepy grin.

"Morning."

"Hey," Yardley said.

"It's early," Cassie said.

"It is. You want some coffee?"

"Sure."

Yardley dropped some paperwork on a chair inside her office, then led Cassie toward the kitchen.

"Cups are in the cabinet."

Cassie selected a mug and filled it from the Keurig. She hadn't spent much time in the realtor's office, only dropping in when Shelter business required it. Yardley pulled a bottle of water from the fridge.

"Have a nice weekend?"

Cassie paused. "Sort of. I went back home."

"New Orleans?" Yardley asked.

"Yes."

"Do you still have family there?"

She shook her head. "No. I just go to my old house, or the plot where it used to be. Then, I go to my mother's grave. It helps center me."

"Did Katrina take the house?"

"It did," Cassie said. "You ever go back home?"

"To Brownsville? Not much. My parents usually come up for the holidays. My kids go down there more than I do. They were little when we left, so they don't remember much of the bad stuff."

Cassie nodded, sipping from her mug. Yardley watched her for a few moments, observing her reflecting on whatever happened back then.

"Your Keurig is newer than mine, so you didn't come over here for the coffee."

"Alright, Perry Mason. Tell me this. I know we spar a lot, but do you really want to do this?"

"The house?"

"That's right," Cassie said.

"Yes, I do."

"Why?"

"I know it's a stretch," Yardley said. "I know for practical purposes, it's a projection. Will we have the money for the upkeep? Will we be able to staff it? There's a hundred problems we don't have the answers to."

"Then, why?"

"I believe in Julia," Yardley said with a shrug. "She's the truth. I know it sounds corny, but I would lie down in traffic for her. And it's not just what she did for me. She's a special person. She'll have to go far off the deep end for me to not have her back."

Cassie inhaled and exhaled deeply, considering what she heard. "I understand."

"You know I didn't mean all that stuff I said the other day," Yardley said.

"Sure, you did," Cassie replied, "and you weren't all wrong. With the law, I feel so confident in my judgment, I've assessed all the risks going in. There are surprises, but I'm in control. Doing my part for the Shelter, it's the same.

"This house, it's different. There's a permanence, a commitment, a finality to it that scares me. I don't know why."

"We all have our issues. Everyone has to deal with them in their own way," Yardley said, striding toward the door. "I'm going to get back at it. Help yourself to more coffee. There's some to-go cups in the next cupboard."

"It's not like we don't have coffee in our office."

"But you don't always get this level of conversation with Julia. Remember, I talk for a living, too."

Cassie chuckled, her heart starting to win over her mind. She guarded against this to help her win at her profession, but couldn't help softening to the idea.

"If we decided to go for it, how much would you offer?"

Yardley told her the dollar figure. Cassie smirked and shook her head.

"What the hell, I'm in. Draw it up."

"Alright."

"Thanks for the coffee," Cassie said, leaving the kitchen.

"Anytime," Yardley said, watching her go.

TWENTY-ONE

WHEN April's vision cleared, the only thing she knew was that it was night. Gradually, her identity came back to her, then her location, then recent history. All of these items were still blurred and hazy, but at least she now knew that it was by design.

The drugs slowed the memories, but didn't remove them. The beatings and virtual captivity living under the constant supervision of an American sports icon, his hired lackeys, and his handler and master, the sinister sports agent who worshipped at the altar of power and money, could not be forgotten in a thousand lifetimes.

Dr. Pelson was a welcome sight at first. April originally thought that her husband tried to make up for his offenses by providing the best in care. She soon realized that the doctor was not her friend. Her senses became dulled with each visit, the memories of her husband's offenses more difficult to parse.

She had attempted escape once before. Tanger was on an extended road trip on the West Coast, three games each in San Diego, Los Angeles and Oakland, and four in Seattle. She enjoyed fourteen hours of freedom, hitchhiking to just past the Oklahoma border before being seized and returned to the compound in Southlake. No telling what deal had been struck with the casino to guarantee silence and a loss of memory regarding the scene she made by the blackjack tables.

The terror she endured upon returning put escape out of her mind, but only for a while. When her spirit retrenched, she began plotting one more chance, and one only. She was determined to plan deliberately and carefully, waiting for the perfect moment to run. If that failed, she would attempt a more permanent solution.

The first step was to regain as much control of her faculties as possible. The drugs dispensed by Dr. Pelson were for more control than healing. April had not given much resistance to the doctor when she dispensed her pills, and was not about to start now. She acted as if she trusted her completely, taking all the pills she was given. As the days turned into weeks, the doctor was less conscientious in watching her consume her pills, giving April some latitude to experiment.

At the very beginning, the dosage began with only one pill. Now there were ten pills, three matching pairs and four different. She began formulating a plan, to test the effects of skipping one pill for a few days, then try another. Eventually, she might stumble upon the right combination. Or, the mix might make it worse. April no longer cared if it would kill her. She would rather die than continue in her present condition.

The large mansion had two master bedrooms, one of which Trent Tanger occupied, at times with his wife, at times with others, but more often by himself. The other master served as April's holding area, where she was kept when he was away, or otherwise occupied. In her bedroom, two large windows with a view of the front driveway were the primary feature, the sights outside tantalizing her dreams for freedom.

April remembered seeing a movie years ago, where burglars broke into a home by rigging the locks on the windows. They used magnets, something she had never forgotten. Months earlier, she noticed the magnets inside the cabinet doors in the bathroom. April loosened one on the door on the far end of the vanity and laid it in the bottom corner of the cabinet. Routine checks of the room by Cash's security had evidently not made notice of it, leaving it tucked harmlessly by the front edge of the door jamb.

Choosing the best date on the calendar was finally all that remained. There would never be a perfect opportunity to escape and stay hidden. After the last session with her husband, any chance would be good enough.

TWENTY-TWO

THE elevator door opened and Julia stepped into the underground parking garage, smiling at what she saw. In the weeks after closing, several upgrades had been added to the list of things to do in getting the compound where she wanted it. The most obvious was right in front of her, several parking spaces cordoned off to create three more bedrooms. Framing studs marking off the outlines of the rooms and the resurfacing of the floors were the only tasks done toward that job, the completion awaiting Cheese's buddy to return from his vacation in the Bahamas.

Julia walked down the hall to the bedrooms that already existed, approaching the sounds of work. Cheese was cutting a PVC pipe, with a variety of materials strewn about the room.

"What are you doing?"

Cheese did not look up from the pipe at her question. "What does it look like I'm doing?"

"It looks like the beginnings of a second bathroom."

"It won't get done if you don't leave me alone. It'll get done a lot quicker if you change into your work stuff and help me out."

"What about Ivan and Chet?"

"Ivan went for supplies. Chet's mother-in-law is in the hospital."

"Oh, no."

"He said it was just a scare. He'll be back tomorrow."

Julia patted him on the shoulder. "I've got one more appointment this afternoon, then I'll be back to relieve Noelle."

Cheese placed the PVC on the ground, turning to her. "Is that how you're going to man this thing? All four of you covering 24 hours a day? That's stretching you four thin."

"Only at first. Molly and some of her friends have agreed to cover during the week. Noelle's a night owl, so she can do a lot of nights, especially once her daughter graduates."

Julia stopped her own narrative, knowing she didn't have all the answers. Cheese watched her ruminating over the problem. Realized dreams are never the same as you originally pictured it in your mind's eye. You don't see the unintended consequences, the complications, the payments that come due on the debts incurred along the way.

"I don't know. We'll just figure it out."

"Of course, you will. Now go finish that appointment and hurry back. Me and the fellas didn't bargain to do this all ourselves."

"You've been whining about losing that gut of yours. Look at it as a workout."

Cheese gave her a disgusted glance, as she walked away. "You also didn't say anything about knocking out those load-bearing walls upstairs."

"And you know better than to trust me."

"Never again," he said, returning to the PVC. She left him with a wink and a smile, disappearing down the hall.

When the elevator door opened back on the ground floor, she found Sophia standing in the kitchen, wiping down the counter. Though they had not worked on the kitchen, it looked spotless, something that would have been difficult to imagine when they first saw it weeks earlier.

"What are you doing?" Julia asked.

"Not much," Sophia said. "Molly put me on light duty now that I'm nearly four months. I'm restricted to the kitchen."

In the den outside the kitchen, Yardley sat, sipping from a water bottle. She had her hair in a ponytail, with safety glasses sitting atop her head. Julia joined her on the couch.

"She's stuck on KP, huh?" Julia asked.

Yardley nodded. "That kitchen is as neat as a pin. Everything in the fridge and pantry is in order, with the labels facing out. The counter is clean, all the appliances are faced out, everything at right angles. When I grabbed this bottle from the fridge, she wiped the handle down, along with the rest of the door."

"She's bored and she's got OCD. Didn't you say you were short-handed at the office?"

Yardley looked at Julia and could see the wheels turning, knowing exactly what she was thinking.

"Look, keeping things tidy in an old kitchen is one thing. Working for me is another."

"Watch this."

Julia went to the Keurig and filled her mug. In doing so, she shifted the Keurig slightly and left the box of coffee pods open turned away from their original position. Sophia saw how she had left the counter and gave her a sideward glance as she returned the coffee maker and box to their original positions.

"Well?"

"You're right. She burned a hole in your back, then put it back exactly where it was. Even wiped clean the Keurig of your fingerprints, if you even left any."

Julia smiled and took a sip of her coffee.

"See you later."

As Julia left through the front door, Yardley walked to the kitchen and refilled her coffee mug. Sophia leaned against the counter, a blank stare on her face.

"Had enough of this?"

"It's okay," she replied, unconvincingly.

Yardley motioned toward the door. "I think I can do better. Come with me."

Sophia folded the towel and placed it squarely on the counter, eager for something different than basic cable and KP.

"Were you pissed she left the counter in such a mess?" asked Yardley.

"Actually, yes." Sophia replied.

"Don't be. She may have just got you a job."

Sophia was confused, but followed Yardley out the door.

TWENTY-THREE

THE idea was only in the germ stage of Gil Hawthorne's mind when he saw Trent Tanger and his wife on the red-carpet weeks earlier. Watching him and his flawless image, it was a striking difference between John Skilby, the quarterback who was now retired, even though he hadn't officially claimed that status. Every team in the league had passed on him when he was waived and his agent wasn't saying a peep. Only Skilby didn't know his career was over.

Their agent was the story that kept Hawthorne fascinated. Damon Cash had assembled an incredible array of talent in both the sports and entertainment industry. He spoke with brash authority in every spoken word. His nightlife exploits at the parties of every major event in America were legendary.

The self-destruction of John Skilby and the picture-perfect life of Trent Tanger were polar opposites, but Hawthorne suspiciously detected a common thread, perhaps wrapped around Cash's finger.

The reporter could usually be found with earphones plugged in, his two computer monitors filled with sports video clips on YouTube, or on some analytics website with complex statistics. He had spent his childhood poring over the sports pages, then the internet. He had dreamed of being a general manager of a big four sports team. Writing about it, like most sports journalists, was an acceptable consolation prize.

Hawthorne was confident that he could discover the next big thing, whether it be the next Michael Jordan, or the next "Moneyball" theory that would revolutionize a sport. Once his assigned articles were written, he went spelunking for new sports knowledge, much like he did when he was a child.

As he got older, his interests started to take a turn towards conspiracy. How can the most penalized team in pro football not get one penalty flag in the championship game?

How can an undefeated heavyweight champion get knocked out by a diminutive 50-1 underdog? How can an undefeated college basketball team get drilled by 30 points in the Final Four?

He spent years chasing down the blind alleys of conspiracy, never fully satisfied with what he found. Either there was nothing to it, or the sports powers that be were just too good at covering their tracks. He finally concluded that whatever the truth was, it wasn't worth the effort to search, especially when his bills were paid by a media machine that relied on healthy sports leagues to feed it content.

The editor of Neon Mega was only a few years older than Gil Hawthorne, but he had enough journalistic skins on the wall to be his mentor. He broke the story of a pay-for-play scandal at a perennial college football power, then a sex scandal that forced a sitting governor to retire weeks before an almost certain reelection. He parlayed the attention into a venture capital investment of several million dollars into his idea for the next big thing, an online tabloid that would change the face of 21st century journalism.

Five years later, he had drifted from rabid reporter to lazy administrator. He looked at potential stories in terms of clicks and advertising appeal, quickly rejecting ideas that didn't fit his business model. He could still appreciate a good story, but with the VC nest egg steadily dwindling, he couldn't afford to swing big and miss. Even the slightest chance of a lawsuit meant the answer was no.

While Gil Hawthorne saw himself as a savant, the editor did not share his opinion. He had been a reliable enough hand, delivering decent copy enough to keep paying him with nominal raises. He appreciated Hawthorne's bent toward conspiracy theories, but he could chase that rabbit into the woods and not resurface for days. He had to work to keep his young reporter focused on the story right in front of him, and not roaming in the shadows for monsters that might not exist.

Hawthorne walked into his office, interrupting a round of online poker by the editor. The editor saw the grin on his reporter's face and knew what was coming.

"What is it this time?"

"I have a proposition for you."

"No. The answer is no."

"You haven't even heard it yet."

Some dufus bullied him out of a decent hand and he folded, turning to his employee.

"Okay."

"I'm due two weeks of vacation. I'm asking you to give me that and another week paid to go to Texas."

"Cash?"

"That's right."

The editor laughed. "You're not going to stop, are you?"

"Nope."

"Alright," the editor sighed. "Save your receipts. Enjoy yourself, but don't go crazy. Two weeks from Monday, I want a legitimate, verifiable story on Damon Cash. If it doesn't pass muster, I don't want to ever hear about it again. Deal?"

"Deal."

The editor opened his hand in resignation and Hawthorne darted out of view. He was so worn down by the reporter's persistence, he realized the best way to end the matter is to let him pursue it, then submit whatever he produced to such a high bar that it would never be seen.

Hawthorne knew that was his editor's plan, but he had supreme confidence on what he already had found in his research. He had accumulated a sizable number of instances where Cash had parted ways with clients and they had come to remarkably bitter ends. There were also plenty of examples of contracts, some astounding, some curious, that were truly illogical. While he had to admit that much of it was circumstantial, he also realized that he wasn't investigating a crime, just a sports story.

The book on Cash was that he was a willing, engaging interview at events, but that he shied away from in-depth personal pieces. Hawthorne had to break down whatever barriers and get Cash to let him in. He was possibly the most powerful person in the entertainment industry and his story would make Hawthorne a new career of his own.

An hour after his editor's blessing, his bags were packed and his bills were paid for the next month. His worn Nissan Sentra passed 150,000 miles as he picked up I-10, heading east toward the desert.

TWENTY-FOUR

TOM waited in the atrium of the restaurant, scrolling through the news on his phone. Waiting in life was a given, especially with a woman. He prided himself on not dragging his knuckles through life, but he was also a realist. Men and women had certain characteristics, good and bad. Stereotypes were generalities not to make assumptions about, but to also not be surprised by. The smartphone had made passing time much more convenient, if not better.

He had met Julia for a drink a couple of weeks earlier. She was as he had originally suspected. She did indeed act with a purpose, and was driven in her life. But over a glass or two of wine, Tom saw the other sides of her. Again, it was all by intent, and never out of her control. She carried herself regally, but casually. By appearances, she knew exactly who she was, and where she was going.

He was unsure what exactly she thought of him, but he was long beyond losing sleep over such things. He had taken the marriage ride shortly after graduating from college, and endured the divorce ride a few years later. His one child, a daughter, was now fully grown and living out of state. His ex-wife, with who he maintained a friendly relationship, lived in Illinois with her fourth husband. Privately, her track record made him feel better about how things had turned out, even though he had to admit he wasn't the best husband either.

The single life suited him, for the most part. The advantages were obvious. No one to check in with, no reason to not run to Vegas or the Caribbean whenever the hell he wanted to, and no guilt in embracing the night when a lovely maiden beckoned.

There were lonely stretches, with or without a steady lover, something he knew marriage would not change, and might possibly make worse. He hoped that someday he would find the woman he wanted to grow old with, but he wasn't sure he would ever walk the wedding plank again. His dance card was active enough to keep him from being too wistful about those possibilities.

"Hey."

Suddenly, she was in front of him. He rose to his feet and they embraced casually, just as they had parted from the wine bar.

"Hello. You ready?"

"Yes."

The Roaring Fork's hostess led them to a booth in the back, and they sat looking over the menus handed them.

"Long week?"

"Yes," she sighed, "but good. It just doesn't slow down."

"You don't really want it to, do you?"

The question stopped her in the middle of a drink decision. "How do you mean?"

"I just get the impression you thrive on the activity."

Julia considered this for a moment, then nodded. "Perhaps. I like what I do."

"The investigation work, or your charity work? Or both?"

"Both," she said. "When you meet these victims, it just stays with you."

She had told Tom about her work with domestic shelters, but only in general terms. It was reasonable that she would assist victims with her professional services. It was unlikely he would guess the wide scope of her activities, unless she somehow slipped and said too much.

"How did you get started with it?"

Tom casually took the first sip of his beer. The question was ventured on a tender subject, with potentially personal ramifications. His casual tone allowed her the freedom to put the brakes on the line of questioning, or redirect the narrative to a course more to her comfort.

A less perceptive person wouldn't have picked up on it, but Julia did, and appreciated it. It spoke volumes about Tom, something good.

"Well, I did experience it firsthand."

"Wow. Are you okay talking about it?"

"I am. It was long ago. It was a boyfriend, and I quickly got rid of him after the last time. What actually got me involved was a friend who suffered much worse than I did. I kept meeting more victims, one after the other. I guess the cause found me."

Tom nodded. "It's a good thing you're doing. It's unfortunate that it has to be done."

"It is."

"So, did the guitar player get what was coming to him?"

Julia laughed, appreciating him smoothly changing the subject. "I don't know. Not yet, I'm sure. The insurance company had been trying to nail his ass for a long time before hiring me. Even if my findings help them, it's a long, drawn out process."

"I imagine you get called to testify on stuff like that."

"Once in a while, but usually not. I'm paid to observe, report and document. What they do with it is up to them."

The waiter arrived with chips, queso and guacamole.

"Enough about me. A system analyst for a consulting firm is all I got from you last time."

Tom crunched a chip in his mouth while shrugging. "It's not that interesting. My firm evaluates companies who are trying to improve their technology in some way. There's a more technical description for it, but you'll fall asleep on me. I basically stay up on all the current coding languages so that I can troubleshoot best practices."

"I have a friend that does that stuff. I envy you two. I can't even keep my email inbox clean."

"That doesn't solve that problem. Mine is about to break. If someone other than a client sends me something, it will sit there for weeks, if not months."

"But you know where to find it, when you need to."

"Usually."

"So, how do you keep your dating life in order?" Julia ventured.

Tom nodded, not surprised by a direct approach. Anything else would have broken her pattern.

"I don't always. I do tell the truth."

"An honorable man," Julia said.

"Not so noble. It's easier to not have to keep track of a catalog of lies, other than, 'No, that dress doesn't make you look fat.'"

Julia laughed and Tom grinned. They watched each other as they drank, without words for a moment or two before resuming the conversation. The waiter came by to check on them as Julia finished off her glass.

"Another, please."

The waiter nodded. "And you, sir?"

"Me too."

TWENTY-FIVE

THE press conference in New York for Trent Tanger receiving his second straight league MVP award wasn't remarkable on its own. The gathered media wasn't interested so much in the award as the subtext of the free agent tour he was about to embark on. The slugger smiled wide, his joyous expression only matched that of Damon Cash standing next to him. Not much notice was taken of his wife, sitting off to the side, a manufactured grin affixed to her face. She played her role correctly, a trophy wife that attracted only the attention deemed warranted by her husband's machine.

The trip was a bit of a setback for April, causing her constant depression to deepen further. Travelling was a dehumanizing process, as she was firmly led with a grip on her upper arm wherever she was supposed to go. Worse, she had been poised to make her break from the Tanger compound. The anxiety of waiting for the perfect moment had been replaced with the indignity of being carried like baggage.

She had successfully used several weeks of experimentation to determine which pills did what, and how difficult it would be to wean herself off them. After two weeks she realized the blue pill, given twice daily, was causing her to be disoriented. She started by only taking one for a few days, then none. The tradeoff for the lucidity was a dull headache that throbbed, but was otherwise tolerable. She decided to continue with the others, as long as her faculties remained relatively stable.

Her medication was not the only testing she was conducting. With a clearer head, she began studying the shift patterns of the security staff. There were four men who were regulars, with a few others who filled in sporadically. The advantage of the regulars was that they had established patterns and routines she could recognize. She knew which of them slept when on sentry duty, which of them played games on their phones, and which of them got lax watching the cameras. The substitutes stuck to their instructions. However, they appeared not to be privy to the specific details of who they guarded like the regulars. She had to match those weaknesses to potential opportunities.

Once the press conference was over, the party of seven left the hotel, splitting into separate limos with separate travel itineraries. Cash and Bonner accompanied Tanger to several media appointments in the northeast. Gordon escorted April back to Texas, with Sandy awaiting them at the airport.

Of all the security members, Gordon was the most pleasant. He had been polite, even prompting light conversation in the past. Sometime back, he had clearly been disciplined for this, and he was now much more aloof. She could tell this was counter to his nature, as he subtly showed kindness to her. Little things like grasping her arm much more gently than the others, or extending a handkerchief when no one else was around, did not go unnoticed.

April could also sense he was the least alert of the group. His mind wandered and he always appeared relaxed when he should be at attention. His size was intimidating, a factor that trumped his other shortcomings in Vance and Junior's assessment. At least the trip back would be a gentle break from normally indifferent treatment.

After landing and deplaning at DFW, Gordon accompanied her into the concourse. April saw the ladies room to their left. She grabbed the forearm of the bodyguard, like grasping the thick limb of an oak tree.

"Restroom?"

Gordon nodded easily. "Sure."

She didn't need to go, but she wanted as much time alone and away from the estate as possible. Gordon would allow her 10-15 minutes without any repercussions. The others would brace her after five.

April walked in, following behind a woman about her height. She had a bright floppy hat, with whatever hair she had tucked inside. She also wore sunglasses and a long, red overcoat. She saw her stop at the mirror, take off the sunglasses, and look inside her purse for cosmetics.

The moment took her breath away, freezing her where she stood. This was her chance.

April moved around the woman to the far side of the counter, away from the door. She gently but firmly placed her hand on the woman's arm.

"What—"

The woman saw April put a finger to her lips. There were plenty of other ladies moving back and forth from the restroom, but it was a force of habit.

"What do you think of this ring?" April whispered.

The woman looked it over. Her eyes quickly brightened.

"It's gorgeous," she said, taken aback by the question. The square cut was at least 5 carats, and as clear as you could imagine. It had a double row of bead set diamonds encircling it. The matching platinum band was also covered in diamonds. It was caliber of the set the woman always hoped her husband would replace her original one with on an anniversary.

"Give me your hat, glasses, and coat, and it's yours."

"What, is it stolen?"

"No, it's mine. And I paid for it."

She extended her arm, displaying the bruises, swallowing the shame she felt. The woman watched her for a moment, and quickly understood.

Moments later, April summoned all her nerve and walked out wearing the new attire she had acquired. Gordon stood several feet in front of the doorless entry, looking at something on his cell phone. She walked calmly away at an angle, toward the baggage claim. She joined a procession of travelers walking through revolving doors, leaving the secure terminal.

As she left the door, she saw Sandy standing ten feet in front of her. He was looking straight past her, giving her a start for a split second. She took a deep breath and kept marching forward, like just another North Dallas socialite fighting off jetlag.

She jumped into the cab outside, slamming the door so fast and hard the driver jumped in his seat.

"Go!"

"Where?"

April stopped, not having thought through the next move. "West, I guess. Just go."

The driver eyed her strangely, then nodded. The cab rolled away from the terminal harmlessly with her captors still inside.

"You have an address?"

"How far can you take me?"

The driver looked into the rearview mirror, measuring her again.

"To the edge of town. Farther than that, it would cost you more than you'd be willing to pay."

April took off her glasses and leaned over the seat.

"How far will this get me?"

He looked at the diamond studded watch. The Rolex was too perfect, too gleaming to be the real thing.

"That's fake."

"It's not. I swear."

April was almost crying, something not lost on him. He could tell she was frightened.

"What are you running from?"

"My husband. He'll kill me if he catches me." April knew this wasn't true, but she would wish for death rather than fail in her attempt to flee.

He took the watch and held it across the steering wheel.

"You have any money?"

"No."

The driver sighed. "I can drop you in Weatherford. From there, you're on your own."

"Thank you." April fell back, dropping against the seat.

The driver wasn't sure if her currency was real, but her fear was no act. He knew that domestic violence was painfully underestimated, even with the recent media attention. His son was a police officer and had told him numerous stories about calls he had answered over the years. His niece had narrowly escaped an ex-boyfriend, who was thankfully serving time on drug charges.

He took his cell phone and scrolled through his contacts. He found a number and dialed.

"Henry. It's me. What are you doing, you lazy ass?"

They began to laugh like old buddies, catching up on shared friendships. April only faintly registered the conversation, still ruminating on how to get from Weatherford to even further away from her pursuers.

"Hey, I got a favor to ask."

The driver saw the frazzled woman in the rearview mirror and smiled, hoping to be the next link in a successful chain of an escape plan.

TWENTY-SIX

CASSIE felt a brief sense of accomplishment at having reached the end of the front wall of the living room. One look at the remaining two walls, both much larger than the one she just finished, tempered her enthusiasm. She kept in shape with weight training and martial arts, but the repetitive motion of the manual labor exposed muscles she didn't know she had.

Noelle emerged from her base of operations at the other end of the house with two bottles of wine and a stack of plastic cups, strategically setting them on a stack of sheetrock that served as a coffee table. Cassie saw her leaving the house.

"Where are you going?"

"I need some more connections. I'll be back in an hour or so."

"Alright."

"I told Yardley the vino was up here with you. Enjoy."

The look on Cassie's face turned sour. "I know what you're doing."

"Good, then don't fight me on it. Behave like two adults until I get back."

Noelle departed before the attorney could get the last word. She surrendered for the moment, descending the ladder and grabbing one of the bottles. The elevator door opened and Yardley appeared, removing gloves from her hands.

"Did she leave us anything worth stopping for?"

"Right now, I'd stop for warm, stale beer." Cassie looked over the bottle and nodded. "Not bad. Good enough for now, at least." She took the opener, popped out the cork, and poured portions into two cups. The two women each took a sip after the obligatory swirl and sniff.

"Did you get the grown-up speech?"

"I did."

"Maybe we'll get along better drunk."

Both ladies laughed and a bit of tension left the room. They took their cups and the bottle and took seats on opposite ends of the old couch, putting their weary feet on top of the drywall.

"How is your rookie doing?"

"You mean Sophia? You heard about that?"

Cassie nodded.

"Not bad. Give her another week or so and she'll be at least as good as who she replaced. She's sharp and a quick study."

"How much longer do you think this will take?" Cassie asked, waving her hand above the construction around them.

"Forever," Yardley said. "Lots of moving parts on this thing. You have a condo, right?"

Cassie nodded.

"Your HOA, POA, or whatever may seem like a pain in the ass at times, but they handle a lot of things. This property will require a fair amount of upkeep. I don't know."

"Don't tell me you're having doubts, not after you three sold me on it."

Yardley shrugged sheepishly. "Sure, I have doubts. Nothing wrong with that. All the best decisions I've ever made scared me to death."

Cassie took another sip of wine. "I understand."

"How do you think she's doing?" Yardley asked, while grabbing the bottle and motioning for Cassie to extend her cup for more wine. Cassie nodded, accepting the refill while considering the question.

"Depends," she said with a heavy sigh. "We all carry some baggage, but she carries more than her share. Much more than she will ever let on."

"Yes, she does."

"Do you know what happened to her?"

Yardley shook her head. "She never said. She'll give you the shirt off her back, her last breath of air, but not her past. I asked once. From the way she said no, I'll never ask again."

"She knows ours though, doesn't she?"

"She does. I didn't have much choice. She spotted me from afar, running from hell."

"She's good at that," Cassie said.

"Yes, she is. My husband had thrown me across the room, broke my arm, gave me a concussion. My father put me and my kids on a one-way bus to San Antonio that night. He then went to our house and put a gun to my husband's head. He told him if he ever came near me or his grandkids again, he would pull the trigger. I haven't seen him since."

"Lovely."

"So, did your boyfriend try to kill you?"

Cassie chuckled. "Try stepfather."

"Oh no."

"That's not the worst of it. He thought I was unconscious, so he decided to try and rape me first."

"What?"

"Yep. I got lucky with a flimsy end table, knocked him out cold."

"That's horrible. What did your mother say?"

Cassie took a sip from her cup. "I never told her. As far as I know, she thought he died in the storm."

Yardley sat up. "That happened during Katrina?"

"The night before."

"Unbelievable."

"The next day, I took the bus to Houston. Our friend Julia picks me out of the Astrodome crowd."

"Uncanny how she does that."

"It's her gift."

"And her curse," Yardley said, rising to get the other bottle.

"Do you think this place will kill those demons?"

Yardley shook her head. "It's just an obstacle. We replace those demons with the obstacles we put in front of us. Every house I sell pushes the past further back, but it doesn't go away. It's still back there. Is it that way for you?"

"I wish it was," Cassie stammered. "It drives me, too. It shuts the world out, makes me resist anybody that doubts or dismisses me."

"Like some flashy realtor who's always on stage?"

Cassie looked up and saw Yardley smile. She smirked, allowing a chuckle.

"I actually respect that, in an odd way. It's better than someone blowing smoke up your ass. When you get old enough, you start caring less what others think."

Yardley nodded in agreement. "You actually relish pissing people off, don't you?"

Cassie shrugged. "I'm an attorney. I like to tussle."

Yardley looked at the bottle. "Well, that one's done. Are you ready to crack open the other one?"

"Let's hold off. I'm actually starting to like you a bit, so I may have already had too much."

At this, both the women laughed.

"Good point. Let me go get us some coffee instead."

TWENTY-SEVEN

THEY were both laughing as they stumbled through the door of Tom's condo, holding each other. Julia was laughing more than Tom, and was more responsible for the stumble, because she had consumed much more alcohol.

"Wow, this is a nice condominium."

"Thank you," Tom said with a chuckle as he locked the door behind them.

"Thank you for parking my car for me. That was sweet."

"The least I could do for my neighbors. They don't appreciate people taking up four spaces with one vehicle."

She burst out laughing, even snorting, then covering her face with her hands. Now Tom laughed aloud, embracing her.

"Maybe I shouldn't have driven myself over."

"I told you not to."

"You told me not to," Julia repeated, "and you were right. But I make my own decisions. I am my own woman, and I can take care of myself!"

As she announced this, she nearly tumbled over his coffee table, saved from the fall by him not letting go of her hand. He gently pulled her back upright, and she reflexively embraced him.

"Let's sit you down over here."

"Okay," she said, letting him guide her to the couch.

"Would you like coffee or some water?"

"You don't keep alcohol at your house?"

"I do, but that's not what you need right now."

"Yes, sir," she said with a mock salute.

Tom shook his head with a smile, and brought over two bottles of water, sitting next to her.

"Besides, I'm not going home tonight. I'm in no condition to drive, or so I'm told."

"Correct."

"So, Mr. Tom. You've got me here in a very pliable condition. Whatever will you do with me?"

They watched each other curiously, taking in the moment. Tom looked into her eyes, and saw hints to her soul. It was a deep well, filled with scars, regrets, hopes and dreams. Despite being inebriated, nothing had changed from the night he met her. Every action was on purpose, including her release of control tonight. Perhaps the rigors of her pursuits required such a rigid hold, that only here, with a virtual stranger could it be eased.

Julia saw in his face and expression a tenderness and an understanding. He was right about it all, and she knew that he knew. Her instincts, honed by countless errors of the past, could spot the jokers in the deck in moments. She knew she could trust him, at least for one night.

Tom gently pulled Julia closer and kissed her slowly. As the kiss grew into an embrace, she felt herself melting in his arms. She wondered if she would feel the same the following morning. As the passion started to rise, he sensed her consciousness waning. Before he knew it, she was passed out in his arms. He laughed to himself, then watched her dozing.

Even in her unkempt state, she was beautiful. He sensed there was plenty of history and pain behind her eyes, but still a strength and a serenity, a poise that could not be defeated or broken. Nothing had changed from the night he first saw her, only more complexity and detail had been added to the picture in the frame.

Tom carefully lifted her into his arms, and carried her to his spare bedroom, softly lying her on top of the bed. He took off her shoes, and spread the covers over her. Julia stirred just enough to nestle into the bed comfortably. He turned on a night light in the far corner, then pulled the door without closing it.

He shook his head, considering the evening. Julia seemed dead set on consuming alcohol well past the point of self-control. He wondered how she would sleep, whether she would have a hangover, or even remember what had happened.

Tom quickly undressed and got in bed, and soon was dozing slightly. His mind drifted back to this woman.

What was it about her?

He shook it off and started falling deeper into slumber.

Julia opened her eyes and knew everything that had happened. The only thing she didn't know was how much time had elapsed. There was a small window to the left of the bed and it was still dark outside, so at least it wasn't morning yet.

She wasn't exactly sober, but the clarity was returning. There was a bit of blur on her last few waking hours, but she was cognizant of it. In fact, she was not quite as out of control as she let on. Perhaps a test for Tom, perhaps for other reasons.

Julia was an alcoholic, and she knew it. She didn't want to change, at least not yet. She had been strong enough to rise above the damage of her previous life, but had not been able to let it go. There was plenty of psychobabble to explain it all, but the truth was, she still didn't like herself. She worked tirelessly, striving for some pinnacle that would erase all of the damage and justify everything that had been done to her, and by her.

When the day was done, Julia still wasn't happy with who she was. Some days she was disgusted with what she saw in the mirror, some days she was halfway content. Most days, she grudgingly accepted what was there.

The attention shown her by Tom was no novelty, as men approached her regularly. Some she would entertain, some were rejected outright. But she never believed in whatever they saw. A life of being single combined with the aging process and built on her insecurities, trumping even the most genuine praise.

Tom's attention was real, and he was a gentleman, two things that set him apart from most. In his eyes, she saw clarity and confidence, things she wished she felt in herself.

She took a deep breath and emerged from underneath the covers. She quietly walked to his room, where the door was slightly open. It was dark, and Tom was sleeping on his side, faced away from the door. The clock on his nightstand said 3:20.

Julia began to disrobe slowly, as quietly as possible. Once she was naked, she approached from the far edge of the bed and submarined under the covers, slowly making her way toward him.

He sensed the covers shift slightly, twitched, then felt the touch of cool, smooth skin against his legs. He turned over and she was naked and on top of him. He pulled her hair back, to see her face. It was the same woman, but with more poise, more intent, more clarity in her eyes.

"Hey," she cooed.

"Hello. Did the spare bedroom not meet your expectations?"

"It was okay. The bed was a little cold, a little lonely."

Tom was ready for Julia earlier, but her bold, controlled approach was exhilarating. He drew her closer, kissing her firmly. After a few moments, he looked in her face again, and saw something different.

She felt something different. Before she was chasing something that had nothing to do with him. Now, she wanted to be with him, for him. The alcohol and the ghosts of the past were no longer present.

They both smiled at the realization. He pulled the covers over them, and they met again for the first time.

TWENTY-EIGHT

HENRY took the 281 exit off I-20, gazing longingly at The Gilbert Pecan Company, but knowing their treats would only expand his growing waistline. His wife had rightfully grilled him about his diet on the road and he was trying not to cheat.

His passenger looked awfully frail and could stand to eat hearty. It wasn't as much about her weight as it was her look, pale and worn, like she had been running for her life for years, not hours.

"You need to stop for anything?"

April shook her head. "No, thank you."

"Alright. Let me know if you need to. There's a few snacks down in the cooler you're welcome to."

She nodded as he turned his rig south. April was still getting used to the ride. It was too reminiscent of her bus rides throughout the country when she first arrived in the States. The fears were in lock step with her memories, being ushered back and forth between men who treated her as they pleased. She was a piece of property and frequently reminded of it. She shook off the horrors as they rolled down the road, putting as many miles between her and her most recent tormentors as she could.

As a child, the idea of America had always been a magic and mystical fantasy. Her parents talked about it like a dreamland, having experienced the days of the Iron Curtain when you could not travel from place to place without papers. If she could have transported herself back to those childlike memories, she would have. She was still in survival mode, not trusting the present to enjoy it just yet.

There were many lonely stretches of road in the Ukraine, but Texas was somehow different. The miles of deserted country looked inviting instead of barren, full of promise instead of foreboding. The lights of each passing town were beacons instead of warnings. Even the names of the towns were filled with character. She hoped to discover these observations were not a deception.

He neared a town called Hamilton and turned into a convenience store on the east side of the road. When the rig came to a stop, she dropped out of the cab and looked around the empty lot. Across the road, the clock on the bank's display was 1:37 AM. The store was right next to a cemetery. The realization shook her briefly, but she realized that the people chasing her were much more frightening, and death was preferable to how she had been existing in virtual captivity.

Henry approached from the other side of the truck.

"My friend should be along in a bit. Do you need to go inside for the powder room?"

"I do."

He nodded in understanding. She stopped, hesitating.

"Are you okay?" Henry asked.

"Can you come in with me?"

He looked at her and understood. She trusted him, and any space left between the two of them was a risk she didn't want to chance.

"Sure."

Henry walked in with her and she walked briskly to the restrooms. He nodded at the clerk and stepped over to the snacks, scanning for something that wouldn't send his blood sugar through the roof. After a few minutes of browsing, nothing qualified.

"Look out for this guy," a voice said to the clerk at the counter. "He's a known troublemaker."

Henry turned to see a familiar face. It was a man in his seventies, slim but sturdy. He wore overalls and running shoes, clearly unconcerned about dressing for anything but his own comfort.

"Sonny."

"Hello, pardner. How have you been?"

The two men hugged.

"Doing good. Good to see you."

The older man saw a young woman approaching cautiously.

"Is this the damsel in distress?"

"It is. April, this is Sonny."

"Hello."

He took her hand gently and the group left the store.

"Sonny and his wife are going to take you in for a bit. I'll check in on you in a few days. Between the three of us, we're going to help you get things straightened out."

"Okay," she said to Henry. "Thank you."

"No problem."

Sonny opened the passenger door of his pickup for a woman who could have passed for a high school girl, then closed it behind her. He then walked a few paces away from the truck toward Henry's rig.

"Thanks again," Henry said. "Here's something for your trouble. There's more coming."

Henry stuck a roll of bills into his old friend's hand. Sonny flipped through and saw several $100 bills.

"You don't have to do that."

"Yes, I do. Look what she gave me for the ride from Weatherford."

Henry pulled a diamond necklace from the pocket of his windbreaker.

"Oh, shit. Who is she?"

"I don't know. The man she's running from must be loaded. He also roughs her up pretty good."

Sonny nodded. "She's scared, isn't she?"

"Uh huh. Watch your back."

"I will."

They parted with a hug and a firm handshake. The man walked back to the pickup and hopped in.

"April, I hope you're hungry and not too finicky. Wanda has supper waiting."

April nodded in relief, suddenly realizing how starved she was.

He turned the truck south thru town, moving his vehicle at a much slower pace than his friend in the semi. Their trip ended at a farm house a few miles away. It was not nearly as grand as where she slept the night before, but it was a home for people, not a castle locked from the outside for a prisoner.

Sonny rolled the truck into a garage with the door already open. After stepping out of the truck, he extended his hand and she took it. He noticed the woman was fragile, even beyond the physical feel of her touch. By all appearances, she would disintegrate in front of him.

"Why did you do this?"

"Beg your pardon?"

"Why are you helping me? It's not just the money he handed you, is it?"

Sonny looked her dead in the eyes. "Of course not. I could tell you needed it. Whatever you're running from, Wanda and I can visit with you about it tomorrow. Tonight, relax and rest yourself."

"Okay."

He smiled with a comforting nod. She slowly walked into the house, letting the fatigue and the fear roll off her. She was finally inside walls that would protect her instead of imprisoning her, for the first time in years.

TWENTY-NINE

VANCE and Junior sat at the end of the dining room table, with Vance staring intently at his laptop and another monitor, clicking his mouse every few moments. Hacking into the airport network to obtain the video feeds was only a few minutes work. Spotting April in some sort of disguise out of over a hundred camera feeds was taking much longer. Vance didn't like Junior looking over his shoulder, but he could use the second set of eyes, so he allowed it.

They heard the door chime sound, followed by Gordon and Sandy trudging toward them, exhausted and disheartened. The bodyguards were fully aware of their disastrous mistake, glancing sideways at each other forebodingly as they approached the table.

They found Vance staring intently at the computer screen, not bothering to glance in their direction. Junior locked eyes with them, sending a clear message. He could no longer vouch for them, even if he wanted to. Their fate was out of his hands. The two men started to pull chairs from underneath the table.

"Remain standing," Vance ordered.

The men did as they were told. Their uneasiness would be humorous to anyone watching without stakes in the matter, two huge specimens afraid of losing their jobs, if not worse.

"What did you find?" Vance's eyes had still not left the computer screen.

"We've been searching since we called you. We—"

"I didn't ask how long you've been out there," Vance snapped, interrupting Sandy's attempt to ease into the explanation. "I asked what you found."

"Nothing," Sandy replied. "We canvassed every terminal and the loading areas outside."

Their instructions to make a painstaking search of every inch of the airport they could legally access was more about punishment than utility. Vance correctly surmised April

Tanger was gone from the area, something he confirmed well before the two men were called back to the estate.

"How long after Mrs. Tanger went missing did you make contact?" Vance asked, finally turning to face the men.

Sandy paused tellingly. Gordon shrugged, opening his mouth.

"Before you answer, I strongly suggest you not lie to me."

Vance had detected in Gordon's body language signs of equivocating. The man's posture changed, straightening like the answer he would give.

"Approximately 15 minutes."

"Approximately?"

"That's correct. I'm not sure of the exact time."

"What were your instructions in the event you cannot determine Mrs. Tanger's exact whereabouts?"

"To make contact."

"To make contact immediately. Not after stopping to think about it, not after a cursory search. Immediately. Because you did not follow instructions, Mrs. Tanger is in the wind."

After watching them for a few moments more, Vance returned to his computer.

"Go home. Wait there until I decide how to deal with you."

"We can go find her," Sandy said earnestly.

"Can you? You lost her out from under your noses. Why should I believe you can find her after several hours head start? Your job was simply to provide security, which you failed to do. The task now is acquisition and extraction of a potentially hostile party, a far more demanding task, which neither of you have the training or discipline to execute. And even if I still had any confidence in you to provide security, Mr. Tanger won't return for several days. There is no one for you to guard."

Vance saw them from the corner of his eye, allowing the silent pause and them standing motionless to add to their discomfort. Finally, he dismissed them with a backward wave of his hand. Junior confirmed the directive with a nod. Once the two men marched out, he turned back to Vance, pen and legal pad in hand.

"They made a mistake, Vance. They could be chasing down what you have."

"This is no longer a job for bouncers, Junior."

Junior watched Vance continue clicking through screens. After another 30 minutes, Vance found a woman with a large floppy hat and sunglasses leaving the terminal and entering a cab. The attire is what caught his eye, but in his second look, he watched the gait and mannerisms. Then, he played it again.

"Is that her?" Vance asked.

"I think so," Junior said.

"Looks right and left leaving baggage claim, then almost jogs to the cab."

Vance focused in on the cab number, then the license number. He minimized the photos, then opened another screen. The selection's pixels slowly focused until the seven digits of the license plate could be read.

"Can you track the cab via GPS?" Junior asked.

Vance picked up his cell phone. "There are several companies that provide GPS services. Without knowing which one that company uses, it would take time. I have a quicker option."

As Junior considered this, Vance put the phone to his ear.

"Lieutenant Casper, please."

Junior looked over Vance's computer display, and well over a dozen windows scattered across the screen. It made him wish he was more computer literate.

"Hey, Ghosty. It's your friend from across the pond. How are you? Good. Hey, I need a favor from you. How soon can you get me an LPR?"

Vance doodled on his notepad, waiting for an answer.

"Absolutely. I'll be at this number. Thanks, mate."

He hung up the phone. Junior looked at him quizzically.

"License Plate Recognition."

Junior nodded in response.

"I meant what I said," Vance continued. "This is no longer a job for bouncers. I now require operators, disciplined men who can do anything I require. With no mistakes."

"How long will that take?" Junior asked.

"They're already en route. When we get the location, you're going to lead them to where the path ends and bring her back, if possible."

Junior measured Vance, considered what he hadn't said. Operators meant mercenaries, people who were accustomed to taking lives and disappearing.

"Is this a part of a larger plan?"

Vance said nothing, closing his laptop and walking to the kitchen. His silence and the look on his face told Junior the answer. April Tanger's fate had been sealed long before today's events unfolded.

THIRTY

THE alarm on Tom's phone sounded, rousing him from his slumber. He could feel himself fading in and out, his body and mind relishing the comfort of a bed on Saturday morning. It took a few moments to take stock of the fact that he was alone, and that he hadn't been when he fell asleep.

It was quiet. He couldn't hear any sounds from the bathroom, the kitchen or anywhere else. Looking around his room, there was no evidence that Julia had been with him.

Interesting, he thought. At every turn, she surprised him. Alternately strong and vulnerable. Firmly in control, and yet letting go of the steering wheel deliberately, as if tempting fate. Perhaps even taunting fate, a dangerous habit to have.

Whether by accident or by design, he wanted to know more. Where did she go?

Julia had successfully slipped out of bed, taken a quick shower, and exited Tom's bedroom without him waking up. She truly hated the morning after pleasantries, especially when she had made a regrettable decision in an alcohol-fueled fog of war.

She had developed a strategy for easy, seamless exits from such situations. First, her phone was set to vibrate at 5 AM sharp. Once settling in for sleep, she tried to place the phone strategically, out of view and feel from the man, yet something that would shake her awake. Once awake, she would slip out of his arms, discreetly shower, dress and tiptoe out of the bedroom.

She now had time to inspect the entire condo, taking stock of the man in ways where he could not monitor her or affect her opinion. The place was appointed well, in sophisticated yet masculine ways. There was enough dust to ensure Tom wasn't some OCD nut, but not so much that he was a slob. The spare bedroom contained some free weights, a recumbent exercise bike, and a small computer desk with a few photos. Most of the photos were with a female, her age ranging from 6 to 20.

He had talked about his daughter. His physique testified to the fact that the weights got a lot more work than the bike.

So, what was she missing?

Maybe nothing. Maybe he was a simple man who was simply what he appeared to be. Maybe most available men were a fraud, but maybe this one wasn't.

Julia usually left without a word and never regretted it. For some reason, she turned back, walking back to his bedroom. She looked in and he was awake, looking at her.

"Morning."

"Morning."

"I thought you had left."

"I almost did. I have a lot going on today."

"I see," he said, nodding. "Did you want some breakfast before you run?"

"I took the liberty of raiding the fridge and pantry. You're now out of granola bars and grapes."

"Not a problem."

"And your milk expired last week."

He chuckled. "Noted."

"See you," Julia said with a smile and wave, as she turned to the door.

"Wait."

"What?"

"I want to see you again."

Julia took a deep breath, hesitating. "Maybe."

Tom laughed out loud. "I guess that's better than no."

His easy manner and transparency broke through her defenses. Flawed enough to be real, and real enough to frighten her with hope. Hope that had always failed in the past.

He watched her slowly approach him, her eyes lowered. She sat next to him on the bed, and looked into his eyes. She surprised herself by reaching for his stubble laden face, caressing it with her hand.

"You're very sweet, Tom Ashby,"

"Why do you say that?"

"You know."

They returned smiles. Tom recognized last night as a test of sorts by Julia, which he had evidently passed. Untold damage lay behind her, which wasn't remarkable. There were few, if any people unwounded by love and life.

"Alright. I've got to go."

Julia offered one more smile, then turned for the door, and quickly opened and closed it.

Tom considered the last 18 hours and the woman he had just spent it with. Julia was a whirlwind, driven by unseen sources inside her. She was well aware of them, and it wasn't hard to guess what they were. But the risks she ran in her life were a conscious decision, regardless of how wise or foolish they were on their merit.

He did not waste time with psychoanalysis of every woman he slept with, but Julia was no ordinary woman.

THIRTY-ONE

AFTER a meal and a hot shower, April slept until past noon. When she woke, she felt refreshed, but still exhausted.

The guest room was lined with paintings of all sizes, most of them unframed. They included a sunset, a mountain range, and houses. The houses were of all shapes and sizes, from shotgun farm houses to Frank Lloyd Wright inspired mansions.

April was relieved to see several changes of clothes sitting on the dresser. She tried on a t-shirt and a pair of jeans that were a bit baggy, but close enough. She eased her feet into a pair of water sandals on the floor that fit just fine.

She walked out to the kitchen and saw a note. She read it and walked out the back door of the house. An elderly woman was working in a garden about the size of a basketball court, with a section of an assortment of leafy vegetables. She watched her for a few moments, until the woman turned to see her and waved.

April walked out to her. The woman had a basket at her side, full of some selections from the garden.

"Good morning."

"Good afternoon, sweetie," the woman corrected.

"Oh," she groaned, the pain of the previous days eroding her clock.

"Your timing is perfect. I was getting our lunch together. Take this."

The woman handed April the basket full of assorted leafy greens and other vegetables. April had never maintained a healthy diet, so a natural, fresh meal sounded great.

"Whose clothes are these?"

"My granddaughter's. She always leaves a few things behind. They fit?"

"They're fine. Thanks."

They walked back to the house, where April opened the door for her. The woman took the basket back from her and dropped it on the counter.

"I just don't know how to thank you for—"

"Don't mention it, honey. You thanked us a dozen times last night, and that was more than enough."

"Okay."

"We're gonna keep feeding you and getting you good sleep before you have to face whatever has you so scared."

Wanda produced a cutting board and more vegetables from the refrigerator and began assembling lunch.

"Hope the bed wasn't too stiff for you. The mattress may be older than you are."

"It was fine."

Wanda looked at her, measuring her spirit. April wore a lifetime of burdens in her twenty-something years, and it wouldn't easily be shelved for even an afternoon.

"You want some cheese with this?"

"Sure."

"There's some shredded cheese in the middle drawer," Wanda said, motioning for April to get it. April walked over and found the cheese after taking a brief inventory of what was inside. She hadn't perused a fridge without being monitored in a long time.

"Where are you from?"

"Dallas."

Wanda dished out some salad for her guest and then for herself.

"Big city. Is that where your family is?"

"No," she replied. Whatever bond she and Trent Tanger had once shared, it was never family. "They are too far away to run to."

The conversation gave way to crunching into the salad. Wanda let the meal speak for a while. April would take a bite, then look around the room, taking in her surroundings. She was like an animal that had been trapped for countless days, then released when the cage's door was accidentally left ajar.

"Where is Sonny?"

"He went to Waco to pick up some things. He'll be back this afternoon."

April nodded, a shiver rolling down her back.

"What are you running from, honey?"

"My husband."

"My goodness. I'm so sorry."

April stopped, dropping the fork into her salad bowl, lowering her face. Another wave of her reality hit her.

"It's all my fault. I don't know what to do."

Wanda saw that she was still shaken. She reached across the table and firmly took her hand.

"Look at me, honey."

April slowly looked up at her.

"Take a deep breath. Use your lungs and stretch it out as long as you can."

Wanda inhaled and exhaled in demonstration. April followed suit and the effect of the exercise made her close her eyes for a moment. Incredibly, she felt a bit more relaxed.

"Remember, it's not your fault."

April nodded, accepting the encouragement.

"We are going to deal with all that soon enough. First, we'll keep you safe, then get things right."

Wanda squeezed her hand before letting it go, as she marched to the fridge and pulled a business card out from underneath one of the magnets.

"My niece had a nasty boyfriend a few years back. One of those bullies that suck the life out of you. There's a group not too far from here that helped her out."

Wanda handed April the card.

"The Shelter. 24/7/365."

April reading it aloud made Wanda smile.

"We'll reach out to them in the morning. Until then, you're going to relax and think only good thoughts."

April would have doubted that was possible, but the earnest, bold confidence of a woman old enough to be her grandmother sparked the first bit of hope she had entertained in years.

THIRTY-TWO

TACODELI had been a default lunch spot for Robert Chisum since it first opened nearly two decades before. He was partial to the Cowboy, although he had a few other selections he would opt for to mix things up. His allegiance to the establishment had cost him over the years as many of his fellow officers would end up in line in front of him by the time he arrived.

Today, the line extended out the front door. After another ten minutes, he finally saw the familiar gray pickup roll into the adjacent parking lot. Julia Caldwell had owned that truck for as long as he could remember and it somehow fit her. She walked toward him in line and they embraced.

"Hey, sister."

"Cheese."

"What's shaking, sweetie?"

"The usual."

"I got that tile you wanted, along with that medium grade mortar. Are you sure you want to spend that much?"

Julia nodded readily. "I don't want the cheap stuff. I plan on this place lasting forever, or at least as long as I'm alive. We'll cover it."

Cheese was thankful she turned to move up as the line progressed, as his face would have exposed doubts he had chosen not to express. He wanted to ease into his misgivings, making her more receptive to what he would say.

They caught up on the news for each of them. It wasn't until they sat down with their orders and they began eating that the conversation stalled. Julia watched her friend, picking up on the hesitation.

"What is it?"

Cheese took another bite of his taco. "Are you sure you know what you're getting yourself into?"

Julia took a sip of her drink from the straw. "How so?"

"This unicorn of yours, this fortress you're spending money on, that I'm spending my off hours working on—"

"You love doing it and you know it."

"What is your endgame?"

"Explain."

"What happens when you get backed into a corner?"

"How would I get backed into a corner?" Julia asked, pulling some cheese from her tray and putting it in her mouth."

"Let's say the abuser has more power and more money than you do. Let's say he has more brains and nerve than you."

"That would never happen because the last two aren't possible, which makes the first two irrelevant."

"That's incredibly arrogant."

"Play devil's advocate. You're an abuser, and I have your significant other. What are you going to do about it?"

Cheese nodded in agreement. "Let's say the abuser and abused live in the area. The abuser has unlimited funds."

"No such thing. Give me a number."

"Multi-millionaire."

"So, he starts paying his fancy lawyer hundreds per hour for weeks, then months. All of a sudden, his business loses three of its top five clients, like that."

Julia snapped her fingers for emphasis.

"Next, he gets sideways with somebody at a club, gets his ass kicked. Or, he's pulled over after one too many drinks. DWI. That means more money for his lawyer. So, he finally pulls up his financials to take stock of his resources and realizes his identity has been stolen. Some thief on the internet got his social security number and opened a dozen accounts in his name. Of course, by now the abused is long gone, maybe even with a new identity. All these resources, wasted in a futile effort."

"I didn't hear any of that."

She shrugs in response. "It's a dangerous world out there, far more dangerous for the victims of domestic violence than the perpetrators. It was only a matter of time before someone tipped the scales in the other direction."

Cheese gave her a sideways look before returning to his taco, shaking his head.

"C'mon, Cheese. Don't act like you didn't know, or at least suspect."

"I was hoping to maintain plausible deniability. Somewhere there is a line you shouldn't cross."

"For the sake of those abused, thankfully someone does."

"Someday, the abuser may have enough money for legal counsel who's not afraid of Cassie Snow," Cheese said. "That attorney will find out who she hires to do her investigative work. And, he may not run out of money until that attorney gets to the end of the line. What then?"

"We'll see it coming," she promised. "If not, shit happens."

Cheese watched her closely. "You are wired today, almost glowing."

"Am I?"

"If I didn't know better, I'd say you were in love."

This caused her to laugh out loud. Julia realized she was riding high, feeling invincible. She realized it was just that, a feeling. She wanted to revel in it for as long as it lasted, for she knew professional success and romantic love were both temporary states with no guarantees.

THIRTY-THREE

CASH saw four burly men sitting in the waiting area of his offices. He looked to his receptionist and threw up his hands in frustration. She shrugged and motioned toward the conference room.

"He's back there."

The agent burst into the conference room and saw Vance sitting with his laptop, facing the large flatscreen TV on the wall.

"I told you not to bring those mercenary types around the office."

"They're just sitting out there, Damon. They'll only be there a few minutes."

"Why do they have to be there at all?"

"Because we don't have time," Vance protested. "Let me show you what I have, and what my plan is, and they'll be gone."

Cash shook his head and grudgingly sat down. Vance clicked the remote and the TV came to life. The grainy video feed showed a cab, pulling up in a truck stop across from a big rig. The driver and passenger walked out and approached the semi. A man jumped out of the semi and shook the woman's hand. The woman pulled something off her neck and handed it to the man.

"There goes fifty grand," Vance quipped.

Cash didn't like his glib tone. "If we don't retrieve her quickly, you can add several more zeros to that number."

"We tracked that rig's path, before and after this video. The driver left Weatherford, went south to this little town called Hamilton, then went back up northwest via a state highway to I-20 where he continued west, finally stopping in Odessa."

"Hamilton was out of his way," Cash said.

"Making that his destination."

"What's your plan?"

"Bring her back," Vance said. "Quickly and quietly, if possible."

"If possible?"

Vance shrugged. "I have no idea what we'll find down there."

"It better not come to that. I have too much money about to change hands. I can't afford to have them make a scene."

"We'll try."

Incredibly, Hawthorne arrived on the outskirts of the Dallas–Fort Worth metroplex in just over 27 hours. He had stopped for gas only, subsisting on snacks and caffeine on the way. He checked into the motel just after 4 PM and woke with a start at 2:30 AM. He pulled his computer from the bag and began reviewing his questions.

He left at 6 AM for Cash's office in North Dallas. He picked up breakfast on the way and listened to sports talk in the car as he munched on his bagel sandwich. The station went from debating the college football rankings to some idiot talking about buying Lee Harvey Oswald's furniture at an auction and displaying it in his living room.

Shortly after 8, he slipped into the office building and used the restroom before walking toward the elevators. A burly security guard quickly stepped between him and the doors.

"Sir, you need a visitor's badge to access the building."

"I work here."

"Let me see your access card."

Hawthorne froze for one moment, just enough to expose his guilt.

"Dammit, I left it at my desk upstairs. I just need to go get it."

The security guard chuckled. "Nice try, slick. I memorize faces, especially everyone with a desk in here. You don't have one. Who are you, really?"

"Gil Hawthorne, Neon Mega."

The reporter extended his hand, which the guard ignored. He firmly led him by the arm to the front desk.

"You will need an appointment. This is Farah, who will be happy to help you."

Gil looked across the desk at Farah who grinned, having overheard the exchange.

"Who would you like an appointment with, sir?"

"Damon Cash."

Farah nearly burst out laughing, but caught herself. "All media requests with Mr. Cash have to be made in advance. Here you go." She handed Hawthorne a generic business card with the main number.

"Okay, thanks."

Hawthorne did his best beaten dog impression while the receptionist and the security guard grinned at each other, sharing a knowing look. People tried sneaking into the Cash castle for any number of reasons. It took a lot more than a smooth talker to get by them.

The reporter walked back to his car, plotting his next move. He remembered the parking garage had a security checkpoint also. He cranked up the car and did another circle around the perimeter. On his second trip, he spotted his opportunity. A truck was using the service entrance, delivering or picking up something.

He pulled up behind a dumpster, ignoring the fire lane restrictions and jumped out. He caught the door right before it closed behind two men entering. He dashed in and quickly found the nearest door, darting inside. The utility closet hid him neatly until security escorted the delivery men back out. He waited a few minutes then stole back outside into the hall.

Hawthorne wisely elected to use the stairwell, avoiding drawing attention in the elevator. He huffed and puffed his way up the five floors, taking a moment to catch his breath before continuing. He finally left the stairwell and found himself in a posh, well-lit hallway.

He knew that the key to fitting into forbidden places is acting like you belong. Hawthorne looked at his ruddy leather jacket, khakis and worn loafers and knew his best non-verbals would only take it so far. He had to find Cash's office quickly, then boldly make his play.

He didn't know the layout of the building, so he was not sure whether he was getting colder or warmer in his search. His best guess was that his office would have a clear view of both the atrium and workout facilities below on one side, and the grandest view of the outside on the other, which would probably be the tollway a quarter of a mile to the east of the building.

He approached a larger entry, which had double doors and glassed walls to the office inside. He walked toward it, then darted out of sight when he saw four men leaving the office. The men walked toward him, stopping just short of his position. They were grim, hardened and squared away.

"Where the hell is Hamilton?" asked one of the men.

"An hour west of Waco," said another voice, authoritatively. Several men replied affirmatively and began walking toward Hawthorne. The reporter took a deep breath and jumped out in front of where he guessed they would be. His timing was perfect as he ran into what felt like a brick wall.

"Hey!"

"Whoa!"

"Watch where you're going."

"I know. Sorry."

The burly man shook his head looking back at him before continuing with the other three men. Hawthorne looked at his empty hand and nodded, satisfied. Hopefully the man wouldn't check his coat pockets until the reporter had what he needed. He continued into the glassed office, bursting in. At the receptionist's desk stood Damon Cash himself, with another large man standing next to him.

"Who are you?" Cash demanded, before his receptionist could even speak.

"Gil Hawthorne, Neon Mega. I just want a few minutes of your time, Mr. Cash."

"Get his ass out of here."

Vance grabbed Hawthorne so forcefully and so quickly, it took his breath away. He literally threw him out the double doors to two security men who caught him and dragged him away. They took him down the freight elevator and dumped him outside.

"Don't come back."

Hawthorne's shove to the ground was painful. His arm was twisted in an odd position, taking the brunt of his fall. He shook it off, pulling his smartphone into view. He found the app he had been experimenting with for months, connected to the small, button-sized GPS gadget he snuck in the man's coat pocket during the collision. Just as planned, the red dot was speeding west, ostensibly on its way to Hamilton.

Cash's stormtroopers urgently traveling to a small town wasn't routine. The reporter's instincts told him they were in pursuit of precious secrets. And uncovering a powerful sports agent's secrets could mean the story of a lifetime.

The charity event was like any of the dozens Trent Tanger attended every year. He would lend his name to some worthy cause, his people would coordinate all aspects of the event, he would give a speech, auction off several autographed or game-worn jerseys, caps, balls or bats, sign more autographs, then smoothly disappear into the presidential suite where a woman of his choosing awaited him.

He walked into the suite and made his way to the bedroom. Underneath the covers of the bed was a woman, with only her long blonde tresses, a wine glass, and a giggle showing.

"It's about time."

"I'm sick of this shit. I travel a million miles a year for the games. A damn check should be enough."

"At least you get to visit me," she cooed.

"Yes," he muttered, unbuttoning his shirt without emotion. It was another night, with another woman, in another town.

The tone of his phone's ring was particular to one caller. While he would never admit it, this was one call he couldn't dare ignore.

"Yeah."

"Can you talk?"

Tanger walked into the other room and closed the doors behind him without a word to the woman. She watched him go curiously.

"What is it?"

"Your wife is missing."

"What? How could you let that happen?"

Cash bristled at his tone. "Relax, Trent. We will find her."

"She could destroy me," he growled under his breath.

"Yes, she could."

"It's that dumb shit Vance's fault."

"Trent, that dumb shit Vance has bailed your ass out of more fires than you'll ever know. Get your head together."

Tanger sighed deeply, staring into space. Without any hair-trigger reaction to take, he was lost.

"Relax," Cash said. "We will update you when you need to know."

With that, the line went dead.

Tanger loved April, at least what passed for love according to him. He didn't think he could live without her. He didn't want to try.

THIRTY-FOUR

THE two vehicles left the Metroplex in a more direct path than April had taken hours before, using the tollway to cut through the city and its outskirts to save nearly an hour. They paced each other approximately a half mile apart. The silver sedan and the grey Tahoe drew no attention on the way, driving only a few miles above the speed limit.

Junior studied the tablet in front him, fighting through the rural dead spots for data coverage. Between the dead spots, he learned the basics of Hamilton, the seat of the county with the same name. He estimated the size of the local police force and their likely response time.

Of the three county sheriff vehicles, two were parked in front of the court house. One of the cars remained parked off the square, where the cars could easily be seen. The Tahoe parked across the street where its occupants could keep an eye on the marked cars. Inside, they tuned the radio to the police band.

The sedan circled the square, then made its way back north to the convenience store just south of the graveyard. One of the men stepped out and darted into the store. A young teenager manned the counter alone.

"Evening."

The teen nodded. "How are you doing?"

"Tremendous."

The man flipped out a badge. "I just spoke with Sheriff Dunham. He said I could take a quick look at your camera feed from last night."

The boy nodded quickly and motioned to the office in back. The sheriff wasn't an altogether unpleasant sort, but he had arrested him for an MIP earlier that summer, and he wasn't anxious to do anything to anger the lawman again. Inside the office, the boy sat down and logged into a computer at a desk against the wall. He quickly pulled up the feed from the previous day.

"Here they are, sorted by the hour."

"Great," the man said, quickly patting the boy on the shoulder. "You can go ahead and return to your station. I need some privacy anyway. Thanks."

"No problem."

The teen scurried out and the man settled in. He had a general idea of the timeline based on the marks he was given from the license scans Vance had provided. He quickly found the clip needed and froze on the pickup as it turned away from the store, its license plate clearly shown. The man texted the plate's numbers and took a deep breath.

Behind him were boxes of crackers, cookies and chips. He pulled a bag of potato chips out and pulled it open. He stuffed a few chips in his mouth, licking his fingers clean of the salt.

The return text arrived quickly, with the name and address connected to the pickup. The man quickly found the address, only minutes down the highway. He spun the chair around and darted out of the office. He marched to the counter where the boy was waiting.

"I munched on some chips back there," he said, pulling a $5 bill from his wallet and handing to the boy. "No time to eat."

"That's cool. I'll take care of it."

"Thanks for your help. I'll be sure to mention it to the sheriff."

"Thank you. What are you looking for, anyway?"

The question briefly stopped the man at the door. "Bank robber in Houston. He has family west of here, so we're doing our due diligence."

The boy nodded as the man left the store, taking solace that the sheriff may cut him some additional slack if he got caught in a similar situation again.

The man jumped into the sedan and it rolled south, to the home of Sonny and Wanda Breyer.

* * * * *

Sonny loved the country. Wanda was a city girl when they married 49 years earlier, but he converted her quickly. What finally got her was the same thing that he could never find with his brief attempts at life in the city.

Quiet. Every living thing made a distinct sound which differentiated it from the others, but the sounds still blended together. With the visuals, it formed a masterpiece which you only had to walk outside your door and take in.

The front porch of their house was small and plain, but what a view. From the rocking chair, he could easily see someone approaching the house, not that it was ever a concern. Crime in the area was minimal. He never gave violent intruders much of a thought, as his hearing was as good as it ever was. Wanda often lamented the fact that he could hear a sparrow blink in his sleep.

The slight crackle that he heard gave him a start, the sound unnatural for the time and place. His first suspicion was the gravel of the rural road at the edge of the hill had been slightly disturbed.

Sonny kept rocking for a few moments, then took a deep breath. He had no idea who it was, but he had a reasonable guess why whoever it was had come.

He slowly rose from the rocker, walking as casually as possible. He entered the house and motioned to the two women talking in the den, and put a finger to his mouth.

"Somebody's out there."

Wanda took a deep breath, then looked at April.

"No," April muttered.

"Stay here."

Sonny walked to the bedroom and retrieved several of his weapons. He took his rifle and ammo pouch, flung them over each shoulder, then holstered two of his pistols. He took two more pistols and their respective magazines and waved the women into the hall, out of view of any windows.

"Can you see him?" asked Wanda.

"No, but I can tell you there's more than one of them," Sonny said, passing his wife in the hall, marching towards April. "You ever fired a gun before?"

"No."

"There's no external safety on this one," he said as he placed it correctly in her hands. "Use both hands. There's your trigger, but keep off it until you're ready to shoot. Okay?"

April nodded.

"Wanda, go grab one of the kitchen chairs and sit in it behind the recliner. April, kneel right here behind this wall. Both of you face the front and shoot anyone that comes in."

"Where are you going?" Wanda asked.

"Back behind the shed. Don't look behind you because anyone coming from the rear is gonna get their ass blown away."

Wanda nodded, watching her husband as she tried to walk calmly. As April started to kneel, Sonny grabbed her arm firmly and pressed a chain of keys and a basic flip cell phone into her free hand.

"When you've either shot everyone who's broken in, or your first magazine is empty, go to the garage and to the pickup. Don't bother with the door. Crank it up, crash through it and haul ass."

"Where?"

"You came from up north. Go south."

April took them and hesitated. The elderly man's firm push of her back toward the floor removed any doubt he was serious. Before she had time to realize it, he was gone and the lights had been turned off.

It was a simple rural plot, with the house set up on the hill. Any vehicles were parked in the garage or back in the barn behind the house. There was no activity outside and dusk was not far off. Shortly after nightfall, they would move.

The farm house was non-descript, but well kept. Junior took a night vision monocular and saw what appeared to be an elderly man rocking on the front porch. The lights were on in the house. No sign of their prey.

Junior pointed to the man on his left and the two on his right. They disappeared in the darkness to make their approach. All seemed to be going perfectly.

He noticed the man in the rocker hesitate. It was nearly imperceptible, for barely a count. He kept rocking for a few moments, then rose casually.

His crew was good, but somehow, he heard them. They were made.

"Tallyho," Junior softly spoke. "We're live."

By the time, the lights went out, the men were at their assigned positions.

Sonny watched one of the intruders stealing his way across the pasture, then through the crack in the wall of his barn. The old man had his share of combat in Vietnam, but he no longer considered himself an expert in battle. Still, as he watched the man approaching, he could tell he was of a different sort. Either born or bred, he was a hunter, a killer, and well-seasoned. His moves had intention and discipline. Whoever his guest had escaped from, they were powerful, and they had formidable resources to bear. All this meant they were in grave peril.

There was no way for him to determine the best time to attack. Since the one intruder he could see was obviously not alone, he figured he would make his move when his opponent was most vulnerable and when it would give the two women the best chance to defend themselves. He decided that was once he appeared to have taken his assigned position, or before he was out of range.

The crash of a window changed everything. The assault was on and he had to join before it was too late.

He left his rifles and slipped through the barn door with his two pistols. He was able to fire off three rounds at the intruder before he turned the weapon on Sonny.

Sonny recognized the MP5 on sight moments before the bullets tore through him. He dropped limply, considering his fate for a few moments before passing. Knowing one of his rounds was a fatal wound for his target would not have been solace. His last thoughts were of his precious Wanda, and hopes she would somehow survive, and not mourn him for the rest of her days.

The flash-bang was predictable, but not welcome. Wanda fired several shots through the window before ambling to April's side.

"Go to the truck," she snapped under her breath. "Do it."

"I'm not leaving you!"

"Go!"

Wanda punctuated her order with a shove down the hall. April hesitated for a second, then obeyed, regretting it immediately. She crawled, navigating by leaning up against the wall, then reaching up to open the door only slightly enough to slide through.

The floor of the garage was dusty and wet with some sort of fluid, but these were the least of her concerns. She crawled into the cab of the pickup on the passenger side. Fortunately, the truck was facing the door. It was a dusty farm pickup with all the requisite smells that accompanied it, but it cranked like a champ. She put it in drive and floored it, crashing through the door as instructed.

The next few seconds were surreal, and seemed to take forever. A short spray of bullets peppered the windshield, and she ducked instinctively, low enough to barely see. Finally, she emptied out onto the farm to market road, then whipped onto 281. She sped south, as instructed. Looking behind her, she saw nothing.

April sped down 281, pressing the pedal, speeding as fast as she dared, hoping to avoid anything that would slow her down. After a couple of minutes, with no headlights appearing in her rearview mirror, she retrieved the cell phone. She pulled the Shelter card out of her pocket and texted the five-digit code.

THIRTY-FIVE

THE weather had turned cold, more like one would expect from a November evening. Mother nature habitually spoiled Austin residents with mild temperatures, but that had ended the previous evening, chilling the workers to their bones. Noelle went to the nearest big box home improvement warehouse with four space heaters added to the list of supplies for continued updates to the house. The supplies were paid for by one the abusers from which they had rescued a victim. Noelle usually did the shopping because she had the funds, obtained surreptitiously from those with the misfortune of coming into their radar.

With the roof repaired, the structural bones of the house were set. The landscaping near the house had not been extensive, as they had opted for more stone and rock. Most of the surrounding acreage would be mowed as needed, but kept like the house, appearing worn and having seen better days.

The linoleum floors weren't in great shape, but the carpet was in far worse condition. The group agreed to do the carpet and lay tile in bathrooms and kitchen later. The tiling would require professional help, but they could save and do the carpet themselves as Julia had done it several times before. She knew the common mistakes, having learned the hard way in past efforts.

She was on her knees in one of the bedrooms downstairs, working the electric seaming iron at the door of the room, when she heard the door to the stairwell open and close. Yardley appeared around the corner.

"What is it?" Julia asked.

"You better get up here."

The women took the elevator up and walked to the corner of the house where Noelle was tapping furiously on her computer while talking excitedly on her headphones with Cassie at her side.

"Where are you?"

Julia and Yardley couldn't hear the frantic cries of the caller, but they could see the strain and urgency on Noelle as she listened.

"And you're going south?" Noelle asked as she punched up a map on her laptop. She nodded, clearly letting her ramble. "How much gas do you have?"

Julia pulled Yardley back a step.

"What happened?"

"Her husband is trying to kill her."

Julia considered the developing scenario, then clued back in to Noelle's words.

"If he doesn't catch up to you, call me when you get to Lampasas. Otherwise, call me immediately."

Noelle kept making hand motions, as if to calm her down.

"I understand, April. Just try to remain calm and drive safely. We're coming to get you, okay? Bye."

She tore off the headphones.

"What is it?"

"She's okay for now, but if he catches her, she said he'll kill her. And she was adamant about no police."

Julia looked at Cassie, and they nodded to each other. Both women dropped their tools and grabbed their purses.

"Where is she, exactly?"

Noelle watched her computer screen. "South on 281. She's coming up on Lampasas."

"Okay. Check our coms in ten."

Noelle nodded. Yardley watched them march out the door.

The women moved directly for Cassie's Cadillac, and jumped in. Once Cassie had plugged in her earbud, she cranked the car and spun it away from the property in one motion. Julia connected her earpiece as well, attempting to ride with the centrifugal force of the XTS taking the hairpin curves out of the development. Once out on the freeway and speeding north, Julia found her pistol and snapped in a clip. She found Cassie's purse, found her weapon and did the same.

Their phones both buzzed and they clicked on.

"Noelle?"

"Yep. What are her instructions?"

"Tell her to find the Whataburger and ditch the vehicle off the highway a block or two away, preferably somewhere darker and out of sight. Then, walk inside the Whataburger and barricade herself in one of the bathroom stalls. We'll come pick her up."

"Got it."

"If he catches up to her, go ahead and call in the cavalry. Understand?"

"Roger that," Noelle replied, closing the line.

Cassie looked at Julia who was looking at her phone's GPS, measuring something. The ex-cop was matter-of-fact about what was happening, even though each rescue had potential for untold danger. She continued pushing the XTS, tearing up 183 towards Lampasas.

THIRTY-SIX

JUNIOR hesitated to call Vance with the results of their assignment. They had failed miserably, although he had no reason to expect to face the resistance they encountered for what seemed like a routine task.

The problems that occurred during the attack were largely due to losing his operator covering the rear. What he suspected was confirmed when he found the corpse of his operator and his killer, the old man who died defending his home. He was probably one of those wily war veterans who had never lost his extraordinary senses, and retained all his tactical reasoning. He bought a few more minutes for his wife, and an improbable escape for their guest, the prey they were pursuing.

The wife knew how to handle herself as well, providing ample cover fire for the girl, who crashed through the garage door and tore away at top speed. One of his operators attempted to pursue her, but reached the nearest town empty handed. The leader instructed for him to wait until the rest of them arrived. Due to the messy nature of their assault, they were forced to move the old man's corpse into the house next to the body of his wife, and then destroy the house by opening the gas lines, causing an explosion. The authorities would arrive more quickly, but their causes of death would take longer to discover.

They found the getaway pickup sitting innocently enough in Lampasas, one street over from 281. A string of fast food and convenience stores lined the highway and she could be in any of them. It was only then that Junior called Vance. The profanity laced lecture he received was no surprise, but he preferred that to calling sooner, wanting to be closer to a solution when that conversation took place.

Junior and the remaining two men split up, taking every establishment until their prey was captured. One of them entered a Whataburger, with only a group of high school kids standing in line. He quickly scanned the dining room before checking the restroom. An older woman nearly ran into him at the door.

"What's the matter with you? This is the ladies' room!"

"Oh, I'm sorry ma'am. I didn't know there was more than one."

"You need to pay attention."

The burly intruder left the ladies' room and moved to the men's room to play out the ruse. Inside the stall, the woman turned to April, standing on top of the toilet, coiled defensively. Knowing she could do no more for her than play out the act, she nodded and closed the stall door behind her.

With no one in the men's room, the man nodded to his partner outside and they quietly moved down the street to check the next establishment.

April wasn't sure if she was hyperventilating, but if she wasn't, this was what she thought it felt like. Her heart was pounding, and she didn't know how much more she could take.

The door opened again. The shoes didn't look like a woman's, more like the loafers of a man on a weekend getaway.

"April?"

The stall door shook.

"April Tanger?"

"Go away!" she snapped, realizing she was found. "If you don't, I'll scream!"

"No, you won't. I can help you, get you out of here."

It wasn't one of Cash's storm troopers. She wasn't thrilled about trusting anyone, but she didn't have great choices.

She cracked the door open and found an odd, yet ordinary man of about thirty.

"I'm Gil Hawthorne," he said, extending his hand. "I can help you, April."

"How do you know me?"

"It's my job to know. I'm a reporter."

She drew back and stiffened. "Oh, shit!"

"I'm on your side. Let me get you out of here, and I'll tell your side of the story."

The door to the restroom opened again. The man turned.

"What the hell are you doing in here?" another woman snapped.

"I'm sorry. My daughter is very sick and—"

April heard a loud thud and the reporter dropped to the ground in front of her. A woman appeared, pistol in her hand. April looked at her eyes. They were fierce, but she sensed a trueness.

"April?"

"Yes."

"I'm Julia. I'm the help Noelle sent," Julia said while finding the man's wallet and briefly looking over his ID before motioning toward the door. "C'mon."

Julia opened the restroom door and led April out. She noticed April looking around as if more threats existed. A worker mopping the other end of the dining area watched them oddly. Outside, she saw nothing.

"You okay?"

"Uh, yeah."

Moments later, the Cadillac appeared by the door.

"This is us."

April scampered through the door and almost dove inside the car. Once Julia jumped in, Cassie gunned the accelerator and they disappeared into the night. They turned south on 281, away from the direct route to Austin where she guessed pursuers would follow. She silently watched the rearview mirror and saw no one.

"Was that him in the restroom?"

"No."

"So, your husband could still be back there."

April paused, breathing heavily. "Maybe. He's got a gun."

"Is he crazy enough to chase after us?" Cassie asked.

"Yes."

"That's Cassie at the wheel," Julia said. Cassie waved to their new passenger.

April measured them and nodded with a sigh.

"Did you know that guy?" Julia asked.

"No. I've never seen him before."

"Who is he?"

"I don't know."

Cassie looked at Julia who shrugged, unsure of what to make of it. They would figure it out once at the safe house.

"Relax and rest back there," Cassie said. "We have a ways to go."

THIRTY-SEVEN

THE two SUVs screeched to a stop in the empty parking lot in a warehouse district just south of Dallas/Fort Worth airport. Once they stopped, a limousine rolled into view a few yards away. Junior and the two remaining operators left their vehicles. Vance darted out, waving away Junior before he could speak. He handed the other two men a manila envelope. Inside were one-way plane tickets, each with different airlines, and different destinations.

"Leave the vehicle in long-term parking, and don't return to Texas for the next 90 days. Do not contact me. I will contact you, if needed."

The men returned to one of the SUVs and rolled away.

"Vance, I—"

"I don't want to hear it, Junior! Go back to the estate and stay there."

Vance turned away, running back to the limo before Junior could say anything else. Inside the rolling limo, Vance did not wait for any words from his employer sitting across from him. Cash noted the role reversal, watching Vance work his cellphone like he was the only volunteer at a telethon. There was little the agent could do but watch him work his connections. It was delicate work, obtaining secure data and surveillance video from law enforcement without raising red flags. Vance had a considerable list of contacts to call, but answers would not be instant.

Finally, Cash saw Vance reach a stopping point, just as his four men in that small town in central Texas had. He stopped moving, looking blankly ahead, as if contemplating a math problem with several missing variables. An answer was not possible, at least not yet. A crime scene had been created for no good reason, and April Tanger was in the wind.

The limousine finally stopped in front of Cash's office building. The two men stepped out and paced to his office in silence until reaching Cash's empty conference room.

"What now?" Cash asked.

"I need to review the data," Vance replied. "Until then, we're just guessing."

"Then, get to it." Cash snapped. He paced back and forth along the conference table. "Where could she go? She has no money, no ID. She's strung out on meds."

"She has quite a tale to tell, though."

Cash turned and glared at Vance. They both knew the enormous risks that her escape presented. She knew the dark side of Trent Tanger, something the public did not. Her story, and his, could ruin them.

One of Vance's cell phones rang.

"Vance. Yes. Good, send it straight away."

He hung up the phone.

"It's coming now," Vance said to Cash. The agent marched back behind Vance on the other side of the table to see what it was. An email message arrived with several attachments.

"This is the video from three different traffic cameras, the 580 intersection on the north side of town, the 183/190 intersection and the 281/Plum intersection on the south. She arrived at around 11:00 PM, so I'll start there and start working my way forward."

"What are the chances you'll find anything?"

"I'm not a psychic, Damon. I'll let you know."

Vance didn't have any easy answers, and he could tell Cash was about to explode. He could have reminded him that he had strongly advised Cash to engineer a divorce between the Tangers. It would have been so easy, sending April away with enough money to live comfortably and stay quiet for the rest of her life. Instead, he wisely let the silence fill the room as he worked the video.

Cash left, snatching his coffee cup and leaving the room for a refill. He knew the same things that Vance did. The Tanger affair was a mess, but every time he considered separating them, the potential collateral damage from loose lips kept him from acting. He kept massaging the situation in the hopes of landing the historic contract he had visualized the first time he saw the kid effortlessly launching baseballs into the outfield bleachers as a prep-school prospect.

He punched the Keurig button and served up another steaming dose of adrenaline. He found some cookies on the counter and stuffed a couple into his mouth. He normally counted calories and carbs fastidiously, cherishing his well-earned six-pack. But desperate times called for desperate measures.

He returned to the conference room to find Vance looking at him expectantly.

"Find something?"

"Yes. It's good news and bad news."

"Okay."

"I went through the plates of twenty vehicles. All but three of them are registered to local addresses. One of the three is from San Antonio, another is from Lubbock. The registrants look like simple travelers. The third is from Austin, a 2015 XTS registered to a Cassie Snow."

Vance punched up the driver license and registration for Cash to view. He also clicked open a website with a professional photo. He saw an attractive black woman. Her look was serious and focused.

"She's an attorney specializing in family law. I also found several news articles where she was interviewed regarding her activities as an advocate for domestic abuse victims."

At this, Cash turned away and dropped into a chair next to Vance.

"You're shitting me."

"No."

"She reached out to somebody."

"That's what it looks like."

Cash took in the body blow. If their conclusions were correct, their fate was no longer in their own hands. Strategically, they were now on offense, instead of defense.

They couldn't afford to be passive, waiting for new opponents to make a move.

"What's our play?" Vance asked.

"The attorney will protect her while she does her due diligence. Then, based on the merits of the case, she will act."

"April may be too scared to tell the truth."

"At first. Until then, we have that long to put our plan in motion."

Cash walked to a white board on the wall and grabbed a marker. He didn't write anything, instead snapping the cap of the marker on and off, a nervous habit he used when brainstorming. He thought back to that fateful day eight years earlier. Tanger had his choice of dozens of sorority girls, and he picks one of the Russian mail-order brides. Unbelievable.

"She'll eventually find out about Tanger, and that he is on the verge of the biggest contract in team sports history."

"Leverage," said Vance.

"Right. And then she'll try to bleed us dry, with as much money as she can extract. Or else parade her through the press and crucify our golden goose."

"Can we negotiate?"

"If we're negotiating with the attorney of a domestic abuse victim, maybe."

Cash purposefully paused, turning to look at Vance.

"But if the attorney is representing a victim of sex trafficking born on the other side of the globe, that's not a risk we can run."

"Which leaves what?" Vance asked.

"That leaves it in your arena. Extraction or elimination."

After saying this, Cash realized he had not thought through these contingencies, and he should have. The remote possibility that April Tanger could escape and tell the world the true story of what her life was like, how she met Trent Tanger, and where she came from, had not been considered. He had thought plenty about the endgame with her, but had not counted on it being this messy.

He had engineered many hush-hush deals in the past. It was part of dealing with celebrities who operated without governors, leaving vast collateral damage in their wake. The abuse element was tricky, especially with how she had been handled medically. To get April to quietly cooperate with a relatively nominal settlement after Tanger's big payday was the plan. Quietly eliminating her was always an option. Granted, it was a risky option, but it wouldn't be the first time.

"You need to prepare for the more difficult possibility," Cash said. "What do you need?"

"She was rescued in a relatively remote area," Vance said, "with stealth and precision. My instincts are telling me that this is no ordinary legal counsel, and she is not alone. It's not a paid by the hour staffer that mans the desk of one of your rival agents."

He stopped talking, watching Cash take in his words. His employer was truly listening, something he did not do by default. He did not make it to the top by playing therapist. He listened only for cracks in the narrative of who was speaking, faults he could exploit in his rebuttal.

"I'll need to go down there with additional reinforcements," Vance continued. "I'll also need someone with a high level of operator experience and sensibilities, but also an IT skillset. I can't lead a team doing everything that's needed and work on collecting the intel we need at the same time."

"You already have the person in mind, don't you?"

"I do."

"Tell me about him."

"He's local, at least he was. From what I hear, he's no longer in the States."

"Is he good?" Cash asked.

"The best. The only question is if he will be willing to risk returning."

"What's he running from?"

"His last job was here, in town, troubleshooting for a mobster," said Vance. "When the feds came crashing in, he slipped away just in time. From what I hear, the mobster was his own worst enemy, wouldn't take his advice."

"By mobster, do you mean Davis Morgan?"

"That's the one."

Cash paused, recalling the details of the case.

"Okay. See if you can find this guy. Hopefully, they'll negotiate and he won't be needed. If they won't, we have to get this cleaned up quickly, so that we can cash the Tanger check and be on to other things."

THIRTY-EIGHT

APRIL heard the Caddy's rumble and felt its forward motion waning. After a sharp turn, she felt the car descending, as if down a steep hill. The car finally came to a stop.

Julia turned toward the backseat passenger. "You can remove the blinds."

April removed the cover and found herself in another parking garage. This one had no sunlight, only fluorescent lights between every other beam holding the concrete underground together. In one corner of the garage was a row of framing studs, construction of several rooms in progress.

Cassie waved her toward an elevator door with a flight of stairs. The three women entered the elevator and it raised one floor.

"You okay?" Cassie asked.

"I don't know yet," April replied absently.

The door opened to reveal what appeared to be a reception area in the process of being finished. A can of paint and assorted tools and supplies were scattered on the desk and on the floor. Two more women approached them.

"April, this is Noelle, who you spoke with on the phone."

Noelle reached out and hugged April. This was not standard practice, but something compelled her to break through the touch barrier. Fortunately, the rescued responded well. Yardley approached, looking her over.

"I'm Yardley. Looks like you have a couple of scratches there."

Yardley gently grasped her face, inspecting a scrape on her nose and a gash above her left eyebrow. The nose would heal easily, but the gash was deeper.

"Really?"

"It's the fog of war, sweetie. C'mon, I'll get you fixed up."

Yardley led her to the bathroom, looking to the others with a nod who waited until they were out of earshot to begin.

"Any trouble?" Noelle asked.

Cassie shook her head no. "We slipped in, picked her up and snuck out."

"There was one little issue," Julia said. "I had to rescue her from some guy. She said it wasn't her husband, but he was trying to talk her out of the stall in the women's restroom."

"Did you get a name?" Noelle asked, walking back to the nerve center and reaching for the keyboard.

"Gil Hawthorne."

A few clicks later, her screens exploded with information. "A reporter for Neon Mega."

"What's that?" Cassie asked.

"It's like a tabloid magazine for sports. Mostly crap. A bunch of slideshows with a lot of invasive ads."

Julia and Cassie exchanged confused looks.

"Something's wrong," Cassie said.

Julia nodded in agreement. A few minutes later, Yardley brought April back in and they sat in a makeshift circle. April sat on the couch, warming her hands around a mug of coffee Yardley had made for her. The four women sat around her in folding chairs.

"We want to get you downstairs to get some rest," Julia began, "but we'd like to get some information from you, if you're up to it."

April nodded hesitantly, clearly pensive about revealing much.

"What's his name?"

"My boyfriend?"

"Your boyfriend," Cassie repeated. "I thought it was your husband."

April's lie was subconscious, the defenses of her nightmare continuing even after rescue. The attorney quickly brushed this away.

"Well, sort of."

"Okay," Cassie said, allowing the silence to fan the flames of inconsistency. April looked around at the four women, who desperately wanted to help her. She still saw strangers, who were potential enemies.

"I never really had a choice. I've never really had many choices."

"Tell us about him," Julia ventured. "Your husband, boyfriend, whatever."

"His name is Trent."

"How long has he been abusive to you?"

At this, April retreated further, glaring at the women as if they were threatening her.

"I—I think I've made a mistake. I want to go."

"April," Julia said, "the more you tell us, and the more truth you tell us, the better we can help you."

She had heard this before, but never had it proven true. It had only fueled more deception and manipulation by those who controlled her life. Her newfound hold on that control was precarious. The friends she had met hours earlier had only received trouble in return for her trusting them.

"I need to go."

With that, April shot up from the chair and bolted for the door. The women reached out for her, trying to stop her as gently as they could. Julia restrained them, letting April dash out the door. She ran out to a cold, starry night in a rural area. Wherever she was going, it was going to take some time.

After running about a hundred yards, she bent over crying. The women approached, Julia leading the way, waving at the others to keep some distance.

"April, we're not going to hold you."

The beaten woman fell to her knees, crying. She was still in shock, afraid of anything and everything. The only constant she knew was the steady, sure pain of her tormentors.

"April?" Julia continued, gently putting a hand on her shoulder. After a few moments, her cries subsided and she looked up.

"I'll take you wherever you want to go. Can we just talk about it first?"

"Wherever I want?"

"Except for back to that asshole. If you're going there, you can keep walking."

April struggled to her feet and collapsed into Julia's arms. She nodded to the other women and they went back inside.

"C'mon."

Julia motioned to her pickup, and led her to the passenger side opening the door for her. When she sat inside, a cascade of papers fell into the floorboard.

"Just throw that stuff in back."

April did so. Julia reached into the glove compartment and produced an eye cover.

"This location is a secret. Wherever we're going, you can't know how to get back."

April took the blindfold and dropped it into her lap. Julia cranked the car and rock music began to blare.

"I never loved him."

April's words didn't register, so Julia turned down the radio. The truck remained in park.

"What's that?"

"We married seven years ago, two months after we met. I never loved him."

Julia sensed a detachment, but not from loss or disappointment. It was merely a formality. April looked out into the darkness, seeing only shapes of trees, or maybe hills.

"I don't know what love is. If I've ever felt it before, it does not interest me."

Julia watched her and understood. She sensed that she had never had it as rough as her new client, but she also wondered what true love felt like. She also heard something odd in April's patterns of diction and pronunciation. It was doubtful she was from Texas.

"Why did you marry him?"

"I grew up with nothing. He had money and treated me nice, at least at first. I had not experienced much of either in my life. Once he found out I had nowhere else to go, he changed."

April's hands covered her face and she began to sob softly. With her defenses weakening, Julia thought it was time to push her out of her comfort zone. She shifted into drive and started rolling down the gravel driveway.

"Put on the shades. Once we get far enough, you can tell me where you want to go."

"Wait."

Julia pressed the brakes and the truck eased to a stop. She looked over at her passenger, who watched her with wet, pleading eyes.

"I'm really hungry. Do you have anything to eat back there?"

Julia looked at April whose weary face had a spark of earnest hope. She smiled and put the truck in reverse.

THIRTY-NINE

BEFORE Hawthorne opened his eyes, it was the sharp, stiff pain in the forehead that awakened him, just above the bridge of his nose. Then, the pain in the back of his head registered. When he reached for the back of his head, the expected gash with stitches was clearly felt.

When he did open his eyes, he was surprised to find himself in a hospital room. It took his conscious mind a few moments to register that he hadn't fallen asleep in his apartment in Southern California, or at his desk at the Neon Mega offices. He was in Texas, chasing a story that would have seemed absurd to any of his peers.

Then he remembered what landed him in the hospital. He had followed Cash's enforcers to Hamilton, and watched in shock as they opened fire on a farm house. He followed someone escaping the house in a pickup to the next town. The woman in the fast-food restaurant looked a lot like April Tanger, clearly shaken by a run for her life. He sat at a booth inside, waiting for her to come out, casually looking at his phone to seem inconspicuous. Only a few minutes of waiting brought a large man who stormed into the restroom only to be chased out by a different woman. Once the large man left, he thought he could play rescuer and get her story in return for the favor.

The plan was sound, until it was ruined by a woman who pistol-whipped him for his trouble. Whoever the woman was, she was skilled with the maneuver. He must have dropped to the bathroom tile in such a state that he had no ability to brace his fall.

"Good afternoon."

"What?"

"They said you came in late last night. How are you feeling?"

When his eyes began to focus, he saw a nurse in scrubs watching him carefully. The thick Texas drawl refreshed his memory further, bringing back details of his evening.

"Like shit."

"No offense, but that's about how you look. Concussions will do that to you."

Hawthorne looked beyond the room and spotted a police officer outside the door.

"What's with the cop?"

"You'll have to ask him. He wouldn't say."

It occurred to Hawthorne that lying unconscious in a women's restroom would not be easy to explain.

"Am I clear to go?"

"Medically, I'll have to go get the attending to agree and sign you out. Legally, that's up to Lampasas' finest."

He nodded. "Let me talk to him."

She handed him a cup of water, then spoke to the policeman. He said something to her and walked in once she had left.

"Gilbert Hawthorne?"

Hawthorne nodded painfully.

"What happened to you?"

"I was doing research on a story. I'm a writer for Neon Mega."

"What were you doing in the ladies' restroom of our local Whataburger?"

He was now alert enough to spot the danger points in the questioning, danger beyond what the cop knew. It was bad enough that he had witnessed the burning of the house and the resulting chase to Lampasas. Even the pure, unadulterated truth would sound flimsy.

"I must have made a mistake. Those signs on the doors aren't as clear as they used to be. By the time I realized it, another customer decided to show me. Forcefully."

The officer didn't buy it, and Hawthorne didn't expect him to. That was all he planned on saying until he knew more. More about where April Tanger was. More about why

Cash's goons were chasing her, even though he had a pretty good idea.

What he really wanted to find was the lady who knocked him out, and why.

The officer walked away from the room and past the nurse's station, pulling out his cell phone. The call was likely to his superior, to tell him about this out-of-towner who was up to no good. A few minutes later, the officer returned, evaluating the contents of Hawthorne's wallet.

"California, huh?"

"That's right."

"Here."

"Thanks."

"When the doctor releases you, leave town and don't come back."

The officer punctuated his order with a glare and walked away. Two hours later, he was released from the hospital and walked the mile to his car, sitting across the highway from the Whataburger where his troubles began.

As he recharged his cellphone via the cigarette lighter, he went back to the reason he had driven halfway across the country. The story was no longer about Damon Cash, super-agent. It was about April Tanger and whatever secrets had driven Cash to send stormtroopers to commit cold-blooded murder in their mad pursuit of her across Texas.

He then remembered that Trent and April met in Austin, 75 miles down the road. He threw his cellphone on the passenger seat and cranked the car, moving it south. The story got juicier with each passing mile.

The best baseball player of a generation, poised to sign the largest contract in sports history.

His wife, running for her life in rural Texas from armed commandos.

The most powerful sports agent in the world, willing to commit murder to bury an explosive secret.

The clues were tantalizing, but formed no pattern. Wherever they led, the truth would form a story that would make his career. He wasn't going back to the West Coast without it.

FORTY

JULIA trudged into her office slowly, the previous night's activities taking their toll. She was envious of her younger partners who seemed tireless in comparison. She took a bit of solace knowing they would someday discover what 10 to 15 more years on the odometer would do to their energy levels.

As she reached for the flask in the lowest drawer of her desk, she acknowledged that her fuel wasn't exactly pure. Merely the vision of whiskey blending with her coffee gave her a bit of calm. She wasn't strong enough to do without it, at least, not yet. Leading this mission was a rewarding endeavor that enabled her to sleep at night, but it was taking its toll in small but incremental pieces.

It was just after 9 AM, so she didn't expect company for at least another hour. As expected, Cassie was next, a few minutes later. She appeared in Julia's office shortly thereafter, with a mug of coffee in her hand. She set it down on the table across from Julia's desk, sitting while massaging her upper arm.

"I don't know if I can do this HGTV stuff every day."

"How's that? You're in better shape than I am."

"It's different. That work uses different muscles than in the gym."

"It's a good change of pace. Besides, we're getting tangible benefits. That scared girl out there is the first of many to come."

Cassie watched Julia's fire and wondered if her vision for the property would suit their purposes as fully as she imagined. They were merely guessing at the costs of maintaining such a property. Even Noelle could not accurately predict whether their underground activity would consistently be able to fund it.

"Anything bother you about the girl last night?" Cassie asked.

"Bother? No."

"Nothing?"

"She did seem a little out of the ordinary."

"Why would she lie about the husband, boyfriend thing?"

Julia shrugged, dismissing Cassie's concern. Ever the litigator, she was quick to identify and point out any inconsistencies, something Julia had become quite proficient at as a cop. But her approach to victims had softened, and even she had to admit her guard dropped a bit, where Cassie would remain vigilant. It was one of the reasons she was so valuable.

"Maybe she's just spooked."

"Maybe she's hiding something, something that still makes her vulnerable. Too vulnerable to trust anyone, including us."

"Okay, I'll play along," said Julia. "What are you suggesting?"

Cassie paused. "She's running away from someone, driving south on 281 to Lampasas. Is her car still in Lampasas? Is it even her car?"

Julia laughed. "Oh, now she stole a car?"

"Okay, smartass. Take off your rescue hat and put on your cop hat."

Julia shrugged and shook the mouse on her desk alive. Her laptop lit up and she typed Lampasas, Texas in the search engine. The local school district superintendent announced his retirement after 15 years of service. A tech company announced they were moving to the city from California.

"Nothing on Lampasas."

"Try the other towns north on 281 from there."

Julia's third try was Hamilton, Texas. She saw the stories appear and looked at the screen with interest.

"Got something?" Cassie asked.

"A Hamilton couple was killed."

Cassie moved behind Julia where she could see.

"Authorities found Sonny Breyer, 70, and Wanda Breyer, 68, dead in what was left of their home off FM 1241, just outside of Hamilton. Authorities are still investigating an apparent gas explosion."

"Coincidence?'

Julia shrugged. "Perhaps not."

Noelle entered the room, turning them away from the screen. It was typical of her to be nonchalant and lighthearted about her business, while making great efforts to seem like it was nothing. This provided the other three a great deal of amusement. As Julia watched her now, she seemed unusually focused.

"What is it?"

"Trouble," Noelle replied, motioning with her head toward the conference room. They followed her into the room, where the screen was already on. Yardley had arrived as well, fiddling with her cell phones.

"I ran fingerprints on our new arrival."

"And?"

Noelle punched a few keys and the Texas ID of April came on the screen.

"April Marie Tanger."

"Tanger?" Julia asked.

"Wife of Trent Tanger," said Noelle.

"The baseball player?" Yardley asked.

"That's the one."

"Whoa," Cassie said.

No one said anything for a few moments. Noelle continued as photos and documentation appeared on the screen.

"April's maiden name is Smith. She graduated from Conroe High near Houston. She registered to attend St. Edwards, but never attended a class. Her high school transcript is unremarkable. The only record in any of the school's yearbooks or periodicals while she was there was her senior photo, which had no activities listed next to it. No sports, no clubs, nothing. Her parents are listed as Bill and Susan Smith. My research on them turned up zero.

"She met Trent Tanger at a UT frat party in the fall of 2008. I'm guessing she was invited to help entice him to sign with the Longhorns that November. He decided to go pro instead, compelled by a $10 million signing bonus, still the largest rookie contract in baseball history. Internet reports their marriage year as 2009, but no date. I couldn't find any license records.

"After one year of minor league ball, he was promoted to the majors. Shortly after his debut in 2010, he established himself as one of the best players in the game. He made the All-Star team in 2011, and every year since. He was also voted the league MVP the last two seasons, and this season led Nashville to their first playoff appearance since their expansion season eight years ago. He is now a free agent and likely to sign the biggest contract in baseball history.

"As for April, information about her is notably scarce. Google search only turned up eight photos for the wife of a baseball superstar."

"Eight?" Yardley said. "There's more photos of my toenails on Instagram than that."

"One of those eight photos are from the senior yearbook," Noelle continued. "All the others are from one of his many charity events. She is rarely seen at any of his games."

"A trophy wife that's kept on the shelf." Julia's words were aloud, but as if she were talking through it alone. She watched the woman carefully, as if to decipher some clue hidden somewhere in the pixels of the screen.

"You like baseball, don't you?" Cassie asked Julia.

"I do. I pass a lot of summer nights at home doing stuff around the house with it in the background. My dad took me to games when I was young. He loved the sport."

Julia had not spoken much of her past. None of them had. Once they had reestablished psychological footing in their new lives, away from their abusers, it was easier to act as if they had been born the day they declared freedom from their captivity of violence.

"How good of a player is he?" Yardley asked.

"You heard Noelle," Julia replied. "As good as they come. When he got to the majors as a rookie, he looked like he had been playing for ten years. No holes in his swing. Power at the plate, range in the field, and a rifle for an arm.'

"Will he stay in Nashville?"

"No chance in hell. It's a small market and they can't afford him. He'll go play in New York or California and break the bank. He's perfect."

Julia let the words hang in the air, then turned back to the group.

"Maybe too perfect. When he's interviewed, it's like he's reading from a script that projects the ideal marketing image. He's too neat, too rehearsed."

"He's got a lot to lose, doesn't he?" Noelle asked.

"Absolutely," Julia said. "That image is very controlled. I remember a couple of years ago, the cameras caught him dog-cussing a teammate in the dugout for dropping a fly ball. It was a big deal. The next day, no mention of it. I remember looking on YouTube for it. His tirade was nowhere to be found."

"Any reports of violence?" Cassie asked.

Noelle shook her head. "Not that I could find."

"How old did April look to you?" Julia asked the group.

"Maybe 25," Noelle ventured.

"Or less," Yardley said, emphasizing the intent of the question.

"DMV says she's 30," Noelle continued. "Her public appearances are rare. Several links on the internet that once had their photograph are now broken. Perhaps a request was received to remove them."

"Flimsy background," Julia said to herself. She looked back to the group. "Thoughts?"

"He's very tightly managed," Cassie said, "understandable as much money as he's worth. If his agent's reputation is accurate, he's the one in charge with many handlers at his disposal."

"Who's his agent?" Yardley asked.

"Damon Cash," Cassie said. "You won't have to work very hard to learn about him. One click of your mouse will tell you plenty. He loves the camera and he's ruthless."

"As ruthless as we are?" Noelle asked.

The group chuckled, breaking a bit of the tension. Julia shook her head, taking in the information. "It seems to me a cold-blooded businessman like Cash will convince his boy to cut his losses, give her a decent divorce settlement and move on."

"Why wouldn't he?" Yardley wondered aloud.

"I don't know that he won't," Julia said, "but chasing her out of town with guns blazing suggests there's more to the story."

Cassie's cell phone rang. She picked it up and heard the voice of her assistant. Cassie lowered the phone from her ear.

"It's Damon Cash."

FORTY-ONE

VANCE opened his laptop and turned on the video screen on the wall. The monitor came to life, but showed nothing. Vance took off his sport coat and hung it on the back of his chair. He looked quizzically at the remote, pushed a couple of buttons, then his computer's desktop appeared.

"Here we go."

Cash watched Vance navigate through the icons, finding the one he wanted.

"I confirmed the possibility from the Lampasas traffic cameras."

Vance clicked the desired icon and facial photos of two women appeared, side by side. One was a black woman in her thirties. The other was a white woman perhaps ten years older. Their demeanor revealed the women were two of a kind, focused and fierce.

"Cassie Snow, on the left, is well regarded. It's said that she often employs an investigator by the name of Julia Caldwell, on the right. Caldwell is ex-Austin PD. Her work is primarily insurance, workers' comp type cases, but she does get some work from Snow.

"The worst kept secret in town is that these two run a domestic abuse underground railroad of sorts. Most simply refer to them as The Shelter. The authorities know about it, but will only speak in generalities, probably to protect them. It's not officially connected with anything because they routinely cross the line to protect their clients, the victims.

"I believe The Shelter operates on two levels. The public face is that of a benevolent group that cares for and assists victims of domestic abuse. The secret side is a rogue group of vigilantes that attacks abusers, with or without the law.

"Starting in 2011, the domestic abuse rates in Travis, Williamson, Hays and Burnet counties began dropping sharply, year after year, until now. Over that same period, those counties' prosecutors have enjoyed a remarkable conviction record, with stiffer than average penalties than anywhere else in state. Word quickly spread to the accused that they would be wise to plea out. Those convicted also faced an inordinate number of civil suits, almost all settled out of court. While most of the settlements are sealed, we have learned that the settlements were hardly a compromise. Cassie Snow was the attorney of record more than anyone else, and it wasn't close.

"Additionally, rumors are rampant that these men were subjected to extensive fraud and blackmail prior to their civil settlements. Abusers also suffered remarkable misfortune before, during and after prosecution. Bankruptcies, assaults, freak accidents. This group isn't just a women's shelter. It's a pack of wolves attacking guerrilla style and these two are their leaders. If these women get to them, the abuser's life is systematically destroyed. Judge, jury and executioner."

At this, Cash grinned, pulling a cigar from his jacket and lighting it. He already had an odd admiration for his opponents.

"For an individual attorney and a private investigator, their technology is extremely sophisticated," continued Vance. "I conducted several dry runs to penetrate their firewall and communications with little success. The few hits I had were detected and eliminated quickly. Whoever runs their electronic world has their bases covered and is very good."

"Anything more on their background?"

Vance clicked a few keys and produced more documentation. "Snow was born in Houston. She received both her Bachelors and JD from the University of Texas, and was a member of their esteemed Chancellors honor society. She graduated from La Marque High School, according to her resume and school records. However, other than a degree, no other evidence of Snow's attendance at La Marque exists.

"Julia Caldwell was born in Fort Worth. She obtained her degree in Criminal Justice at the University of Houston, then promptly joined the Austin Police Department. Her records indicate a GED, and no scholastic info prior to that."

"What do you have on either of them prior to high school?" Cash asked.

Vance let a smirk escape, then removed a stack of papers from one of his file folders. He opened the empty file folder and laid it flat on the conference table.

"Cute."

Vance shrugged in response to Cash's quip. "Even with only a couple of days, my research was very thorough. It's likely their history has been sanitized."

Cash nodded. "They've got something in their past that they're hiding. What?"

"A crime?" ventured Vance. "An abusive lover? Or both?"

Cash pounded firmly on the table, then pointed. "We're getting somewhere. Let's make some educated guesses. Since they're runners, their origin is not anywhere near here. Do you have any audio or video of either of them?"

"There's a few hits on YouTube for Snow. I haven't found anything on Caldwell yet."

"Let's see what you've got."

A few clicks later, Vance produced an Austin news clip. It was a generic piece on domestic violence, where the attorney was a subject matter expert. Only a few seconds of her speaking elapsed before Cash motioned to Vance.

"That's enough."

Vance paused the video. "What is it?"

"Houston, my ass. Snow is from New Orleans. Probably the Ninth Ward."

"Really?" Vance asked. "Are the two accents that different?"

"No question," Cash replied confidently. "It's in their words, their speech patterns, and their inflection. It might as well be DNA to my ears."

Vance shook his head, part in amusement, part in amazement. Cash was fond of bragging about being able to tell someone's origin within 100 miles after just a few seconds of audio. In the major metropolitan areas, he claimed he could name the cross streets. With potential clients from all fifty states, every province in Canada, and every country in Central America, it was unwise to bet against him.

"The badass mercenary you were telling me about. How is that coming?"

"Still trying. Like I told you, he doesn't want to be found."

"Is he really that good?"

Vance looked at Cash, who was staring straight at him. He nodded.

"I was trained by one his protégés. Heard a lot of tall tales. I have no reason to doubt them."

"Make it happen. Promise the world if you have to. He may be needed."

Vance nodded in understanding. Cash stepped closer to the screen, looking intently at the faces of the women.

"Actually, I can't help but admire these girls and their brazen approach. The one thing they don't have is money, at least not much of their own. Domestic shelters are no different than most charities, begging shamelessly for every penny they can get their hands on. Maybe they can be bought, and save us all some trouble."

"Do you think these two know what they have?" Vance asked.

"Let's find out."

Cash looked in his phone and easily found Cassie Snow's office number. He dialed the number and turned to Vance, who watched him to see what results a connection would bring.

FORTY-TWO

THE four women briefly debated the merits of Cassie taking the call versus having her assistant take a message. After a few moments of discussion, they agreed the best thing to do is have the attorney take the call and give her best poker voice. Any reticence might show weakness. Maintaining even the slightest doubt as to whether they had learned the truth could weigh in their favor.

Noelle quickly patched her computer into the call to record it. Once Noelle nodded in the affirmative, Cassie told her assistant to send it through.

"Cassie Snow. Can I help you?"

"Cassie, this is Damon Cash."

"What can I do for you?"

Cash sighed audibly, purposefully. "I have a unique legal matter I need your assistance with. I'm in town and I'd appreciate the chance to consult with you."

Noelle waved Julia and Yardley over in her direction. She handed them each a pair of earbuds to listen in to the conversation.

"I have a pretty busy week, Mr. Cash. Can you tell me what this is concerning?"

"I'm sorry, but I'll have to discuss it in person. I'll be here for several days, but the matter is extremely urgent. I am willing to compensate you generously to work me into your schedule as soon as possible."

"One moment." Cassie paused for effect, having the next month of her calendar committed to memory. The exercise bought them a few precious moments to silently strategize. Cassie mouthed "tomorrow" and they all nodded.

"I can do 1 PM tomorrow."

"Does the W Hotel downtown work for you?"

Cassie paused at the planned location, looking at the others. Julia and Noelle looked at each for confirmation that would work. They nodded at each other, then to Cassie.

"Alright."

"Good. Please also invite Julia Caldwell to the meeting. My understanding is she usually assists you as an investigator. Her input would be vital to me as well."

The women saw a quizzical look grow on Cassie's face. "I don't know her schedule, but I'll see if she can make it."

"Excellent. I will see you then."

Cassie ended the call, staring at her cell phone.

"What do you make of that?" Julia asked.

"He's feeling us out," Cassie said. "He's also too smart to say anything on the phone."

"So, we have the battered wife of a baseball player, whose public image is as pure as the driven snow," Julia said, sitting back down at the conference table. "He's a couple of weeks away from signing the richest contract in professional sports history."

"She's a threat to it," Noelle said.

"And so are we," Julia said. "If he knows our names, he knows what we do."

Cassie nodded in agreement. "He only has two plays. Pay her off, or—"

The room fell silent.

"Or what?" Yardley asked.

"Or eliminate the threat," Noelle replied.

Noelle's words confirmed the grave tone they all now felt.

"He knows more than we do," Cassie said. "The only place we'll get it is from her."

"Noey, what else do we have to work with?"

Noelle clicked her mouse several times. "I still have problems with her age and background. She doesn't look 30 to me."

"She also doesn't come off as a Texan," Julia said. "Her accent has an odd edge to it. Almost European."

"She's not from Texas," Yardley declared. "I doubt she was born here, and she certainly wasn't raised here."

"Why?"

"Phrasing she uses, I guess. It just doesn't sound right."

Yardley's Hispanic accent was still evident, but it wasn't thick. It flowed and she enunciated well. Her parents spoke little English growing up, but in school she had excelled in English. She could easily identify an ill-fitting voice.

Noelle raised a finger while clicking a mouse in the other hand.

"How about Russian?"

"Why?"

"I put her face into this program I've been experimenting with. Her features definitely match many Slavic characteristics."

Cassie slid her chair over to where Noelle was. The photo of April had dozens of laser-like streaks pointing between two points on her face. To the right, Slavic heritage was listed as a 77 percent likelihood of being within three generations.

"What about her voice?"

She nodded, and with a few clicks brought up the call during her escape.

"Her mouth moves a lot less than the typical American when she speaks. Another telltale sign is a harsher emphasis on certain sounds, which would be more likely exposed while under duress, like last night."

A few more clicks, and Noelle clicked on the screen at the end of the conference table.

"With the voice, the Slavic heritage is even more likely. 86 percent. Wherever she's from, it's not Texas."

"That's enough," declared Julia. "Let's talk to April again, and see if we can get the truth this time."

Julia and Cassie left the office and jumped in the Cadillac. Cassie rolled out of the parking lot and sped down Mopac, toward the compound.

"You're the attorney. I'm going to let you cross-examine her. We have to know what she knows."

"Don't you worry," said Cassie. "I'll get it."

"Just don't make her shut down. If she crawls into a shell, it will take us forever to get the truth. And we don't have time."

They stopped talking for a few moments, with the ambient sounds of an afternoon drive as a backdrop for their thoughts.

"If they know we have her," Cassie finally said, "what's to prevent them from coming after us to take her back?"

"Nothing," Julia replied. "Only the convenience of writing a check to get rid of us, as opposed to a messy tug-of-war."

"One they would win," Cassie ventured.

"They think so," Julia shot back.

With that, the silence continued until they arrived at the compound. When the XTS came to a stop, both women darted out. They exchanged nods with the off-duty policeman sitting in his truck before marching inside. They rode down the elevator, then found her room, Cassie knocking firmly on the door.

"April, can we talk?"

"Yes."

They opened her door and found her curled in bed.

"We have a problem."

Cassie's words were a directive. April cautiously removed the covers and sat up.

"I just received a call from Damon Cash."

Her eyes exploded in fear.

"You know him?" Cassie asked.

"Don't believe a word he says. He's evil, pure evil."

"What does he want with you, April?"

She began to cry, almost wailing, falling back to the bed, her face buried in the pillow.

"April?"

Julia's voice was tender, but it had no effect. April continued sobbing, almost hyperventilating.

"April!"

Julia voice was firmer and she grasped her shoulder. She turned to face them, but retreated, backing against the wall.

"April, we want to help, but if you don't tell us the whole story, we can't even start."

She shook her head. "You can't help me. I'd be better off if you just killed me."

"That's nonsense, April," Cassie said. "I'm an attorney. We can negotiate a divorce settlement, get you away from your husband for good."

"It's not that simple."

"Explain it to us," Julia said.

"That would take so long," April said, looking up at the ceiling, as if the mere mention of her story would be excruciating.

"We've got nothing but time."

April lowered her head in resignation. Julia took this as an affirmative cue and retrieved two chairs from the room next door. Cassie and Julia sat across from her.

"How did you meet Trent Tanger?"

"It was a party on campus, a college party. I wasn't a student, but they would take us girls there to see if we attracted anyone interesting."

"They? Who is they?"

"The men who owned us."

Julia and Cassie looked at her, dumbfounded.

"Owned?" Cassie asked.

"They called themselves sponsors. They told us what to do. If anyone argued or misbehaved, something bad happened. We didn't dare."

"Where are you from, April?"

She hesitated, then looked down. She had told too much already to hold anything back now.

"I was born in the Ukraine."

Julia and Cassie did not respond.

"I was fourteen," she continued. "There was an advertisement, auditions for modeling in America. I went and they said I was exactly what they were looking for. One month later, I was on a boat with dozens of other girls who were all told the same thing. Since my English was good, I got to go to America, but modeling was only a small part of the job."

"Prostitution?"

April nodded. "We were shown pictures of our family. We were told they would be fine if we did what we were told and made no trouble. Otherwise—"

She stopped talking. Cassie took a beat to let April collect herself and to release some tension.

"How did you get to that party?"

"We spent a year travelling around the country by bus. I guess moving around avoided suspicion. We were told to tell anyone that asked we were exchange students. We were stopped by police two times that I know of. I don't know whether they had the right papers, or paid off the police, but nothing happened."

"Talk about the party."

"Three or four of us were taken to this party. This man started talking to me. I didn't know anything about him."

"Tanger?"

She nodded. "He was barely a man, he looked more like a boy. But he had kind eyes and had these huge hands. Everyone seemed to be watching him, as if he was the most important person in the room, but I didn't know why. He said he wanted to see me again."

"What happened to the handlers?"

"I don't know. After only a few weeks, I moved in with him, and I never saw them again. Trent treated me well at first, compared to what I was used to. Cash never liked me, but I didn't understand why until later. Trent and I flew out to Vegas and got married without Cash knowing."

"When did he start hurting you?"

"After a few months. I took it for a while, but once, I tried to fight back. That's when I met Cash. He told me he purchased me because he had no way of getting rid of me. I was treated just like I was on the tour. The only difference is the food and shelter were better.

"The last time I fought back, they brought in a doctor to give me drugs to control me. It kept getting worse and worse until I decided I would rather die than go on. That's when I decided to escape."

Julia leaned back in. "So Cash knows where you came from. Does Tanger?"

"He does. Cash won't let him forget it. He keeps threatening to expose him if he does not comply with all of his instructions."

"How old were you when you married Tanger?"

"Sixteen."

"What happened in Hamilton?"

The question made her look up in alarm. A nerve had been touched.

"Sonny and Wanda Breyer. Do you know those names?"

Her face fell. "That's the farmer and his wife who took me in."

"So Tanger chased you down there?"

"Cash's men. They attacked us. I don't know what happened to them."

Julia and Cassie stole looks at each other, then looked back at April. When she realized what their looks meant, she put her hands to her face, crying.

"They were so good to me. They gave me their truck, made me run for it. I left it in the town where you found me."

The three women fell silent. Julia and Cassie looked at each other forebodingly. Now they knew.

"April," Julia said. "I don't care how powerful they are. We will protect you."

"They won't stop," April replied, unconvinced.

"Try and get some rest, okay?"

April nodded in response. The two women left her and went back up the elevator.

"What have we gotten ourselves into?" Cassie asked.

"A mess," Julia said. "A big mess."

FORTY-THREE

A T the corner of Lavaca and 2nd, a man in a sport coat sat
at a table and watched the street corner with his back to
the W Hotel. Behind the shades, he could have simply been
looking at the statue of Willie Nelson, guitar in his lap,
welcoming visitors to Moody Theater. Instead, he was on
assignment, looking for two women, their photos queued on
his smartphone. One was a thirtyish black woman around 5-
7, the other a white woman in her mid-40s, about 5-5. He
was merely to note their entrances and any relevant details.
When they exited, he would follow. Another man with the
same assignment was stationed at a bench outside the
Starbucks at the other end of the block.

It was a typical midday in downtown Austin, people
milling about in a variety of attire, ranging from business
suits to shorts and flip-flops. This helped the Hispanic
woman with Ray-Bans, a sweatshirt, and a baseball cap
blend in with the scenery. She sat on a bench, looking at her
tablet. Anyone walking by would dismiss her as someone
enjoying a mild fall day in the state's capital, relaxing by
catching up on her email or social media.

Instead, she had a handheld camera hidden inside her
hand, wirelessly connected to the tablet. She could move the
camera in any direction by simply moving her hand in the
desired position. She also had an extra set of eyes on her
camera feed, helping her navigate the entire area in front of
the hotel.

"Can you slowly pan to your left?" Noelle asked, seated
back in her office seven miles away.

"Alright," Yardley replied, adjusting her position in the
bench.

"I said left. And slowly."

"Hang on! I wasn't sitting at the right angle."

"Okay," Noelle replied, backing off.

"This is very nerve-wracking," muttered Yardley.

"Tell me about it."

Yardley shifted, then adjusted the camera in her left hand.

"Alright, what do you need again?"

"Just slowly move your hand from nine o'clock to twelve o'clock."

She did so as subtly as she could.

"Good, now switch hands and do twelve to three."

Yardley transferred the camera to her right hand, repeating the motion.

"Good."

"Now what?"

"Just watch for what we're looking for. Suspicious looking bad guys, loitering, I guess. If you see it, just point in his direction and describe him."

"Got it."

Julia and Cassie entered the hotel an hour earlier than the two hours prior to the meeting. A former survivor happened to be the assistant director of guest services. She lined them up with a suite to use and a chef salad lunch while they prepared for their meeting.

At 12:54, a limousine dropped off Cash and Vance. Across Lavaca, a small camera hanging from the balcony of the second-floor apartment went unnoticed. Noelle watched their enemies enter the W on one of her screens. A couple of minutes later, she saw them enter the empty conference room and sit down. She picked up her cell phone and typed a quick text. In the hotel suite, Julia and Cassie received the message.

"Showtime," Cassie said.

"Let's do it," Julia replied.

They lifted their purses and folios, left the suite and entered the elevator. As the door closed, Cassie looked at Julia. Neither was in the habit of letting the stress of their work show, but they could each see the gravity of their meeting on the other's face. They rode in silence.

When the elevator door opened, they marched out with purpose, walking down the halls to Studio 2, and opened the double doors. Inside, two men rose from their seats and approached them. One was around 5-10 and fit. The other was about 6-3 and as solid as an oak tree.

"Hello," came an eager greeting from the shorter man.

"Hello," answered Cassie.

"Damon Cash," he said, extending his hand.

"Julia Caldwell."

"Cassie Snow."

"This is Rudolph Vance, my associate."

They shook hands. Cash's handshake was firm, but Vance's was incredibly strong, and borderline rude. He squeezed not quite hard enough to be painful, but strong enough to communicate his power. Those huge, thick hands had committed violence. From the expression on his sinister smile, he wanted you to know it.

The four sat at the conference table, the opposing sides facing each other. Julia appeared serenely confident, unlike how she felt. Cassie seemed just as poised, but with perhaps a touch of defiance. If the ladies were intimidated, they didn't show it. Cash knew from his research they wouldn't be. They had an impressive record of defending their clients and destroying their enemies.

"What can we do for you, Mr. Cash?" Cassie asked.

"Please. Call me Damon."

"You said you had a unique problem."

"I certainly do. As I'm sure you're aware, my job entails far more than negotiating the best deals for my clients. It also involves solving some of their more unsavory personal issues."

The two ladies nodded slightly, while jotting something down on their notepads. They watched him intently.

"One of my clients is Trent Tanger. I'm sure you're aware of him."

The ladies nodded affirmatively with mild interest. They had rehearsed verbal and non-verbal responses to a variety of questions.

Don't play dumb. Don't overact. Show casual, measured recognition. When in doubt, stay silent.

"As you ladies may or may not know, he is now a free agent. He is in line for quite a payday."

"I don't suppose an expansion franchise in Nashville is willing to break the bank for him."

"Quite correct," Cash replied to Julia. "Are you a fan?"

Julia shrugged. "I follow the sport."

"So, Julia. If you were Trent, where would you go?"

"Depends on what he wants. Given that he's your client, there will be no discounts, hometown or otherwise. If he's interested in pursuing records, he should go to New York. Los Angeles is not much of a hitter's park, but that's his best chance to win a championship."

Cash smiled. He knew the ladies would do their homework, but he doubted Julia's comments were rehearsed talking points.

"Not bad."

"I doubt you've come here to get our baseball expertise," Cassie said, deftly redirecting the conversation, while reminding Cash they were on the clock.

"Our client's wife, April Tanger, has gone missing."

"Missing?"

"She may have been kidnapped," Vance interjected. The two women turned to him and considered him. He said this gravely, but it sounded hollow.

"How long has she been missing?" Julia asked.

"Three days."

"Have you called the police?" Cassie asked.

At this, Cash and Vance looked at each other. Unlike the ladies, they hadn't put much effort into their routine. They feigned confusion and uncertainty about what to say next.

"I don't say this lightly. Mrs. Tanger has a drug problem."

Julia and Cassie did not react to Cash's response, something not lost on him. They simply nodded, waiting for more.

"It's something we've tried to keep out of the press, with Trent's big year coming up. We've tried to get her help, but she has fiercely resisted our efforts."

"We fear her habits have helped her fall in with the wrong crowd," added Vance. "Once someone with bad intentions learns her identity, they view it as a quick, easy payday."

Cassie considered Vance for a moment. "What is your background, Mr. Vance?"

Vance stiffened. "I handle security for Mr. Cash, among other things."

"I see."

Across town, Noelle noted the background interrogatory, a prearranged cue. Accordingly, she focused one of the two cameras on Rudolph Vance and captured several screen shots for research later.

"What exactly are you wanting from us, Mr. Cash?" Julia asked.

"Please, call me Damon," he insisted. This was something that Julia hated, but she kept poised. "We have reason to believe that April is in Austin."

"Her drug contacts are here," Vance ventured. It was a flimsy interjection, that both women had to fight smirking at.

"Yes. And whether she is here against her will, or the better judgment she would have if clean and sober, we are determined to bring her home."

"What kind of relationship do the Tangers have?"

Cash shrugged at Cassie's question. "Well, obviously the stress of his career combined with her addictions have made things quite difficult at times. We work very hard to deal with the obstacles they encounter. Why do you ask?"

At this, Cassie looked at Julia before answering. "I don't know if you're aware of what we do, Mr. Cash."

"Please, Damon."

"I am a family law attorney, with a specialty in domestic cases. That's also an interest of Ms. Caldwell's. You have to know that we have a built-in bias in favor of a woman in the context of a troubled relationship."

"I am glad you mentioned that, Cassie," Cash said, pointing for emphasis. "That is one of the reasons we wanted you. We wanted someone on April's side in this matter. We have no idea the pain she is going through. All of my associates are men. We need your experience as investigators and litigators to make sure we are doing the right thing by her."

Now it was getting very difficult for the ladies to keep a straight face. "Okay," was all Cassie could manage in reply. Julia had plenty to say, but wisely stayed quiet.

"We're asking you to simply find her, make sure she is okay and bring her safely home," Cash pleaded, with all the sincerity of a politician on the campaign trail. "We understand that there may be great expense to your resources of both time and money. We hope this will be enough to serve as both a retainer and an advance for the time being."

Cash slid two envelopes across the table. They looked inside and their resolve to appear composed cracked. The amount of the checks in the envelopes stretched the edges of the blanks provided on the paper.

"Mr. Cash," Julia said, stifling a chuckle. "This is not necessary."

"We have not yet agreed to take your case," Cassie added as she handed back the envelope. Julia also handed hers back.

The men watched the ladies for a few moments before Cash took the checks back.

"Rest assured we will give your offer due consideration. We will contact you once we have decided."

Having reached a natural pause, the four all rose from their seats. Vance walked to the door and opened it for them, with Cash following behind.

"Ladies?" Cash said.

They turned to face him. Vance stood with the door opened, slightly behind them. Cash moved closer, a conversational distance, but still uncomfortable given all that they knew, most of it unspoken.

"Please understand that we are determined to have April back safely, with her husband. There is no price we will not pay to reach that end."

Cassie turned to Vance who looked down at her. There was an aggression, even a malevolence in his eyes. She met it firmly while replying.

"We will let you know of our intentions."

"Good. It was a pleasure to meet you."

The women left the room. Once gone, Cash nodded to Vance and they walked away from the door.

"Was it worth the trip just for that?" Vance asked.

"It was," Cash replied. "I wanted to measure them, search for weakness, vulnerability, or compromise. They would have been worthy adversaries."

"Would have been?"

Cash looked at him with a grim expression. Vance nodded in understanding.

"I'll take care of it."

"You know where to find me."

Cash left the conference room and the hotel. A limousine awaited him outside the front desk. His jet was already fueled for the return to the Metroplex. While he hoped to not return, something told him resolving the Tanger matter wouldn't be quick or easy.

Julia and Cassie walked down the hall and moved directly to the ladies' room. Once inside, they glanced at each other.

"Why do I feel like I just talked to a demon from hell?" Cassie asked.

"How about the devil himself?" Julia agreed. "Let's get out of here."

They retrieved their com units from their purses and put them in their ears. They left the restroom and marched in the direction of the stairwell.

"Noelle, Yardley. You get all that?"

"Absolutely."

"Copy that."

"We'll see you two back at the office."

They descended the stairs and entered the parking garage. Without realizing it, they were half-walking, half-jogging to the Cadillac, quickly getting inside the car.

"Let's take the long way. In fact, go north up Mopac for a bit, then turn back."

"Think there's any chance we're being paranoid?" Cassie asked, cranking the XTS and wheeling out into the sunshine.

"I'd rather be paranoid than naïve," Julia replied.

Cassie nodded in agreement. She watched her rear and side mirrors for any vehicles behind them resembling a tail. Julia kept her eye on her mirror as well. At the ramp to enter the highway, they saw nothing. Predictably, Mopac began to stack up, as it often did regardless of the time of day. The benefits of living in Austin had costs, and traffic was one of them.

The Cadillac was the last car in a long chain that seemingly extended to Oklahoma. No one was behind them for a few moments, then a truck came into view. Julia and Cassie both saw the truck drawing closer, seeming to pick up speed rather than slowing for the jam. The truck had a large, worn grill guard that looked heavy, and strong enough to survive a nuclear blast.

Once both Cassie and Julia realized the truck had no intention of stopping, the split second needed to get out of its way had elapsed.

"Move!" Julia yelled just as Cassie floored the accelerator while cranking the wheel to the right. The quick reaction kept the truck from crushing the car into the vehicle in front of it. The lost split second left the back-right corner of the car in the truck's path. The impact of clipping that corner was so massive, it sent the Cadillac spinning like a top, off the shoulder of the road and down the grassed embankment. When the car landed, it tipped on its side, then slowly fell over.

Julia and Cassie both came to at the same time, a few seconds after the car finally stopped.

"Jules. You okay?"

"I'm okay. I think."

As their senses refocused, they took in mostly sound, since they could see very little with the airbags deployed. Sirens wailed in the distance, growing closer.

FORTY-FOUR

JULIA watched as a nurse tended to a large gash on Cassie's forehead. Incredibly, cuts, bruises, whiplash, and maybe mild concussions were the only injuries the two suffered. Just as Julia felt fortunate to not have any wounds to her face, another nurse resumed work with her, applying a bandage to her chin, which she did not realize was streaming blood.

"You two are lucky."

"Do you feel lucky, Jules?"

"Not exactly."

"Well, you are," the nurse said. "I've seen lesser accidents do far worse."

A familiar face appeared outside the door of the room.

"Who did you piss off this time?"

Robert Chisum's voice was a dead giveaway, his slight grin making her realize they would be okay.

"What are you doing here?" asked Julia.

"Dispatch knows who you are, knew we were tight. He gave me a buzz."

Julia nodded. Cheese looked to Cassie.

"I thought having competent legal counsel like Ms. Snow here would keep you out of shit like this."

"I try," Cassie replied. "It doesn't always work."

"You know who did it?"

"We do."

"You want to share it with me?"

"Maybe later. For now, can you check something out for me?"

"What is it?"

"There was a gas explosion up in Hamilton with two fatalities a few days ago. It may be connected."

Cheese smiled. "I'll see what I can do."

"For now, help me up."

"What?"

Julia began to strain herself, getting out of bed. When Cheese could see that she was serious, he darted over to the other side of the bed.

"I don't think you're in any condition to move."

"I'm not ready to die, either," she replied. "Can you move, Cass?"

Cassie followed suit, grimacing in discomfort. "I can go."

"You two are nuts."

"Drive us to the nearest car rental place. We'll take it from there."

"Are you going to at least check out?"

Julia shook her head. Cheese led the two women out, both of them shuffling along as if they were recovering from a hangover, or the flu. He helped them into his truck and they drove off.

"You can't give me anything more on this?" Cheese pleaded.

"Not yet. Have to do it my way."

"As always."

Cheese quickly pulled into a car rental lot and let them out. Each of the women selected non-descript sedans. Julia's truck would be as useless as Cassie's totaled Cadillac with targets on both of their backs.

Cassie waved to Julia and drove off, their plans already discussed. Julia took her phone, which had incredibly avoided a scratch in the wreckage.

"Noey."

"Hey. Where are you two?"

"We got run off the road. By guess who."

"Oh, shit. Are you two okay?"

"I think so. We just left the hospital. Can you pull up Cash's client list?"

"Hang on." Noelle punched a few keys and clicked her mouse a few times. The long list appeared. "Got it. What next?"

"See if you can find a client who's had a domestic run-in. Preferably, one who's on a contract year and about to break the bank."

Noelle ran off the first two names. Julia dismissed them both.

"Okay, here's one. Jeremy Wickes, linebacker for Arizona. 5th round pick four years ago, currently 2nd in the league in sacks. Unrestricted free agent next year."

"And his priors?"

"Beat up his girlfriend his junior year in college. She dropped the charges. He also served a four-game suspension last year for substance abuse. Rumor is he likes the weed."

"Perfect."

It had been a banner year for Jeremy Wickes. His new defensive coordinator had recognized his abilities in his first season, moving Wickes like a queen on the chess board in the front seven, terrorizing quarterbacks from every conceivable direction. 14 sacks in 12 games had nearly cemented his status as one of the prime free agency targets the following spring.

His path to the eight-digit payday had not been without its bumps in the road. The wrong woman nearly derailed his career before it started. Sure, there had been similar incidents before and after her, but it wasn't really his fault. After all, lesser players had gotten away with much worse in earlier years, right?

Despite her agreeing to drop the charges, he still dropped like a stone in the draft. It was hard enough for a small school, Division II player to get drafted high. A character red flag tacked on to his resume made him a risk at any round, he was told.

Then, the third positive drug test. The team had warned him, got him help, even paid for "friends" to entertain him safely once he left team facilities. Those friends could not watch him 24 hours a day. They also could not medicate the mounting pains he pushed through every week to take the field and make plays. The weed did the trick if you gamed the testing schedules like the veterans coached you to. But the previous violations dispensed with the predictable schedule, leaving him to play roulette with random testing.

The current year, free of scandal and drama had left all that behind. He had been assured, through back channels, that the random tests were over. All he had to do was make it to the opening of free agency, and he was home free. He even felt free to toke up once and again to dull the pains of combat and finish the season with a flourish.

The church on North 68th was an ideal location for Scottsdale police to set up a speed trap. The officer had used it many times while on traffic duty. Today was a different matter. He was given a vehicle to watch for, monitor and pull over. The likely times of spotting the motorist in question had been provided.

As advised, the red Escalade sped past. Conveniently, the SUV was more than 20 MPH over the speed limit. No other probable cause would need to be manufactured.

After a short chase, the Escalade pulled over on McDonald, just past the canal. The routine traffic ticket turned into much more once the officer noticed the pungent smell of marijuana inside the vehicle.

By nightfall, Jeremy Wickes had bonded out of the Scottsdale jail. But the damage was done. A year-long suspension awaited him, and tens of millions of dollars had evaporated into thin air.

At the police station, the captain drew a satisfied breath watching the player processed. Upon returning to his desk, he picked up a framed photo of a young teenager. She would forever be that age in his heart, tragically taken away from he and her mother, thousands of miles from his current post.

His daughter had been brutally raped by the son of a prominent businessman. He served a nominal sentence, all but 10 days of it probated. Tormented by the entire affair, his daughter took her own life, overdosing on sleeping pills. Threatened with firing and worse if he did not end his protests in outrage, he and his wife moved west, and started again.

It wasn't right, and it wasn't pure justice, but his daughter didn't get it either. And he slept well at night and wasn't about to apologize for it.

FORTY-FIVE

CASH looked over the city from his office, considering his life. The drama of his client's lives had made things interesting over the years, but even that had become routine. The prospect of taking on a group of domestic violence advocates was oddly exhilarating. Despite all the risks that Tanger and his wife currently posed, he would have relished entering the ring with the scrappy vigilantes. A small part of him actually hoped he hadn't knocked them out with his first punch.

His cell phone rang and he picked it up.

"Cash."

The agent listened. He wasn't surprised at what Vance reported to him.

"Maybe just as well. Their injuries may overrule their nerve after a day or two. They're in the deep water now, and they know it. Let's sit tight and see what they do. Alright."

He ended the call. His assistant appeared at door of his office.

"What is it?"

"He's ranting and raving. He says he won't leave until you tell him where she is."

"Where?"

"In the conference room."

Cash knew who it was, without a name being spoken. He walked to the conference room, where his most valuable piece of property paced frantically, retracing his steps over and over. When Tanger saw Cash, he charged him like a lion in a cage who was just tossed raw meat.

"Where is she?"

Cash stared him down. "She's in Austin, T."

"You've found her?"

"No. Not yet. Sit down, T."

"I can't think straight, I can't—"

"Trent."

Cash grabbed his arm in a strong clench. The agent's grip got his attention.

"Sit down."

Tanger looked away from the agent feebly and dropped into a chair, putting his head on the conference table. Cash sat next to him.

"It's over, T."

"It can't be."

"It is. She's unstable, she's a drug addict."

"You're the one that keeps her doped up all the time."

"Because of the beatings you have subjected her to. We're in this position because of you, and only you."

The slugger began to weep. Cash had to keep himself from shaking his head. The best player in baseball was incredibly weak between the ears and inside the heart. Unable to control himself, he was subject to Cash's manipulation.

"You got involved with the wrong woman. It happens. You have to move on."

"I'm not sure I can."

"Yes, you can. I've introduced you to a lot of women the last few months, haven't I?"

Tanger sighed, nodding reluctantly.

"Monogamy is not something that suits you right now. Go home, sleep it off. Someday soon, your wife will be a bad memory."

Something in the way Cash said this sent a chill down Tanger's spine. The slugger looked up at his agent's gaze, as cold as ice. He knew he had seen his wife for the last time.

"Go home," Cash said again, patting his prized client on the shoulder. Tanger slowly rose to his feet and staggered out of the office.

The agent rubbed his face, suddenly ready for the Tanger issues to be over. Battling with the women vigilantes was fun sport, but the inconveniences of the side items kept getting in the way.

His assistant marched in again, urgency on her face.

"Not now, Shain."

"You need to turn on the news."

"Which one?"

Before he could answer, she rushed in and turned on the TV, changing it to a sports channel. It showed Jeremy Wickes, waving off reporters outside the Scottsdale jail. The crawl below the video gave the short description of the drug arrest after a routine stop.

"—Arizona linebacker was taken into custody for drug possession early this morning and bonded out this afternoon. The perennial Pro Bowler was surrounded in turmoil last season when the commissioner gave him only a two-game suspension after assaulting his wife three days prior to the start of training camp. The commissioner, already under fire for controversial changes to the league's conduct policy, is sure to be criticized now that—"

Once his attention was frozen to the screen, Shain wisely left him alone. He stood silently for a few moments, then found his cell phone.

"It's me. Find that bad-ass dude and get him here."

The response set Cash off like a firecracker, shaking his fist.

"I don't give a shit how much he costs, Vance. Get him here, whatever it takes. We need to start applying pressure on these bitches. Now."

Outside the conference room, Shain heard his voice stop and heard glass breaking, crashing against the wall.

At the end of the day, his assistant swept up the remains of the frame holding the baseball jersey of Trent Tanger. Per her instructions, she bagged the wreckage and the jersey along with the other trash in the office.

FORTY-SIX

JULIA entered the conference room to find the other three waiting for her, that in itself a surprise.

"You three are up early."

"Ready?" asked Noelle.

Julia nodded, taking her seat. She saw a solemn, focused group. The stakes had changed.

"Let's start with who you met yesterday. Damon Cash was born and raised in Orange County, California. Attended the University of Southern California and graduated with his bachelors as well as his JP. After leaving school, he began his career under the tutelage of Graham Younger. You may remember Younger as the legendary sports agent who was behind the strikes in both pro football and baseball in the eighties. After five years with Cash, Younger was convicted of wire fraud and tax evasion. Younger insisted he was innocent, finally taking an 11th hour plea bargain to avoid heavy jail time. Rumors persist Cash set up his mentor so he could take over the business, which, of course, he did. By the way, Younger is penniless and lives in a nursing home in Florida.

"He's the biggest and the most powerful agent in the country. His agency has over ten percent of the baseball players in the major leagues. He also counts athletes from football, basketball, hockey, golf, boxing, tennis, and several gold medalists from the London games. He also represents actors, rock bands and one rap group.

"Cash helped Tanger launch his own brand as a rookie. In two years, it ranked behind only Nike and Under Armour in revenue. Tanger's athletic earnings represent only a fraction of his stream of income, which will be even bigger in a few weeks when he signs his contract. Cash is known for not compromising at negotiations. He generally walks away from the table, finds leverage, and then returns when conditions are more to his liking."

"Surely Cash has lost before," Yardley said.

"Not very often. He also takes playing dirty to an incredible level. In 2002, one rival agent accused him of solicitation of his client. An investigation resulted in no action. Eight months after the conclusion of the investigation, the agent crashed his Mercedes into a telephone pole and is permanently disabled from the injuries. The agent was well noted as a teetotaler, but had a blood alcohol level twice the legal limit. The agent also claimed he was run off the road."

Noelle began rolling through a lengthy list of similar instances. In each, Cash's enemies met with remarkable tales of misfortune. Athletes, entertainers, front office personnel, even some politicians. She shut off the video screen.

"So, we have a survivor who can jeopardize a half-billion-dollar payday and put two superstar celebrities behind bars for life," Noelle said, neatly ending her presentation.

"What about a divorce?" Yardley asked. "Why wouldn't they give April a seven-digit settlement for a quiet, no-fault divorce?"

"Too much risk," Cassie said. "Just because we reach agreement on a dollar figure doesn't mean they quit looking for her. With a half-billion-dollar war chest, you could pay mercenaries for years until they hunt her down. Besides, being threatened, then run off the highway isn't exactly a negotiation."

"Threatened?" asked Yardley.

"They used the term 'kidnapping' under the guise of asking us to investigate April as a missing person," Julia said. "That's a threat."

"How much was in those envelopes?" Noelle asked.

"$200,000," Cassie said. The group took this in quietly. Each of the four was used to relatively large money changing hands in their professions. Being offered what amounted to blood money was a first.

"Noelle, did we get anything useful from video?" Julia asked.

"Not yet. No record of a Rudolph Vance that seems to match. We couldn't get anything on Yardley's friends outside the hotel either."

"What about Vance's face?"

Noelle shook her head. "No, that's Hollywood. Even the black-market stuff out there isn't foolproof. And even if I could hack into something like the FBI's database to use their toys, there is no guarantee that there is a photo to match."

"And there's a good chance Vance is a mercenary of some sort," Cassie added, "meaning you'd never find a trail of bread crumbs leading to anything other than a dead end."

"That's right," Julia agreed. "He's probably got a half-dozen identities. Cheese came back with the report from Hamilton. A gas leak is the suspected cause of the house explosion. No shell casings, no evidence of anything close to what she described, which confirms what we already know. These guys are professionals, and very good at cleaning up after themselves. They know what they're doing."

"Cash and Tanger are public figures," Yardley said. "Don't we have anything we can fight back with?"

"Any leverage we had was lost when they ran us off the road," said Cassie.

Julia nodded in agreement. "Our move with Wickes was just a shot across the bow, a move to keep Cash wary. He knows he's got more money, more guns, more men. The only question he has left is whether or not we'll bargain."

Cassie's cell phone sounded, vibrating against the conference table. They watched her pick up the phone to see who it was. The look she gave them confirmed their suspicion. She sat the phone back on the table.

"Cassie Snow," she answered, putting the cell on speaker mode.

"Cassie, this is Damon Cash."

"What can I do for you Mr. Cash?"

"I've received word you and Julia Caldwell were in a horrific traffic accident. Please tell me you two are okay."

"We've got a few cuts and scrapes, but we're okay."

"That's good to know. I'd hate to hear that the two professionals I attempted to hire had come to some tragic end."

"Let's cut the shit, Cash," Julia interjected. "What do you want?"

"The same thing that I wanted yesterday, Julia. April Tanger."

"We haven't come to a decision yet."

"Yes, you have. I heard your response loud and clear, all the way from Scottsdale, Arizona. Fair enough. I am prepared to make a counter offer. This offer will be my last."

"My new XTS will run seventy grand," Cassie said. "Our injuries, combined with all the pain and suffering we'll endure could cost much more."

"$2 million should be enough to cover all your expenses, provided you bring Ms. Tanger to us."

The four women looked at each other, taken aback at the dollar figure. The silence hadn't changed anything, just surprise at how high the stakes had reached.

"It's amazing what one more zero will do, isn't it?"

"We'll take it under consideration," Cassie said.

"No, you won't. I'm not about to let you string me along while you work out an exit strategy for my property. She belongs to me and my client. We either strike a deal right now, or I will have to resort to other measures."

"There aren't enough zeros to do that, Cash. We can't help you."

"You can't win. You know that. I have more connections, more money, more manpower. Your black hat hacker can pull every trick in the book. We'll still find April."

They looked at Noelle, whose eyes widened at the reference. She and Yardley had been insulated from most of the dangers of their efforts. The threat may have been offhand, but it was invasive, achieving its intent.

"And don't think Louisiana and Florida won't come find you two, and anyone else over there with a secret. Someone would have exposed you eventually. I'm afraid now it will have to be me."

The four women looked at each other. They all had seen enough to believe the agent could make good on his boast, bringing their past back to life.

They also saw something else, rising above their fears, a steely resolve. It was in each of the others' eyes. Once they all nodded in acknowledgment, Cassie snatched the phone from the table.

"We're done here, Cash. The answer is no."

Before Cash said anything else, she ended the call. The four women took in what they heard silently for a few moments.

"So much for stalling," said Noelle. "How long do you think we have?"

"Maybe a week to get her a new identity and get her out of here," said Cassie. "We can only hide in the shadows so long."

"Once she's gone, they won't quit coming after us," Yardley said. "Then, what?"

The question was asked of the group, but they slowly turned to Julia for the answer. In response, she rose from her seat purposefully, her expression hardened in determination.

"Then, we bury the fuckers."

The words sounded the alarm in each of them. There was no turning back now. The four women looked at each other in silent agreement. In each of their eyes was firm conviction, and no hesitation.

"Alright," said Julia. "We've got a lot work ahead of us. Let's get to it."

FORTY-SEVEN

THE man currently operating under the name Grimes stepped out of the limousine in front of Cash's office building, an ostentatious, gleaming middle finger to the rest of the world. Being money-whipped to take a job was usually a bad sign, but surviving several such jobs had set him for life. Returning to the United States was a risk he never imagined taking, regardless of the price tag.

He shaved his goatee, grew his hair out, dyed it and obtained a new passport. The new identity hadn't been questioned. Even in Dallas, only a handful of people remained in town who would remember who Skip was and what he looked like. Any of them would probably pass him on the street without a clue.

The driver handed him his bags and thanked him. He had barely taken a step when a young man from the office building approached him purposefully.

"Mr. Grimes, good morning. Mr. Cash is awaiting you for lunch."

Grimes took in the information awkwardly. "Okay."

Behind him, the hatch of an Escalade parked next to the curb opened. The young man took Grimes' bags, placed them in the back and closed the hatch.

"Here is the key to your vehicle. It's the Executive Steak House. Just follow the access road. It will be on your right just before the light. Tell them you're there to see Mr. Cash and they will take you to him."

Before Grimes could say a word, the young man darted back into the building. He wasn't sure what to make of it, but he shrugged and jumped into the Escalade.

Cash sipped from his glass, in a dimly lit private room. The 2007 Caymus Special Selection was exceptional, and he made a point of savoring it while waiting for his summoned guest to arrive.

The door opened and a man with dark hair with streaks of silver stepped inside. He watched Cash at the head of the table on the far end of the room carefully, taking a moment to assess the situation before approaching and stiffly taking a seat to the agent's right.

"Good afternoon, Jason. Thank you for coming so quickly and on such short notice."

"I postponed a very important meeting for this," the senator replied, bristling at the sound of his first name from one of his constituents.

"I apologize. The matter is very urgent. Would you like some wine?"

"What do you want?"

Cash glared at Jason Kent purposefully, slowly setting down his drink.

"What do you know about domestic violence shelters?"

Kent shrugged. "I suppose what everyone else knows. They are in short supply. It's a serious problem."

"No argument there, Jason. Unfortunately, there is a rogue group down in our great state's capitol that has taken their advocacy a bit far. They break the law, and the local authorities look the other way."

"That's in Austin. What does this have to do with me?"

"You have friends in Austin, I'm sure. And I'm counting on having a friend in you."

The senator measured the agent, his irritation at his disrespect starting to show. "Okay, what does this have to do with you?"

"That is not your concern. You simply need to reach out to your people and apply pressure where and how I say. When the threat is gone, I will let you know, and you can thank your friends for me accordingly."

"You haven't convinced me any of this is my concern."

"Plenty of people's lives have been ruined by domestic violence. Including yourself."

"Beg your pardon?"

"Your quiet divorce seven years ago. Joann gets more than the usual financial assistance, doesn't she? A 5000 square-foot mansion overlooking the Pacific Ocean had to cost a pretty penny."

Kent took a wine glass from the table and snatched the bottle. He poured himself a serving, shaking his head at what he was facing. The deal with the casino in Reno was supposed to be a hush-hush arrangement, but he should have known better that someone like Cash would be tipped off to such a tasty secret.

"Which would you choose, Jason? Losing the next election because of domestic abuse allegations over a decade old, or going to prison for multiple years for accepting bribes from some less than reputable gaming interests in Nevada?"

The senator lowered his gaze to the table.

"Imagine every network leading with your sorry ass being led out of the capitol building in Washington in handcuffs!" Cash said this with a hearty laugh, taking another swig of wine.

"What do you want?"

"All the protection those women enjoy, I want it removed. Send out the word that their days are numbered. Have all your media moles start dropping bread crumbs to their door. I want all their powerful friends gone. You know how to do it. I'll take care of the rest."

"What does that really buy me, Cash? What assurances do I have that shit doesn't come out anyway?"

Cash looked straight at him. "None. From my vantage point, you simply have no choice."

The senator stared at the agent, unable to speak, frozen in submission.

"You picked the wrong woman, Jason. Raised in a good family, taught right from wrong by example and not just words, they have self-respect. They haven't been twisted enough to devalue themselves. It's in the eyes, the posture, the demeanor. It all screams, 'I'm worthless! Take advantage of me!' Then, when a man of means like yourself or myself takes them in, they take whatever you give them. Their daddy, uncle, older brother, or whoever treated them like shit, they laid the groundwork for you. So, you feed and clothe them, show them the high life. That girl will put out, and then put up with whatever. It's their lot in life, and there's worse out there."

Kent realized that he and Cash were just as sordid, the only difference being that the agent had no shame. He had no choice but to keep his skeletons locked in the closet, hoping they never escaped.

Behind the senator, the door to the private room cracked open and Grimes entered.

"Jason, my lunch appointment has arrived. You may leave now."

The senator looked at the visitor, a large intimidating man, then back at Cash. The agent had already returned to his steak, as if he was no longer there. He stepped out of the way for Grimes, and stumbled out meekly. Grimes replaced the senator in the seat across the table.

"Did you do that for my benefit, or his?"

"Both. I wanted to humble him, and impress you. How did it work?"

Grimes said nothing, waiting to see if he would say more. A waiter came by and handed him a menu.

"It's all good," Cash prompted, pointing at the menu.

Grimes ordered salmon. Cash ordered more wine for each of them, and the waiter left the room.

"Did you recognize him?" Cash asked.

"He looked familiar." Grimes knew, but didn't want to admit that.

"You should. He was more than just an acquaintance of your previous employer."

At this Grimes stiffened, irritated by Cash's reference to his history. "I appreciate the lunch, Mr. Cash. But I didn't return to the States for a meal. Or a walk down memory lane."

"I know. Your fee for this meeting has already been wired to your account. I'd appreciate you hearing out my situation. Skip, isn't it?"

"The name is Grimes," he corrected sharply.

"Of course," Cash replied, realizing the nature of who he was speaking with. "You come highly recommended."

The man nodded acknowledgment. Even if the agent's reputation hadn't preceded him, he would have quickly taken stock of Cash as a talker. He would be paid well, so he would have to endure it.

"I am told you don't lose."

"It's bad for business," Grimes replied. He didn't add that the claim was incorrect. He regretted his mistakes of six years earlier, even though he knew it wasn't really his fault. When a mobster pays you that well for your advice and doesn't take it, he only has himself to blame.

"Of course."

"What can I do for you?"

"One of my people has a missing wife."

This brought a curious look to Grimes's face. "Missing?"

"Yes."

"Missing as in kidnapped, or a runaway?"

"Does it matter?"

"It could."

"My client has an anger management problem," Cash explained. "Understandably, his wife tends to run out of patience with his issues."

"So, she won't be returning by her choice."

"No."

Grimes sighed. He had seen all types of scenarios. Instances like this weren't worth the trouble, regardless of how well he was paid.

"And, her captors are two women?"

Cash produced their photos on his cell phone and showed them to Grimes who looked at them curiously.

"Vance said you had a theory on their origin."

"Not a theory," said Cash. "I know. The attorney, the sister, she's from New Orleans. Probably Lower Ninth Ward. The PI is a former cop. She's from Florida, somewhere south of Orlando."

Grimes considered Cash and saw his confidence. "Nice trick."

"Occupational hazard."

"So, what are you asking me to do?" Grimes asked.

"Their identities are as phony as yours. I need you to expose them, get their dirt. Whatever demons they have, I want to resurrect them. I'll need that and a few other things to flush them out of their hole, and get my client's wife back where she belongs."

"What is your superstar client planning on doing with her, locking her up in the ivory tower?"

"If that's what it takes."

"Who is the missing party?"

Cash held up a finger to pause the conversation. The waiter brought in more wine and filled up a glass for Grimes. He swirled the glass a few times, stuck his nose inside the glass briefly, then drank.

"Not bad, huh?"

Grimes nodded in agreement as the waiter left the room.

"The missing party is April Tanger," Cash continued.

"Tanger, as in Trent Tanger?"

"Yes."

Grimes considered the many implications, and snorted a small chuckle.

"He's only in about 20 charity PSA commercials. What a prince."

"You don't know the half of it."

"He can't live without her?"

Cash paused. "It's a complicated matter."

"How complicated?"

Cash bristled. "You charge a great deal, Mr. Grimes. A marriage counselor costs much less. Do you want this job or not?"

Grimes was quiet and unmoving for a long time, long enough for Cash to start fidgeting. Grimes finally removed a folded sheet of paper from his coat pocket and slid it across the table.

"That is for my retainer. It's non-refundable, of course."

Cash stared at the amount on the paper then frowned. He looked up at Grimes and his face was stone. Evidently, the amount was also non-negotiable. Cash studied him for a few moments, then nodded.

"The money will be there by close of business tomorrow."

"Good."

"Time is critical, so I'll want you to get right to it."

Grimes intended to fly in, consult for 24-48 hours, then fly out. This job appeared to be a bit longer, but the money that suggested the extra time would be worth it.

"Very well. Once we're done here, I 'd like to see the house."

Cash stopped. "The Tanger residence?"

"Yes."

"Why?"

"It's part of the job."

Grimes' expression was steadfast. Cash sighed, as if considering it. What he was calculating was if there was something there he didn't want Grimes to find. He was hiring him as a consultant, which put limits on his need to know.

FORTY-EIGHT

THE first bedroom downstairs had been turned into a makeshift conference room. The bed and chest of drawers had been removed in favor of a folding table and four used office chairs. April sat with Cassie and Noelle on either side of her at the table. Noelle had her computer ready for use, while Cassie produced a binder of large photos inside sheet protectors. She laid the binder in front of April and opened it.

"In these pictures is every Cash client around the time frame of the party. Look through them and see if any of them look familiar."

April nodded and began to look over each one. Cassie and Noelle knew there were plenty of decoys in the stack, several that looked similar to his clients, in an effort to confirm that her memories of eight years before weren't imagined or manufactured. They both watched her carefully to detect even the slightest bit of response.

She studied them slowly, passing through half the binder until she stopped at one, a large black man.

"Him. He's the rapper."

"Rapper?"

"That's what people were saying. I didn't know who he was."

Cassie put a small tab on the photo.

"Alright. Keep going."

April nodded, continuing. She turned over only two more until she stopped again.

"Him. He was there too."

"Are you sure?"

"Yes. They said he was a football player."

April went through the rest of the photos, then closed the binder.

"Is that it?" Cassie asked.

"Yes. Those are the only ones I remember from that night."

"Are you sure about those two?"

"I am."

Cassie nodded, touching her on the shoulder. "Good job. Let's go upstairs and eat something."

They went up the elevator and April went to the kitchen. Noelle and Cassie quietly went into the living room, walking around the stack of drywall still sitting in the middle of the floor.

"You know them?" Cassie asked.

"I do. They are two of Cash's clients," said Noelle, "or they were."

"Were?"

"The rapper is Redd "Line" Vernon. He went by "Redd Line" before he stopped performing to start producing and managing clients."

"I remember him," Cassie said. "One big album with a couple hits, then he disappeared. What about the football player?"

"Barrett Nohlen," said Noelle. "Broke every passing record in Division II. He was drafted in the 2nd round by Cleveland. Had a good rookie year, then tore up his knee in the last game. They waived him the next year. He played in Canada for a couple more years, then quit."

"Nothing out of the ordinary about that."

"Except that both of their careers took a nosedive shortly after the party."

"Maybe Cash realized the threat April posed—"

"—and kicked these two out of the limelight to reduce the risk of anyone asking them questions about who was there, and what was happening."

Cassie and Noelle looked at each other, considering the possibility.

"You're the lawyer," Noelle said. "You have a case?"

Cassie shook her head. "No judge would consider it. But justice won't be dispensed in a court on this one. We have to go get it on our own. We'll start with approaching those two. If they refuse to cooperate, we'll encourage them accordingly."

"Blackmail?"

"Can you hack into their social media?"

Noelle chuckled. "I could take your smartphone and post anything on anyone's profile as easy as ordering a pizza. I don't know what good that will do, though. The best part of Nohlen's life is over. His wife left, took the kids and most of the money. He doesn't have anything left to lose."

"What about Redd Vernon?"

"Do you think bullying a hip-hop producer is wise?"

"Is his street cred legitimate or manufactured?"

Noelle shrugged. "He killed a rival gang member at a club. The cops screwed up collecting the evidence. With no one willing to testify, he pled to involuntary manslaughter, served 18 months of a four-year sentence. He's legitimate enough for us to tread lightly."

Cassie winced, feeling continuing after-effects of the wreck.

"C'mon," Noelle said, noticing her discomfort. "You need something to take the edge off."

Sophia focused on the computer screen, keys snapping at 70 strokes per minute, followed by several clicks of a mouse. The work was overwhelming and engrossing, but exhilarating as she realized she had a knack for it. She never applied herself much in school, so her memory had never been put to constructive use until now.

Her regrettable past and her compelling surroundings pushed her to master her new craft. When Yardley brought up the possibility of being a transaction coordinator for a realtor, it sounded interesting enough. After spending two weeks sitting at a desk in a plush office, the thought of returning to working in a salon was gone. She didn't enjoy the work, only doing it because she learned it from her mother. She also noticed the sore back and feet her mother came home with every day, and didn't enjoy the prospect of facing that in twenty years. The idea that she could work for someone like Yardley was enticing. A walk through her house and a ride in her cherry-red Mercedes didn't hurt either.

"Okay," Yardley said, marching out of her office to Sophia's desk. "Make sure you have these finance dates noted in the database. Otherwise, the alert won't come up and we won't have done our check with the lender."

"Got it."

"And you remembered the signatures," Yardley said with a smile, clapping her hands gently in congratulations.

"Can't let the option period expire when negotiating repairs."

"Very good," Yardley said, walking back to her office.

Sophia lowered her head. "Are you ever scared?

Yardley turned back toward her. "Scared of what?"

"Scared he'll come back?"

"Every now and then, I'll have a nightmare. But they have faded over time. I've stopped looking over my shoulder."

"What happens when he gets out?"

"We get alerted when he's released. Then, we track him everywhere he goes. We also scare the shit out of him when he steps out of prison. Twelve months from now, you'll be well into your new life, and he'll have much bigger things to worry about."

"Is that how it happened for you?"

"Not exactly. Mine is a similar story. But the Shelter has come a long way from those days. You'll have a much bigger head start."

Sophia smiled, but it was a fragile, fearful smile. Yardley moved closer and took her face in her hands gently.

"You're going to be okay, sweetie. We'll see to it."

She smiled, releasing some of the tension. She hoped with everything in her heart it was the truth.

FORTY-NINE

GRIMES didn't enjoy mindless conversation, thankful that wasn't necessary with Cash. The agent was more than happy to talk about himself, needing nothing more than a casual nod of the head from his captive audience. The food arrived and was finished, with the only interruption to Cash's narrative enough time to send several text messages.

They finally left the restaurant, the valet delivered a Bentley to Cash at the door.

"You ever driven one of these?"

"No."

"I'll take us there and let you drive back."

They dropped into the car. Cash fiddled with a few things on the display.

"I only drive this once in a while."

He finally put the car in drive and wheeled out to the frontage road and then the freeway.

"Your boys are probably finished cleaning up Tanger's place by now."

At Grimes' statement, Cash feigned confusion. "What are you talking about?"

"Your texting. Your phone was in your coat pocket until I asked for a tour. Once you agreed, you sent off twenty messages."

"I'm a busy man."

Grimes returned a glare. It was clear he wasn't buying the act, so Cash shrugged it off. He was caught in the act, but it demonstrated the man he hired was no amateur.

He continued talking about everything coming across his line of vision. *This client lives there, that client had his DWI right there, I used to have my offices there, I know the guy that stole the contract for that there.* Grimes began to tune him out, simply waiting to arrive at the destination.

They finally reached the Tanger mansion, Cash retrieved a remote from the glove box to open the gate. He parked right by the front door and showed Grimes in.

Grimes took off his glasses and soaked in the sight. It was what you would expect from a superstar athlete's house, ostentatious and opulent, with no useful purpose for much of it. He paced around for a few moments, while Cash looked at his phone, keeping the man in the corner of his eye.

"Show me her room."

Cash walked in that direction, not showing how reluctant he was to do so. He opened the door and Grimes looked around. The bed was made and all was tidy, but there were always things that could not be hidden.

Like many clients, Cash thought he knew better than to give Grimes all the information requested. Some had better reasons than others, and Grimes suspected this was probable now. To combat this, he would gather data subtly, in ways the agent would never spot.

A few blades of carpet showed the last remnants of what might be blood near the wall. He knelt near the wall as if looking at it. When Cash took a glance at his phone, Grimes' steel grip right hand easily pulled the strands and dropped them into his coat pocket in one fluid motion.

"How did she get away, exactly?"

"Slipped out of the airport bathroom," Cash sneered. "Good help is hard to find."

Grimes shook his head. *Amateurs.* He opened the window and the alarm sounded. Cash's first impulse was to go shut it off, but he didn't want to leave Grimes alone.

None of this mattered to Grimes. When he opened the window, in both of his hands were two pieces of clear film. The film was mostly covered by his hands and nearly imperceptible to anyone not watching from a foot or two away. After closing the window, Grimes closed his hands, hiding the film completely from view.

"Okay."

Cash nodded at Grimes and followed him out of the room. Once Cash passed him to lead him to other parts of the house, Grimes glanced at his hands and spotted the color change in the film. It was fingerprints, perhaps of the runaway wife testing her boundaries.

Grimes humored the agent by asking to see most of the remainder of the house. Once he was satisfied with the time spent, he told Cash he was done and they left the house. Cash handed the keys to Grimes for the drive back. Grimes cranked the Bentley and rolled past the gate.

"Nice, huh?"

"It is," Grimes confessed, forced to appreciate the tastes of a sports agent with no governors on anything in his life. "I still don't understand something, Mr. Cash."

"What's that?"

"Why?"

Cash said nothing, irritated at the question. The big, bad mercenary was simply supposed to go dig up the skeletons on these women so that he could crush them. His insistence was another demonstration of his instincts, despite it not serving the agent's purposes.

"Why, what?" Cash asked dismissively.

"Why not cut her a check and send her on her way?"

"It's not that simple. She knows too much."

The agent's last response sounded ominous to Grimes. "About Tanger or you?"

"Don't be silly. We would love to pay her off, but she is completely unstable. We want some assurances she won't continue to be a problem for my client."

"Tell me what I don't know about Trent Tanger."

"How do you mean?"

"What's not out there that I need to know?"

"Such as?"

"What aren't you telling me?"

For once, Cash was stuck for words, or at least pretending he was. He paused purposefully before answering.

"Athletes are like stocks, Mr. Grimes. Their worth can skyrocket overnight, and plummet even more quickly."

Grimes nodded.

"Professional sports leagues have recently started embracing more stringent personal conduct policies in light of recent embarrassing events. In particular, domestic violence has become a very costly mistake to a career."

"Of course."

"I am intent on making history with Tanger's next contract."

"How much?"

"Won't take less than half a billion dollars."

For the first time, Cash saw something close to surprise on Grimes' face.

"Really?"

"Really. He's about to turn 26. With all the advancements in diet and workouts, I expect him to get that much for no more than a 15-year deal."

"Tell me about the girl."

"Her name is April. He met her at a party down in Austin when Texas was trying to get him to play college ball."

"Was she a student there?"

"No."

"Where is she from?"

"I don't know. She claims she grew up in a foster home."

"Claims?"

Cash nodded. "That's right."

"From what you said, she rarely ventured outside of this domicile."

"Correct."

"So, he was keeping her more or less prisoner in the house?"

"Prisoner is a strong word. She had a lot of, shall we say, psychological issues. We did the best we could to keep her safe."

"Medical records?"

"I can have them sent to you."

Grimes pulled the Bentley next to the Escalade in the parking lot.

"And, Mr. Cash?"

"Yes?"

"I want nothing redacted from your data. No secrets."

"Okay."

"I'm serious, Mr. Cash. I have many successful clients who swear by me. I also have a few that didn't follow my advice, and some of those few didn't even live to regret it. I can't protect you from what I'm not aware of."

"I understand."

"Looks like I'm off to Louisiana. I'll be in touch."

Grimes left the car, handing the keys to Cash with a nod as he passed. Once Grimes had left the scene, Cash retrieved his cell phone and dialed.

"It's me," Cash told Vance. "He appears to be as promised, at least sharp enough to know we're holding out on him."

He heard Vance's reply, nodding in acknowledgment of his warnings.

"He doesn't know what we're holding out," Cash replied, "Sure, he went over her bedroom like it was a crime scene, but what's there to find? The DNA of a woman who doesn't exist."

FIFTY

TOM Ashby's life was classic Americana, growing up in a time when parents let their kids go out the door to freely roam their neighborhood as long as they weren't late for dinner. The pain of his adolescence was remarkably small, at least in his memory. He was never without friends, male or female. He graduated from high school, college and graduate school in perfunctory fashion, starting and finishing on time. His career as an analyst steadily ascended like a clock ticking.

His personal life had been satisfying, while not without periodic difficulties. Entering the dating scene in his late forties had presented unexpected challenges. He knew better than to expect the single world to be the same as he left it decades before, but the changes in the unspoken rules were still more daunting than he imagined. The dynamics of a relationship were as varied as the number of women in the dating pool.

With several years' experience in this new world and a keen perceptiveness about people, the complications of a woman like Julia Caldwell were not as off-putting as it would have been a generation before. The single again crowd put a premium on experiencing life as well as keeping the heart under lock and key. Blurred lines and grey areas dominated, and forging a committed relationship was an involved process, if not totally unnecessary.

After that first night together, he called and left a message which went unreturned. This did not surprise him. Julia was a fiercely independent woman with a past that he guessed had its own set of unique scars. Likely driven in her work by what she had experienced, she would run if pressed. Besides, he knew a relationship was not like chasing a rabbit that did not want to be caught. It was a dance, and each dance had its own pace.

She finally returned his call several days later and suggested they meet for lunch downtown. Tom realized he was already taken with her, and was guarding against becoming too invested. There was a purpose for everything in her life. But he did not want or deserve the taxing of his life to untangle her issues, probably against her will. If all he did was serve a purpose, fighting to be more would be a fruitless, losing battle.

Hawthorne wouldn't have taken her for an ass-kicking, domestic abuse advocate, even though he didn't have any pre-conceived notions of how such a woman would appear. She was a lady, but she had a serene confidence about her. She could clearly handle herself, just by observing her walk down the street. It was no wonder she and her work had achieved such noted impact.

The long walk up 6th street to wherever it was she was going allowed him ample time to take plenty of photos. The pictures themselves were not necessary, but they helped frame her in his mind. She would not easily be accosted by a stranger, let alone cornered, without exactly the correct approach. Otherwise, she would slip away, or attack with ruinous results.

He finally chose an aggressive approach, a public ambush in the light of day. The damage would be limited to what she would do with others watching, giving him the advantage of choosing the venue.

He darted across the street, dodging traffic, reaching the door of the restaurant right as she did, grabbing the door handle at the same time.

"After you, Ms. Caldwell."

Julia looked up and saw a familiar face. It wasn't until she connected the recent events with the scar between his eyes and purple bruising on his eyelids that it came back to her.

"Hawthorne?"

"You remember? I'm honored." He saw the healing scar on the left side of her forehead. "You meet a customer tougher than me?"

"Not that difficult. Get lost."

"Wait! You don't even know what I want."

"I know exactly what you want, Gilbert Alden Hawthorne of neonmega.com. You want a story that will break the internet, regardless of what damage it does to the lives of the subjects of your story."

"But—"

Hawthorne grabbed her by the arm, and Julia froze. She looked down at his hand, then up at him with a glare. The reporter felt her coiled strength and quickly removed his hand, extended his open hand apologetically.

"Sorry about that. Look, judge me all you like, but I'm better than all that shit you probably Googled over the last three days. That's all the editor will give me. I have to go spelunking for the big story on my own."

"That's not my problem, Hawthorne."

"I know, and I know I can't bullshit you. I also can't bullshit my way into being the next great sports columnist. I have to earn it the hard way."

"What does that have to do with me?"

"April Tanger," he ventured. "What's the deal with her running from all those guns anyway? Give me something. Otherwise, I'll have to get Damon Cash's side of the story first."

"Good luck with that."

Hawthorne began to say something else as she turned away from him, but fell silent. A relatively large man eased up to Julia.

"Hey."

Julia saw Tom and smiled. "Perfect timing."

Gil Hawthorne quickly resettled himself. "Hi, I'm Gil Hawthorne."

"Hello."

The men exchanged handshakes. Tom's grasp was firm. While he had a pleasant demeanor, he was an imposing figure.

"Looks like your rescuer has arrived."

"I think I rescued you," Tom corrected the reporter.

"Goodbye, Mr. Hawthorne." Julia snapped, ending the conversation.

"Think about it, Julia."

"You'll be the first to know if I change my mind."

Once the man trudged out, the couple hugged warmly.

"You alright?" he asked.

"I'm okay."

"What was that all about?'

"He's a reporter for one of those online tabloid websites. I'm not all that anxious to discuss my work with the press."

"Understandable," he replied. It figured that there were always fires to be put out in her work. He perceived her high work ethic, but not at a pace that was manic or frenzied. It was like the steady beat of a metronome, which made her behavior even more curious. There was a method to her madness, and she was aware of every risk her dysfunctions ran, even if she didn't have the desire or will to control it.

She ordered a drink. The waiter asked Tom if he wanted another and he shook his head, content with the beer already on the table. He looked over her face and noticed what he thought were a bruise and a couple of cuts, neatly hidden by makeup. He elected not to ask about them.

"That guy seemed scared of you."

"Did he?" Julia said with a laugh.

"When was the last time you were scared?"

His question raised her eyebrows. "Scared? How so?"

"Not scared like having a snake jump out, or a near miss car accident. Scared like your career, your life is at stake."

"It happens, but I don't think much about it."

"I don't usually pursue things that have high risk prospects like yourself."

Julia fell silent. While this wasn't unusual, he could tell her contemplation was serious, even grave.

"I know there's a lot of things you can't tell me about what you do," Tom said. "I would guess that's because of the danger."

She nodded. "It comes with the territory. We face a lot of threats and we manage them. But there's one coming up that I'm not sure about. One that might be unmanageable."

Tom did not speak, instead taking a long draw from his beer bottle. He would not pry, which was one of the things that kept drawing Julia back to him. The message he left was unhurried and relaxed. He would make no demands, but she also figured he would firmly guard his personal boundaries.

"There are types of threats. Some are lethal, but their deadly nature is due to a lack of control. Those are easier to manage because I know I can control my actions and my environments. I must have control because most of my opponents do not. The ones that do, they are deliberate and even more dangerous."

"Is that uncommon for you, opponents that are more focused?"

"As a cop or investigator, no. In regard to domestic violence victims, yes."

"What's the difference?"

"The difference is that I am willing to go outside the law for victims. The stakes are too high and precious. I would lay down my life for someone in my charge."

She looked at him. He considered her words, then nodded. The nod was neither approval or disapproval. Acknowledgement.

"I don't know why I'm telling you this. I don't share this with people outside my circle."

Julia smiled at him. Her cell phone rang inside her purse sitting by the bar. She drained her glass as she reached for it.

"Hey."

She listened intently at her caller, then finally nodded.

"Okay. I'll finish up my lunch and be right over. Bye."

She looked up to see Tom smiling, almost suppressing a laugh.

"What?'

"Reporters, dangerous opponents. You enjoy it, don't you?"

"I do," she replied.

He didn't reply right away, as if anticipating for her to expound on her thought. He was good at this, and it irritated her after the fact. She ended up revealing more of herself than she planned.

"When I was younger," she continued, "I spent a lot of energy being afraid. When I got to a certain age, I decided I wasn't going to be afraid anymore. I attacked my fears. It's given me a better life. Not a perfect life, but one where I choose my destiny and not my circumstances."

Tom nodded in approval, but Julia covered her face in mock embarrassment.

"Ugh! I probably sound like a self-help guru."

"You did, but I bought it."

"There are days where I have to tell myself that to get through. It isn't always easy."

Julia stared into her drink, knowing that there were demons that still hung on, taking their toll. To Tom's credit, he acted like he didn't notice.

"Look, I know this sounds horrible," she started, "but I can't do this right now. I've just got so much going on."

"Can't do what? What are you talking about?"

"A relationship. I'm horrible at them, anyway. You deserve better, and—"

"Whoa! Time out," Tom said, waving his hands, even using his hands to stop the clock like a referee. "I didn't ask you to marry me. I just hadn't seen you in a while."

Julia caught herself and chuckled, hanging her head in embarrassment. Tom laughed out loud, gently grasping her hands.

"Have you enjoyed spending time with me?"

"Yes. Yes, I have."

"Do you want to continue spending time with me, at least when your world hits the pause button every once in a while?"

"Yes."

"Then don't worry about it. I'm not a teenager. I'm not going to pound on your door, asking where you've been."

"I'm sorry."

"It's okay. Really."

Her head tilted to the side, half embarrassed, half exhausted.

"You have something big coming up, don't you?"

Julia nodded. "Maybe my biggest fight yet."

"A fight?"

"That's what we do. This one, this one is going to be a son of a bitch."

"I don't think I'd want to be on your bad side."

"No, you wouldn't. Doing what I do, you have to play rough."

FIFTY-ONE

CHEESE kept a messy desk, almost as bad as his old partner. It was one of the things he could needle Julia about when she was a rookie detective. Now that she was her own boss, she could keep her desk as cluttered as she wanted, while he still had superiors to answer to.

Cheese's desk belied his competency as a detective. He closed cases and stayed out of trouble. Homicide was interesting, but he enjoyed breaks when he was asked to fill in for someone in Robbery or Narcotics. The variety appealed to him, as did the adrenaline rush when the heat turned up on a case.

He could see retirement from where he stood, but didn't think he would take it at the first opportunity. He enjoyed the work and the comradery. And, while he loved his wife, the variety and the rush would be gone. 24/7 with her would drive him crazy. He would be looking for reasons to leave the house. Why surrender his built-in excuse?

The phone buzzed mid-morning, breaking the monotony of reviewing a cold-case file from 1989. It was thick, with a steady stream of docs that, by appearances, led nowhere. The phone screen showed his commander calling from his office. This was unusual, as the commander would usually just retrieve him from his desk in passing if he needed something. The commander was not a micro-manager, especially with seasoned officers.

"Homicide, Robert Chisum."

"Chisum, come see me."

"Yes, sir."

Cheese walked down the hall and stepped inside.

"Morning, Commander."

"Have a seat."

Chisum sat at one of the chairs across from his desk, looking earnestly at his boss, curious as to what this was about. He had not been alone in his superior's office in months.

"I'm sure you have probably heard rumors about this domestic violence vigilante group."

The commander measured Cheese after his leading statement. The detective nodded casually, giving away nothing.

"I have."

The commander sighed deeply. "The media treats them like superheroes. 'Working outside the law to do what the system can't.' All that crap."

Cheese nodded again, with no apparent interest, waiting for his superior to continue.

"The mayor has advised me that several prominent citizens have been recent victims of blackmail from this group. These prominent citizens also happen to be key supporters of the mayor."

Supporters meaning campaign donors, Cheese thought. He nodded again calmly with a slight grin. *I understand, sir.*

"Obviously, the mayor wants to keep this quiet. However, he does want it made clear to the rank and file that there will be no more assistance, however subtle, from officers in the department."

"I understand, sir."

"These women, however well-meaning their intentions, are reckless in their breaking of laws. And, our officers' assistance, while for a very worthy cause, is just as illegal. Do you understand?"

"I do, sir."

"Very good."

The commander nodded and rose from his chair. Cheese followed suit, rising from his seat. They met at the door of his office with the commander holding the door closed.

"Off the record, I know you and Julia Caldwell are still close."

Cheese shrugged. "We keep in touch."

"It might be a good idea to go off the grid regarding her for the foreseeable future. If she doesn't rein her efforts back within the legal boundaries, it will cost her."

"I understand, sir."

"You're one of our very best, Chisum. Let's make sure that stellar record of yours stays that way."

"Thank you, sir. I will."

The commander patted him on the shoulder as Cheese left the office. It was an odd exchange, especially in its formality. He routinely gave him shit about putting on a few pounds or wearing a tie that looked like his old couch. A meeting like this one was out of the ordinary.

The meeting was a directive from on high. The Shelter's efforts and the use of off-duty officers was no secret. Cheese was one of many who assisted, but he felt the commander's speech was more pointed than other officers would get.

The lunch with Julia at Tacodeli had been prescient. Cheese had hoped she would avoid picking a fight with the wrong enemy. His old partner wouldn't be scared off by the lack of support from Austin's finest. He just hoped the storm, whatever it was, would blow over soon.

FIFTY-TWO

CASSIE had conducted many depositions over the years, but asking a court reporter to be taken to and from an unknown location while blindfolded was a first. The court reporter hesitated at the request, but eventually agreed based on having a trusted history with Cassie.

The conference room's subtle lighting was gentle and warm, especially important when guests were aware of being underground. Sleeping in a hidden bunker was less off-putting for April than it would be for most, especially knowing she was being guarded for her protection, not to prevent her escape. Solid meals, rest and relaxation had made her more vibrant, but the fragility was still all too obvious. She sat in a firm chair with a manila folder in one hand, sitting in the center of the conference table. Her eyes still darted back and forth when someone entered the room, as if enemies were liable to burst through the door at any moment, taking her back to hell.

Cassie entered with a newcomer in tow, a woman with a business suit.

"April, this is Sharon, our court reporter."

She greeted April, then took a seat at the far edge of the conference table. Noelle fidgeted with the small camera sitting on the table, adjusting the settings to make the most of the surroundings. Cassie talked briefly with Sharon, explaining what she could regarding the unique circumstances. The court reporter finally nodded in acknowledgment. Once Noelle pointed to Sharon, she cleared her throat.

"Raise your right hand."

April raised her hand as instructed.

"Do you solemnly swear to tell the truth, the whole truth, and nothing but the truth, so help you God?"

"I do."

Cassie considered her approach once more, even though she had carefully scripted it. Because having a representative from the opposing side was out of the question, the deposition would be viewed more critically if it ever came to light. Like a nuclear weapon, the power was in the threat it posed. It would have little, if any, power in a court of law. Leaking the video to the media would be a desperate last resort.

"State your name for the record."

"April Marie Tanger."

"Ms. Tanger, what is your birth name?"

"Taina Rustev."

"Where were you born?"

"Donetsk. In the Ukraine."

"How old are you?"

"Twenty-four."

"How long did you live there?"

"Until I was 14."

"What happened when you were 14?"

"I responded to an advertisement to audition for modeling jobs in America."

"Is that when you came to America?"

"Eventually. I spent the first several months in Europe working."

"Were you working as a model?"

"No."

"What were you doing?"

"I was a prostitute."

"Did you choose this work voluntarily?"

"No."

"So, you were forced to be a prostitute?"

"Yes."

"What was used to force you to do this?"

"I was shown pictures of my parents and younger sister. I was told they would be killed if I refused."

Cassie saw April's countenance wavering. She paused strategically, looking over the next few questions. She made eye contact with April and took a deep breath. April took the cue correctly and mimicked her. Cassie nodded approvingly and continued.

"How did you come to America?"

"The men and the conditions in Europe were very bad. Coming to America was motivation for the girls to perform well. Those who did eventually were sent here."

"How old were you when you got to America?"

"Fifteen."

"How soon after you arrived in America did you meet Trent Tanger?"

April paused thoughtfully. "Around twelve months."

"How did you meet?"

"There was a party in Austin."

"What kind of party was it?"

"It was a party with college students."

"Was it on a college campus?"

"I don't think so. There were students from several schools there, I believe."

"How did you meet Mr. Tanger?"

"He introduced himself."

"What did you think of him after meeting him?"

"He seemed nice. He asked to meet me again sometime, and I agreed. He asked for my phone number, and I did not have a phone. So, I asked if I could call him."

"When did you call him?"

"The next day."

"How did you call him without a phone?"

"The men who owned me gave me a phone to use. They told me they would send me back to the Ukraine if I did not make him like me."

"And he did like you?"

"Yes."

"How long after meeting him did you marry?"

"Two months."

"Where were you married?"

"Las Vegas."

"Did you love him?"

"I don't know. He treated me better than the men who owned me, so it was not a difficult choice."

"When was the first time Mr. Tanger hit you?"

April looked up in memory. "Maybe three weeks after we married."

"After you married, how often would he hit you?"

"Sometimes, he would not hit me for a month or two. There were times when it was every day."

"Ms. Tanger, are these pictures of you, taken four days ago?"

Cassie pointed to pictures displayed on a monitor to the side of April.

"Yes, they are."

Noelle clicked through each of several pictures, showing the cuts and bruising they saw on her when she first arrived.

"Who gave you those wounds?"

"Trent Tanger."

"How many days after he hit you were those pictures taken?"

"Four days."

"Has Mr. Tanger ever raped you?"

"Yes."

"Did it happen often?"

April shook her head. "If I ever fought back, that was his way of punishing me. I tried not to resist, but sometimes I couldn't help it."

Cassie paused, changing the direction of the questions. "Did you ever consider leaving?"

"All the time. I tried once. After I was caught, I was watched closer and kept home more often."

"Who watched you?"

"Cash's men."

"By Cash, you mean Damon Cash."

"Yes."

"Did his men keep you in Mr. Tanger's house?"

"Yes."

"Were you ever able to come and go if you chose?"

"Never."

"Did Mr. Cash ever speak to you?"

"He did."

"How would you describe your conversations?"

"They were mostly threats."

"What would he threaten?"

"He threatened to give me back to my owners and send me out of America, to a worse place, with worse customers."

"So, Mr. Cash knew how you got to America and where you came from?"

"Yes. He told me he had to pay for me."

"Did he know your age?"

"Yes. He knew that my identity and age on my identification were fake. He knew I was only sixteen when we married."

"Did Mr. Cash ever drug you?"

"Yes."

"Describe how that happened."

"After Trent had beaten me really bad, a doctor came in to give me medicine. She said it was for the pain."

"Did the medicine help?"

"Some, but I kept getting the medicine. After a while, I realized the medicine was to control me, not help me."

"Do you remember the doctor's name?"

"Pelson, I think. Dr. Pelson."

"How did you escape?"

"I experimented with the drugs and figured out which ones made me blurry and sleepy. I pretended to swallow them and I gradually became more alert. After returning from a trip to a public event for my husband, I escaped at the airport."

"Where did you go?"

"I hitched rides to escape town. I finally found a place to stay in Hamilton, Texas."

"Any reason you went there?"

April shook her head. "No. I was just trying to get as far away from where I was as possible."

"Where did you stay?"

"I met a man named Sonny Breyer. He and his wife Wanda took me in."

"Why did you leave?"

"Several men with guns attacked the house one day later."

"How did you escape?"

"Mr. Breyer gave me the keys to the truck and made me leave."

"What happened to Mr. and Mrs. Breyer?"

"I heard later they were killed."

"Thank you, Ms. Tanger."

Cassie nodded to Noelle and she shut off the recording. They thanked the court reporter, and Noelle left with her to take her back to her office.

"Good job," Cassie said. April didn't seem all that encouraged.

"Do you think this will make any difference?"

"It's all a part of the process. Hopefully we won't ever have to use it."

"You know he'll never stop, don't you?" April said confidently. "He may pay you, but that won't mean it's over."

"We don't let anyone off the ropes, either. You leave him to us."

Cassie squeezed her shoulder gently as she left to go back upstairs. April hoped Cassie was right, but feared she and her friends didn't realize what they were facing.

FIFTY-THREE

GRIMES braced for the landing of the Hawker on the tarmac at Louis Armstrong. In another life, New Orleans was a city he would visit for both business and pleasure. He could no longer afford the luxury of recreation for several reasons. His time and his anonymity were treasures too precious to risk at the moment. Cash had lured him by money whipping him. The money would do him no good if his cover was blown and one of his many enemies blindsided him, leaving his corpse in a Bourbon Street alley. Even stepping off the aircraft was not in the plan.

Near the hangar, a man in a sport coat smoked a cigarette, watching the plane descend. It was far more peaceful watching aircraft touchdown and glide down the runway than taking the ride. He hadn't taken a plane ride in many years, and wouldn't anytime soon if he could avoid it.

The plane taxied to a stop and the door opened. When the pilot looked at him and nodded, the man tossed his butt to the side, walked to the plane, and passed the pilot up the staircase.

He saw the man now calling himself Grimes sitting in a seat near the cockpit. Grimes nodded to him.

"Grimes?"

"John Crowney."

Crowney nodded and took a seat across from Grimes, the man he knew years before. He looked a bit leaner and no longer had his long locks of hair, but it was still the legendary wetboy he had once worked with. There were plenty who would pay handsomely to be alerted to his new identity. Crowney had a healthy fear of what might happen if Grimes survived such an attack, and then tracked him down. It served both parties to honor whatever agreement would be made in the next few minutes.

"Still working, I hear."

"Reluctantly. I take less chances than when we last crossed paths."

"Old age?"

Crowney chuckled. "Yes, that and two grandchildren. I want to watch them grow up, and remember me fondly."

"Of course. This is far safer than anything we did in the past."

"What is it?"

Grimes produced a folder and passed it to Crowney. He opened the folder and saw a photo of a young black woman. She was beautiful, but the look in her eyes was fierce. Her spirit was striking and leapt off the page.

"You're looking for her?"

"Not who she is. Who she was."

Crowney looked up. "How do you mean?"

"She's a person of interest. Currently an attorney in Texas. She has a history that likely originated here. A history she's tried very hard to hide. I need you to find it."

"You have anything else on her?"

Grimes produced a file folder and gave it to him. Crowney briefly perused through its contents, then nodded.

"Okay."

Crowney wasn't going to require an advance, although he often did when the client or the case merited such caution. Grimes was a man of his word, but he could disappear into thin air in a moment. Still, Grimes produced a stack of bills and handed them to the investigator, well above what he would have asked to begin working.

"If you get results, there will be more."

Crowney nodded. "Any idea when she disappeared?"

"I'm not certain, but her history begins in 2006."

"Katrina? Possibly assumed as dead?"

Grimes nodded. "That's where I would start."

Crowney paused and massaged his goatee, considering the task.

"I have relationships with a couple of cops who know their way around. I'll have them look into some things. I do know that the body count is sketchy at best. There's plenty missing that have long since been written off as deceased."

"Dark days?"

"Very. I was down here, back when I was still with the feds. Danziger Bridge, Henry Glover, and probably dozens more like it that we'll never know."

"Anything else you need?"

"Nope. I'll be in touch."

"Thanks."

Grimes rose and they shook hands. Crowney walked out the way he came. Halfway to his car, the pilot returned from the hangar with a cup of coffee. Before Crowney had driven away, the Hawker's door was closed and the engines fired up, ready to take its passenger further east down the Gulf coast.

Once landing in Florida, Grimes would have to deplane, not able to afford errors or wasted time. The weight of being stateside and vulnerable to exposure was worth Cash's payday, but only if the work was expedited.

FIFTY-FOUR

AMID the burgeoning hip-hop scene exploding on both the West and East coast of the United States, another faction was steadily gaining traction in the South. The styles shared common roots, but the results were disparate, in a way that excited fans of the music as well as the record executives who stood to make money on the trend.

Houston held its share of artists, some of which still thrived today. Many rappers who flashed during the halcyon days moved on to the rest of their life after the star had flamed out. Redd "Line" Vernon was the rare case of the artist who flamed out, refused to give up on his passion and reshaped a career to his choosing. After the tiny residuals had dwindled to pocket change, he started to find and produce other younger artists, guiding them through the perils of the business. Vernon had his share of scrapes with the law in his early years, but his word was considered solid throughout the industry. His clients trusted him because he invested in them, seeing them as more than a one-time transaction.

Vernon's signature sound was noticeable to trained ears in the business. He was noted for a simple, minimalist style that didn't overly rely on sampling, but still demonstrated influences from all musical genres. As his reputation grew, so did the variety of musical acts that enlisted his services. While the bulk of his work was with hip-hop acts, he was the guiding hand behind a lengthy list of rock, pop and country hits. He did not receive public credit for many of them, letting higher profile names accept the accolades. After pride had nearly bankrupted him as an artist, he chose financial compensation over the fame as a producer. The important people in the business knew Vernon well and he was in constant demand.

His early mistakes served him well, especially trusting the wrong people. He took the ride of fame, deferring the marketing and financial details to managers who talked smoother than any of his artists free styled. When the record companies moved on and he was broke, he promised himself he would build it back. He retraced every squandered opportunity, every gift to friends, and every liberty taken by his managers. Today, he was aware of every penny that changed hands and knew his books better than his accountant.

Julia had only scratched the surface of his biography, reading over the links Noelle had sent her to review before driving to Houston. The information there wasn't much to go on as she drove into the industrial park southeast of town, finally arriving at the address, a corner unit with several vehicles parked next to a nondescript building. There was no name, no hours of operation, not even the complete address on the windows to the lobby. The number "819" was the only clue that she had found the right place.

Inside was a reception desk with a phone, a leather chair and nothing else. There was only one door to the rest of the unit, guarded by a small doorbell and the simple instructions "Ring for Assistance" stenciled on the wall.

She rang the bell. After a few moments of silence, she could hear footsteps approaching. The door opened and a large black man appeared.

"Can I help you?"

"I'm Julia Caldwell. I'm here to see Redd Vernon."

The man glared at her for a count or two, then motioned her in, holding the door for her. They walked down a short hallway where the man opened another door for her. She walked into a sitting area with about a dozen chairs and three large windows situated on the wall in front of her. The walls to either side and the area above the windows was covered with gold and platinum records. If she wasn't focused on the task at hand, she would have started counting them to satisfy her curiosity.

"Wait here."

The man disappeared through a side door. Through the windows, she could see three separate rooms. On the left was a room with several electronic components situated around two turntables. On the walls were hundreds of vinyl albums, enough to stock an old record store. On the right was a sound proofed room with a drum kit, a few guitars and several microphones. In the center was the production section with even more electronic components and a huge mixing board. The waiting area was designed to impress, and with Julia it succeeded.

Four men were talking in the production area. Two of the men were black, and two were white. She didn't know much about hip-hop music, but she realized her own stereotypes in noting the colors she observed. The man who had greeted her in the lobby finally entered the production area, pointing through the window to where Julia stood.

They all looked through the window, but one man with particular interest. It was Vernon, who she recognized from photos in her assigned research. He stared at her for a few moments, then left the room with the others filing out behind him. A minute later, all five men approached her, with Vernon at the front.

He was dressed well, with a thin ribbed sweater revealing his ripped physique. A simple gold chain with a large cross hung from his thick neck. He raised his head, indicating Julia's time had arrived.

"Redd Vernon. I'm Julia Caldwell."

"I know," he replied firmly. "What do you want?"

"You know why I'm here?"

"I was properly warned. Damon Cash said you tried to blackmail him. You think I'm an easier mark?"

Julia sighed. Cash had guessed her next move.

"And you believe him?"

"Over you? Yes."

"You should know better than to trust him."

"He's the devil I know."

"Seven years ago, Rolling Stone said he bailed once you refused to honor your contract with the record company. You sued him."

"We reached a settlement."

"And you promptly filed for bankruptcy. That's not much of a settlement."

Vernon shook his head. "Be careful, Ms. Caldwell. You might not be the devil, but you're no saint. There's no honor in bleeding Cash dry, holding his client's drugged out, deranged wife for ransom."

Julia took a step forward. "Have you talked to him since that party back in 2008?"

At this, Vernon closed the remaining distance between them so that Julia was looking up at him. He glared down at her.

"Austin," she said, "college girls. Any of that jog your memory?"

"I have no idea what you're talking about. But if you try to place me somewhere that would be embarrassing to me, or subject me to liability, I will deal with you swiftly and severely. Is that understood?"

"He's got you scared shitless, doesn't he? A tough-ass rapper taking his cues from a man who sold you out."

"You want to see how tough I am, you come through my door spouting shit like that again. Right now, you're about to leave the same way you came. You come back in here, that won't be the case."

At this, each of the men drew closer to the two of them. Julia tried not to be physically intimidated by their demeanor and numbers, but it was impossible. She was a threat.

Julia couldn't tell if he was truly loyal to Cash, or if he had simply been bargained with or threatened. It did not matter either way, as he would not move. Neither were any of his posse, their eyes glued to her.

"If you change your mind," Julia said, producing her business card and dropping it on a nearby side table before turning away and walking out.

Vernon watched her go, then picked up the business card and looked at it for a few moments before producing his cell phone.

"Damon Cash."

He heard the assistant deflect his call.

"This is Redd Vernon. You tell him I want to hear back from him today. It's urgent."

He clicked the phone off. Cash had screwed so many people, it was only fitting that someone would target him. He wasn't sure he wanted to help the agent, but he was determined for his career to not fall into someone else's hands again.

FIFTY-FIVE

THE unforgiving mattress in Hawthorne's motel room had done a number on his back, making him feel like he was much older than his thirty years. He was used to unusual sleep schedules, but one of his few indulgences back in California was a luxury king size bed that barely fit into his one-bedroom apartment.

He had many clues, but nowhere near enough for a routine article, let alone the feature he was dreaming about. He was desperate to come up with something to salvage the trip, something to hang his hat on to see if he could convince the boss to give him a few more days without firing him.

Since Cash was back in Dallas, Hawthorne decided to go back to Julia Caldwell, who was in Austin. He had searched the internet for anything he could find about the private investigator, only coming up with a few minor news stories. Most of them were regarding fraud and insurance claims.

He searched her office address, then something clicked. She was in the same office complex with Cassandra W. Snow, an attorney at law. A Cassie Snow had appeared in one of the news stories he had found on Caldwell, a civil suit brought against a wealthy husband who had been physically abusing his wife. The investigator was one of Snow's witnesses.

Hawthorne drove to the building where their offices were located. All the parking spots in front of their side of the building were empty. He stepped to the offices and tried both doors. They were locked and closed for business.

He backed his car into a space facing their doors. Maybe he would try his luck with Cassie Snow instead. The attorney might tell him to go to hell, but she also might give him something, taking control of the narrative before Cash did. Either way, baiting her might give him some shred of information to go on.

The trash in Hawthorne's car was beginning to pile up. Neon Mega wasn't a dream job, but it was a job. He wasn't about to return to that spare bedroom in his mother's house in Omaha. As he settled in to the broken-down driver's seat, he concluded that it wouldn't be much less comfortable than the motel bed. If need be, he would live out of the car for a few more days.

His attention perked up watching a beautiful Hispanic woman walking from the opposite building to the door he had been watching. She opened the door and disappeared inside. Across the way, another woman left the Mercedes and entered the adjacent building, carrying files inside. A quick internet search confirmed the offices were for Yardley Ramirez Realty, with a photo that matched the woman now in the investigator's office.

The lights inside the office came on for a few minutes, then the woman walked back out with what looked like a few days' worth of mail. She was as casual as one would be in their own office. She belonged there. Maybe she would know something.

It is possible both were working at the same time.

Or, they could be working together on behalf of April Tanger.

Sophia walked into Yardley's office with another stack of documents, all collated and notated properly. She had turned out to be a quick study, enough that Yardley selfishly wished she could keep her. Her other two assistants were already overwhelmed, and one of them would graduate from UT in the spring. Good help was hard to find.

"I got those last two contracts done."

"Good, thanks."

Yardley saw Sophia sigh deeply.

"You think you're ready?" Yardley asked her.

Sophia stopped at the door. "I really don't know," she replied, still unsure of herself. "You tell me."

"You are. I told Tina what we're doing. She's already got someone who's graduating from Lamar in the spring. She said she's perfect to show you the ropes until May. By then, it will be your show."

"What's Tina like?"

"She's nice. She's a bit more demanding than me, and she sells even more than me. But I've sent two others like you her way over the years. They both became realtors themselves."

"Really?"

Yardley nodded. "By the way, there's an excellent daycare half a mile away. When the young one arrives, he or she will be set up. It's all out there for you, kid."

She nodded solemnly, still clearly unnerved by the coming change.

"Tomorrow is going to be scary, but don't worry. We've got your back, and we'll watch him. You shouldn't ever have to look over your shoulder for that bastard again."

The door to the offices was opened so gently that Yardley didn't realize they were no longer alone. They looked up to see a non-descript man in his thirties.

"Hello, what can I do for you?"

Hawthorne looked her over carefully while trying to not appear creepy.

"I need a house. I searched around and this popped up on the map."

"Good. Have a seat and we'll be right with you."

Sophia followed Yardley back to her office, then suddenly turned around, running into Hawthorne.

"Whoa!"

"I'm sorry!" Hawthorne exclaimed. "How clumsy of me. I was just admiring this painting."

"No, it's okay. I just forgot to ask if you wanted some water or coffee."

"No, I'm fine."

Sophia nodded. "Yardley will be right with you."

Hawthorne took a seat, waited the few requisite seconds, then pushed his smartphone to make a buzzing noise. He took a quick look at the phone.

"Oh no! My wife is tied up and I need to go get the kids. Can I just take her card and call her tomorrow?"

"Sure," Sophia said. "Here you go."

Hawthorne took the card. "Thank you so much. I'll see you tomorrow."

"I won't be here. Today's my last day."

Hawthorne turned back. "Oh no. I didn't run you off, did I?"

"No," she said, with a giggle.

Hawthorne smiled and waved. "Well, good luck then."

"Thank you."

He turned and walked out.

Tomorrow is going to be scary, but don't worry. We've got your back, and we'll watch him. You shouldn't ever have to look behind you for that bastard again.

The conversation he eavesdropped on between the realtor and the departing employee seemed to match. The woman was running. A quick glance at his smartphone confirmed that the GPS dropped into her purse was working fine.

He now had a bargaining chip. His story had just come back to life.

Neon Mega be damned. California could wait.

FIFTY-SIX

THE weights clanking against each other made almost as much noise as the high school kids yelling and carrying on. One of the two coaches assigned to monitor the room thought about many things throughout his day. He never aspired to be a coach, but had taken to the job. Working with kids was a labor of love. He wasn't crazy about teaching algebra, but it allowed him to be the quarterback's coach for the football team. The game was his true love, an addiction that never left him.

He tried not to think about what it had cost him. He and his college sweetheart married just a week after he was drafted by Cleveland late in the 2nd round. He was a small school project with a seemingly bionic arm. The team figured it was a good risk for him, allowing him to be third string behind two veterans, learn his craft and then emerge in his second season to show what he was made of.

Predictably, both veterans were lost for the season in consecutive weeks, leaving him to navigate an encyclopedia for a playbook, an iffy offensive line, and two diva receivers more concerned about their reality shows than winning football games. Four years later, he was out of the game.

It didn't shatter him, losing his chance, or his exile to Canada. Even as a rookie, he went into the league with eyes wide open. With all the effort he could muster, he was still battling incredible odds. He considered himself lucky to have a few highlight moments on YouTube, a decent start on retirement savings, and a tall tale or two to tell at the bar when he was an old man.

His college sweetheart had turned into a bitter wife, however. Entitlement built up quickly, jading her heart and killing her affection for him. Less than a year after his career was over, she packed up his daughter and served him with divorce papers, riding away in a car that would far outpace his salary as a coach and teacher years later.

Despite all this, he had made peace with his lot. He had seen the bright lights and felt the warmth of a handful of national television interviews after a stirring victory. His lawyer had fought for and won a just amount of time with his daughter. His reputation alone secured his place on the staff at his high school alma mater just outside of Houston.

Julia watched him go about his business from the door to the outside, talking to students, spotting them on lifts. She wondered before the approach if she could get him to talk, especially after her meeting with Vernon.

The man saw the woman standing in the doorway and marched toward her. The outsider stuck out, something she had anticipated.

"You have a visitors' pass?"

"No, I don't."

"I'll kindly ask you to leave. We've had some security problems in the past. I'm sure you understand."

"Actually, I came to see you. Barrett Nohlen."

Julia's words raised his interest. "Are you media?"

She shook her head no.

"What then?"

"I'm Julia Caldwell."

"And?"

"I'm an investigator."

He shook his head. "No, no. You can call my attorney. I'm not giving Courtney another—"

"I'm not here about your divorce, Mr. Nohlen. I represent a young woman, a domestic abuse victim."

This struck a chord in him, she could tell. His eyes and posture softened.

"Her abuser is a professional athlete, represented by Damon Cash."

He lowered his head, grunting. "So, that's it."

"That's what?"

"That son of a bitch called yesterday. Haven't heard from him in years. He's got two dozen messages on his voice mail from me over the years that he couldn't bother answering."

"What did he want?"

"He told me if I talked to you, he would destroy me."

Julia saw the strategy. Cash lied to and warned Vernon. He simply bullied Nohlen.

"Can he?"

He turned back to her. "Can you possibly imagine the invasion of your life when a professional team is about to hand you over a million dollars? Every one of those teams employ federal agents or cops to crawl up your ass and find every secret you've ever tried to hide. The agents, at least the good ones, are even worse.

"But Cash, he uses it against you. Every traffic stop with dope you got dismissed, every girl you went too far with, he's got it all. Once you sign with him, he owns you. Only a fool refuses him."

"So, the answer is no?"

"I don't know anything. Is he a merciless bastard? Yes. Did he go behind my back to teams, in favor of one of the newer, shinier toys in his stable? Probably. That won't help you. The only thing that will help you save your client is to keep from taking him on in battle. You will lose."

"What do you have to lose by helping me?" Julia asked.

"What are you talking about? Look at this," he said, spreading his arms. "My luxurious lifestyle doesn't impress you?"

"You could tell your story. Especially about that college party in Austin."

She could tell this gave him a jolt. "Look, I left that party ten minutes after I got there. I may have been a simple hick from the woods, but I could tell something was wrong with that scene. There's nothing I could tell you that would help you. And it would only hurt me."

"You don't know that."

"Yes, I do. You bring me in, Cash will destroy me, and then you."

"I could subpoena you."

"It won't matter. I'd rather risk a little jail time than Cash getting with my ex's attorney and stripping me of my visitation privileges. My daughter is all I care about. I won't risk the little life I've crafted out of this shitstorm for you."

He walked toward the locker room, not waiting for her to reply.

"I don't think you'll ever forgive yourself for not helping me."

Nohlen turned back. "Actually, I think someday you'll thank me for warning you to quit. That is, if you take my advice."

He paced back to the locker room. Julia watched him go, realizing she didn't feel any sympathy for him, but wasn't sure why.

The drive back to Austin was joyless with only the sounds of the road and the truck's engine in the background. The doubts started to creep in and she did her best to fight them off. When she finally reached the clearing in front of the fortress, the doubts were shouting a chorus.

The house was usually a beehive of activity, with several vehicles scattered in front. Only Cassie's Cadillac was there, parking in front of the entry to the garage. Cassie met Julia at the truck as she jumped out.

"Where is everybody?" Julia asked.

"Yardley and Noelle are seeing Sophia off tonight," Cassie said, wiping her hands with a towel. "Your buddy Cheese hasn't been here since Wednesday. His guys haven't been here all weekend."

Julia's expression told the story. She wasn't expecting the resistance this fast, this invasive.

"Cash?" Cassie asked.

Julia nodded. "Running us off the road was just the beginning."

FIFTY-SEVEN

THE theory hit Grimes shortly after takeoff from New Orleans. When Crowney mentioned Katrina, it occurred to him how many people unsatisfied with their current life might have just checked out. A young woman from the Ninth Ward who never surfaced after the storm could easily be dismissed and forgotten by the authorities with minimal resources to respond in such catastrophic conditions. Only her loved ones would wait for closure, with the passage of time making hope of her survival unrealistic.

What if the cop, who appeared to be the founder of the guerrilla group, recruited the attorney by rescuing her from circumstances similar to her own? Caldwell was 47, which would have put her at 23 during Hurricane Andrew. According to Cash, the record storm hit in his predicted area of origin. He would begin by investigating disappearances from this age range.

Grimes did not consume much media, but he often laughed at some of the ways Hollywood simplified and dumbed down complex processes in the effort to compress events for narratives that would fit neatly into an hour of television or two hours of a movie. One of the trendy concepts was facial recognition. Two detectives pull up a photo, compare it to a ready database, and voila, you have a match.

The truth was that private entities were actually far ahead of the authorities, or the authorities weren't willing to admit that they had delved that deep into the private lives of its citizens. The libertarian instincts of the tech companies were holding firm to principles, probably because the dollars had not been stacked quite high enough.

Fortunately for Grimes, he was not a sovereign state. He was a free agent, with no restraints in his personal bill of rights. He had also collected enough favors to get an audience with people in the tech community. On his laptop, he had a variety of toys for use at his disposal. Facial recognition was one of the tools neatly stored behind one of the icons on his desktop.

The tool itself was exquisite, but it was unable to access a database and simply roll through hundreds of images a second. He would have to manually select photos from a database and paste it into the program next to the most recent photo of Julia Caldwell. Once done, it would take a few seconds for the algorithm to run and give the two photos a numerical probability of a match.

A quick review of Florida high school enrollments from the Department of Education gave him a guesstimate of roughly 100,000 high school seniors per year, so roughly 50,000 females. Removing the panhandle and the Miami-Fort Lauderdale areas reduced that number to less than 10,000. Grimes began browsing the high school annuals online for the schools in those sections from 1987–1989. By the time the plane touched down in Orlando, he had selected three dozen photos as possible matches.

He closed his laptop and stuffed it into his backpack before exiting the aircraft. When the pilot handed him his suitcase, he only had to wait a few moments before the car service arrived. The driver took his luggage and opened the door for him.

"Where to, sir?" the driver asked when he was back behind the wheel.

"Downtown."

The driver nodded and took off. Grimes was confident he would soon find Julia Caldwell's identity, but the answers he really wanted were downtown with another contact. This was not in his job assignment, but he was determined to get them before supplying Cash with anymore of his services.

The car stopped in front of the Amway Center. Grimes paid the driver, directing him to a nearby hotel to deliver his bags. He then walked across the street to police headquarters. Reliable sources in law enforcement that remained throughout the years were hard to come by, but a few had proven steady and could be called upon in times of need.

Grimes stepped to the desk and the officer on duty took his request and politely asked him to wait. A few minutes later, a short, heavy-set man in his fifties stepped forward, both his buttoned shirt and sport coat straining to keep in the gradual change in sizes. He looked over the man carefully, unsure of who he was. When he stepped closer and saw the man smirk, the memories came back to him.

"Is it you?"

"It is. The name is Grimes."

The detective laughed and eased across the counter. Grimes followed suit, allowing their quiet words to remain private.

"How many names have you got, man?"

"Hopefully enough for one more move."

"What are you doing here?"

"I need a favor."

The detective straightened up, measuring his old acquaintance.

"C'mon back," he said, motioning towards his office. The detective dropping into the chair behind his desk, Grimes sitting across from him.

"What do you have in the way of DNA proofing?"

"Not much. We have to go to the feds for that stuff."

"Do you have someone who can run these without too many questions?"

Grimes dumped the bags with the strands of carpet and the plastic transparency with the fingerprints on the desk. The detective eyed the items curiously.

"Whose are they?"

"I want you to tell me. I know her name. I want you to find out who she really is."

"Where is all this going?"

Grimes opened his hands in resignation. "I have a client I don't trust. There's something he's not telling me about this woman."

The detective took the bags. "Alright. No promises, but I'll let you know."

FIFTY-EIGHT

THE Yardley Ramirez real estate offices were closed, but from the outside it still appeared active. All the lights inside were on and Yardley's red Mercedes sat out front. This was not unusual, as the real estate agent worked tirelessly, especially now that her children were mostly independent.

Headlights broke through the darkness outside, shining through the windows, letting Yardley and Sophia know that their expected party had arrived. Noelle jumped out of the Mini, a large padded mailer under her arm. She opened the door and saw Sophia sitting at her desk, Yardley leaning up against it facing her.

"Alright," Noelle said breathlessly, "I finally got it all set up."

She slapped the parcel on the desk, and emptied out the contents.

"Your name is now Sophia Thomas. It's not a new identity, we just had Social Security and DMV change your last name. Your ex is a loser with very little means and several more months in prison, so we feel the risk is relatively low. However, we've got him on our radar screen and he'll stay there, forever. He comes within twenty miles of you, we'll take the necessary precautions."

Sophia nodded, having covered these particulars with the ladies previously. She wanted to return to her family and didn't want to start over with a new life and no connections. In her circumstance, they felt this was not unreasonable.

"Your checking and savings comes through this," Noelle continued, showing the plastic debit card. "There is $2000 in your checking, and $7000 in your savings. There is also a Visa and American Express in there, but it's only for emergencies. If you must use it, let us know."

Noelle continued with all the newly installed elements of Sophia's life. Yardley had traded some favors to get her new employer to insure her as of her first day of work. Noelle had already transferred her medical records to two doctors, a GP as well as a OB/GYN. She found a house ten minutes away from the realtor's offices. The first year was rent-free, the landlord a domestic violence survivor herself. The cable and utilities would also be paid the first year by gift cards from their stash. There were also two burner phones, cleaned and ready to use.

"Are you ready?" Noelle asked. Sophia nodded, turning back to Yardley.

"Thank you so much."

"My pleasure, sweetie."

They hugged warmly. Noelle took her suitcase and they loaded into the Mini just as a cold, winter rain began to pour. Yardley waved to them as they pulled out.

The rain did not let up all the way to the used car lot in Bastrop. The dealership was closed, but a man stepped out of the lobby, clearly waiting for them, covering himself with an umbrella. The man motioned toward the Mini and Noelle rolled down her window.

"Go back to the service department. I'll meet you there."

Noelle nodded and wheeled the Mini around to the back. Underneath the cover in the shop was a used blue 2005 Chevrolet Impala. The Mini pulled inside next to the Impala and the ladies stepped out.

"What do you think, Noelle?"

She opened the driver's side front door and took a quick look inside. She then popped the hood and opened it.

"How many miles?"

"Just over 90. My mechanic replaced all the belts and hoses, gave it a once over. Tires are decent. It's ready to roll."

Noelle nodded, apparently satisfied, then turning to Sophia. "Will this do?"

"Sure," she said, not sure how else to respond.

"Good. We'll keep it under my name at first, then transfer the title to you once you're settled."

The manager handed Sophia the keys, then looked at Noelle, motioning to his office. "I've got the paperwork all ready. It should just take a few minutes."

"Great. Thanks."

The man nodded, leaving the two women alone. He knew the purpose of the transaction, as it was not his first with Noelle and her associates.

"Let's get your stuff," Noelle said, retrieving the suitcase out of the trunk and putting it in the Impala. Once she slammed the trunk shut, she looked at Sophia, whose eyes were wide with uncertainty.

"Are you ready?"

Sophia shook her head. "I don't know. Probably not."

The two women hugged. "You just relax, take it slow. And I'm not just talking about the drive."

"I don't know how to thank you."

"You just be on the lookout for the next you, the new you. Then pass on the card you were given and keep it going."

"I will."

Sophia stepped away slowly, then fell into the car. The Impala cranked crisply and rolled east down highway 71. Noelle smiled watching her go, then walked to the office to buy a vehicle she would likely never see again.

Neither of the women spotted the worn Nissan Sentra that had followed them from Austin, waiting at the end of the parking lot. Hawthorne was tired of the waiting game, already out one week of pay. If needed, he would make the story happen himself. He followed the Impala southeast on 71, wondering how far the lead would take him.

FIFTY-NINE

FROM the outside, the pool hall looked to be a relic preserved from before she was born. A faded Dr Pepper sign with an empty two-line marquee stood on the corner leaning slightly toward the intersection. The dated appearance of the establishment was too authentic to be quaint, the wear on the structure and surroundings too haphazard to be calculated. Despite its condition, the parking lot overflowed with vehicles once night fell.

Julia vaguely recalled the place from her days on patrol. The burgers, ribs and catfish would often run out several hours before closing time. There were also a few tall tales she remembered, of celebrities who had visited, of barroom brawls that had ended with one or more lives lost. In the early days, Cheese would bring her here, showing off his status as a regular by ordering his "usual" and hamming it up with the other patrons.

She maneuvered her truck into a parking spot across the street and walked toward the door. The cars closest to the door fit into the old drive-thru spots that still had a menu board and speaker attached. Inside, she saw four pool tables in the center of the room. Restaurant booths lined the edges of the room. The bar was immediately to her left. She walked to the bar as the bartender watched her approach carefully.

"Chisum."

"Beg your pardon?"

Out of the corner of her eye, she saw a figure moving in the back, slipping through the exit door.

"Never mind."

Julia darted back out the front door and marched to the far corner of the building. When she turned the corner, she was met by Cheese, who stopped abruptly a few feet in front of her.

"You want to tell me what the hell is going on?"

Cheese turned away from her glare, unsure of how to respond.

"What happened?" she persisted. "Why are you running from me? What happened to you, Powell, and the other guys?"

"You finally picked the wrong fight. I told you."

"C'mon, Cheese! With your reputation? They can't do anything to you."

Cheese laughed. "You are so naïve. My captain told me to stay away from you, period. You know what it's about, don't you?"

Julia nodded.

"I told you this was going to happen. You never listen. Kidnapping, extortion? Really?"

"It's not what you think."

"Then, what is it? How am I supposed to stand by you when you keep giving me cards from the bottom of the deck?"

"I can't always tell you the specifics of what we do and who we deal with. You know that!"

"You can tell me when it suits you, when you need a favor or two to corner the little guys. When you get a fish on the line that's too big to handle, it's all hush-hush."

"So, when the temperature gets turned up just a little, you run and hide."

"Don't give me that shit. I have been covering your ass every day on and off the force until now."

She threw her arms up and turned away.

"The only reason the captain would do that is if you were part of an active investigation. I'll do what I can to cover you, but you have to tell me straight up. I can't afford to get any more heat on this. I have a family to support."

"I understand, but I can't tell you. It's probably better you stay clear, anyway. At least until all this blows over."

"Will this really blow over? Something this big, it's not going away."

Julia's eyes shifted, the gravity of the mounting battle growing.

"Is it worth going down for? For good?"

Julia's expression hardened. "If I pick a fight, I intend to win it. I damn sure won't quit it."

They shared a knowing look. She turned away, walking back to the truck.

"You have to quit this, Jules," Cheese said.

"Quit? Quit what?"

"This crusade. You've taken it too far for years, and now it's caught up with you."

"Too far?" she snapped, marching back to him. "How far is too far, Cheese? Which victims am I supposed to pass over? I don't make those decisions. That's why I don't work for the city, or the county, or the state anymore. I don't do all this shit to make the stats look good for politicians. I do this to save the lives of people who can't do it themselves. There is no 'too far' for them in my book."

"This isn't just about them, is it? It's about you. You can't abide by any rules except your own. You couldn't follow orders on the force, and you can't follow the law working for yourself."

"Cheese."

"Back then, it only cost you your badge. This time, it will be your life."

"Stop it!"

"And that flask you carry around with you won't change any of it!"

At this, Julia slugged him in his jaw. Cheese absorbed the blow, falling back, surprised at the power she packed. She bent over, shaking the pain from her hand.

"After all these years, if that's really how you feel about me, you can go fuck yourself."

She turned away, marching to the truck. To know that your friend never believed in your cause, that he always had doubts about you, was far more wounding than any physical blow she would absorb.

Cheese watched her go, pissed at Julia, pissed at himself. He hoped their friendship would survive this, but he was more worried about his friend's fate at the moment.

SIXTY

THE calm was unnerving to Cash, fidgeting in his office. He had made all his calls, checked in with every potential client and connection, and was left with waiting. Ordinarily he would have jetted off somewhere, mixing the business of working his clients and their employers with pleasure. But the Tanger matter required him sitting tight, with nothing to do but watch his phones for messages that would resolve the matter. Only a $25 million-dollar payday, done with the stroke of a client's pen, could cause such inertia in his behavior.

There was still the media left, but even most of his work there was done. He had used every member of the fourth estate, dropping hints and creating smokescreens to shift the narrative to fit his interests for his clients, especially Tanger. The best and most reliable media sources had long since quit playing along with his games, seeing through his strategies. By now, even the hacks who called themselves "insiders," simply regurgitating things they had heard second or third hand, wouldn't bite on the chum he threw on the water. The handful of teams in play now had everything in front of them, as long as a bombshell didn't catch them all unawares and destroy the biggest contract in team sports history.

The phone on the desk buzzed and he picked up the receiver, thankful for a break in the quiet.

"Yes."

"There's a call you might want to take. It's Gil Hawthorne."

The name sounded familiar, but he wasn't sure why.

"Where do I know that name from?"

"He's that reporter we threw out of here a couple of weeks ago."

"Dammit, Shain. Get rid of him. What are—"

"Damon, you might want to take this. It's about Tanger."

Cash smelled some sort of ploy. He sighed deeply, before deciding he better at least hear the pitch.

"Alright. Go ahead."

The call connected.

"Damon Cash."

"Damon, this is Gil Hawthorne with Neon Mega."

"I know who are. You have sixty seconds. Go."

"Still having trouble with those domestic violence freedom fighters? I can help you."

"I have no idea what you're referencing, Hawthorne," Cash said, not yet piqued by the reporter's clues, and not about to take the bait.

"I'll bet you already have a full workup on all their clients over the years, don't you?"

"Thirty seconds."

"Does the name Sophia Ricks ring a bell?"

Cash paused tellingly. "And if it did?"

"Your freedom fighters just set her up with a new location and a new identity, one which I know."

Cash was now clicking through his computer, looking through emails that Vance had sent him. There were three lists, each in its own email message. He had browsed them enough to remember Sophia Ricks name, but not enough to have her details committed to memory.

"Hold, please."

The second email held the name Hawthorne had referenced. Cash clicked the link and spent a minute scrolling through the particulars.

Maybe the press can still help me after all.

Cash picked up the line.

"For the sake of argument, let's say I'm interested. What do you want?"

"You give me an exclusive, behind the scenes look at Trent Tanger in the days leading up to his big payday. I paint a clean, wholesome picture of both you and Tanger, leaving all the ugly stuff on the cutting room floor. You see every word before it's printed and get full editorial control. You help broker the story to a major outlet, and help me get a job. In return, I give you her location, and forget it ever happened."

"Have you shared this with anyone? Your editor, your girlfriend, anybody?"

"Nope."

"Keep it that way, or you get nothing."

"Understood."

"Give me a number where I can reach you."

Cash jotted down the number.

"Alright. Be ready for my call."

With that, Cash hung up the phone. He took a moment to take in what just happened, considering the risk that he was being played. He thought through all the possibilities, making sure he could employ the necessary safeguards to prevent disaster. His face turned from steely focus into satisfaction, his pursed lips morphing into a malevolent smile as he retrieved his cell phone.

"Judge Prosser, Damon Cash here."

The two quickly began to laugh like old friends, recounting their fun months earlier in the Caribbean. With the benefit of no cameras, eyes or ears to report what happened there, they shared a bond of secrecy that had proved mutually beneficial over many years.

"I'm sure they'll have the greens back to championship level by the time we're ready to go back. We definitely need to make that a standing event on the calendar."

They continued talking, Cash clearly reveling in the judge's animated enthusiasm. Once the pleasantries ended, he took charge of the conversation.

"I'm interested in a case coming up in the docket of one of your contemporaries. I'd like to provide some information that would prove pivotal."

Cash smiled at the judge's response, putting his feet on the desk in satisfaction.

"The name of the accused is Brad Benton. I would certainly appreciate you looking into it yourself and advising the presiding judge accordingly."

SIXTY-ONE

JULIA slept late, which was telling. The alcohol usually afforded her rest regardless of the hell she had endured the previous day.

Seemingly hopeless situations were nothing new. There was always an answer, she told the others. It wasn't necessarily easy or appealing, but there were options to choose from. Late at night, after a grueling day with everything against you, was the worst moment to assess your prospects. The light of the next morning broadened your perspective, opened your eyes to things despair had clouded your mind and heart from seeing.

It was morning. She didn't feel rested. She didn't feel like getting out of bed. And she felt worse about their chances.

This wasn't the first time an abuser had pushed back. She should have known Cash would be far more dangerous than others they had dealt with. That they so quickly got to Cheese was disheartening and frightening. That they had targeted and overpowered Julia's staunchest defender concerned her. While she might not have done anything differently, underestimating his nerve and his reach made her angry at herself.

Surrender was not an option, especially with April's life at stake. They could send April away with a new identity and passport, but with what resources? If the authorities hemmed them in and Cash bled them dry, she would be stranded far away with no support. Then Cash would hunt her down, something Julia promised her wouldn't happen. He had countered their every move, and now had them on the run. She wasn't sure what to tell her three partners, but being overpowered was a very real fear she was not ready to admit to them.

Julia knew the answer wouldn't be found in her bedroom. At the office, maybe there was a thread to pull and unravel the net Cash had spread around them.

She quickly showered and made herself presentable, then left for the office in the rental car. The birds had shown what they thought of her rental, or her judgment in leaving it in the driveway overnight. The collection of junk in the garage only allowed room for her truck. She wondered how long she should continue with the rental and if it really offered any protection from their enemies. Cash isn't omnipotent, she concluded, dismissing the thought.

Right after turning out of her neighborhood, she saw red and blue lights approaching behind her. The stop sign she was in the habit of rolling through had finally caught her.

"Shit," she muttered, pulling into the parking lot of an empty strip center off 71 just outside of the Austin city limits. An officer appeared at the side of the car.

"License and registration, please."

Julia handed them over without even looking directly at him. He took the items from her and looked them over.

"Could you step out of the car please, Ms. Caldwell?"

"I beg your pardon?"

"Please, ma'am. Step out of the car."

Julia shook her head, just anxious to get it over with. She showed her hands freely.

"Hands on the car, please. Spread your feet."

Now that her hands were up and she was vulnerable, she sensed something wrong.

"What is the charge, officer?"

"Do you have a permit to carry that weapon?" he asked, noting the gun at her side.

"Yes, I do," Julia snapped. "Will you please tell me what this about?"

"You're under arrest. Lace your hands behind your back."

"I have a right to know the charges before you take me into custody."

A second officer appeared, moving around the far side of the car and the front hood, to her other side. His weapon was drawn and trained on her.

"Do as he says. Now!"

By now, Julia knew her instincts were correct, alerting her a moment too late. She was in trouble, as these were not lawmen. She realized further resisting could not help her now. Her only hope was to play along and act naïve, while searching for some weakness. She slowly put her hands behind her.

"Again, what am I charged with?"

"Kidnapping. Aiding and abetting a fugitive."

They loaded her into the squad car and proceeded into town. Predictably, they passed where an officer in that jurisdiction would turn.

"How much farther is the station, officers? I need to pee."

The men laughed. "Ms. Caldwell, you have much bigger problems to consider."

"Such as?"

"You'll soon see."

Once 71 connected with 290 and passed under 35, they turned into the empty parking lot of an office building. The car sped into the parking garage, making its way up eight floors to the top of the garage and open air. Three more vehicles awaited them, two SUVs and a limousine.

The police car stopped abruptly and the men stepped out. They quickly shed their uniforms, then pulled Julia out of the car, removing her cuffs. She turned around to see a dozen large men circled around her.

"Alright. Any of you assholes want to tell me what this is about?"

"That's my job."

Emerging from the limo with a shit-eating grin on his face was Cash. Julia laughed at the sight of him, the theatrics he was employing overcoming her tension. She looked at him pitifully.

"What do you want, Cash?"

"The same thing I wanted the last time we spoke. As promised, I'm prepared to deal with you fairly."

Cash snapped his fingers and two nearby men pulled a large duffel bag out of one of the SUVs, dropping it to the ground in front of her with a heavy thump.

"Gee, I wonder what's in the bag."

"Take a look."

Julia stepped forward, knowing what was inside before she unzipped the bag. Stacks of bound $50 and $100 bills sat in a scattered pile.

"How much?"

"Two million. As promised."

She stared at the money, hard to believe how tantalizing it was, despite knowing she could never take the money.

"See how differently you feel about the offer when the money is not figurative? Nine times out of ten, it closes the deal with these dumbass jocks. They can't resist."

Julia took a deep breath and refocused on Cash.

"But you're not like them, are you?" Cash continued. "You're a crusader, a true believer. You'll never sell out, and you'll die without a penny to your name. But your conscience will sleep well at night."

"I'd like to think so."

"Then consider this. How will your conscience sleep when I take back April by force from you, and you get nothing? You stand on your principles, all in defense of a drugged-out street girl whose only motivation is to make a play for my client's money."

"You forgot illegal alien, taken for sex trafficking against her will."

Cash shrugged. "None of that matters. You're not going to risk having her show up anywhere near a courtroom. Because you know and I know, she belongs to me. It's just a matter of when I take her from you."

Julia just stood there, staring him down, unmoved.

"Two million dollars. Think how much good that would do for domestic violence victims in the Austin area. Just tell me where the girl is. I promise I will get her away from Tanger very soon, and take care of her."

"Take care of her. Is that what you call it?"

"Besides, you have no choice."

Julia pulled one of the stacks of money out, flipping through the bills. This was part curiosity, part stalling, part considering her options, all of them quickly dwindling. She didn't think they would kill her, since she still had something Cash wanted, but that was no guarantee. But there was pain ahead, and she braced for it, preparing her mind and spirit.

"Sorry, Cash," she said, rising to her feet, tossing the single stack of bills back inside the bag.

"Very well."

The man lifted the bag back into the SUV. She stepped toward Cash, and the men formed a half-circle around her, leaving Cash standing just outside, leaning against the limo. Behind Julia was twenty yards of concrete to the wall. From there it was fifteen floors down. The twelve men varied somewhat in height and build, but they all appeared to be in excellent physical condition.

Cash nodded to one of the men. A lean but muscular man stepped forward. Julia guessed his height at 6-2. He was no older than thirty. He removed his jacket, flexed his trapezius muscles and cracked his knuckles. She appeared scared, frail and vulnerable to him, so he walked slowly to her. He took one step too many, and quickly realized his mistake.

Before the man knew what had happened, he crumpled on the ground, holding his destroyed knee. He never expected the speed of Julia's precise kick. She quickly swept him off his feet, his back slamming to the pavement. The stunned man shook off the pain and rose to defend himself, but was staggered by a blow to his chin and another to his sternum. He fell to one knee and Julia drilled him again in the mouth. He fell again, blood dropping from his mouth.

She took a step back and realized the man's colleagues were chuckling, enjoying the spectacle. This didn't give her any comfort, revealing their lack of concern. It was still their eleven against her one.

The defeated man wearily rose. His friends' enjoyment only angered her further and she grabbed his head and drove it into her knee, then kicked him squarely in the crotch. At this the man fell for good, and the rest of the men laughed. Cash began to clap slowly.

"Excellent, Julia! This was much better than I could have hoped for. Bring him over here."

Two of the men dragged their beaten colleague back to Cash, who produced a pistol and screwed a silencer in place atop the barrel.

"Sorry, Clay."

"No! Don't—"

The man's pained protest ended as several muted bullets plunged into his chest and head. Julia jumped back in shock, falling to the ground.

Cash motioned to the vehicles and the men lifted out a stack of body bags, dropping them to the ground with an even heavier thud than the money.

The men fit the corpse into the bag while Cash smiled watching Julia. She realized she was missing an opportunity to go on the attack against another man, but she was still catching her breath from her first bout.

"Patrick."

Another man stepped forward. He was balding and around forty. He was a couple of inches taller than Clay and at least twenty solid pounds heavier. Unlike Clay, he had no neck.

"This one may be a little tougher to drop, Julia."

She tried to hide it, but Julia clearly showed despair after seeing her next opponent. Patrick would not take a false step, having had a preview of her abilities. She coiled defensively, measuring him for any weaknesses. He smiled, revealing nothing.

Julia feinted a few kicks to measure his responses. The large man was lighter on his feet than expected. While his flexibility appeared to be a minor weakness, he easily extended his arms to block the kicks anticipated.

She finally decided to test his knee and he turned to have the kick hit his thigh. It felt like her foot hit a brick wall. She tried to hide a reaction, but it was impossible.

"Patrick is a bit sturdier, wouldn't you say?"

Julia's grimace exposed her poise starting to fade. She forced herself to bounce on her toes, probing for a weakness, displaying more energy than she really had. The muscled mass slowly drew closer, erasing her advantages of speed and space.

The man stepped a bit too close and got his nose popped by her foot. Blood oozed from a nostril which he shook off. A few times he was tardy in a block and got drilled in his side. But he knew from Julia's reactions that her body was paying a heavier price than he was with every blow.

Julia couldn't be sure, but about five minutes had passed. Her footwork was lagging and the distance to the ledge of the roof had been cut from 20 yards to 10. The men had been slowly closing the circle with Cash leaving the side of the limo for a closer look. Whatever slim chance she had in pushing back the behemoth in front of her was to attack now.

She wasn't quite sure how she did it, but she leapt and got his head locked inside her legs. He wasn't prepared for it and stumbled. When he fell to a knee, she began pummeling him with head shots as many as she could. She got five or six in until he finally wrested himself free and unloaded a full fist on the side of her face.

Everything went dark, then dizzy as she lost her balance and toppled on her side. Sprawled on the concrete, she reached out her hands and arms, trying to brace herself to rise. The problem was the world was still spinning. She rose and fell back down, unable to regain her bearings.

Once her opponent picked her up, she regained her perspective. He had her by the throat with both hands and she tried to twist away. When she got her face nudged up against his forearm, she bit down as much flesh as she could as hard as she could. He finally grunted in pain, loosening his grip. She pushed against him to try and gain more space, but his weight and her strain finally collapsed her knee and she fell in a heap back to the ground.

On her knees, she crawled away from him, but didn't get far. He lifted her up again, then drilled her on the other side of the face with a left. She dropped again, this time conscious enough to the feel the full measure of pain. She told herself to get up, but she was exhausted.

"Don't get up, lady," her opponent said.

"I don't want him to hurt you permanently, Julia," Cash said with mock concern. "If you keep getting up and coming after him, I can't help what happens."

She turned over on her knees and looked at them. Patrick, her opponent, was standing straight. His forearm was bleeding profusely from her bite and his nose was red. Other than that, and the beads of sweat on his forehead, he was no worse for wear. The looks on the faces of the other men were a mixture of respect and pity. She was valiant, but still the loser.

Sensing she had accepted defeat, Cash parted through the men, kneeling next to her.

"Did you really think I wouldn't anticipate your next move? I own Redd Vernon, just like all the rest of them. And just like you."

Julia looked up at him, still panting for breath.

"One more little news update for you. Remember your friend Sophia Ricks? About now, the charges against Brad Benton are being dismissed."

"You bastard," she muttered, sweat and blood dripping from her mouth.

"I think those two love birds deserve one more chance, don't you?"

Cash smiled and walked away from her. Julia screamed and lunged for him a moment late, grasping air and stumbling back to the ground. The men would have restrained her, but her adrenaline was only able to provide energy for that final move. She began to cry in a mix of grief and fury as the men walked away. They walked to the car and one of the men popped open the hatch. They pulled another body bag from the SUV, this time struggling with it, since it was full.

"Gee, I wonder what's in the bag."

Cash's words prompted the men to unzip the bag and pull out its contents, standing Cheese on his knees facing her. A mixture of blood and sweat covered his face, and duct tape was wrapped around his mouth.

"No!"

"This is my last offer," Cash said, pointing his gun at her, stopping her from crawling any closer. "Robert Chisum has served this community for so many years, several of them by your side. Are you really going to trade his life for hers?"

Julia fought back tears, grunting to keep from screaming. Cheese's eyes met hers, and he shook his head no. She started crawling toward them, even though she was powerless to change anything.

Cash sighed and shook his head before pulling the trigger at her friend's temple. The sight of the blood and the sickening sound of the impact sent shockwaves through her body.

"NO!!!!"

Julia screamed, struggling to her feet one last time. Cash marched forward and decked her with the butt of his pistol. He then grabbed her by her hair and put the gun to her head. His men returned Cheese's body to the bag, zipping it closed and putting it in the SUV.

"Let's take your friend away from here. I can't have the police bothering you with questions until you return my property."

Cash threw her back to the ground, then followed his men back to their vehicles.

"24 hours, Julia. I'll keep moving up the food chain, until there's no one left but you."

He jumped into the limo and the vehicles darted away. Julia fell back to the concrete, sobbing and delirious, her mind slowly accepting the reality of what she had just seen.

She finally rose to her feet, staggering towards the exit door at the far end of the rooftop. She made a few more strides before she lost consciousness, her exhausted body overruling her adrenaline, dropping her back to ground.

SIXTY-TWO

GRIMES sipped on iced tea in his hotel suite, reviewing the data from his email inbox. Two simple inquiries had netted the possible identities of the Shelter's leaders. He sat back in his chair, considering the information.

Patricia Scott was last seen at her job as a waitress the day before Andrew hit Florida. The bodies of her boyfriend, Neal Carroll, and her friend, Beth Worley, were discovered in Lake Okeechobee several days after the hurricane landed. The bodies of Carroll and Worley were found inside Ms. Scott's car. Ms. Scott's body was not found and she was later declared dead by the authorities, assumed to have perished with her friends.

Grimes put the photo of Julia Caldwell and the latest photo of Patricia Scott prior to her disappearance, side-by-side. Her hair was shorter and the color was a much darker brown. Nearly three decades had aged her gracefully, the lines being minor and the skin still tight. He didn't need his fancy programs to tell that the two photos were likely of the same person.

Hannah Willard being the same as Cassie Snow was even more conclusive in his mind. Her aging had actually transformed her from a fragile teenage girl into a steely, formidable woman. The most significant change he noticed was in her demeanor facing the camera. The woman today was a force to be reckoned with, to be dismissed at your own risk.

Her stepfather was found in the flood waters a week after Katrina hit. Ms. Willard's death was not made official until around Thanksgiving. Her mother passed away the following year, not surprising after her tragic losses.

There appeared to be no controversy regarding either of the deaths. The two women neatly fell off the radar screen and were evidently reborn halfway across the country. The only detail that still piqued Grimes' interest was that the bodies of Mr. Carroll and Ms. Worley were discovered near Patricia Scott's car, but without Ms. Scott. He returned to the obituary and began searching through the names of the surviving relatives. The only one of note was Carroll's father, a county judge who had retired in 2014.

Grimes quickly found contact information for the judge and began to dial the number, but an email message popping up on his computer screen distracted him. He studied what he saw there for a few moments then cleared the numbers for the judge and dialed another number in Florida.

"Tell me what I'm looking at here."

The detective on the other end of the line laughed. "I figured you would say that. Have you never looked at one of these before?"

"Years ago. There's a lot more to these things than I remember."

"What do you want to know?"

"I want to know what you know about this person, just looking from this report."

"Well, this woman was not born in the States. Probably somewhere in the old Iron Curtain."

"And what if I told you that this woman, who is supposedly 30, barely looks old enough to drink?"

"Then I would tell you she is likely a victim of sex trafficking."

Grimes sighed. "That's what I was afraid of."

"Do I need to know anything more about this? I don't want my ass hanging out just because I ran a DNA test on a nameless person."

"No worries. My liability in the matter is now over, and so is yours. I appreciate it."

Grimes hung up the phone.

So that's what this Tanger thing is about. Cash is trying to hide the woman until he can safely get rid of her.

He punched up the airlines and found the next flight out of the country to his permanent home. Once he had purchased the tickets, he took one last look at the documents on Patricia Scott and Hannah Willard before deleting the emails.

Thirty minutes later, Grimes left the hotel suite for the airport. There was no nostalgia in leaving the States for the last time. The Cash affair convinced him he should have never resurrected his old life in the first place. He had been many ugly things including a killer for hire many times over. But he was not about to take another penny working for someone who had any dealings in sex trafficking. Cash would have to figure out how to dispose of the Shelter on his own.

SIXTY-THREE

HAWTHORNE loitered in the W Hotel lobby, waiting for the call he was promised. This was the day his life would change. He would get the story of the year, Trent Tanger signing a half billion-dollar contract with superagent Damon Cash at his side.

The phone rang.

"Hello."

"Good morning, Mr. Hawthorne."

"Mr. Cash."

"I am en route with Trent. You'll have thirty minutes. How well that time is spent will determine if you ride on with us."

"Ride on?"

"We expect there will be a few days of negotiations, then the press conference announcing the signing. I assume you're ready to travel."

"I am."

"Where is Sophia?"

Hawthorne paused. He was now at the poker table with the champion. The pause was fatal and he knew it.

"As soon as I see you and Mr. Tanger, I will give you the location."

The line went silent for a few seconds.

"Go up to suite 518. One of my associates will let you in. Take a bite of the caviar and a sip of the bubbly, then have a seat. Call me back with her location. We will be there shortly."

"Okay."

"Remember the rules I sent you. You bring up any of the forbidden subjects, the interview is over and I will personally end your career."

"I understand."

Hawthorne paced to the elevator and went up. On the 5th floor he turned to the left and found the suite. He knocked and a very large, muscular man in a sport coat big enough to cover his car opened the door. He walked in and looked inside the ice bucket, lifting the bottle and nodding as if he was a seasoned veteran of the high life. Next to the bucket was a tray with a feast, including caviar. Satisfied, he dialed his phone.

"Okay, I guess you're not playing me."

"The address," Cash demanded.

"6181 Forest, in Houston. It's just a mile off Highway 6."

"Good. Relax and we'll see you in a bit."

The phone went dead. Hawthorne breathed a deep sigh and sat on the couch with a full glass of bubbly. He took a long sip and relished it before moving back to the table to sample the food. A few minutes later, another very large man walked in and took a seat across from him. The other man stood there watching him.

"You two work for Mr. Cash?"

The man sitting across from him made a sideward glance to the other before answering.

"Yes."

"I guess you never can have enough security."

"No, you can't."

The two men were eerie and a bit disturbing. Hawthorne tried not to think about them and went back for more food. As he did, the man sitting across from him took his phone and put it to his ear, moving to another room in the suite.

Hawthorne considered the food again. He had experienced very little of the high life so he was far from an expert. The cheese was a bit dry as was the meat. He wasn't about to complain because the selections further along the trip would improve.

He looked up from the tray in his lap just long enough to see a very large pistol with a silencer pointed at him. He didn't have time to be scared, to scream or to protest as the bullet snapped into his head a moment later.

The men quickly paced out of the suite, hanging the Do Not Disturb sign on the door as they left.

SIXTY-FOUR

SOPHIA pushed away from the desk, finally reaching a stopping point. Tina Redden did so much business, even more than Yardley Ramirez, which would have been hard to imagine before her first day. Her first transaction coordinator was a college student named Claire who was unfailingly polite and patient. Claire had already reported to Tina that Yardley's endorsement was just as advertised. Sophia had hit the ground running, her skills even more advanced than they had expected.

It was Thursday, her fourth day of work. It was the first time she had been the last to leave, so she had to set the office alarm. She pulled the handwritten instructions out of her purse and punched in the code. When the green light appeared she sighed in relief, locking the door and stepping outside into the air. It suddenly struck her how she was alone, outside in an urban area at night, and was not afraid.

The Impala was clean and comfortable, although she had eaten in the car a few times. She reminded herself to not do that. Whatever she would eat on the run wasn't good for her, and a clean car seemed to make a difference in her spirits.

The drive to her home was only 20 minutes, not bad for Houston. But there were too many fast food temptations on the way to resist. She relented, reasoning that she only had salad fixings and peanut butter left in the kitchen and that wouldn't satisfy her overwhelming cravings. As if approving of her turning into the drive-thru, her child made its first noticeable movement from inside her belly. Sophia began to cry in sheer joy.

6181 Forest appeared before her. She hit the garage door opener and rolled inside. The house was on a worn residential street that had seen better days, but the interior was immaculate and the neighborhood had a relatively good crime rate. The alarm system was working, but the contract had expired months before. She made a mental note to call and get the service returned.

Vance saw more traffic than he preferred, but he had canvassed the area and was confident there would be no issues. He looked back at the man in the rear seat who was clearly taking everything in.

"Mr. Benton, you understand?"

"I do."

"You have to make your girlfriend understand. She belongs with you, and no one else."

"Damn right."

"Here's some cash to help you get back to Austin without incident."

Benton shook his head. "But what about that legal shit? What about my probation?"

"It's taken care of."

"Why are you doing this?"

"You don't need to know. Just consider it a stroke of luck."

Benton paused, still confused by the oddity of the situation. He finally nodded and bolted out of the car and across the street. He marched straight up to the closed garage door and looked back at his new friends. As if on cue, the garage door opened. Benton darted inside.

Sophia heard the door open and gasped. She took a deep breath and tried to collect herself.

Relax. It must be some sort of malfunction.

When she opened the door to the garage and stepped out, suddenly there was her nightmare, alive again. She opened her mouth to scream, but only got out half of it, as his fist snapped through her jaw. She dropped and continued screaming, crawling back into the house to get away from him. Benton tackled her on the kitchen floor, quickly covering her mouth.

"You thought you got away with it, didn't you? You and your lawyer friend setting me up."

Sophia struggled desperately, but his weight kept her pinned to the tile, unable to move. He slowly raised up from her, realizing her body had changed.

"Are you—"

She closed her eyes, fighting back the tears, trying to wish away what had just happened.

"You were never going to tell me, were you? You bitch!"

He raised his hand to hit her and she screamed, using every ounce of space in her lungs. He covered her mouth again.

"You belong to me! That baby belongs to me!"

Inside the garage, a large man stood on the other side of the doorway. He was told to simply wait until given instructions. The man was accustomed to violence, but even he didn't enjoy hearing what was taking place inside the house. Finally. Vance's voice sounded in his ear.

That's enough. Clean it up.

The man stepped forward and whipped Benton on the head with a revolver, dropping him on top of Sophia. She was now able to scream again, but her cry was short as the man quickly covered her mouth and hit her as well.

The doomed couple lay there next to each other and the man considered them for a moment. He took the pistol and stuck it underneath the chin of Benton and fired, sending the inside of his head exploding against the wall. He then fired into Sophia's head, ensuring both would remain down. He gently wedged the gun into Benton's curled hand and then ran back out the garage door, jumping back into the driver's seat of the waiting car.

From the passenger seat, Vance nodded in satisfaction. The driver floored the accelerator, speeding out of the neighborhood.

SIXTY-FIVE

JULIA'S eyes opened and slowly focused. As expected, she was in a hospital bed. It took only a few moments for her to remember everything, in excruciating detail.

She turned to her right side and saw Tom watching her.

"Hey."

"Hey. How are you feeling?"

"I don't know yet," she mumbled. "I take that back. I have a monster headache."

Tom watched her carefully. To him, she was still beautiful, despite multiple facial lacerations and a black eye.

He gently raised his hand toward her, brushing strands of hair out of her eyes. Julia felt guilty about him being there. She had deftly avoided him, pushed him away, and here he was.

"How did you know?"

"Your friend Noelle called me."

Julia felt herself fading, like she wanted to sleep.

"I may not last long."

Tom laughed. "The doctor said you should be fine. You're not going anywhere for several days though."

That's what he thinks, she thought. "No, I mean I may drop right back to sleep on you."

"That's okay."

Though her head pounded, she felt sleep coming on, the slumber that was more powerful the harder you fought to stay awake. She heard herself saying words, words she herself didn't understand.

Tom watched her drifting back to sleep. A few minutes later, three women appeared in the room. They were all attractive, but not in a uniform way. The black woman appeared to be the leader of the group. She and the Hispanic woman were dressed like professionals. The white woman was dressed more casually.

"Hello," Tom said, rising from his chair and approaching.

"Hello. I'm Cassie Snow."

"Tom."

"Yardley Ramirez."

"Noelle."

"We spoke on the phone."

"Yes."

"Good to meet you," he said as they shook hands.

"How is she?" Yardley asked.

Tom nodded reassuringly. "Doctors say she should be fine."

"Has she said much?" Cassie asked.

"Other than she has some enemies, not much."

"How do you and Julia know each other?" Cassie ventured.

"We met a few weeks ago."

The ladies nodded in acknowledgement. They had only met a few of her significant others, if you could even call them that. Julia was cagey about her private life and those meetings were unplanned, chance meetings that she probably would have preferred never happened. He appeared to be a friend, or at least someone to be trusted.

"She just conked out. I'm going to get some sleep myself. If she wakes up, tell her I'll see her tomorrow."

"We will. Thank you."

He nodded and left. The ladies shared a brief, mischievous smile before moving toward her bed where the mood quickly changed.

"She looks better than I thought she would," Yardley said.

"Do you think it's safe to leave her alone?" Noelle asked.

"Probably not," Cassie said.

They continued watching her for a few moments until the three moved together toward the chairs on the far edge of the room.

"What should we do?" Yardley asked, looking at Cassie.

The attorney was quiet for a few moments, then looked to Noelle. "How long can we finance April abroad?"

Noelle shrugged. "For a while. Eventually we'll need some of that Tanger money. Otherwise, she'll be on her own."

Cassie nodded. "I say we try and get April out of town and out of the country now. They can do what they want to us, but I'll be damned if they get her. That's exactly what Julia would say."

"I agree," said Noelle.

Yardley nodded. "Absolutely."

The women gravely nodded in agreement. They were making life-and-death choices while their leader was lying unconscious in the hospital, lucky she wasn't in the morgue.

"I've got an idea," Cassie said.

"What is it?" Noelle asked.

"Remember how you said you could hack anyone's social media with your smartphone?"

"Yeah, why?"

"Just be ready. Get April out the way we talked about before." Cassie said, turning away from them.

"Where are you going?" Yardley asked.

"It's better if I don't tell you. That way you can't tell anyone if I crash and burn."

They nodded in agreement and Cassie left quickly. The other two women saw that Julia was still sleeping. They left to accomplish their prearranged plan.

As soon as they left, Julia opened her eyes slightly. She had heard enough of what they said to know their plans. They had come to a logical conclusion, but she wasn't about to tell them how she was going to change the script.

First, she tried to assess her physical condition by subtly moving her torso and limbs. There was plenty of soreness, but she felt able to move. She also felt the pinch of the IVs sticking in her arm.

Next, she took in her surroundings. She saw her clothes in a laundry bag in a nearby chair. On the counter was gauze and tape.

Julia took a deep breath, then removed the IVs with a pained groan. She was sure someone in scrubs would see or hear her and try to stop her. Fortunately, no one did. She stumbled out of bed and nearly lost her balance. She quickly applied the gauze and tape, clumsily winding it around the punctures. She ambled to the door, picking up the laundry bag along the way. She found the stairs, descended one flight, then found a unisex bathroom to change into her old clothes.

It wouldn't look pretty, as they were the same clothes she had gotten her ass kicked in yesterday. They would have to do, as the patient's gown would not get her very far. Fortunately, her cell phone remained. Once she had navigated the staircase down to the ground floor and snuck out of the hospital, she stepped outside and rested herself against a pillar.

A shiver ran from head to toe. The weather had turned colder while she was bedridden. A shuttle finally appeared and she hobbled toward it, waving. She gave her address and the driver shook his head.

"That's out of the radius."

"Get me there and I'll make it worth your while."

The driver watched her for a second, then waved her inside.

"You okay?" he asked, watching her curled in discomfort.

"I'm alright."

Once at her house, Julia limped inside. She found some money and limped back outside to pay him. He thanked her, but she had already turned away, dragging herself back in the house. She reached her bedroom, dropping on the bed from exhaustion. She fell asleep then roused back awake suddenly, wondering how long it had been. A glance at her alarm clock told her she had dozed for less than an hour.

Julia went to her closet and unlocked the safe. She grabbed her two remaining pistols and clips and placed them on the bed. She looked at them for a few moments, then nodded, her mind and body reaching agreement. She then found a spare burner phone and dialed a number she somehow retrieved from her memory.

"This is Julia Caldwell."

She heard the reply.

"I know what you said before. I have a deal for you. Do you want to hear it or not?"

SIXTY-SIX

NOELLE sat on the edge of the bed, a packed duffle next to her. She looked at the time on her cell phone again, counting the minutes until she left. The plan ahead had options that branched out into other options, creating a countless number of contingencies. If Plan A worked as scripted, the duffle wouldn't be opened until she returned home.

She knew the risks of what she and the others did. Their respective tasks were not always equal in their danger, and she was shielded from most of it. Now that she was called upon to get her hands dirty, she had no reservations. Her eyes closed, praying she would return, praying safety for her daughter if something happened.

"Mom?"

Megan watched her sitting there, her solemn nature a clue to the gravity of the night ahead.

"Hey, honey."

"I'm ready," her daughter said, her own bag hanging from her shoulder.

"Don't forget that—"

"The deed to the house, the will, and the insurance policies are in the lockbox. Bottom left-hand drawer of your desk. I've got it."

Noelle nodded in approval. Megan sat next to her mother on the bed, watching her.

"Do you ever wonder what would have happened if my dad hadn't been in one of the towers?"

Her mother shook her head slowly. "I try not to. Once your grandma sent the obituary, it was a big relief. I hope you don't blame me for being happy he's gone."

Megan smiled. "I don't. It would be nice to have a father. But you're more than enough for me."

At this, they hugged each other tightly. When the embrace ended, Noelle looked at her cell phone again.

"Okay, we better go."

Mother and daughter grabbed their bags and walked into the living room. April sat on the couch and watched them enter. She thought about her parents and how much she had missed them. The horrors she had endured had distanced her from that pain, but watching Noelle and Megan allowed it to resurface.

"Ready?" Noelle asked. April nodded and they went to the garage. April tucked herself in the backseat, scrunching down to where her head wasn't visible. Noelle opened the garage door and cranked the car.

The Mini backed out into the street, then advanced a few yards to the next-door neighbor's house. They hugged again.

"I love you," Noelle said.

"I love you," Megan replied. "Be careful."

"Thank Nancy for me."

"I will."

At the door, Nancy waved to her and then closed the door. The neighbor's instructions were to not let her daughter leave the house until she returned or contacted them.

The Mini zipped away to its destination. One block away a sedan slowly rolled forward, the headlights coming on once it had passed the neighbor's house. The sedan's passengers made note of the neighbor's house before speeding off in pursuit of its prey.

Yardley sipped on a bottle water, watching the cell phone sitting on the kitchen counter. She had debated telling her children that she was leaving town, but that wasn't necessary. There was nothing productive they could do with that information, and it would leave a trail that only enemies would follow. If all went well, she would be back before they knew she was gone.

She looked around at her home, admiring it. It was custom built, paid for with hard-earned commissions while ferrying two children back and forth from every conceivable ballgame, recital, and doctor's appointment. She cherished her life and the loved ones she shared it with. The house was merely the frame of a beautiful painting she had spent years crafting.

That masterpiece required a rescue from domestic violence. Julia saving Yardley and her children was far less dramatic than April's journey, but no less necessary. Lives were at stake. Her conscience forced her to act, passing on the gift she had received. Not every survivor was called to make the sacrifices she and the others made, but it was a part of her heart now.

The incoming text finally arrived, the phone vibrating against the counter. She saw the message she was expecting on the screen. It was time.

Yardley grabbed her backpack and stole out the back door, pushing out of her mind the number of ways their plan would backfire. She ran to the gate on the far end of her yard and out into the alley. She jogged to the end of the alley where the Mini rolled to a stop just long enough for her to jump in before speeding off again.

Noelle navigated her way to I-35, well out of the city limits. She and Yardley said little, which made April nervous.

"Sorry to put you through this."

"Don't mention it," Yardley said. "It's what we do."

"Can you tell me where I'm going?"

"Nope. Even we don't know all the details. Just know that you are going to be okay."

"I just never want to see his face again."

"We will make certain of that."

They fell silent for a while. The changing of speeds was jarring to April. They maintained a fast pace, quickly slowed without notice for a few minutes, then sped up again. Noelle had a radar detector that she watched carefully, adjusting her speed as necessary. The other variable that factored into their speed was their pursuer. Yardley kept looking out the rear window.

"Distance?" Noelle asked.

"About a quarter mile," Yardley replied. April heard this exchange several times. She correctly guessed there was a car pacing them. When the distance closed, Noelle would accelerate to maintain distance. When radar required them to slow, Yardley's watch intensified. She even took hold of the pistol a couple of times, as if readying for a gun battle on the interstate.

April started to doze off, then was awakened by another report.

"Three hundred yards."

Their speed increased suddenly. Several miles later, the pace relented. April correctly supposed there was some strategy at work. Yardley had stopped looking back through the rear window, instead watching a small computer in her lap intently. Noelle had given her a crash course in using the DOT cameras to spot specific vehicles' license plates, then using their database to identify which vehicle was giving chase. She now knew the make, model and color of their likely pursuer, and knew from their GPS exactly how much distance was between them.

Noelle and Yardley had decided against trying to lose them, instead keeping a safe distance while tracking the enemy's location. The pursuers never closed enough distance to attempt an ambush. Keeping them close might give them another crucial advantage once they neared their destination.

April floated in and out of sleep, finally surrendering her fears to the fatigue. When she roused, she saw they were surrounded by the lights of the big city.

"I was about to wake you," Noelle said. "Ready?"

"I guess."

A large sign read DFW airport, the very place she had run from weeks earlier. The memory of her escape chilled her, wishing there was another way than this airport to free herself.

"Distance, Yardley?"

"Two hundred yards."

JEFF WISHARD

"Since we have company, we'll go with Terminal C."

Yardley reached into her bag, pulled out a manila envelope and handed it to April.

"Here it is. Wherever you're going, it's in there. You know the drill."

Yardley nodded, prompting April. Accordingly, she recited her instructions back from memory.

"Excellent. Good luck."

The Mini slowed at the passenger drop-off at Terminal C, fitting into a small space crowded with travelers, unexpected for this time of night.

"Good luck, April."

"How do I do this? I don't know—"

"And you won't know. But you'll make it."

Noelle and Yardley grasped and squeezed her hand from the front seat.

"Thanks."

April grabbed her small suitcase and jumped out, putting on the fedora they had given her. The Mini quickly darted away.

Per her instructions, she went directly to the restroom, found an empty stall and locked the door. She tore open the padded envelope and pulled out the contents, one by one. She found a note, written with very strict, definitive instructions. After reading it three times, she dropped the package back into her purse, then opened the door and walked out, suitcase in tow.

Despite the fedora, there was no doubt about the woman's identity. He had watched April Tanger for months in his duties at the Tanger house, often with less than honorable thoughts. It was her.

Tailing them had not been difficult, hanging a quarter mile behind them to the Metroplex. For as formidable as the group had been up until now, that was a surprise. All that remained was to follow her until an opportunity presented itself.

"Step out of line please, sir."

The man looked and saw her. It was a short Hispanic woman, discreetly flashing a badge of some sort. The surprise at both the badge and her beauty had distracted him. He looked back to where April was standing. She was gone.

His options were now limited. Escalating matters by challenging the woman would guarantee April Tanger would escape to parts unknown. Even a simple text message to alert his employer would be difficult. His right hand casually slipped into his pocket.

"Don't move. Hands out of your pockets. Now."

Yardley's words were firm, but not loud. Only the handful of people in the immediate area took note of the confrontation. He saw Yardley's hand behind her back. Was she really a cop? If not, how did she get a gun through security?

"Now!"

Her words were deeper, with a harder edge. He realized his best bet was to go with her and somehow get away. He finally obeyed, slowly moving away from the line. He glanced back toward where April had been, as if hoping he had simply missed her.

"Move it!"

Yardley shoved the man, easily twice her weight, away from the gate and towards the ladies' restroom. Once inside, she shoved him again, against the wall.

"Spread your legs. Hands behind your back."

He almost moved against her right then, but he saw two other women moving past them, and complied to avoid making a scene. In a moment, she had the cuffs applied like a pro, using her body and movements to negate his size and strength advantage. His chance had come and gone. She had to be a cop.

With his face planted against the wall, Yardley took his legs out from underneath him, and he dropped with a thud on the restroom tile. She produced a large, thick zip tie, fastening his bound hands to one of the stalls.

"Bye."

"Hey."

Yardley smiled, reminding herself to thank Julia for drilling her on subduing much larger opponents. She never guessed such a skill would come in handy, but it had.

On the other end of the concourse, April handed her ticket to the gate attendant, who scanned it. Before boarding, something made her look back behind her. She saw both Noelle and Yardley watching her go. She saw the satisfaction in their expressions and smiled in return, nodding goodbye.

Once they saw April board, they took a seat near the gate where they could watch each face that followed. The red eye was only half full, mostly business travelers and families, many weary of the battle to simply board a domestic flight with a reasonable expectation of arriving safely. Finally, the door to the plane closed and the jet bridge retracted back to the concourse.

"You ready?" Noelle asked.

"Yep," Yardley replied. "Let's go."

SIXTY-SEVEN

THE limousine rolled into the parking garage of the Omni Nashville and stopped in front of the VIP entrance. Two burly men dashed out and opened the door for an older gentleman who slowly eased out. They escorted him through the doors and into the lobby by a side entrance. The few who passed by didn't recognize Herbert Nason, the 77-year-old owner of the local major league baseball team.

Raised in relative poverty in the southern cotton fields, Nason left the farm for the city as a teenager and began selling cars. At thirty, he bought his own dealership. His holdings quickly grew into a large network of dealerships throughout the south. His fortune enabled him to win the bid for Nashville's expansion franchise. He was a quiet, gentle soul who had already won over Music City with his pleasant nature. The public persona belied his inner fires, which were evident once the other side negotiated with him inside the board room.

Public sentiment regarding the potential loss of Trent Tanger had been tilted in the club's favor from the beginning. Nason had said and done all the proper things regarding negotiations, but stopped short of admitting that the big market teams would take the bidding to an absurd amount that was simply foolish to try and match. Nashville's fans had accepted losing Tanger as a given, preparing to use the compensatory draft pick to continue building a young team long on youth and depth, and short on free-agency dollars.

The owner had never missed the kickoff event for Tanger's charity held every year at the downtown hotel, and the almost certain loss of Tanger would not change that. Nason was an honorable man and one of his word. He fully planned on deflecting any questions regarding free agency, helping his young star out of a potentially awkward situation.

The elevator door opened at one of the upper floors where Nason would rest for a bit before heading back down to the ballroom for the event. When he and the men stepped out, they were met by a strikingly beautiful black woman, walking purposefully toward them.

"Herbert Nason?"

The older gentleman and his two bodyguards stopped in their tracks. There wasn't supposed to be anyone else on the floor this evening.

"Do I know you?"

"Cassie Snow. Did you receive my message?"

"I did."

"Is it worth a few minutes of your time?"

Nason looked over the woman, measuring her. He had dealt with his share of con artists over the years and prided himself on spotting them long before he struck the deal for the Nashville baseball franchise. He finally nodded, then looked over his shoulder to the two large men waiting for his orders.

"Wait out here," he said, motioning Cassie into the suite.

The Broadway Ballroom of the Omni Nashville had been the location of the press conference announcing the details for the SafeTNFamily.org charity golf tournament and fundraiser since the charity's beginning five years earlier. The tournament was held in the spring, but the presser was routinely held in December. The keynote speaker was always Trent Tanger, founder of the SafeTNFamily.org charity. The benefit helped Tennessee families in need due to poverty, tragedy or any other notable misfortune. Ironically, the charity staffed crisis counselors specifically trained to deal with domestic violence cases.

Tanger walked into the men's restroom and stepped up to a urinal. Once he was finished at the urinal, he walked to the sink to wash his hands. In the corner of his eye he saw a woman appear from one of the stalls.

"What the hell?"

"Hello, Mr. Tanger."

"I think you have the wrong bathroom."

"No, I don't. I'm the attorney representing your wife."

Tanger was taken aback for a moment, then waved her away.

"I ain't got shit to say to you. Call Cash and he'll put you in your place."

"He's been trying that for weeks. It doesn't seem to be working," Cassie snapped. "We need to have a little talk before you go out there with your PR mask on."

Tanger reached into his coat pocket for his cell phone and touched one of his speed dial options. "I'll solve this damn quick."

Cassie leaned against the counter, watching the superstar listening to the line ring, over and over. A smirk began to appear with each moment that his call wasn't answered.

"Not used to that, are you?"

"Just misdialed," he said, shaking his head, reexamining his phone, unable to process the possibility something was amiss. As the second call continued to ring, he looked back up at Cassie, stunned.

"What are you doing to my phone?"

"Nothing."

Tanger bolted for the door.

"Get your ass back here."

"Fuck you."

When Tanger opened the door, he was met by two of Nashville finest, in uniform. The two officers glared at him, arms folded, seemingly blocking his exit. He froze for a moment, then slowly paced back into the restroom.

"What's going on? I'll have you disbarred."

"I don't think so."

Tanger's face was quickly turning red. His hands were curling into fists, trembling slightly, as if poising for action.

"What are you thinking, Trent? You want to grab me by the throat, don't you? Or maybe toss me against the wall and start punching me?"

Now his teeth were bared and his breathing more labored.

"I really wish you would try. Because even though your wife and I weigh about the same, I can handle you. There's also a couple of cops that would laugh their ass off while picking what's left of you up off the floor, clicking you up and taking you to jail."

Tanger looked around the restroom, like an animal suddenly trapped in a cage. There was no escaping whatever she had planned for him.

"You care a lot about your image, don't you? Do you ever Google yourself, Trent? Try it now. See what the word on the street is about you this evening."

He watched her for a few moments before turning to his phone. He punched up the browser and searched himself. The headlines he saw listed dropped his mouth open.

Tanger and superagent at odds
Cash to lose baseball's best player?
Tanger to change agents before payday

"How did you do that? How the hell did you do that?"

"Your boy Cash isn't the only one who can create headlines out of thin air."

"It's bullshit!"

"Tell it to Cash. He doesn't appear to be taking your calls right now."

Tanger wanted to slam the phone as hard as he could on the tile by his feet. The policemen outside kept him tethered to as much self-control as he could muster. If he wasn't so filled with rage, he would have realized that he could control himself, despite the excuses he routinely made for his behavior. He simply needed enough motivation.

"What do you want?" he hissed.

"I had a nice conversation with Mr. Nason. I showed him a few photos of your wife after you assaulted her, as well as a deposition we took from her. I explained that we had the same conversation with Damon Cash, which is probably the reason the agent is distancing from you, just like he always does when he senses his investment is no longer justified.

"I also told Nason that his worst suspicions were quite correct. You don't have any intention of re-signing with Nashville and you never did. But now that you no longer have the leverage, or the most powerful agent on the planet at your side, Nashville can retain your services at a much cheaper salary."

Cassie produced a small stack of papers clipped together and handed it to him. He took it from her and leafed through it. As he read it, he shook his head incredulously.

"That's your deal, take it or leave it."

"No fucking way!"

"We're letting you off easy, Tanger."

"I'll get another agent."

"Not before signing."

"You can't make me."

"Oh, yes I can. Nason is waiting in a meeting room 100 feet away. He has the original copy of the contract ready for you to sign. If you don't, I start tweeting these pics to every news outlet in the country. You're the leading story tonight. The only question is what the story is."

Tanger slumped over the counter, defeated. He took in the body blow, then looked over the papers once more.

"I do this, we're done. Right?"

Cassie nodded. "We'll send you the divorce decree. The judge has already previewed it, and agreed to sign off."

He took the paper, wadded it up, and threw it in the trash. He pushed the door open.

"Oh, and one more thing," Cassie said.

Tanger turned back to her.

"We'll be keeping tabs on you and any woman you socialize with. If so much as a hair on her head gets moved out of place, we will end you."

Tanger glared at Cassie as he left the restroom. Twenty minutes later, a stunned crowd heard the superstar announce his one-year extension to stay with Nashville. The $25 million-dollar salary was a relative bargain, but the public would never know the full extent of Tanger's sacrifice. Only three parties knew of the $10 million payment cut off the top, sent to a numbered off-shore account.

As a subdued Tanger announced the signing, the other two people who knew the details locked eyes. Nason subtly nodded to Cassie standing to the far right of the stage. She nodded back, then disappeared through the exit.

SIXTY-EIGHT

A firm but gentle nudge from the flight attendant is what awakened April. When she came to, she nodded and said thanks. She took a few moments to collect herself before unbuckling her seat belt and rising to retrieve her carry-on bag from the overhead bin.

Your name is Jill. Jill Stuckey.

April was sure she would forget. She had to get it firmly planted in her brain. Once she deplaned in Chicago, the change to Jill would become official.

In the restroom, she took a quick look at her face and head, making sure her brown tresses of hair were still secure underneath her fedora. She stepped out of the restroom, putting on her sunglasses, and took the short walk to the spa. An attendant at the desk greeted her.

"Is Duane here?"

The attendant looked at her computer screen. "Jill?"

"Yes."

"Right this way."

The attendant led her to a private massage room. "He should be with you shortly."

"Thank you."

She closed the door behind her. About five minutes later, the door opened.

"Jill?"

"Yes?"

"I'm Duane. Sorry that this is the best we can do here. I was told we're going from long brown to short honey blonde."

"That's right."

"Have a seat."

Duane began spreading clear plastic all around the chair. Once done, he retrieved several liter bottles of water, a pair of scissors and a small kit from his duffel bag.

"Alright. Lean back and relax. We'll be done in no time."

She did as instructed, closing her eyes while he worked. She exhaled deeply, as if she hadn't taken a breath in weeks. To Duane's credit, he didn't stretch his claim by much. She was taken aback when he finally spoke.

"Open your eyes and tell me what you think."

She rose and turned toward the mirror. She still saw the same woman, but it was a different woman, a woman redeemed from a lost life. The hair was merely the frame for a picture with beauty she had never seen before.

"Jill?"

She smiled. "That's right. Jill."

"I'm sorry?" Duane asked, unsure what she meant.

"Nothing. This looks different."

"Different bad or different good?"

"Different good."

"Excellent."

"Thank you. How much do I owe you?"

"Nothing. It's already the most profitable job I've ever had."

April stepped out of the chair, then realized she needed one more favor from the stranger. She produced her driver's license and outbound plane ticket.

"Can I borrow those scissors?" she asked.

"Keep them. Good luck."

"Thank you."

Once he left, April took the scissors and cut her license and plane ticket into as many pieces as she could. She took the remains to the bathroom and flushed the confetti down the toilet.

She donned her fedora, leaving the spa looking just like she did when she arrived. Inside, she felt transformed. The path designed by her new friends was illegal in a dozen or more ways, but it was righteous. And exhilarating.

She glanced at the new driver's license and passport to see how closely it matched her new style. She expected to spot the tell-tale signs of a computer in the photos, but was instead surprised at the quality. If she was forced to remove the fedora, the hair would not be what gave her away.

SIXTY-NINE

CRUISING south at 90 MPH on 130 was quietly disturbing, especially on an overcast day. Development had not yet caught up to the tollways that had been constructed to connect the southern border of Texas with the rest of the country. Julia's trip and destination was eerily appropriate for meeting her fate.

She slowed to take an exit ramp, turning southeast. A couple of miles from the tollway, a dozen warehouses sat in a grouping, with no trucks or other vehicles in sight. She parked her truck just inside the complex, backed into a space a few yards in front of a loading dock.

She popped the top off her coffee cup and watched the steam curl out in wisps. After a moment of reflection, she laughed to herself and found her flask, emptying what was left of it into the cup. She took a long, slow swig, then checked her pistols, snapping magazines in each of them before leaving the truck.

Julia's feet landed painfully on the pavement outside, still feeling the ass-kicking she endured two days earlier. She had taken four Advil to diffuse the discomfort, but she still could not walk without a slight limp. If it came to running to or from a fight, she had no guess how far she could manage.

She placed her weapons in the holsters at either side, then leaned against the truck, waiting to see if her opponents would arrive as agreed. Julia had seen the morning's headlines about Trent Tanger's shocking decision to stay in Nashville on a one-year deal. With Tanger and his big payday gone, Cash no longer had any reason to barter for April's life, and she doubted they would believe Julia would give her up. Her own survival was preferred, but wasn't a given. She only knew how she wanted the meeting to end.

Cash had to die.

How her three cohorts fared with getting April away safely, and then protecting themselves, briefly crossed her mind. Julia took solace in that they would fight just as hard as she would. She was also comforted by the fact that she had no idea which out they would give April. If forced to reveal her location, she would have nothing to give. The pain she might experience before convincing Cash and his men of that forced her to move her thoughts to something else.

Vance stole a subtle glance at his employer sitting next to him in the back of the Escalade. Cash was quiet, which was unusual. He was also stubbornly defiant, which was not. They both knew that the women vigilantes had won the war by separating Tanger from his master. Cash would order that they hunt down Tanger's wife and the women who had hidden her, but their deaths were not worth the millions they had cost him.

Perhaps that was why Cash was insistent in bringing the two million in cash used in his previous confrontation with Julia Caldwell. It sat in a duffle between them on the seat, and this concerned him. It wasn't the risk of reprisal, because he didn't consider it possible for the woman to defend herself against them. It was the sign of an employer whose reckless pride trumped his judgment, making him vulnerable to more dangerous threats in the future.

The SUV entered the warehouse complex and saw a truck parked at the far end with Julia Caldwell leaning against it. Her poise increased Vance's reservations about the move as they eased to a stop.

"Are you sure about this, Damon?"

"They're like cockroaches. These bitches won't go away unless we kill them."

As the four men left the vehicle, Julia felt like a gunfighter in the old West. The overwhelming odds stacked against her removed any romanticism she might have felt about the moment. It was not a movie, and her death would barely be a blip on the world's radar screen. The only drama remaining is how exactly Cash would deal with her, having lost his payday. If nothing else, it bought her partners and April some time to run and hide.

"Julia."

"Cash."

One of Cash's men was carrying the same duffel bag from her abduction at the parking garage. He dropped the duffle on the ground and unzipped it so that Julia could see the money inside.

"Congratulations on Tanger. You fucked us pretty good on that one."

"Did we?"

Cash nodded. "You did. Sounds like you managed to get April out of town and into the wind."

"What did you do, suicide Benton and Sophia?"

"I had to get to April somehow. Still didn't get it done, did it?"

"What did you bring the money for, to taunt me?"

"Taunts are an effective intimidation tool. You and your girls know that as well as anybody. Stealing from people, ruining their lives."

"Ruining abusers' lives."

"The ends justify the means, huh? I understand that. We are not that different. In fact, we're the same."

"No, we're not."

"Yes, we are. The only difference is that my ends are money. Yours is your self-righteous moral high ground. This money is not what you came for."

"You're right."

Julia parted her leather jacket open with both thumbs, revealing the two pistols.

"I knew it. Look at this, boys. She means business."

His mockery didn't faze her. Cash and the two men stepped toward, closing the distance slowly.

"It didn't have to end this way," Cash said. "Sophia and Chisum would still be alive, the Shelter would have been set for decades. Instead, you had to play God and judge."

"Spin it any way you want to, Cash. You have to go down. Hard."

Cash smiled with a shrug, opening his arms. "I don't see that happening, Julia. You won't do it. You may have done it in a previous life back in Florida, to save yourself, or to save someone else. But to kill me, frontier style? No way."

The men were now fifteen yards away, almost close enough to rush her before she could draw on them. Julia held firm, but her inside was wavering. She wasn't sure if she would be able to from the beginning. She wasn't sure her conscience would let her do it, and hoped he would provoke her into pulling the trigger. He was daring her to do it, confident she wouldn't.

The sound of approaching vehicles pierced the tension. From either end of the complex, two SUVs rolled up to the scene. Six large men got out of the vehicles and approached them.

"Look who finally decided to join us," Cash said with a shrug, almost strutting, backing off a step.

A large black man came up behind Julia.

"You're late!" snapped Cash.

"But not too late," replied Vernon. "Ms. Caldwell."

She didn't look behind her, recognizing the voice. "Redd Vernon."

"I warned you. You didn't listen."

"Did you really think Vernon wouldn't tell me?" Cash asked. "How stupid do you think I am?"

Julia raised her eyes to meet his, letting a wry smile escape.

"I knew he would tell you. That's what I wanted."

Cash looked at Vernon and was surprised to see him glaring back unpleasantly.

"I told Redd I was going to meet you here and kill you. He had two choices. He could either warn you to keep me from killing you and take whatever cut of the money you offered."

Julia's grin got bigger and she took a step toward Cash.

"Or, he could back me up and take all of it. Either way, he makes out. Redd, how much did he offer you?"

"$200,000."

"That's all? That bag looks about as big as it was the day you killed my friend. There's a helluva lot more than two-hundred grand in there."

By the time Cash realized he had been set up, Vernon's crew had subtly taken a few steps forward and beyond, circling Cash and his three men. They had more guns, and they were in better position.

"I knew you couldn't resist taunting me with money one more time."

Vance was the first to notice the movements of Vernon's men, but it was a moment too late. One of Vernon's men had been assigned to take Vance out first. He had his eyes fastened on the mercenary, waiting for him to move. Once Vance moved, the shooter drilled him in the chest. Vernon's other men followed suit, dropping Cash's other two men.

As for Julia, she was insistent that Cash belonged to her. She drew smoothly and quickly, and her aim was true. Cash barely grasped his weapon before the bullet tore into his chest.

She took a deep breath and stepped forward. Cash reached for the pistol he had dropped next to him, but Julia kicked it away. She kept the pistol trained on him, breathing through bared teeth. After a few moments of watching Cash fighting to breathe, the mania slowly drained from her. She measured him, then lowered her gun.

"You stupid bitch," Cash mumbled. "You'll pay for this."

"I doubt it," she replied, kneeling next to him. "No one cares about you, Cash. And now, no one is afraid of you."

Julia considered watching him die, then thought better of it. She struggled back to her feet, taking the hand of Vernon who had reached out to help her.

As she turned away, Cash reached down his leg and unsheathed a knife. Julia turned back, having only taken a step and fired several bullets into his chest. Vernon and one of his men had already drawn their weapons, but she had beaten them to it.

"You okay?" Vernon asked.

Julia nodded. "I saw the knife and I knew he'd go for it."

The pair shared a knowing look before walking back to the clearing and the rest of the carnage. She saw the bodies of Vance and the other men lying harmlessly on the concrete.

"You gave him more of a chance than I would have."

"Sorry to steal your thunder."

"It's your show, Julia Caldwell. Happy to assist."

Vernon picked up Cash's bag and began perusing it.

"You were right. It's all here."

"He didn't see any chance of losing it."

"How did you know I would show?"

"I didn't. But I was confident he had dealt you a few cards from the bottom of the deck over the years. I figured that and the money would be enough to flip you."

"But you didn't know for sure," surmised Vernon.

"Calculated risk," Julia shrugged. "I was running out of options."

Vernon flipped through the stacks, doing some quick math. "It's nowhere near what he cost me, but it'll do."

"Good."

He removed two stacks of bills, large enough to stretch both of his huge hands.

"This Shelter of yours, shit like this isn't going to scare you out of the game, is it?"

"Not a chance."

"I suppose a finder's fee is in order. Especially for such a worthy cause."

Julia measured him for a moment, then smiled, accepted the stacks of bills.

"I appreciate it."

Vernon shrugged. "You were right. I had tried to put what he did behind me. But he just kept showing up in the media, day after day, spouting his shit. When you showed up at my door, then had the nerve to call again, I couldn't let it pass. I knew you were in the right. I just needed another push."

Julia nodded. Vernon considered her for a moment.

"Do you think you would have really shot him?" he asked. "If we hadn't shown?"

"I don't know."

Vernon smiled. "I think you do."

She smiled wearily, dropping against the hood of Vernon's SUV, thoroughly exhausted. He began to laugh.

"Long day?"

"Long month. I guess we have to clean this up."

"You leave that to us," Vernon said. Behind him, his men were already zipping up the bodies in bags they had found in Cash's vehicle.

"Thanks," Julia said. "Would you mind walking me to the truck?"

Vernon nodded and took her by the arm, pacing with her gently to allow for her limp until they arrived at her truck. Julia's adrenaline must have been wearing off because the pain was mounting.

"Julia Caldwell, it's been a pleasure." he said. Julia and Vernon clasped hands, his huge meaty hand nearly covering hers.

"Same to you."

"You get any blowback from all this, you holler at me. And keep up your good work."

"Will do."

Julia strained to lift herself into the cab, and then dropped her head onto the steering wheel. She stayed in that position for several minutes, allowing herself to take a few breaths. When she lifted her head and cranked the truck, all the other vehicles were gone. No evidence to those incredible events moments before had been left behind.

She put the vehicle in drive and left the complex, heading for home.

Sophia and Cheese, that one's for you. Rest in peace.

SEVENTY

THANKFULLY, April slept most of the remainder of the trip. The pills Noelle had given her did the trick. She was now in another world, hopefully safe from being discovered.

She deplaned through the gate and made her way to the bar of the Auckland airport. April ordered a vodka tonic in the Auckland airport bar. The drink arrived and she took a small sip as she looked at the model planes on the wall above the bar. Taking a deep breath, she turned to the seating and selected one of four leather chairs surrounding a small table. Her instructions were to set the drink on the table and wait.

She did not wait long. A tall woman appeared out of nowhere and sat in the chair next to her. She placed a coffee cup an inch away from the vodka tonic, then produced her purse and retrieved her cell phone from inside. When she touched it, it lit up and she began tapping on it purposefully.

April stared straight ahead, anxious for some clue. The instructions were clear and the paper cup was part of the plan. But the woman kept fiddling with her cell phone and didn't seem to have any other purpose.

Finally, the woman grabbed April's drink and took a sip. She set the drink back on the table, grabbed the paper cup and shook it twice, the contents of the cup jingling like metal. She sat the cup back down and rose from her seat.

April cut her eyes up slightly and saw the woman nod before she walked off. She waited until the woman disappeared before taking the cup from the table and walking out of the bar.

She quickly found the ladies' restroom and occupied a stall, locking the door behind her. She popped the cover off the cup and reached inside, retrieving a ring of keys. A laminated fob simply had "A14" shown. She put the keys in her purse and left the stall and the restroom.

In long-term parking, slot A14 was occupied by a silver sedan. She opened the door, tossed in her suitcase and purse and saw the steering wheel on the right side. She circled to the right side and climbed in. She cranked the vehicle and it rumbled reassuringly. The odometer read just over 8000 miles.

April reached into the glove box and found an envelope. Inside was a travel itinerary, directions and a handwritten note.

Hello, Jill. Welcome to New Zealand.
Remember to drive on the left side of the road.

She smiled and gently eased the car out of the terminal parking and out of the airport. She held the wheel firmly, trying to navigate unfamiliar roads with her limited driving experience, while driving on the wrong side of the road. As the cars and buildings decreased and the green of the land increased, she began to relax.

The directions finally led to an open gate. A woman stood next to the gate and waved, motioning for her to stop. April slowed the car and rolled down the window.

"Are you Jill?" the woman asked. April recalled her new persona and nodded.

"I'm your contact. Mind if I hop in?"

"Okay."

The woman circled to the left side of the car and hopped in. She was pretty with brown eyes, and shoulder length hair that was dark red. She extended her hand.

"Call me Jackie. I've already got you checked in and ready to go."

Jackie pointed forward and April took her foot off the brake. Her passenger navigated her to the Turehu cottage. She helped April with her bags and led her inside.

"The store is almost half an hour away, so I stocked your pantry and fridge for a few days. I hope you can live with what I picked out."

April did not respond, walking through the doors to the outside lawn. Ahead of her stretched the beach and the water.

She stopped in front of a table with a bench and sat down, gazing in wonder at the Pacific. Jackie trailed behind her.

"Are you okay?"

"I'm alright. I'm just a little frazzled from my life changing so quickly."

Jackie nodded. "I understand."

"Jackie isn't your real name, is it?"

April wasn't sure why she asked this. She simply had a feeling that this was not a new experience for her contact.

"As far as you know," she replied sweetly, sitting down across from her. Not much of the local accent had rubbed off on her. She was clearly an American, with perhaps a Texas drawl that hadn't quite disappeared.

"You live here?"

"No, just vacationing. I work with the same travel agents as yours from time to time. I also started out leaving the States, dropped across the globe out of nowhere, running from my past."

April watched Jackie, hidden under the large sunglasses, wondering what her story was.

"I could be a terrorist that gave up my superiors for immunity. I could be the wife of some banker who made hundreds of millions off the mortgage crisis."

Jackie lifted the glasses from her face. Her eyes twinkled, and she smiled tellingly.

"Or, I could be the daughter of a mobster, who got out just in time to save herself."

April considered this for a few moments. "Any advice?"

"Some of it gets easier, some of it doesn't. Just embrace your new self as best you can. Lots of people want to start over and never get to. You do. Don't think it will solve all your problems. It's just what had to be."

The advice seemed part soliloquy. "Do you ever worry you'll be found?"

"Not really. I'm actually dead. There's a gravestone with my given birth name engraved. Of course, I've only seen the pictures. I'll never set foot in the country it's in again, let alone the cemetery where it's located."

"Do you miss it?"

"Parts of it, every day. Especially one person. I had hoped he would come find me, but I've stopped waiting. But I do still dream at night."

"I don't really want that."

"I understand." Jackie reached into her beach bag and handed her a stack of maps with an envelope inside. "I was told to bring you these items. Don't look them over now. Later, when you are alone and indoors."

"Thanks."

"You're welcome. Good luck."

"Will I see you again?"

"Not for a while. I'm going back to my place in the world. I may drop in, check on you from time to time. Never regular enough for the people chasing us to spot a pattern."

"I'd like that."

"Take care."

Jackie waved goodbye, walking down the shore until she disappeared out of sight. April wondered what had happened to make her disappear. She could sense she had wounds as well, but they were different than hers. Unlike herself, Jackie seemed sadly resigned to her fate.

Once her guide was gone, she went back to the cottage and took a bottle of water from the fridge. She then found the path to the beach and walked until she reached the shore. In all her travels, she had never set her feet in the sand of a beach. The moist goo in between her toes felt as good as she had always imagined it.

SEVENTY-ONE

JULIA watched the Shelter house, leaning against her truck, feeling the cold breeze blow her hair across her face. It had even less curb appeal than before, the overcast skies dulling its muted colors. She still wasn't sure if she wanted the house to look more inviting. Its non-descript looks and the surrounding trees would prevent the curious from investigating, keeping their rescued survivors safe from intrusion.

Her tour of the interior was predictably like they had left it days earlier, a variety of materials and equipment strewn about, waiting for work to resume. Julia found the state of transition oddly appropriate. Humans were never perfect, always in a transitory state. Life was under the constant struggle between hopeful construction and tragic demolition, a process that wouldn't end until the last breath.

The question of whether their investment was worth the return was now irrelevant. The four women had bought into a cause larger than themselves, but they had also staked their futures on each other. There were far more risks than Julia had known before they started, yet she would do it all again.

Satisfied, she limped back into her truck and drove to the office. When she arrived, the rest of the parking lot was empty, just as she wanted it. She knew her partners would interrogate her, so she wanted as much time undisturbed in her office as she could get.

She set her coffee cup on the desk, then picked up a pile of mail from the conference table and dumped it on her desk, along with everything else. She then dragged the trash can and her shredder to the side of the desk so she would not have to keep making trips to unload it each time. She reflexively reached for the flask in her desk drawer, then realized it was still in the truck. She would have gone back to get it, but then remembered it was empty.

As she cut open the junk mail, dumping and shredding, she felt pain with even the slightest movement, every muscle and every joint still aching from the beating she had taken days earlier. Though wounds healed so much more slowly at 47 than they did at 20, 10, or even five years earlier, they would heal.

A little over an hour later, the three cars rolled into the parking lot, one after the other. Individually and collectively, they had survived the war.

"Where have you been?" Yardley asked as she burst into her office. "You're supposed to be in a hospital bed."

"They released me."

"Bullshit!" Noelle snapped, following behind her. "You snuck out."

"I released myself."

While Yardley and Noelle peppered Julia with questions, Cassie trailed behind them, watching the scene. Julia did not predict everything that had happened, but she nailed the end result. If they survived, they would be unified in a way they hadn't been before.

"Head injuries are serious," Noelle said. "You need to see a neurology specialist. Today."

"I'm fine," Julia insisted.

"Are you a doctor?" asked Yardley. "I don't see a medical license hanging on your wall."

Julia let them fuss over her for a few more minutes, until she saw Cassie sitting on the table behind them, fighting off laughter.

"Okay, that's enough. I'll go see my primary sometime this week, if you shut up about it right now."

Yardley and Noelle continued talking as they backed out the door, promising they weren't done. Once they left, Julia dropped back into her chair with a sigh, then laughed along with Cassie. She returned to the mail on her desk.

"So, what do you have to say to me?"

Cassie's expression changed, turning serious. "I know today isn't the best day, but there are a couple of things you should know."

"What is it?" Julia said without looking up, still tearing open envelopes with a letter opener.

"Renee left over the weekend."

"What?" Julia dropped the mail and looked at Cassie who met her eyes, then dropped them to the floor.

"She asked to leave. Molly tried to talk her out of it."

"She went back to him?"

Cassie nodded. It wasn't a surprise, but it didn't make it any less painful. You rescue someone, protect them, help them process the pain and horrors they endured, and yet they don't break free. You don't win all the battles. You take heart in the successes, and you take stock and learn from the failures.

Julia had told Cassie this dozens of times, so there was no need for either of them to say it. It was still defeating. The victories rarely seemed to last long enough to savor, even after the war they had just won.

"What's the other?"

"Robert Chisum's funeral is Thursday."

Julia's eyes fell. Her friend hadn't left her mind, but the fog of war had masked her psychological pain just as effectively as her physical pain.

"They found his body in a wooded area off Mopac near Zilker Park. You're probably going to start getting some calls."

Julia glanced at her cell phone and saw 12 voice mails, more than she usually received over a weekend.

"Looks like I already have."

"You worried?" Cassie asked. "You're a logical place to start asking questions."

"Maybe I should be," she replied, "but I've barely had a chance to grieve over it."

"Will you go to the funeral?"

"I don't know."

"Was it worth it?"

Julia thought for a moment. "Is April safe and sound?"

"As far as we know."

"Then, yes."

Cassie nodded in understanding. "I'll leave you be," she said, walking back toward her office. After a few strides, she turned back. "By the way, sounds like Damon Cash is taking losing Tanger pretty hard. He hasn't been seen or heard from in several days. He's not taking calls, and his office doesn't know where he is. His clients are getting pissed."

"Interesting. We dealt him a tough blow. It will take a while to make up the money we cost him."

Cassie watched Julia carefully, detecting a subtle change in her demeanor.

"You never know," Julia continued. "He may have more problems than a declining revenue stream."

There was a gleam in Julia's eyes that told Cassie there was more, something she didn't know, something she may not learn until months, perhaps years from now. She wouldn't be telling that story today.

"See you later," Cassie said. "I'll let the other two play mother, but don't go running off on us again."

"I promise."

Cassie shook her head and disappeared out the door. Once she was alone, Julia felt numb, unsure whether to laugh or cry. She knew each impulse would arrive without warning in the days ahead, but she also knew her three friends would be there for her, every step of the way.

She took another long sip from the mug, knowing the contents wouldn't provide its usual comfort, and returned to the envelopes stacked on her desk.

ACKNOWLEDGMENTS

Thanks so much to the people who helped me with the research and editing of this book. Only some of them are listed below.

Deborah Biggers
Ld & Bobbie Herzog
Frances Laengrich
Derrick Lee Sr
Dionne Minor-Adams
Cecily Shull
Erin Wilde
Amy Wishard
Kevin Wishard
Larry & Sheila Wishard

Most importantly, thanks to my wife, Donna Wishard, who makes the impossible possible.

And, of course, all the mistakes are mine.

JDW

ABOUT THE AUTHOR

Jeff Wishard is the author of *Redemption Avenue* and *Domestic*, both from Port Fannin Publishing. He lives in Texas with his wife, Donna, and their two cats, Jasper and Calvin.

Follow Jeff on social media:

Online: jeffwishard.com
Twitter: @jeffwishard
Facebook: facebook.com/wishardjeff

www.ingramcontent.com/pod-product-compliance
Lightning Source LLC
Chambersburg PA
CBHW030337120726
47901CB00007B/1820